"Can I have

"Kell Jameson." She narrowed her eyes at him, waiting for a reaction. "Perhaps you've heard of me?"

"Should I have?" he remarked quizzically, well aware of who she was. Not that he could remember much beside his own name right now. Up close, the caramel porcelain skin carried a scent that teased his senses, appearing and disappearing on notes of spice and sex. A fist of heat punched at his gut and his tripping pulse sped to a gallop.

Luke hurriedly straightened and scribbled the name on the pad, added his signature and ripped off the white cover sheet. "This one is because you're parked in front of a hydrant, Miss." He passed the ticket to her through the open window.

By Selena Montgomery

RECKLESS
SECRETS AND LIES
HIDDEN SINS

RECKLESS

SELENA MONTGOMERY

AVON

An Imprint of HarperCollins*Publishers*

This is a work of fiction. Names, characters, places, and incidents are products of the author's imagination or are used fictitiously and are not to be construed as real. Any resemblance to actual events, locales, organizations, or persons, living or dead, is entirely coincidental.

AVON BOOKS
An Imprint of HarperCollins*Publishers*
195 Broadway
New York, NY, 10007

Copyright © 2008 by Stacey Abrams
ISBN 978-0-06-137603-0
www.avonbooks.com

First Avon Books paperback printing: July 2008

Avon Trademark Reg. U.S. Pat. Off. and in Other Countries, Marca Registrada, Hecho en U.S.A.
HarperCollins® is a registered trademark of HarperCollins Publishers.

Printed in the U.S.A.

10

For Mom and Dad,
Andrea, Leslie, Richard, Walter, Jeanine,
Jorden, Faith, and Nakia.
With my enduring love and admiration.

ACKNOWLEDGMENTS

With gratitude to Mirtha Estrada Oliveros, my very own public defender; to Dr. Andrea Abrams, an anchor and reminder of what can be done; to Lisa Borders, a stalwart and a respite; to Jeanine Abrams, my science gal; to Erika Tsang for the extra days and Marc Gerald for the timely touches. And, most essentially, to Leslie Abrams, my judge, jury, and perfect sentinel.

PROLOGUE

August 11, 1991

Smoke billowed from the warehouse and flames licked the metal roof with sharp red tongues, lighting the night sky. Kell raced ahead of the conflagration, sneakers slapping the unpaved road with a steady beat that echoed her thudding heart. Scraggly trees with branches gnarled from meager rain lined the road, providing scant shelter from prying eyes. Kell calculated they had a couple of minutes at best to find a place to hide. Assuming it wasn't already too late.

She spared a jittery glance behind her. Findley ran smoothly with the lean, graceful strides that had won the state track championship in April. The satchel strap across her chest, and the bulging tan bag it supported, appeared to have no affect on her ability to run like a gazelle. But Julia stumbled, her petite frame unused to the exertion. Or the panic. Her sherry brown eyes grew impossibly wider. Terror gripped the younger girl, born, Kell understood, from more than their current predicament. Julia was recalling the last fire, the last frenzied flight that had taken away all she'd known.

Kell shortened her stride and fell back. Automatically, Fin took the lead. Reaching out, Kell captured Julia's arm, as much to propel as to comfort.

"Come on, Jules. Just a little farther." In the distance, sirens wailed toward the burning warehouse. With a quick pant, she instructed, "Fin, we've got to get off the road. Head for the Grove."

In unison, the trio angled left, leaving the gravel road for a wooded path that snaked from the warehouse through the Grove. The dense copse of trees ran for more than a mile, separating the seedy side of town from the merely downtrodden. Tall shortleaf pines towered over stands of sawtooth oak and hackberry and other trees Kell had learned to name in botany. Fin had teased her only yesterday about her fascination, when she'd made them all go and look at a tree she thought was the mythical *Franklinia* that hadn't been seen since the first settler reached Georgia. A tree that would soon be cinder if the fire behind them reached the Grove.

The thought stumbled her feet and caught in her throat. *How had she messed up so badly?* she wondered wildly. Just two months ago, she and Fin stood on stage, receiving release papers from the prison of high school. Now they were fugitives, on the run from a firestorm that could consume their lives and those they loved.

All because of her.

So it would be up to her to save them. A quarter of a mile into the Grove, she skidded to a stop in a small clearing.

"Fin, we're good," she rasped out to the girl who continued to streak ahead. Fin curved around and returned, while Kell bent over to drag air into her lungs. Beside her, Julia collapsed onto the sun-baked earth. Ragged breaths turned into heaving sobs as the sixteen-year-old wrapped her arms around her legs and wept. Kell knelt beside her and draped an arm over her trembling shoulders. "I'm sorry, Jules. So sorry," she whispered into her hair. "I didn't mean to. I swear I didn't."

The quiet apology brought an oath from Fin. "He didn't give you a choice, damn it. It was them or us. You picked your friends." She braced coltish legs wide and swung the satchel over her head and let the heavy bag dangle from her clenched fist. "And I'm not sorry. Not at all. He was about to—"

Kell jerked her head up and shook it once to silence Fin. They wouldn't speak of that now, not yet. Returning her attention to Julia, she stroked her trembling back, murmured nonsense. Soon, the sobs quieted to whimpers that nearly broke Kell's heart. She pulled Julia deeper into a hug, brushing a light kiss on the top of the short cap of chestnut curls. "You're okay, honey. He's gone." A lump the size of her fist formed in her throat as she choked out the lie. "He can't hurt you."

Fin dropped down to sit on Julia's other side and

wrapped her arms around them both. "It's okay, Julia. Let it out. Let it all out." She dipped her head to brush the other two, and they huddled together, a tight knot of fear and worry.

After a while, Julia raised her head and took a long, slow breath. Kell and Fin eased away, but kept their arms taut around her. Julia wriggled suddenly, playfully. "You two trying to smother me? I can't breathe. Move." She offered a tremulous smile and shoved at the two girls lightly. She sniffed the air delicately, the acrid scent of fire drifting above. Soberly, she added, "But maybe that's for the best."

Grateful the tears had passed, Kell sat and drew her knees to her chin, staring up at the tree cover. "I can smell the smoke, but I don't see anything. Maybe the fire is under control." She didn't mention that this deep in the Grove, with the wind blowing south, the smoke probably wouldn't reach them. Aloud, she instructed, "Fin, get the bag."

Fin dragged the satchel into the loose ring the three girls formed. "Here it is."

Kell tipped the satchel and stacks of bills fell to the ground.

"Is that real money?" Fin whispered in awe.

"Three hundred thousand dollars." Kell stared at the pile she'd poured onto the forest floor. Tentatively, she lifted one of the bound stacks with the white banker's tape that proclaimed it held $10,000. "Have you ever seen this much money in one place?"

Julia picked up a stack and turned it over in her hands. "We have to give this to the police." She cast a distressed look at Kell. "If we do, maybe they'll believe us."

With a snort, Fin dismissed the idea and gathered stacks of the cash, letting them fall. "Three orphans with three hundred thousand dollars and a burnt-down warehouse? You really think they'll believe us? Get real."

"Fin, we have to try," Julia pleaded. "Otherwise, when they find—"

"If they find out," Fin interrupted pragmatically, "then we'll explain. But I know the police, kiddo. Despite the crap they teach us in school, the cops aren't our friends. Especially once they know the whole story."

"Which we can't ever tell." Kell stood up, dropping the money to the ground. Rising, she paced away from the clearing, her eyes shut as she ran through the alternatives. But there was only one option. She turned around, opened her eyes, and pointed at the money. "Fin's right, Julia. We have to keep the money and take care of ourselves. The police won't believe our story. They'll put Fin and me in prison and send you off to juvenile detention."

Julia flinched. "Prison? Why?"

"Because Fin's eighteen and I'm seventeen. You're sixteen and a victim, so they'll probably go easier on you. Maybe."

"But we didn't have any other way out!" Julia scrambled to her feet. "If you hadn't come in there—" She stopped, her breath catching in terrified memory.

Fin leapt up and grabbed Julia's shoulder. "Easy, kiddo. Don't think about it."

"Don't think about it, and for God's sake, after tonight, don't talk about it." Kell joined her friends and clasped their hands. "You two only showed up to help me. This is my fault." She shook her head to stop their protests, sadness roiling in her gut. Mistake after mistake flashed through her mind. If she hadn't gone to the warehouse. If she hadn't listened to conversations that she shouldn't have. If Julia and Fin hadn't followed her, trying to help. *If. If. If.*

"This is my fault. And so is what has to happen next." Kell took a deep breath and linked her fingers with theirs. By habit, Fin and Julia did the same. "A man is dead, guys. And I'm responsible. I'm going to turn myself in and face the consequences. Tell them that I was alone." *Goodbye college. Goodbye brand-new life.*

"No way," Fin spat out. "We're not going to let you cover for us. Not again."

"This isn't breaking curfew, Fin. We're not talking about Mrs. Faraday putting us on kitchen detail for a month. This is murder. And I'm not going to be responsible for ruining both of your futures."

"And you're not going to ruin your own."

Fin and Kell looked over at Julia, her chin lifted in a sign of resolve both of them recognized.

"Julia, whatever you're thinking, no," Kell argued. "This isn't time for your Three Musketeers speeches. This is an adult decision and I've made it."

Shoulders stiff, Julia retorted, "You can't tell me what to do. Like you said, this is an adult decision, and I think I've survived enough to consider myself all grown up."

Fin shrugged. "She's got a point."

"Shut up, Fin!"

"No, you shut up and listen for once," Julia snapped. "For eight years, you've taken care of us. First Fin, then me. You've lied for us, covered for us. Been the best sister either of us could imagine."

"Amen," Fin muttered.

Julia smiled at Fin and continued. "Now, you're in trouble. We all are. There has to be a way to save you and protect us. Kell, you start college in two weeks, and I've got another year in high school. We can't throw that away."

"Besides, I'm the one who's destined to wear an orange jumpsuit."

Kell swiveled her head to look at Fin. "Cut it out. You just haven't decided what you want to do. You have a track scholarship to UGA, if you still want it. And Julia, if they find out, you won't be going back to high school. Don't you understand that? I can't let you two destroy your futures."

"I'm not going to college, Kell. We both know that." Fin shrugged again, and a dimple appeared in her cheek as she smirked. "College isn't for me. Plus, I'm a known hoodlum. Like mother, like daughter. A fact we can take advantage of."

Fin broke the circle and reached down to the money lying on the ground. She plunged her hands into the pile and jerked out three stacks. "Three hundred thousand. Three of us. Do the math."

Joining her, Julia began to sort the money into separate groups and said, "One hundred and fifty thousand for Fin to start her new life. A hundred and fifty for you to pay for law school."

Fin flung the extra stacks toward Julia, who caught them in her lap. "I'm not taking yours."

"I've got plenty of money," Julia countered. "I don't need it."

"Think of it this way." Fin passed her the extra fifty thousand in Kell's stack with a grin. "You take it and you're as guilty as the rest of us."

Julia laughed shakily and looked up at Kell, pleading. "We can do this. Come on, you've always liked the myth of the phoenix, Kell. A new life born from the ashes."

"Those were bad men, Kell," Fin said flatly. "Men who can't exactly go running to the police either. If we skip town, they'd have to spend a lot of time and money tracking each one of us down. Probably not worth it to them."

"They know you, Fin," Kell reminded her bleakly. "Besides, three hundred thousand dollars is a good reason to look for us. That and the fact that we're witnesses."

Fin winced, but shrugged philosophically. "Only if we talk. Which means we'll have to keep our contact to a minimum. I'll head west or something. We'll be in touch four times a year. Our birthdays and the anniversary."

Julia stood, spine stiff with determination. "Are we agreed?"

Kell studied the faces of her two best friends, knowing it would be years before she saw them again. Tears misted across her gaze, blurring the beloved faces. "We do this, it might be for a long time. Your lives ruined just because I got reckless."

Fin caught her hand and Julia joined them in the circle. "Reckless, Kell? See, I taught you good."

CHAPTER 1

He didn't have to look inside the room to know what lay in wait.

Sheriff Luke Calder hiked up the last of the three flights of narrow, rickety stairs, already snapping latex gloves onto his hands. The stench that hung in the claustrophobic stairwell belonged to one source only.

The dead. After a career of standing over bodies gone ripe in sweltering heat, he figured the deceased had been lying undiscovered for at least forty-eight hours. The medical examiner would have to confirm his hunch, but his nose didn't lie.

Luke took the final steps and rounded the shadowed corner that led to the fifth-floor apartments inside the Georgia Palace. A rundown motel straddling the city limits, the Palace had been the site of more than a few visits from the Hallden Sheriff's Department. In cramped rooms rented by the week, acts against nature and the law were commonplace. But visits to the Palace rarely dealt with murder, unlike his time in Chicago.

But murder, if that's what he found inside, would be par for the course this week. Earlier in the week, a construction crew discovered two charred bodies in the basement of an abandoned warehouse. The two had perished more than a decade ago, according to preliminary reports. The county commissioners and the mayor had already begun calling for information, spurred by an overzealous police chief who hated being out of the spotlight.

The three dead men in a week, all in his jurisdiction, would put Chief Graves in a fit. A rivalry between city and county law enforcement wasn't unusual, but Graves was a media hound thinking to challenge Luke in November. With high-profile crimes like these on his plate, Luke would have to keep his eye on the chief.

Long, solid arms hung loosely by his sides, ropy, powerful muscles hidden by a blue cotton shirt bearing a silver badge. He took care not to touch the sweaty walls or pause too long in the corridor. Threadbare carpet of a muted brown hid a myriad of resident sins. Luke counted off doors, as the management of the Palace had stopped rehanging the number plates that fell or disappeared.

Five-O-seven. Five-O-eight. The death stench rammed into him like a fist as he approached apartment 509. He stopped in the open doorway and peered inside. A shoebox of a space, the studio apartment was barely wide enough for four people to fit comfortably across. Two were already inside. The living visitor, his deputy, held a mask over her nose as she knelt near the prone form.

Luke crossed the threshold and stepped lightly around a fallen ladder-back chair. A quick look around cataloged the rest of the furniture. A sunken couch rested against the side wall, with a black milk crate as a makeshift television stand. A sleek plasma television boasted a cable receiver and an Xbox on the carpet in front. Across from the couch, which appeared to double as a bed, a dresser stood bolted to the wall, the peeling white paint serving as a resting place for scattered cigarettes and empty bottles of Budweiser. One drawer was half open, empty of contents from what he could see. The other two drawers remained closed.

Cereal sat on the breakfast bar where the chair had fallen. Milk congealed around oat rings that bubbled in the heat. The kitchen sink held a butter knife bent at the tip and mismatched forks with plastic handles. Mildew crept around the fixtures, black and grimy. The deceased hadn't been much of a housekeeper.

In the center of the room rested the body, blood pooled near the legs and lower torso. A gaunt pale face stared blankly at the popcorn ceiling. The room's only window held a box fan that hadn't been turned on for a while, judging from the smell. Two days gone, and not a soul had noticed. Not until the smell had permeated the next-door neighbor's home, who called in a complaint about the odor.

Moving to his deputy's position, he asked, "Know who've we got, Richardson?"

Deputy Cheryl Richardson glanced up, set down her camera and inclined her head. "No official ID yet, Sheriff, but that weasel, Emmit Purdy, confirmed—" She stopped, seeing movement behind him. "Out. Right now."

"This is my building." A bald head with protruding ears poked into the doorway. When he caught sight of Luke, he hurried forward. "Sheriff Calder! I need to speak with you. I've got a right to my money."

Cheryl waved him back. "Do not enter, Mr. Purdy. I told you to wait for me downstairs."

"The sheriff can make me leave if he wants to, girlie." The super crossed into the room, a bony finger pointing to the body. Sidestepping the overturned chair, he made a beeline for the half-opened drawer, muttering as he snatched at the handle. Luke moved to stop him, but Cheryl was faster.

"Mr. Purdy! This is a crime scene." Cheryl shoved him away from the dresser and clutched his arm to remove him. Purdy aimed his captured elbow at her stomach, which Cheryl easily evaded. Instead, Cheryl hooked a leg behind him and tumbled Purdy to the floor. With efficient motions, she had him on his stomach, a foot planted between his shoulder blades, his hands manacled in hers. "And the name is Deputy Richardson, not *girlie*."

"Purdy." Luke advanced toward the fallen man. "Don't make Deputy Richardson arrest you for assaulting an officer. Again."

Lifting his head awkwardly, Purdy complained, "I just wanted to look in the drawer, Sheriff. That meth-head Clay Griffin, Sheriff, owed me rent, the bum. Coming and going and dealing, driving a new car and buying all kinds fancy equipment, but never able to make the rent on time. I want my money," he announced dolefully.

Luke motioned to Cheryl to release Purdy, and she reluctantly lifted her boot and freed his hands. While Purdy scrambled up, she planted herself between him and the dresser with its half-opened drawer. She gritted out, "Do not enter the premises again, Mr. Purdy. Next time, you're going to the station."

Mr. Purdy sputtered, "Can't keep me out of my own apartment. I watch television. I've got rights." He tried to skirt around her, and when she blocked his path, he spun on his heel and faced Luke, whining, "I think he kept his stash in that there drawer. I've got bills to pay, and he owes me rent. Just let me get what's mine and I'll be on my way."

Hiding a grin, Luke stepped forward and draped an arm around the older man's spindly shoulders. The flush on Cheryl's cheek meant that she had her temper by a very fine thread. With an insistent grip, he steered the super toward the door. "Mr. Purdy. We've been over this before. This is a crime scene. Until we've finished up in here, you can't come inside. You can't claim property, and you can't touch anything. Remember?"

"But, Sheriff, the man owes me money. And if he's dead, how's he gonna pay? You tell me that? People die around here or get arrested and they never have to pay. How's decent folks supposed to make a living?"

"Stop renting to deadbeats and hoodlums," muttered Cheryl as she returned to her post by the deceased.

"Whatcha say?" Mr. Purdy shot an angry look at the back of her head. When she didn't respond, he appealed to Luke, "I just try to make sure everybody's got a place to lay their heads at night. I don't discriminate, not like some folks. I say money's green, you're right with me. I don't put nobody on the street."

"Of course you don't, Mr. Purdy." Luke nodded in support, guiding the man steadily to the door. He didn't add that Purdy's indifference to the source of income explained his high-default rate. "The Palace has just had a run of bad luck."

Hearing the sympathy, Mr. Purdy hung his bald head and shook it limply, glancing back forlornly at the drawer. He stopped in the hallway and glared at Cheryl, who refused to look up. Thwarted, he turned his attention to Luke and fixed his face with a placating smile that revealed yellowing teeth. "I'm trying to make an honest living, Sheriff. Like every man's gotta right to."

"Absolutely," Luke replied, bracing his arm on the doorjamb, effectively blocking the smaller man. "And it's my job to make sure that you aren't constantly bothered by a criminal element intent on preying on your residents."

"Good. Good." Mr. Purdy sidled closer to Luke and whispered, "Any money you find in here belongs to me first, right?"

"I'll make a note in the file." Luke clapped the man

on the shoulder. "If you could do me a favor, Mr.
Purdy?"

"Yes, sir. Whatcha need?"

"Run downstairs and let Deputy Brooks know that he
can head back to the station. Chief Deputy Richardson
and I will handle it from here. Also, please direct the
ambulance to this apartment when they arrive, okay?"

Puffing out, Purdy bobbed his head in assent. "Happy
to, Sheriff. Anything for the law." He started down the
dimly lit hallway. He paused and turned. "You'll check
the drawers for me, right?"

"I'll make sure you get what you deserve, Mr. Purdy."
When Purdy disappeared around the corner, Luke re-
turned to the victim's prone form and squatted beside
Cheryl. "He touch anything else in here?"

"No, sir. Was afraid to come inside until I arrived,
and I had Brooks take him downstairs to pull Griffin's
file." Sliding seamlessly into her report, she continued, "Neighbor called in a complaint about the smells
emanating from the apartment around nine A.M. Says
she came over and knocked on the door, but no one
answered. Deputy Brooks and I responded at nine
twenty-seven A.M. and requested entry. When we received no response, we tried the door and found it un-
latched. We entered the premises with Mr. Purdy and
saw the body."

Cheryl pointed to the corpse. "The victim was stabbed
in the thigh, Sheriff. Severed his femoral artery, from
the looks of it."

"Strange way to kill a drug dealer," Luke murmured.
"Intimate."

"Intimate?"

Nodding, Luke pointed at the ugly gash in the inner leg. "Most stab wounds are to obvious places. The throat, the heart. Easy to reach locations. Stabbing a man in the thigh is specific. Personal. The killer would likely know that the wound bleeds quickly, that a cut there is always fatal if not treated immediately."

"So his killer knew him."

"Probably." Luke continued to study the body. "From the smell and the state of rigor, I'd say he died thirty-six to forty-eight hours ago, but the coroner can confirm."

"The body doesn't appear to have been moved. Whoever stabbed him left him here to die." She gestured to the floor. "He didn't try to crawl to the phone or get help. Just bled to death."

"Any sign of the weapon?"

"No, sir. The only knife in the apartment is in the sink, and this wound looks too clean to have come from something that dull." Cheryl speculated, "I assume the killer took the knife with him."

"Makes sense. Anything else?"

She jerked her chin at the television set. "Sir, that flat screen costs a cool three thousand. My husband James has been drooling over them ever since Hopkin's Electronics got one in stock. And my kids got that Xbox for Christmas. Four hundred bucks."

"Yet the vic's got a broken couch and a crate as furniture. And according to Purdy's rant, he also has a brand-new car."

"A Hummer," Cheryl offered with an arched brow. "Brooks is having it impounded."

Luke released a low whistle. "Have Brooks run a title search and see who offered our local dealer credit or if they took cash."

"Will do." She rose and walked to the drawer that Purdy tried to open. "Last thing, sir. The drawers were empty when we arrived. The top one was shut, and the bottom one barely opens. Whoever was here pulled out the middle drawer and left it open. Purdy thinks it's where Griffin kept his stash."

"So they steal his drugs but not the merchandise."

"Perhaps. I'm dusting it for residue and prints. Purdy got his hands on it before, so we'll have to account for his prints too. I'd like to send it to the lab for testing."

"You thinking this was a drug deal gone sour?"

"Yes, sir. Sad, but not unexpected. Clay Griffin has been in trouble since he was a kid. In fact, I collared him my first day on the job. He lived at the Center for a while when I was there, but even Mrs. Faraday couldn't keep him on the narrow."

From his crouch near the body, Luke lifted one of Clay's hands to his nose. He sniffed once, then took a deeper draught. "Pine oil."

Cheryl frowned. "Sir?"

"His hand smells like pine oil. And there's some residue on the skin." Luke turned the hand palm up. "Under the fingernails and on the tips. There's something sticky. Not meth."

"You could smell pine oil through that stink?"

Luke quirked the corner of his mouth. "We all have our talents, Richardson." He gently replaced the hand and moved down to the shoes. "Same smell here, but mixed with something earthier. There's soil in the grooves. Have the lab run tests on the shoes and whatever is under his nails."

Cheryl took notes and glanced at her boss. "You don't think this is a drug deal."

Rising to his feet, Luke gave a diffident shrug. "Don't know. Just seems to me, if you're going to kill a man over a drug deal, you'd take the three thousand in merchandise and the fifty-thousand-dollar truck and not just what's in a drawer."

Chagrined that she missed the details, she murmured, "Of course, sir. I wasn't thinking."

"Deputy, when a drug dealer dies, nine times out of ten, the killer was one of his own." He walked to the door. "This simply might be time number ten."

Kell Jameson curled manicured fingers on the jury rail and leaned in close. "The prosecutor expects you to believe that my client is a maniac. That the man you watched on Tuesday nights for eleven seasons simply snapped. That a terrible accident, brought on by age and outrage, should be treated as vehicular homicide. Paul Brodie played America's father—both on television and in real life. The Brodie Foundation sends children to summer camp at Lake Harrell, giving them a chance to know a different way to live. When his co-star Denise Terry faced a crippling disease, he donated millions for her care. When his on-screen daughter, Nicole Monroe, struggled with alcoholism and drug addiction, he didn't turn away. He placed her in rehab and stayed by her side. When his nephew, the actor—"

"Objection, Your Honor." Chére Debue, the prosecutor, stood up, head shaking. "This isn't the sentencing hearing, Judge. These facts are not relevant to the case."

Kell turned quickly to face the judge, her face grim. "I disagree. Your Honor, these facts are essential to this case. More importantly, they are central to my closing argument, which is not subject to objection by the prosecution, which she may have forgotten. The Georgia Rules of Criminal Procedure clearly allow an attorney to offer information during closing arguments that may aid the jury in reaching its decision, where such information is not a misstatement, prejudicial, or a personal attack."

The D.A. snorted. "I don't see how recounting Mr. Brodie's humanitarian efforts are germane to a case of road rage that made him leave a man in a burning car."

Before Kell could muster her objection, the judge barked out, "Attorneys, approach!"

In a sleek black suit that stopped an inch shy of inappropriate, D.A. Debue strode up to the bench. In a tight whisper, she hissed, "She's crossed the line, Your Honor. And, I must say, I am surprised that you've allowed her to make a mockery of your court. Ms. Jameson has turned this case into a circus, with you as the ringmaster. Cameras follow everyone. A juror had to be released because he couldn't take the attention. Now, you're allowing her to canonize a murderer because he reads cue cards well and looks like Santa Claus. I expected more of the courts, sir."

Kell watched in silent glee as Judge Harold Post darkened from his normally ruddy hue to a color approaching eggplant. Resisting the urge to speak, she simply stared at the judge and waited for the explosion. It wasn't long in coming.

"Enough." Judge Post clamped his hand over the microphone. "That is enough, Ms. Debue." Sputtering, he blasted in a low voice, "If anyone has crossed the line, you have. I allowed this case to move forward, expecting you to provide some scintilla of evidence that Paul Brodie had intentionally driven that man off the road. Instead, what you have produced is random theory strung together with innuendo. While I have half a mind to grant the defense's motion for a directed verdict, for the sake of the Fulton County D.A.'s reputation, I will allow this farce to come to a merciful end."

"But, Your Honor—"

"Objection overruled, Ms. Debue."

Removing his hand from the mike, he waved them away from the bench. He pronounced again, "Objection overruled."

Kell repressed a look of triumph and turned back to the rapt jury, projecting the mix of sorrow and compassion that had swayed juries in verdict after verdict. She pitched her voice soft, tinged by the traces of Southern honey that she had ruthlessly exorcised in law school and kept hidden until necessary. "Paul Brodie is an elderly man today. One who, on a rainy night, failed to notice that he cut off a driver on I–85. One who drove up beside that driver later to apologize. One who was terrified by the sight of a gun and tried to speed away.

One who will always regret that his SUV slid across the slick asphalt and collided with the truck. One who will never forget the six rolls that ended tragically against the guardrail that night."

She fixed her sights on a man in his early thirties, one who had grown up, like her, with Paul Brodie's *American Dad* spouting clichéd one-liners about family values and loyalty. Juror number seven would never hear about the sobriety test Paul had failed or the spiked levels of Viagra in his system that had acted like adrenaline in a man on too many legal pharmaceuticals. Evidence that had been tossed out because the police got overly excited about meeting a celebrity.

"If you believe Paul Brodie, America's dad, would intentionally drive a man to his death, that he would glory in the sight of a car exploding, then you do not know Paul Brodie. He not only welcomed us into his television home, but he has opened his very soul to you during this trial. Look inside, I implore each of you, and tell me if you see the ugly, bitter man the prosecution describes. If you don't . . ." She paused here, letting the honey thicken and the image linger. "If you don't, then you must return a verdict of not guilty and send Paul home to his family."

The moment on film would have called for her to hang her head, but Kell didn't believe in overkill. Instead, she turned slowly on the Manolo Blahniks she treated herself to last month, made of a supple aubergine leather that matched her Calvin Klein suit with its pencil-thin skirt.

Behind her, Juror Seven focused on the sculpted calves and generous curves that the tailored suit highlighted. Juror Four appreciated the purposeful yet graceful stride that belied three-inch heels made of splinters. For his part, Juror Eleven wondered if the stunning attorney wore more than the bare essentials beneath the jacket that framed her narrow waist in sharp relief.

Kell wasn't privy to the thoughts of the jurors, but none of them would have surprised her. She chose her wardrobe as carefully as her words. All designed to project femininity, accessibility and confidence and to mask the killer instinct that gave her a 90 percent win rate in court. Sliding into the seat beside her partner, David Trent, Kell listened to Judge Post as he offered jury instructions. Paul Brodie was led back to the court's holding cell, with a reminder from Kell to speak to no one.

When the jury filed out of the courtroom and the judge declared a recess, she leaned in to David. "Fifty says they're back in under thirty minutes."

"Come on, Kell, not even you're that good. It'll take that long to get their lunch order straight." David brushed a finger along the back of her hand. "But add a night at my place, and you've got a bet."

Kell and David did this dance at least once a week. Despite her resistance to the idea of expanding their relationship, David tried his best. As she did each time he asked, she queried, "Is the cat gone?"

David scowled. "Pepper has been with me since college, Kell."

Kell's hand disappeared into her lap, while the other

drummed a restless tattoo on the defense table. "As long as the cat is in residence, I'm not. You know the rules."

"You won't come over until I get rid of my best friend?"

Allowing her eyes to go limpid, she touched his thigh lightly beneath the table. "We all have to make choices, David." And he would never get rid of that cat.

"Come on, Kell—"

In her pocket, her cell phone came to life. "Hold that thought, David." With the court on recess, she was free to remove the phone and flip open the receiver. "Kell Jameson."

"Kell? Kell, dear?"

With three words, the past rushed in and crashed through her. Kell stiffened in her seat, her hand falling away from David's leg. "Mrs. Faraday?"

"Yes, honey. It's me. I need your help."

The voice on the other end caught on a gasp that sounded suspiciously like a sob. Kell shoved her chair back and made her way out of the courtroom. "What's wrong, Mrs. F? Is it Finn or Julia? Are you hurt?"

"I haven't heard from Findley or you in sixteen years, Kell." Censure coated her response. "Julia is well, I believe. As am I. For now."

In the corridor, spiky heels clicked on the marble floor as she made her way to the witness prep room. "What's happened?" Mind spinning, Kell forced herself to sit and take a deep breath. It wasn't often that her past found her, and each time it did, it left her reeling. "Are you in trouble, Mrs. F?"

"Yes, I am." Another breath sighed out. "I'm afraid I'm about to be arrested, Kell. I need you to represent me."

Kell stared at the scarred conference table, thinking how quickly she could be drawn again to the place she'd tried her best to escape from. Images flashed in a nightmare she'd thought long behind her. Or concealed in a safety-deposit box. She hadn't realized it took only a phone call. Forcing herself to focus, she asked, "Arrested for what? When?"

"I don't know exactly." Mrs. Faraday's voice trembled slightly, then firmed. "That is to say, I don't know when, but I want to be prepared."

"What's the charge, Mrs. Faraday? Why do you need an attorney?"

"Clay Griffin's dead, Kell. And I might be arrested for his murder."

CHAPTER 2

The sleek silver Porsche slid neatly into the lone space in front of the Magnolia Bed and Breakfast. Kell shifted the gear into park and turned off the ignition. With practiced motions, she stowed her PDA in her briefcase, all the while listening intently to the man haranguing her in her earpiece.

"We don't have time for a *pro bono* case right now," David carped. "But if you insist, at least let me send down one of the interns to take the woman's statement and see if there's even a case."

Kell tipped her head back against the smooth leather seat and grappled for patience. One of the joys of partnership with David Trent was his single-minded focus on the bottom line. His fascination with building their coffers left her free to practice law and burnish their reputation as lawyers to the stars. The downside, of course, came when she took a client without a marquee name or a trust fund. Thinking of the hundred thousand dollars sitting untouched, she corrected, "I can cover the costs, David. Bill me out at my regular rate."

"Using your draw? I'm afraid your new toy has put a dent in your funds," David contradicted. "And a little old lady running an orphanage can't afford you to cover a parking ticket and certainly not a murder trial."

In a placating tone that usually worked, she reminded him, "The woman's name is Mrs. Faraday, and I've known her most of my life. She wouldn't have called if wasn't important."

"I appreciate your altruistic streak, darling, but we have bills to pay. As our rainmaker, I need you here for the cameras. Today."

Closing her eyes behind the wide-framed sunglasses perched on a nose that was just shy of pert, she bit back a sigh. "David, we won the Brodie case with a unanimous verdict. You can handle the press without me. The standard lines about how we knew he was innocent. Blah, blah, blah."

"Brodie is already yesterday's news. That fast verdict didn't even give *CourtWatch TV* time for a verdict clock," he whined. "You're the story here. Kell Jameson, attorney extraordinaire. In the past year, you've successfully defended the NFL's leading rusher, a best-selling author, and now the country's most beloved actor. What if a reporter wants to talk to you? Thirty minutes in a murder trial decision might be some kind of a record."

"Twenty-eight minutes, actually. And if a reporter calls, I've got my cell." Reaching up, Kell slid her hand through dark brown hair that appeared black except in direct sunlight. The shoulder length mane had been duly treated and blown dry by her stylist on Monday, and the silken strands felt cool in the rapidly heating car. If she didn't turn the engine back on in a few seconds, though, the hot, wet Georgia summer would force its way inside.

She twirled a strand around a coral tipped-fingernail. Perhaps logic would work where sentiment failed. "The longer we fight about this, the longer it will take for me to get back to Atlanta. I promised Mrs. Faraday I would drive down today and hear her out. I can't believe the woman I know harmed anyone—and no one else will either."

"Explain to me again why you even need to be there," David demanded, annoyance growing. He had plans for the weekend that included an exclusive spa and over-priced room service, sans cat. Not a meaningless trip to a forgotten hole in middle Georgia. "I made reservations at Barnsley Gardens for the weekend."

Kell felt a twinge of irritation, but only for an instant. David's tenacity was his best feature, so she couldn't complain when it strayed into personal territory. Still, she said firmly, "You shouldn't have, David."

"Give me a chance, darling. We work well in the office and the courtroom. Why not try for three out of three?"

"Because I don't have the patience or the energy to find a new partner if we fail." Which they no doubt would. Kell had a romantic track record that was the mirror opposite of her courtroom success. There was no way she'd let David become the next casualty. "You have plenty of work to keep you occupied this weekend. We got requests this week from L.A., with trial dates starting in November. With you on the Susan Antonetti drug-possession case, and Malikah finishing up the Tengley shoplifting trial, we've got more than enough work to keep the firm afloat while I take a short trip."

"Assuming this isn't a ruse to get something else out of you." David shifted his tone to concerned. "Don't you find it suspicious that a woman you haven't heard from in sixteen years calls you out of the blue, Kell? She hasn't been charged with a crime. Hell, according to what you told me, we don't even know if a crime has been committed. A drug dealer that she ran off her property is found dead."

"Your point?"

"No offense to your friend, but you've been in the press almost every day for ten weeks. Isn't there the slightest possibility that this Mrs. Faraday might not be on the level with you?"

Without hesitation, Kell responded coolly, "None at all. Mrs. F wouldn't do that to me. To anyone." She released a tense breath. "David, she's the closest thing I've ever had to a real mother. I owe her."

Recognizing the steel in her voice, he relented. "Today's Friday. I assume I can expect to see you on Monday?"

"I doubt it'll take that long. I'll talk to Mrs. F, calm her down, and see what I can find out about the police's case. In fact, have Roland run a background check on Clay Griffin. I want priors, bankruptcies, speeding tickets, missed dental appointments, anything."

David grumbled, "You said there's nothing to worry about. Why do you need all this information?"

"Because that's how I win." And because of the nagging headache that had plagued her since yesterday afternoon and the mention of Clay Griffin's name. She didn't add that some of the items on his rap sheet would be very, very familiar to her. "Malikah should contact the M.E.'s office in Macon. Tracy Hoover." Anticipating his question, she explained, "Hallden is a small county. They send their forensic work to Bibb County."

"Will she tell us anything?"

"We're old friends. Just have Malikah give her a call and use my name."

Kell felt a shadow fall across the driver's window, which she ignored. Probably a resident trying to get a closer peek at her car. She'd bought it with the retainer on the Brodie case, and she doubted Hallden's streets had seen a Porsche before.

Patting the leather steering wheel, she rattled off additional assignments. No use in wasting a perfectly good weekend. The associates at Jameson Trent would whine to David about the extra work, then they'd jockey for a seat at the table for trial. Hunger and avarice were essential to her line of work, and neither was in short supply. "I need to get a status update on the McCall investigation. We go to trial in eight weeks. Assign that to Doug Collins. He's pretty good with asking questions."

When a knuckle rapped on her window, she waved the intruder away. "I'll fax you the markup of the Tatum brief, once I've settled in tonight."

"Ma'am." The man outside her car knocked sharply on the tinted pane. "Ma'am, please step out of the vehicle."

She whipped her head to window, startled. "What?"

"Huh?" David asked in puzzlement. "What's going on?"

Kell made the khaki-wearing interloper instantly. "There's a cop at my window. I've got to run. See you on Monday." Without waiting for a reply, she snapped the phone shut. Twisting the key in the ignition, she let the engine purr on and released the window. The glass slid down quietly, revealing a tall uniformed man holding a yellow and white citation pad. He towered over the low-slung sports car, permitting her only a view of an athletic torso and long, elegant fingers busy writing her a traffic ticket.

Pasting on her best smile, Kell peered up at the meter maid. *Darn.* She thought she'd slid under the traffic light unseen. "Is there a problem, Officer?"

"I've been flashing my lights at you for nearly a quarter of a mile."

The bass timbre of the voice matched the powerful build. "Big case," she apologized lightly. "I must have been distracted for a second. Won't happen again."

"It happened three times, Miss."

Three lights? She hadn't noticed. "Are you certain?"

He repeated blandly, "Please step out of the vehicle."

Exasperation crept into her pleasant expression. Stepping out of the vehicle was cop-speak for trouble. Even if she had run a few lights, which she didn't concede, she couldn't imagine why he would be at her window demanding that she present herself like a perp. Indulging him, she asked, "Can you tell me what the problem is, Officer?"

"At the present, it is your refusal to step out of the vehicle, Miss." He paced away and clasped his hands behind him. "Now, Miss."

Kell folded her hands on the steering wheel and studied the officer as he came into full view. Closely cropped black hair curled against a high forehead. Sunlight slanted over his features, revealing a square jawline that dimpled in the center and cheekbones angled enough to cut class. Shades covered his eyes, which were likely glaring, if the tight lips were any indication.

In other circumstances, she might have found the sculpted mouth appealing, the rugged face handsome. "Why don't you tell me what you want? If it's a peek inside the car, I'm happy to oblige. I know folks rarely get to see a Porsche this close."

"Miss." The word bore no resemblance to a question.

Reclining into the seat, Kell switched tactics. In the tone she used with recalcitrant witnesses, she said, "I'd rather not get out of my car until I understand the nature of the problem, Officer."

"Get out of the vehicle, and I'll be happy to explain."

She knew better than to antagonize law enforcement, but something in the gravelly voice raised her hackles. The cool interior had been transformed into a makeshift sauna in a matter of seconds, and her temperature rose to match. "Hallden doesn't have three traffic lights, sir. I must assume you are simply trying to harass me."

"What I'm doing is my job." He placed a hand on the

car door. "Which will include an arrest in about thirty seconds."

Kell bristled. "Arrest on what grounds? Even if I ran a couple of lights, that doesn't warrant more than a citation."

"You must be a lawyer."

The summary left little doubt of his opinion of her profession. To taunt, she corrected, "Actually, I'm a defense attorney."

"Figures." He braced a hand on the roof and brought his face down to hers. "When I attempted to stop you earlier, I intended to warn you about your speed and disregard for traffic safety. My current issue, Miss, is your failure to obey an officer." He smiled then, a sensuous, taunting smile. "Keep talking and let's see what else we can come up with."

With a gasp at the blatant threat, Kell jutted her chin out defiantly. "I'll have your badge."

"You can try." With an easy motion, he unhooked his radio and depressed a button. "Curly?"

Static gave way to a bass voice that could have scratched the paint from her car. "Yes, Luke?"

"Give Jonice a call for me, will you? Have her meet me in front of the Magnolia. Bring Rosie."

"Yes, sir. It'll be about ten minutes, though. She's been out at the Houston place. Something's wrong with the tractor. Coughin' smoke something terrible."

"Don't worry. I'll be here." Sheriff Luke Calder rested his forearms onto the window frame. The lady lawyer shifted away, then returned to her insolent position, eyes staring balefully at him. He admired the audacity of the move, almost as much as the cameo face that looked ready to spit nails. Lord, she was beautiful. And she knew it.

Luke studied his sudden adversary. Masses of sable swept away from a widow's peak and cascaded to shoulders framed by two thin straps. The white top veed into curves that nudged his pulse into attention. Damnably long legs were framed by a flowered skirt that left just enough to the imagination.

But it was the face that drew his focus. Wide-set eyes looked out from a delicate triangle that melded graceful and bold in equal measure. Hers was a face that got a man's attention and held it with melted chocolate eyes and a courtesan's mouth.

When that mouth pouted at him, he took a firmer grip on his thoughts. Midday was his turn to patrol the mean streets of Hallden County. At a population of 6,708, if the welcome sign was to be believed, the circuit took twenty minutes on a good day and ended at the city limits of Hallden proper.

Indeed, he'd been on his way to find lunch when the steel gray 911 Carrera zipped under a yellow light at the county line. Rather than raise the siren, he decided to follow the leadfoot into town. The driver had been too busy talking on the phone to notice his tail. She'd pulled into the Magnolia and still didn't register the flashing blue lights.

Which reminded him—he owed her a citation for parking in front of a hydrant. Luke measured the cocky tilt of her pointed chin and the flash of rebellion in the eyes that were trying to bore holes into him. His guess was that she understood the gift nature had given her with a gorgeous face and body to match. No doubt, she relied on both. Men probably took one look and catered to her every whim. He bit back a grin. *Wrong town, lady.* "Can I have your name, Miss?"

"Kell Jameson." She narrowed her eyes at him, waiting for a reaction. "Perhaps you've heard of me?"

"Should I have?" he remarked quizzically, well aware of who she was. Not that he could remember much beside his own name right now. Up close, the caramel porcelain skin carried a scent that teased his senses, appearing and disappearing on notes of spice and sex. A fist of heat punched at his gut and his tripping pulse sped to a gallop.

Luke hurriedly straightened and scribbled the name on the pad, added his signature and ripped off the white cover sheet. "This one is because you're parked in front of a hydrant, Miss." He passed the ticket to her through the open window.

Grateful he moved away, Kell released a breath she hadn't been aware of taking. With the sun in her eyes, he'd been handsome. Closer in, the ruggedly handsome face was extraordinary. Add in the way he said *Miss* with a drawl that was neither southern nor western, and she nearly forgot what they were discussing.

Oh, yes. Traffic tickets. In defense as much as defiance, Kell folded her arms, refusing to accept the sheet. "I did not run three lights, and I'm not accepting a citation from you."

"Well, yes, ma'am, you did and, yes, you are." He

watched in fascination as color flushed her cheeks
and bowed the mouth that would follow him into his
dreams. A routine traffic stop had become a war of
wills for her. *Interesting*.

Because Jonice wouldn't be here for a while, he
decided to enjoy himself. Fighting with a gorgeous
woman had to be more fun than what waited for him
back at the station. Paperwork, a dead junkie, and
two John Does. Luke extended his hand inside the
window and instructed, "Take the ticket, Ms. Jameson."

"No, sir, I will not." Kell twisted to her right and gestured out the window to the front door of the Magnolia.
"I am parked on a public street, and I'm not in front of
a hydrant, Officer. Perhaps they didn't teach you the
difference in meter maid school."

The insult slapped at him. "Excuse me?"

"No, excuse me," Kell sneered with false politeness.
"*Traffic enforcement officer* is what they call you these
days, right?"

"You think I'm the meter maid?"

Talking over him, she continued, "And one day, if
you harass a sufficient number of tourists, they might
promote you, hmm? A warning, though, Officer. Pick
your targets better. Stay away from the ones who can
read and write. Like me."

Luke gritted his teeth. "Be careful, Ms. Jameson. Be
very careful."

Revving up, Kell taunted, "Or what? You'll write me
another ticket?"

"Absolutely." Pride pricked, he dropped the first citation into her lap. "This one will get you started. Give me a second to make out the next one."

In full righteous outrage, Kell sputtered, "This is a blatant abuse of power. And I'll prove it." She snatched her phone from the passenger seat. "A picture of your incompetence should do the trick."

Luke glowered. He didn't take himself too seriously, but being called the meter maid raised his hackles. "By all means. Take a photo for the judge. I appreciate the help. Maybe you can record yourself talking, and save me the trouble of explaining your attitude problems too."

When she muttered a curse, Luke jerked at the handle, and Kell sprang from the car. The ticket he'd dropped in her lap fell to the asphalt. She ignored the paper and marched to the rear of the car. Glaring over her shoulder at him, she pointed down at the sidewalk. "There's no hydrant here."

From behind her, Luke extended an arm covered in brown khaki. He curled his hand around her forearm and moved it over and up. The skin beneath his fingers felt as soft as a whisper. He gauged her height at 5'7, a full head shorter than his own 6'3. Generously curved, the body in front of his brushed against him, igniting an immediate reaction. *Steady*, he cautioned himself.

He aimed her toward a red valve embedded in the side of the building. "Right there, Miss. See the spigot? That's a fire hydrant." He pointed to the curb, where white paint gave way to more red. "That paint indicates the fire hydrant zone. Your bumper clearly extends past the white and into the red."

"By a centimeter," Kell protested faintly. A muscled chest pressed against her back and the strong hand that clasped her arm nearly shorted her system. That, plus the fact that the centimeter was more like a foot, had her heart drumming. Adrenaline and unwelcome attraction pumped through her in combative unison. She'd be damned if this hick cop was going to be right. Even if he was.

Switching arguments, she insisted, "The hydrant isn't clearly marked. This is obviously a trap for unsuspecting visitors to town. I intend to have a word with the sheriff about this. Unless this was his idea of helping you all make your quotas."

"Sheriff Calder doesn't have quotas, ma'am. And you got your warning when we painted the sidewalk bright red." Releasing her arm with reluctance, Luke scratched information onto the pad and ripped off another sheet. He extended it to her, but she allowed it to flutter to the street.

It landed beside the first one. "Ms. Jameson, please pick up the citation."

"I will not." Kell folded her arms rebelliously and demanded, "What's it for?"

"Refusing to obey an officer of the law." With quick motions, he made out a third ticket. "You going to pick up the other two, Ms. Jameson?"

"Absolutely not."

"Thought so." He tore the paper off and handed it to her. "Littering a public street."

Before Kell could let loose the curses that bubbled up, the radio on his hip beeped imperiously. He walked a couple of paces away and engaged the radio. "Luke here."

"Yeah, Luke, it's Curly. Jonice called in and Houston's tractor is gonna need a new carburetor. She wants to know if the tow can wait until she gets them squared away."

At the mention of a tow truck, Kell panicked. A greasy, dilapidated contraption dragging her brand-new car to some disreputable garage to await the mercy of some justice of the peace. Over her dead body. Thinking fast, she scuttled to the driver's door, crushing the tickets beneath her feet.

"And, Luke? Rev. Palmer called in a vandal out at the parsonage. Somebody egged his house last night. He slept in, so he didn't smell it until the sun got real hot. Wants you to come out and take a look personally."

"Why doesn't he call Chief Graves? The church is on city property." A turf battle with the police chief ranked low on Luke's list of priorities at the moment. "Tell the good minister to call the police."

"He did, Luke. No one answered. Everybody except the dispatcher is on a lunch break."

With an inward sigh, Luke replied, "Tell Jonice not to worry about the tow. And let Rev. Palmer know I'm on my way. I have to finish up here and then I'll head out."

As he spoke, the sound of an idling engine engaging caught his ear. Kell Jameson had slipped behind the wheel and was pulling away from the curb.

"Ms. Jameson!" He jogged to car door and barely

missed being tapped by her bumper. "Fleeing the scene of a crime."

"Write me a ticket," Kell challenged as she streaked away.

"I think I'm in love," Luke muttered, trying to explain to himself why he wasn't angrier.

"What's that, Luke?"

With a self-deprecating laugh, Luke tucked his citation pad into his back pocket and responded, "Nothing, Curly. I'll be along soon."

The silver sports car moved quickly, catching every green light until it faded from view. Luke scooped up the tickets he'd dropped and climbed into the F–10 that he drove through town on patrol. He rubbed at his stomach, no longer hungry for food.

But Ms. Kell Jameson had certainly whet his appetite.

CHAPTER 3

"Who are you?"

The speaker waited impatiently for his answer, scuffing a tennis shoe as he swung his foot back and forth. He'd been stuck on the wooden porch for the best part of the afternoon and would be there until he said sorry to Lara O'Connor for pushing her off the swing. Didn't seem to matter to nobody that he'd called the tree swing first or that she'd jumped him in line when Cody showed him a booger the size of his fist. All because she was a girl and boys weren't supposed to push. Or hit or kick or anything else to get even.

If questioned, he would have explained his justification and lodged a protest at the unfairness of a rule that discriminated based on gender, especially when the girl could punch like Lara. But pushing girls didn't afford the offender the courtesy of explanation. Punishment came swift and fierce. Timeout on the porch—no playing allowed.

But when the cool silver car roared into the driveway, Jorden's day started looking up. The lady driving it wore movie-star sunglasses and was real tall for a girl. She had gotten out of the car and taken the short-cut across the gravel like she knew the place. However, Jorden didn't know her, and Mrs. F didn't like strangers coming around too much. Especially when they looked like social workers.

To Jorden, most adults looked like social workers.

He tapped his foot on the porch, like he'd seen Sheriff Calder do when he wanted a quick answer. Pitching his voice in rough imitation, he demanded, "What do you want around here?"

Kell paused on the bottom step. She wasn't in the mood for impertinent questions or any further delays. Adrenaline from the run-in with Dudley Do-Right bubbled in her veins, tinged with a hint of shame at her panicky flight from justice. Still, she would have given a week's pay to see the officer's face clearly as her tires squealed away.

Yet, the lawyer in her had to acknowledge that her ill-conceived departure possessed a major flaw. As she dashed through the second stoplight, she'd considered—belatedly—that her car, with its *Law Won* license plate, would not be difficult to trace. And Luke struck her as the inquisitive sort. With any luck, though, she'd be safely ensconced in her bed in East Lake in the heart of Atlanta before he tracked her out to the Center.

The little boy cleared his throat determinedly. "I asked you a question, lady. Who are you and what do you want?"

"That's two questions and the answer to both is none of your business," Kell retorted as she climbed the steps to the porch. Her hand curved around the white railing that ran the length of the shallow steps. She'd spent many a summer afternoon repainting the handrails in punishment for some infraction. The memory brought a fond smile. She reached the final wooden plank, only to find her way blocked by the boy, whose posture reminded her oddly of Officer Luke.

More familiar was his insistence that she do as he wanted. *What was it with men in Hallden today?* she wondered in exasperation. Her latest interrogator appeared to be no more than nine years old, his overalls showing signs of a recent brawl. Dust and a darkening bruise streaked below one suspicious brown eye and more dirt held tight to the ripped knees and the red T-shirt beneath the denim straps, one of which hung drunkenly from its mooring. Kell assumed the fight explained his presence on the porch rather than in the backyard with the other children she could hear whooping and yelling.

How many times had she and Fin been confined to the porch prison for breaking one of Mrs. F's rules? Remembering the slippery mix of outrage and disgrace, she sympathized with the inmate, but not enough to remain on the steps in the direct path of the sun. She brushed past the boy with a murmured "Excuse me."

Stopping beneath the fan that circled lazily above her head, she lifted a hand to slip her shades up and into her hair. The boy scurried to place himself between her and the imposing oak door with its burnished brass handle that she suspected he'd polished more than once. Her eyes met the boy's and she inclined her head in polite acknowledgement. "I'm here to see Mrs. F. Is she home?"

Jorden scowled at the lady's easy use of the nickname. Only residents of the Center called her that. Even more suspicious now, he stopped tapping his foot and instead folded his arms and glared at the newcomer. "Where are you from?"

"Atlanta."

At her terse response, the slender young body snapped ramrod straight, alerted by the mention of the capital city. Jorden knew that little good came from visits from there. Atlanta represented power and authority and the worst kind of trouble. Grown-ups from the city didn't bring good news. They had lots of questions but didn't say much worth listening to, he'd learned. Still, he forced himself to ask, "You here to take somebody?"

Kell softened as she recognized the apprehension that lay beneath the question. She resisted the urge to bend and, instead, extended her hand in greeting. When he hesitantly placed his smaller one inside, she shook it formally. "My name is Kell Jameson, and I'm not a social worker. I'm a friend of Mrs. F's and she asked me to come and see her. What's your name?"

"Not supposed to tell strangers who we are," he explained apologetically, impressed by the handshake and the smooth, cool fingers that held his. "Unless Mrs. F or a teacher tells you to."

"That's a good rule."

"Yeah, maybe. Mrs. F's gotta lot of rules. It's hard to

remember them all," came the plaintive reply. He kept his hand very still, hoping she wouldn't notice he hadn't let go. The touch kind of reminded him of his mother's hand when they used to cross the street. Nice. "I'm on punishment for pushing a girl. Can't do that, even if they cheat and skip in line and hit you in the eye."

Kell grinned conspiratorially and bent closer. "I got in trouble for sliding down the banister in the front hall. Flew right into the china cabinet. Had to paint these railings. I also spent a lot of days on the porch for climbing Old Magnolia without permission."

Eyes wide with disbelief, Jorden returned her smile. "You used to live here?"

Pointing up at a window on the third floor of the house, she answered, "Right up there. The yellow bedroom with the canopy beds."

"That's where my sister, Faith, sleeps. Cool." Jorden considered this new information. A former resident of the Center wasn't exactly a stranger. If Mrs. F knew her, then she wasn't strange to them. Deciding to take a chance and break another rule, he offered, "My name's Jorden. I'm nine and a half."

"Nice to meet you, Jorden." Still holding his hand, Kell moved them toward the front door. "Will you take me to see Mrs. F?"

"Sure." He reached up and twisted the knob of the door. The heavy oak swung on its hinges, and he flew inside, pulling her along. Jorden shouted, "Mrs. F! Mrs. F! There's a pretty lady here to see you!"

Kell remained in the hallway, buffeted by memories she rarely allowed to surface. Hardwood floors shone with the dull brilliance that spoke of dozens of children's feet trampling their polished surfaces. The foyer spread wide, its centerpiece a majestic staircase that rose from a broad bottom step and curved up to the second level, where a landing overlooked the main floor. Six spaces carved into bedrooms for children ran the length of the second floor. A second staircase rose to the third floor, where the older children lived in five additional rooms. Two bathrooms served each floor, one for boys and another for girls.

Looking to her left, the mahogany door that guarded Mrs. F's study and the interior entrance to the library stood ajar. A teenage girl sat cross-legged on an ottoman near a towering bookcase in the library, a book open in her lap. Red hair escaped from a baseball cap she wore low on her forehead, despite being inside.

Hungry eyes skimmed the interior, noting a new sofa in the sitting room, a different table in the dining room. Paintings adorned the walls, an indiscriminate mix of masterworks and finger paint. In the Faraday Center, Southern architecture melded seamlessly with Senegalese weavings and Indian sculpture. Kell had been one of the few in her freshman art class who'd been able to correctly identify both Mondrian and Jacob Lawrence. Of course, she could also throw a punch and a party with equal dexterity. Mrs. F believed in raising well-rounded charges who could fend for themselves.

Sometimes too well.

"Here she is, Mrs. F. The lady with the car." Jorden skidded to a stop by Kell and grabbed her arm. Together they turned, Jorden chattering rapidly. "I told Mrs. F that I came inside cause you asked me to—even though I'm supposed to be on the porch until she tells me to come in. And that I was very polite when you arrived," he added hopefully.

At a more graceful but no less hurried pace, Mrs. Eliza Faraday approached their position, hands clasped in front of a salmon pink suit with pearl buttons. A string of real pearls encircled her neck and smaller ones dangled from her ears. Diminutive in height, she nevertheless walked with a carriage that made a person forget she barely topped five feet.

Kell stared, taking in the gray and white hair pulled into a sleek chignon that emphasized the fair brown complexion and direct hazel eyes. A patrician nose too strong for an ordinary woman nicely balanced the determined features that dared comment. At sixty-three, Eliza Faraday wore her years elegantly, as though defying age to stake a claim. She stopped in front of Jorden and Kell.

She looks exactly the same, Kell marveled. *Exactly.* She took a small step forward, unsure of her welcome. Sixteen years had become a lifetime. She lifted her chin and smiled hesitantly. "Mrs. F."

"Kell." The older woman took another step and opened her arms. "Welcome home, honey."

Even as she promised herself she wouldn't, Kell found herself wrapped in a hug that wiped away the years of distance and disappointment. A sob pressed against her throat, but she refused to give in to the threat of tears. "Oh, Mrs. F, I've missed you. So much."

Eliza squeezed once, then slipped her hands up to Kell's shoulders, holding her away. "Well, you're here now, and that's what matters. Jorden."

Jorden watched the reunion with fascination, trying to figure out what trouble Kell had been into that nearly had her crying. When he heard his name repeated, he jolted to attention. "Yes, ma'am?"

"Go on outside and join the others. Let everyone know that evening chores start in an hour."

"Yes, ma'am!" He took off at a dead run for the kitchen door before she recalled that his punishment didn't end for another fifteen minutes.

"Walk, Jorden. Walk."

Ignoring the directive, he careened around the corner and disappeared from view. Smothering a laugh, Eliza hooked her arm in Kell's. "Let's go have ourselves a talk. We've got a lot to catch up on."

Echoing Jorden, she responded, "Yes, ma'am."

Eliza led her into the study, which contained an antique desk and matching captain's seat, flanked by two Queen Anne chairs upholstered in sapphire. A trio of bay windows framed the side garden. Below the panes, a window seat stretched the length of the wall. A carpet of rich goldenrod gave nicely beneath her feet. Crossing to an open doorway, she poked her head into the adjoining library and motioned to the young girl on the ottoman. When she joined them, Eliza made introductions. "Nina Moore, this is Kell Jameson."

Nina's eyes widened in recognition. "The attorney? I've seen you on *CourtWatch TV*. You're good most of the time."

Amused by the summation, Kell nodded solemnly. "Thank you. You're interested in becoming a lawyer?"

Nina bobbed her head in vigorous agreement. "All my life." She shot her a quizzical look. "Mrs. F told me that you used to live here, but I didn't believe her. You never mention it in your interviews. Why not?"

"I try to keep the press out of my private life," Kell equivocated. In truth, very few people in her life knew about the Faraday Center or Hallden, and she intended to maintain the distance between her childhood and the life she'd created. "What grade are you in?" she asked to distract.

Undeterred, Nina pressed, "But I read an article about you in *Glamour* and when they asked where you were from, you said Atlanta. You ashamed of being from here?"

Kell shrugged uncomfortably at the direct question. "Of course not. It's easier to explain Atlanta to outsiders than it is to try to tell them where Hallden is located on a map."

"I guess so," Nina conceded doubtfully, clutching her book to her chest. "Did you really date Patrick Cogan after you defended him in that lawsuit? He's so cute."

Kell grimaced at the reminder, but was grateful for the new question. "Patrick and I are good friends. That's all." To distract her, she glanced at the title of Nina's book. "What are you reading?"

"A biography of Barbara Jordan. I want to be a lawyer and a senator and then president."

"Nina is very ambitious. One of my brightest children." Eliza smiled warmly and laid a hand on the girl's shoulder. "Kell came to visit today, and she'll be spending the night. Will you go and prepare the guest room?"

Kell opened her mouth to protest that she'd be staying in town, but decided she didn't intend to offer Nina anymore proof of her disloyalty. "Thank you," she murmured.

Nodding, Nina sidled toward the door. "Did Mr. Brodie do it?" she blurted.

"The jury found him not guilty."

Nina scoffed knowingly. "That's not the same." At Eliza's warning look, she stopped. "I'll go take care of the room."

"Good. Don't worry about signing your book out, I'll remember." Eliza glanced at the title and made a mental note. "Close the door, please, dear."

When the door shut, Eliza lowered herself into one of the blue chintz chairs and Kell sat on its mate. A Saint-Émilion tray table stood between the two chairs with tea service prepared. "I appreciate you coming so quickly, Kell."

"You needed me."

Neither mentioned that this wasn't likely the first time. Instead, Eliza offered, "Would you like a cup of tea?"

"Thank you." Kell watched silently as the china cups were filled with the strong Earl Grey tea that Eliza preferred. Cradling her cup, she finally asked, "Mrs. F, what's going on?"

Eliza shut her eyes, inhaling deeply. "As I explained on the phone, the police found the body of Clay Griffin yesterday morning. He'd been stabbed to death a couple of days ago."

"I pulled the story from the wire. But you kicked Clay out of the Center before I left. I don't understand what his death has to do with you."

Eliza sighed and opened her eyes, suddenly looking every one of her years. "He's been a nuisance for years. Blamed me for everything that went wrong in his life. He couldn't hold a job, couldn't stay out of jail."

"That's not your fault," protested Kell. "You gave him the same chance you gave everyone. Maybe even more."

"He didn't see it that way. Clay is—was—a drug dealer and he's been trying to recruit some of my more difficult children to join him. As much out of spite as opportunity, I imagine. But Wednesday afternoon, I caught him in the gazebo with Nina. She's only fifteen."

"What happened?"

"He tried to touch her. She ran, but he caught her and had her cornered, his hands on her. When I found them, she was terrified." Eliza shuddered, recalling the scene. "I sent Nina into the house and we argued. He accused me of ruining his life, of tossing him on the streets like trash. He was furious, Kell. Shaking and screaming obscenities. I got angry and I threatened him. Told him if he ever touched one of my girls again or stepped foot on the Center's property, I would kill him. And God knows, I meant it."

Kell felt her stomach sink. "What did you do, Mrs. F?"

"That afternoon, nothing. Honestly." She twisted

the hem of the jacket and crushed the fabric beneath her hands. "But I started thinking about what he said. About how I had treated him differently and that I'd caused him to be like this. In all my years running the Center, I have lost four of my children, but he's the only one that I sent away."

Knowing the fate of the other three, Kell said nothing, waiting for her to continue.

"I went to the Palace later that night to see him. Talk to him."

For as long as Kell knew, the Palace had been a haven for the forgotten in Hallden. A place without security locks or surveillance cameras. "Did anyone see you come?"

"I don't think so. He lived on the fifth floor, and I didn't see anyone in the stairwell."

"How did you know his apartment number?"

Eliza flushed. "I'd visited him before. To check on him."

The rush of color caught Kell's attention, and she filed away that reaction. "What happened next?"

"I knocked on his apartment door and it opened. At first, I didn't see anything. Then I heard a sound and walked inside. He was lying on the floor, blood pouring out of him. I tried to help, but it was too late." On her lap, fingers trembled in horrified memory.

Kell reached out and covered the quivering hands. "Did you call the police?"

"No. Because, God forgive me, I saw what had killed him. There was a knife in his leg. One that looked exactly like mine. I panicked and pulled it out of him, and somehow, Kell, it was one of my knives."

"What do you mean it was one of your knives?"

"Monika Bailey once lived here."

"The chef?" Kell had eaten in one of her restaurants in London. "I didn't know that. But what does that have to do with Clay?"

"She sent me a specially designed set of knives for Christmas. I recognized the handle. So I took it."

"What did you do with it?"

Eliza glanced uncomfortably around the room, eyes downcast. "I hid it."

"Mrs. F, I need to know where you put the knife."

"It's secured, Kell. Once you decide what we should do with it, I'll give it to you."

When Kell opened her mouth to protest, Eliza pointed to the closed door that led to the rest of the Center, speaking aloud her deepest fear. "I thought someone from this house took that knife to Clay Griffin's apartment and stabbed him with it. One of my children may have killed a man, Kell. But I won't let them ruin their lives, not if I can help it. And you won't be responsible either if you don't know where it is."

She turned her hands over and captured Kell's in a strong grip, firm and unyielding. "Will you represent me, Kell?"

CHAPTER 4

A knock sounded at the study door. Kell rose immediately and crossed to open it a crack. Nina stood outside, her expression concerned.

"Yes?"

"Ms. Jameson, Sheriff Calder is here."

Behind Kell, Eliza let out a soft gasp. Kell ignored the urge to turn and comfort. Instead, she leaned forward. "Please show the sheriff to the sitting room and tell him—" She paused and Nina nodded. "Tell him that Mrs. Faraday will be right with him." Kell moved to shut the door, but Nina slapped her hand on the panel to stop her.

"Not Mrs. Faraday. He wants to see you," Nina corrected, not hiding her curiosity. "Said he had something for you. Is it for some big case?"

"I don't know," Kell answered honestly. With the Brodie matter closed, she had nothing on the calendar sufficiently urgent to warrant a contact from the sheriff's office. David hadn't called with any dire messages, and he was not the type to suffer in silence. Which meant that the autocratic meter maid had turned her in to his superiors. "Tell him I'll be right with him."

Closing the door, Kell returned to Eliza's side. Composure regained, Eliza regarded her with a stern look that Kell read easily. She sat down and studied the hand-made rug intensely.

"Kell."

She refused to look up, knowing that she'd see narrowed gray eyes and a mouth firmed into a thin line. "Yes, ma'am?"

Undeterred by her recent confession, Eliza quizzed, "Why does the sheriff want to see you?"

"I had a minor disagreement with one of his officers downtown." With a sigh, Kell forced herself to meet Eliza's censorious look. She took a hasty sip of luke-warm tea to wet a mouth gone abruptly dry. "It seems I accidentally parked in front of a fire hydrant on Terrell Street. Not even in front of really, so much as my bumper nudged into the red zone."

"So you parked in front of a hydrant," Eliza corrected.

Kell waved a dismissing hand. "The point is, this obnoxious man decided to write me not one but—get this—four tickets. Four of them." Indignation in full flower, she railed, "When I refused to accept these unjustified citations, he made me get out of my car. Can you believe that?"

"Where are the tickets now?"

Righteous anger melted into chagrin. "On the street

in front of the Magnolia B & B," she admitted guiltily.

"Oh, dear." Eliza set her cup on the tray table and stood. "My defense attorney cannot be a scofflaw, Kell. Go see the sheriff and take your punishment." She added morbidly, "Then we can discuss my possible imprisonment."

Together, they walked from the study down the hall to the sitting room. The sheriff waited in front of the bank of windows that overlooked the backyard. At the sound of their entry, he turned.

"You're the sheriff?" Kell took an involuntary step backward, until Eliza firmly pushed her into the room. "Sheriff Calder?"

"Hello." Smiling at the infuriated flash of recognition, he advanced to join them. He ignored Kell, instead taking Eliza's hand in his. He raised it to his lips in a courtly gesture that would have seemed hackneyed from someone else. "How come you get more beautiful each time I see you, Mrs. F?"

"Because you refuse to wear your glasses, Luke. Good for me." With a fond pat of his cheek, she turned slightly, toward Kell. "I understand you've met one of my children. Kell Jameson, Sheriff Luke Calder."

Luke folded his arms and gave a short nod. "Ms. Jameson and I have a long and varied history together." One he intended to add another chapter to, he promised silently. At least to see if that decadent mouth could do more than pout at him. He tore his gaze away from the heavy bottom lip and focused on Eliza. With a conspiratorial smile, he explained, "She spent the day engaged in several unlawful activities including running several lights, speeding, blocking a hydrant, littering, obstruction of justice, and leaving the scene of a crime. Quite the lawbreaker for a famous lawyer."

"Actually, I believe you were responsible for the litter." As soon as the smart-alecky words escaped, Kell regretted them. Now wasn't the time to antagonize him, but something about Luke Calder stoked at her temper and jolted her pulse.

"Definitely a defense attorney," Luke commented to Eliza. "Never taking responsibility for the actions of their clients."

Too busy fixing the errors made by the police, she thought caustically. This time, though, she managed to keep her thoughts to herself. Summoning her most placating voice, she offered, "If you'll give me the citations, I'll be happy to make amends, Sheriff."

Luke shook his head. "Usually, with this type of case, I'm required to bind you over until the court can hear your case. We're talking major violations here, Ms. Jameson. In Atlanta, you'd be in jail already."

For the first time, real panic assailed her. "Jail? For a traffic ticket? You must be joking."

"I don't joke about the law, Ms. Jameson. I expect you take it quite seriously yourself." Reveling in her reaction, he reached into his pocket for the sheaf of citations. He riffled through them and shook his head. "I was wrong. I've got you on six counts. Forgot to add failure to obey. Then you told me to write you another ticket for fleeing the scene of a crime, didn't you? According to the sheriff's manual, you pose a flight risk and should be detained in the county's facilities."

He's enjoying this, Kell realized with annoyance, but she'd gotten herself into this trouble. Chastened, she repeated, "Sheriff Calder, I will happily pay all of the fines right now. And offer my most abject apology to you and to the sheriff's department."

"And Jonice?"

Kell acquiesced, recalling the name from earlier. "And Jonice."

"Jonice runs the local auto shop and towing company," Eliza added helpfully.

"Ah, yes. Jonice and Rosie. I assume that's her assistant."

"Her truck," corrected Luke. "Jonice is also the best mechanic in the county. Does excellent bodywork."

"That's good to know," Kell responded politely, relieved that the sheriff no longer seemed predisposed to arrest her.

Luke inclined his head toward the front door. "Thought you'd agree, given that there's a dent on your hood."

Relief slid into stunned disbelief. "A dent? On my Porsche?"

"From the size of it, looks like someone hit a foul ball."

Kell moaned softly, "My car."

She started to rush out to check on the rumored damage, but Luke caught her arm. The heat from his touch cut through her dismay, and she stopped without thinking. She tossed her head back to meet his eyes. "Yes?"

"Stay." The command slipped out on a rasp. "We still need to discuss the fines."

"But my car—"

"I'll go and check on it," volunteered Eliza. "You two get squared away."

"Why don't we have a seat, Ms. Jameson?" Luke started across the room to the sofa, a faded rose silk that had been in the house for years. Because he had not let go of her arm, Kell followed close on his heels.

She sat down and slid over to make as much room as possible between them. "Just out of curiosity, why is the county sheriff giving tickets in the city? Hallden has a police office."

"Of five. Besides, when you ran the red light, you were on a county road. The fire hydrant simply constituted the continuation of a criminal enterprise."

"You'd have made a good prosecutor," Kell complimented wryly. "And how did you find me?"

"The infamous Kell Jameson roars into town and folks will talk. I mentioned your name to one of my deputies, and she told me you'd probably hightail it out to the Center. In my line of work, they call that detecting."

"Who's the deputy?"

"Cheryl Richardson." Luke stretched out his legs, his knee brushing hers, which were primly tucked beneath her. When she shifted away, he resisted the urge to follow. "Been with me since I started here."

Tendrils of sensation shimmered along her bare

legs. In defense, she scooted deeper into the cushions. "Cheryl's a cop?" Kell easily recalled the gangly, shy waif who'd been brought to the Center. "She used to be scared of everything."

"Not anymore. She's my chief deputy."

"Amazing." Filing away that tidbit, she shifted on the sofa away from him. Somehow, the polite distance she'd placed between them had evaporated. Again. She fixed him with a glare. "Sheriff Calder—" she began.

"Luke."

"What?"

"Call me Luke."

"Why?"

"Because you haven't yet, and I want to hear you say it." His honesty surprised him. Yet, at the moment, he wanted nothing more. He enjoyed the smoothly precise way she spoke, trying vainly to smother the sultry hint of southern that grew more pronounced with anger. How would his name sound in the mixture of honey and vinegar. "Say it."

"No."

"Why not?"

"Because we're not friends. We're not even acquaintances. You're the man who has spent the better part of the afternoon harassing me."

"Ten minutes. And it would have been less if you'd simply accepted the first ticket." When she opened her mouth in retort, he simply covered her lips. "I'd hate to have to fill out another citation, Ms. Jameson. I'm already at my quota."

Kell's eyes spit fire, but she nodded once in terse agreement.

"Smart woman." Before he lifted his hand, though, he would have sworn she nipped at the flesh below his fingers. "Ouch."

"Problem, Sheriff?" she asked innocently.

Kell Jameson was trouble, Luke decided, but he liked her. He'd always been one to follow his instincts, to accept the tug at his gut that said duck or the knot in his neck that signaled an ambush. With the feel of her skin still on his and the shallow bite quickly fading, he felt the tug become a yank. To distract, he laid the tickets between them. "Let's tally up the damage."

Eager to be rid of his disturbing presence, Kell snatched the citations up. "I promise to write a check before I leave. City and county."

"And to stay out of red zones and below the speed limit?"

"Absolutely. On my honor."

"Then my work here is done." Luke gained his feet lithely. "Have dinner with me tonight."

"Why?"

He chuckled at the bald question. "Because you are the loveliest and the most exasperating woman I've met in a long while, and I'd like to be annoyed over a good meal."

Amused despite herself, Kell smiled. "Such a flattering invitation."

"Seems appropriate." He watched her closely. "Is that a yes?"

Tempted more than she'd have imagined, Kell forced herself to decline. "I can't. I'm sorry."

Echoing her question, he asked, "Why?"

"Because I don't date law enforcement or men from Hallden."

"We wouldn't be dating. It's dinner. Pasta, a good wine, and an argument or two over the value of the Miranda warning and which *Law and Order* franchise is the best."

Laughing, Kell felt her resolve waver. What would it hurt? If she agreed to have dinner with him, she could subtly pump him for information on the Griffin murder investigation. Find out if the police had any leads or suspects. One dinner and she could leave Hallden with a clear conscience. The fact that he was almost sinfully handsome was simply a bonus. Before she could change her mind, she answered, "Okay."

"That was almost too easy, but I like to live dangerously. Should I meet you here or at the Magnolia?"

With an arched brow, Kell responded, "I think I'm spending the night here. I never quite made it to check-in."

"No place to park anyhow." Luke helped her stand and tucked her hand in his arm. "Seven o'clock too early for you?"

Shivers danced along her skin, mimicking her spirited pulse. "Not at all. I've had a long week."

"Yep, the Brodie trial. I didn't put the two together at first. Nice footwork. Hell of a closing argument." He led them across the foyer. "Does it bother you that he was guilty as sin?"

Kell stiffened, but continued walking. Every defense attorney faced the question each time she stepped into a courtroom. She supplied her stock answer, tone guarded. "Court of law said he wasn't. Unanimous verdict."

"Touché." Luke stopped at the door and faced her. "But you know better, Ms. Jameson. You know that guilt or innocence have nothing to do with a courtroom or a jury box."

"That's all I care about, Sheriff Calder. I leave the philosophizing to others." She reached past him for the knob. Pulling the door open, she tilted her head. "See you tonight."

Understanding he'd been dismissed, Luke tipped an imaginary hat. "Good afternoon, Ms. Jameson." He strode down the steps and out to the black truck he'd driven earlier.

From the porch, she could see the sheriff department insignia embossed in gold across the cab. Before he climbed inside, several boys swarmed around him, pelting him with questions. With an easy laugh, he swung one small child into his arms and rested a hand on Jorden's shoulder. Beneath the touch, the little boy leaned closer, resting against Luke's thigh.

The sun dipped low heading toward sunset. Gold swathed his cocoa skin, danced over the broad shoulders and powerful body. As though he sensed her watching, Luke glanced up and winked at her.

Kell smiled back, gave a short wave, and moved inside. She gently closed the door, her smile fading as her thoughts returned to the conversation with Eliza.

A dead drug dealer killed with a kitchen knife from her house. Murdered the day he attacked one of her charges and hours after she threatened to kill him.

She'd taken on worse cases, but not by much. On the plus side, no arrest had been made and Luke gave no indication that he thought Mrs. F or any of the children might be involved.

One dinner with Sheriff Luke Calder and a few phone calls to the right place, then she'd take her mangled car and traitorous body back to Atlanta where they both belonged.

CHAPTER 5

Luke strolled into the sheriff's office, whistling a name-less tune. Cheryl and the rest of the staff took note of their boss's uncharacteristic lightness. For a week that started with murder, he was unusually good-humored, a fact that didn't pass without remark. Sheriff Calder took police work seriously, not himself, but it was hard to tell the difference sometimes. Cheryl watched him stroll through the office, chatting with deputies, with a casualness he didn't often allow.

During his time at the department, he'd never de-veloped the kind of relationships that strayed outside the office doors. No questions about kids or weekend plans, no shared confidences or personal advice on a bad breakup. Everyone agreed Luke was a great boss, but nobody managed to scale the invisible barrier that separated collegiality from friendship.

Today, however, that wall had come down a few inches, leaving the sheriff more relaxed than she'd ever seen. Not that Cheryl imagined Griffin's death had left his thoughts for an instant. Or the two unidentified victims from the warehouse. Something had shifted in him, but not his dedication to the work. She'd learned his patterns, and despite the easygoing demeanor, his brain was processing clues. Working with Luke taught her that detective work required patience and rumination, taking the time to gather the facts and sift through for the unexpected or the too familiar. With this case, as with every other, Luke's hunches would hold until he'd received a coroner's report from their borrowed M.E. and the chemical analysis he'd sent to Atlanta for evaluation.

In the meantime, though, it appeared Sheriff Calder had found something else to occupy his mind.

Oblivious to his staff's reaction, Luke circled the office, gathering reports on car accidents, petty theft, and a missing cow. As easy as those cases would be to solve, human bodies were piling up. First the discovery at the abandoned warehouse and now this. Luke had good officers, but none who had the experience to handle a murder investigation solo. As much as it rankled, he realized he might have to ask Chief Graves for help, giving the other man another plank in his platform when he challenged Luke for sheriff.

But Luke had neither the time nor inclination to worry about Graves' electoral plans in November, he decided, listening to a recount of a goat-on-pig fight out at a farm, where the pig proved rather fiesty. Instead, Luke accepted wryly, he would rather concentrate on mile-long legs, a smile that morphed seamlessly into a smirk, and a sharp tongue that kept him on his toes. Each encounter with the combative Ms. Jameson left him intrigued and impatient to solve the mystery of his attraction to her.

"What do you think, Sheriff?"

"Hmm?" Luke forced his attention back to the deputy's report and away from Kell Jameson. "Oh, right. Give Mr. Parsons a second warning about his pig. If it happens again, let him know we'll be having a luau the next evening."

"Yes, sir," Deputy Little agreed with a guffaw. He picked up the phone to call the Parson's farm.

Kell would look fantastic in a sarong, Luke imagined, pausing by another workstation. Immediately, the image popped into his head, her curves draped in flowered silk. He stared blindly down at that desk, savoring the picture.

"Aren't they adorable?"

Luke snapped his attention back. "What?"

Jr. Deputy Gallings lifted a photo of twins for closer inspection. "My grandkids. Aren't they darling?"

Focusing on the photo, Luke pretended to be impressed by two squalling blobs appearing to share three strands of red hair between them. "Cute," he managed.

While Gallings beamed, Luke hurried to Sergeant Marane's desk, wondering at Kell's stubborn occupation of his thoughts. He'd never thought he had a type, but Kell was like no one he'd ever met. Or wanted. Something about her stirred his senses and upset his normally even keel. Luke prided himself on his ability to remain dispassionate and observant, to withhold judgment until all the evidence was in. But with her, he found himself jumping ahead to a number of pleasant conclusions.

Determined to put her out of his head, he dove back into murder. "What have you got for me, Sergeant?"

Marane tapped the file on his desk. "Some tips on the warehouse bodies, Sheriff. Mostly pranks, but I intend to follow up on the more promising leads."

"I'd like you to clear those up today. Take Krenicki along if you intend to interview. Tape recorder too."

Marane tried to hide his disappointment. His wife was going to kill him, he thought glumly. "Will do, sir."

Luke caught the crestfallen expression and glanced at the calendar on Marane's blotter. "Tonight's your anniversary, Marane?"

The older man straightened in his seat. "Yes, sir. Thirty-fifth. Thought I'd take the missus to a show up in Atlanta, but I can postpone."

"The tips can wait until tomorrow. Go see your wife."

"Sure thing, Sheriff," beamed Marane.

Luke headed for his office, his movements followed by dozens of bemused eyes. Unaware, his thoughts returned inexorably to the puzzle of Kell Jameson. If pressed, he thought, he could make a few guesses about what captivated him. It had to be the challenge she presented. After all, a car like hers showed a connoisseur's eye for power and control. Kell, he imagined, relished the display and he knew from experience, she rankled at any implication that she didn't exert complete dominance in a situation. Her quicksilver slide from flirtation to defiance spoke of a volatile temper, one he imagined she held ruthlessly in check—unless provoked beyond standing.

He welcomed the opportunity to test the depths of those reactions tonight at dinner.

Luke swung past the reception desk on his way into his office and inclined his head in greeting to the dispatcher. Curly Watson's long sunburned face and grizzled red beard returned the greeting with a canny smile. To Luke's knowledge, Curly had never carried a gun or a badge. What he did possess was an encyclopedic knowledge of Hallden and its workings, from the size of a farmer's crops to the newest comer.

"Hear you had a run-in with the lady lawyer," he offered with a smirk. "Also heard she ran away. You find her at the Center?"

"Yes, I located Ms. Jameson." Shaking his head, he passed the desk, mystified. The speed at which Curly accumulated information constantly astounded him. "Do you have surveillance cameras in town? A tracking device on me?" he asked, giving himself a mock pat-down.

"Don't need 'um. Got eyes everywhere, Sheriff."

"And a mouth like a telegraph," Luke muttered as he walked into his office and shut the glass-paned door.

Chuckling, Curly reclined in the swivel chair that creaked in protest and propped his feet on the battered metal desk that had been there as long as he had. His boots clanged against the corner and echoed through the cozy space. The Hallden County Sheriff's Department employed a staff of eleven, including three sergeants, four junior grade deputies plus administrative staff.

Unlike the rest of the staff, he'd never let Luke's wall keep him on the other side. Whipping the department into shape was hard work, and Curly understood that the boy needed at least one good friend who understood what Luke was doing. And he had to give the sheriff credit for what he'd accomplished with the department. Luke took his time building a solid department, and he'd done a fair job of the thing. The dregs and a few good cops had slunk off to the city police department with Chief Graves, leaving Luke with a lot of empty spots to fill.

Curly knew Graves thought he'd decimate the department and force them to hire him as sheriff once Luke failed. But Luke had blown that plan up but good. Oh, Graves and some folks had grumbled about hiring an outsider to take the place of their beloved Sheriff Patmos, but the county commission dug in their heels and Luke had proven them right.

Like it or not, Hallden was changing. The county sat three hours south of Atlanta. A new exit ramp added to the freeway brought traffic off of I–75, including semis and commerce and regular guests for Magnolia's B&B. Access also brought meth and crack and the sins and pleasures people used to have to travel north to find.

After a string of robberies and Patmos's third heart attack, the political leaders knew they had to have a chief law enforcement officer who'd actually handled real crimes, rather than watching the ones shown on *COPS*. The biggest case Captain Graves had handled was Mrs. Block's attempted murder of a philandering fourth husband with a skillet and a wicked backhand. But when crime came to Hallden, the area had to have a sheriff who didn't flinch at the job. Just so happened, Curly's cousin worked dispatch at the Chicago P.D. and sent an interesting news clipping Curly's way.

Studying the sheriff, Curly rested his hands on a belly protected by a solid layer of fat. In Chicago, a fatal accident had left Luke the sole survivor. The article mentioned Luke's temporary leave of absence, and Curly had seen in the blurry photo the man Hallden was looking for.

Some machinations and a few words in the right ears, and Luke Calder took to Hallden like fish that had been out of the water too long. Gasping and flailing, but settling down quickly. He'd learned not to chase after shadows, even the ones that clouded his own eyes on occasion. Curly hadn't burrowed so deep that he had the whole story, but he had time yet.

He lifted the receiver by his elbow and pressed the intercom button. When Luke lifted his phone, Curly inquired, "How's little Kell doing? Haven't seen her in years."

From behind the glass door to his office, Luke kept his face noncommittal. "Ms. Jameson seems well."

"Good, good. Grew up at the Center. Left town, say, 1991. August, I believe." Curly shook his head. "Shot out of town like a light and didn't look back."

Luke straightened, his interest peaked. "What are you talking about?"

"Just musing. Seems interesting she'd be home again after so long away."

Luke mulled over the information. "Any idea why she's decided to return now?"

"Nope," Curly answered honestly. However, he had his own plans on solving that mystery.

"Didn't the warehouse fire happen in 1991?"

Curly hesitated. "Thereabouts."

Sifting on his desk for the notes he'd requested, Luke checked chronology. "August 1991. Warehouse burned down." *And two bodies had lain hidden since,* Luke thought. "Was there any connection between Kell Jameson and the fire?"

Curly coughed uncomfortably. The story of the two orphans who'd skipped town the week of the big blaze didn't get much retelling. And as much as Curly enjoyed sharing information, he wasn't a gossip. "No solid proof, Sheriff. In fact, Sheriff Patmos took that under consideration when the fire happened, but the evidence didn't amount to much. No sense in spending county funds on account of that place. Whole town knew the only goods run through there had a bad end in mind."

Luke considered these new details. Kell Jameson's arrival on the heels of their discovery had his antenna up. He sent Curly a stern look through the pane of glass and crooked a finger. "Here. Now."

While Curly slowly made his way across the phalanx of desks that stretched between the reception area and his office, Luke punched a series of digits into the phone.

Cheryl picked up her line with a brusque greeting. "Deputy Chief Richardson."

"I need you to pull any files we have on Kell Jameson."

"Right away." On the other end of the line, a frown wrinkled her brow. "Any reason you're asking, Sheriff? I thought you'd given her the citations this afternoon at Mrs. F's place."

Luke scoffed in disbelief. "Does the entire town have radar?"

"This is simple deduction, sir. I assumed after I told you about her connection to Mrs. Faraday, you'd go to the Center to deliver her tickets. Although, I do understand that you're taking her out to dinner tonight. Might I recommend—"

"No, you may not," Luke interjected hastily. "Just grab those files for me. I also want the rest of the records connected to the 1991 fire at the warehouse."

"Yes, sir."

He disconnected the call and rubbed wearily at his neck. The Fates possessed a perverse sense of humor. For the first time in a while, a smart, beautiful woman caught and held his attention. Now, he learns that his ticket-dodger had been considered in a probable case of arson and, now, possibly a murder. Worse, the entire county likely knew by now that he'd made a date with her for tonight.

Absently, he scratched notes onto the blotter on his desk. *Kell Jameson. 1991. Arson?*

"Interesting research project for a date, Sheriff," Curly commented in the doorway.

"Come in and close the door."

Dragging his left leg slightly, the dispatcher came inside and gingerly lowered himself into his favorite seat in the office. Luke inherited Sheriff Patmos's digs, complete with an aged sofa that dipped comfortably in the center. A careful observer would note the deliberate contours that matched the body settling into its embrace. Curly propped his leg on the armrest, where boot black had long since joined the flowered motif.

"You got something on your mind, Sheriff?"

Luke sent the man a pointed look. "Am I going out with an arsonist tonight?"

"Kell? Naw. She and those girls could find trouble in a church, but they weren't criminals."

"Which girls?" Luke flipped his pen in a swift arc over his thumb repeatedly, a habit he barely noticed. "Who were they?"

"Findley Borders and Julia Warner. Now, Fin had no affection for the truth. Or the consequences for that matter. Bald-faced liar with a smile that made you want to believe. Julia, though, there was an angel for you. Only time I knew Fin to even entertain the notion of shame was if Julia made a comment. But Kell was the ringleader. She'd been at the Center the longest."

"All three of them lost their parents?"

"Not exactly." Curly reached into his shirtfront for a stick of gum. He methodically unwrapped the silver foil and folded the gum into a stack. As he folded, he wondered how much he should tell the sheriff. Man hadn't been out with a woman since he broke up with a doctor out of Canton months ago. Much as he enjoyed a good story, Curly felt no call to ruin a perfectly good date with history best kept buried.

Reading his mind, Luke prodded, "I'm not planning to arrest her tonight. But I'd like to know more than I appear to know right now."

Curly shrugged. Sooner or later, some busybody would tell him. Might as well be him. "Kell's parents skipped town on the child when she was old enough to understand what they were doing. Just knocked on the door to the Center and handed the child over. Mrs. F is the only momma that girl ever really knew."

"And the others? What happened with their parents?"

"Julia's family died in a house fire when she was eleven. Child showed up all tiny and frail. Kell took a shine to her and made the other kids leave her be. She and Fin." Curly smiled at the memory. "Girl had a helluva right hook."

"Kell can punch?"

"Yep, but Fin had more fun with it. That's a girl after my own heart. She brought herself to the Center. Marched right up to the door and asked to stay."

"Where were her parents?"

Curly chewed his gum slowly, then he shook his head. "Some stories belong to the folks who made 'em, don't you agree, Sheriff?"

Hearing the reminder, Luke didn't press. "The night of the fire. I discerned from the police reports that some of the inventory ignited and burned the warehouse. According to what I read, Sheriff Patmos and the GBI assumed the illegal contraband in the warehouse exploded."

"The Georgia Bureau of Investigation didn't do much more than sign on the dotted line," Curly corrected with a snort. "The sheriff asked for help in proving arson, but nobody wanted to wade too deep into the mess. A fire marshal from Atlanta agreed with the GBI and the case got closed."

"Then why put Kell and her friends on a question list?"

Curly sat up and swung his legs to the floor, rubbing at his bad knee. "Back then, no one would talk about the warehouse or what it was being used for. Getting information from that side of town was like pulling teeth."

"Fear or complicity?"

"I reckon a bit of both. But no one cried when the fire happened."

A knock sounded and Luke saw Cheryl at the door. He motioned her inside. "So there's a fire without witnesses and two dead men who go unburied for a decade. I still don't see a connection to Kell and the other two girls."

Hearing her cue, Cheryl extended a thick manila file to him reluctantly. *Grove Warehouse Fire* had been typed onto the tab. When he took the documents, she explained, "At the time, Captain Graves took a statement from a young man who claimed to have seen Kell, Fin, and Julia at the warehouse before the fire."

Opening the file to the page she'd marked, Luke read the statement quickly, and his gaze narrowed. Curly joined Cheryl in the doorway. "Now, Luke, this fire happened a long time ago."

"That may be, but I don't like coincidences, you two."

Cheryl and Curly exchanged troubled glances. Cheryl spoke first. "I'd forgotten the connection until you asked for the file, sir."

With a cough, Curly added, "I didn't believe him then and I don't now. He was sniffing after Kell something fierce then, probably trying to make some trouble."

Luke laid the file on the table, he tapped the name at the bottom of the statement. "The only witness to the fire was the recently deceased Clay Griffin. And the report indicates he told Sheriff Patmos that he saw Kell and her friends leaving the scene with a knapsack."

"The sheriff didn't find evidence of a knapsack," Cheryl supplied lamely.

"Did he look?"

"Sure did. Had a team go over to the Center when we got the report."

"Anything at the site?"

"Nope. Didn't find anything. Including those two bodies the construction workers found."

Luke leaned forward, puzzled. "What about the knapsack?"

"By the time the sheriff got around to questioning them, Fin and Kell had gone. No knapsack or the girls. Julia swore they hadn't been near the fire."

Cheryl indicated another tabbed page. "The sheriff found diary entries from both girls discussing their plan to move to New York rather than go to college. Mrs. F got a postcard from them too."

Finishing the story, Curly added, "With no girls and no proof of arson, the fire was ruled an accident and the case was closed."

"Until we found the two dead bodies and suddenly, the only witness dies and the prodigal daughter returns." Luke hissed out an expletive. "I don't like co-incidences."

CHAPTER 6

Hallden felt almost deserted in the deepening shadows. Storefronts posted closed signs, their proprietors long-since departed for Saturday-night dinner. In the center of town, a statue of the city's founder posed, surrounded by lush green park. Flowers bloomed in sunburst profusion, encouraging couples to spread blankets on the lawn at dusk.

Luke slowed the rumbling truck to a stop beneath a street-light and glanced at his nearly mute passenger. She'd said no more than a few words since he picked her up at the Center. The sight of her in a slim column of black that left her shoulders and her remarkable legs exposed had kept him silent while he unswallowed his tongue.

But the ride had continued in the same quiet, unless he asked a question. Although he appreciated she wasn't one to fill the silence with nervous chatter, he was determined to coax out more than a monosyllabic response. On the radio, a saxophone bemoaned a lost lover. He lowered the volume and prodded, "Ever miss Hallden?"

Turning from the passenger window, Kell gave the park a thoughtful look. "Sometimes. Like tonight. Summers in Atlanta, you can visit a park, but there's always noise. Music, cars rushing by. Hallden's different. Same sounds, but softer." As she spoke, he noted how her hands moved with her words, a graceful ballet to accent her thoughts. She spoke as eloquently with her hands as her mouth. "Peaceful."

Weariness and longing wound beneath the response, two responses he hadn't expected. She struck him as self-contained, too busy to notice the distinctions or care. Luke recognized both and could not help but respond. "Hallden isn't idyllic, but it has a tranquility cities can't match. Makes you feel like you can stop running for a moment and simply rest. Be at home."

But you can't rest, Kell reminded herself. And Hallden was no longer her home. An afternoon spent at the Center, reminiscing with Mrs. F, reinforced that fact. She'd made her choice years ago, and this brief sojourn was simply a moment out of time. It wouldn't do to get too connected—to the Center or to Luke Calder.

Changing topics, she asked, "Where are you from?" She'd been puzzling over his accent all day. She considered her ear for regional differences finely tuned, but she couldn't place the mix in Luke's speech. The deep, even timbre carried a veneer of southern polite mixed with a note of western brusque. "I've been trying to figure that out all day."

"So you've been thinking about me," Luke teased. When she stiffened slightly, he continued smoothly, "I'm a navy brat. Parents dragged me across three continents before settling in Chicago. Born in Gulfport, Mississippi, on an Air Force base and lived there until my parents were shipped to the Philippines when I was seven. Then six years in Galveston and a post in France. When their tours ended, we moved to Illinois."

"Both of your parents were soldiers?"

"Mom's a doctor and Dad sailed ships." Luke drove forward, waving absently at an elderly woman inching along the sidewalk. He rolled down the window, "Good night, Mrs. Rasbury."

"'Night, Sheriff," she returned with a palsied wave.

"Mrs. Rasbury taught me fourth grade." Kell relaxed in her seat, amused. "I thought she was ancient then."

"Has the eyesight of a sharpshooter. Calls my office every Monday with a report of the weekend's happenings. Patrols the park until sundown and then keeps an eye on her neighborhood until *Nightline* is off. Between her and Curly, I barely have a job to do around here."

"But you enjoy it." It wasn't a question. Luke spoke of his work with a satisfaction that she envied. Unwilling to explore why she'd be jealous of a small-town cop, she firmly pushed the feeling aside. "You like being sheriff here."

Luke nodded easily. "Best job I've ever had."

"Better than Chicago?"

"Different."

When he didn't elaborate, she asked, "Did you join the military too?"

"Nope. Went to college and studied English lit and creative writing."

"You're a writer?"

"According to my professors, not at all," he supplied unashamedly. "Seems my talents are limited to appreciation of the arts, not participation."

"So how did you go from Shakespeare to law enforcement? To please your parents?"

"Mom wanted me to be a doctor and Dad picked out naval pilot," he corrected. "I don't like biology and I prefer roots to wings. A grave disappointment to them both."

"Roots," she repeated the word, the bite of envy returning. "Is that why you decided to become a police officer?"

"Mostly. That, and I spent a lot of time on base hanging out with the MPs."

"Ah, ha," she smiled. "All the big, shiny guns marching around the base."

"Well, I was a teenager," he concurred with a rueful laugh. "Living on a base, there's a sense of protection. I liked knowing that we were safe, and I respected the men and women who made it true." With a kid's grin, he added, "But the guns were cool too."

She smiled in reaction, but lingered on his mention of protection. "Why did you feel threatened? You're a formidable man. Can't imagine you as a scrawny child afraid of bullies."

"I hit six feet by ninth grade so, no, no bullies. But there are a thousand threats, Kell. Some physical, more of them not."

"Of course."

Luke frowned, contemplating his choice of words. "A child on a base feels safe, but you can't ignore the fact that everyone is on constant alert. The precision of military life and having your mother run off to take care of friendly fire accidents guarantees that you don't get too complacent. When crimes did occur on the base, the MPs tracked the culprits and brought them to justice."

"Military justice," Kell muttered.

"Justice," corrected Luke. "Everybody on base knew the rules. You broke them, you faced the consequences."

Kell watched him thoughtfully for a moment. "Knowing the rules isn't the same as comprehension. And the law has to make space for human error. We make mistakes. Big ones, little ones. Justice has to make some allowance for the fact that we are human. Fallible."

"I suppose. Human error is why we have judges and juries rather than automatons." Luke turned into the parking lot for Hervé's and put the car into park. He shifted, unbuckling his seat belt. "I realized early on that I'm not the one who should decide the penalty. I like making sure that people can go about their days without keeping their guards up constantly."

"The police aren't the only ones who want that."

"True, but it's hard to see how a defense attorney helps the cause, especially when she puts another criminal back on the street."

Feeling her hackles rise, she steamed, "Someone

has to be out there to keep cops from getting too much blood on the Constitution."

"Ouch." Luke rubbed at his chest. "Direct hit. Let's agree that Justice needs foot soldiers as much as defenders and detractors, to my way of thinking."

Kell eased back, muttering, "Exactly which camp do you put lawyers in?"

"I plead the Fifth."

Interior lights illuminated the truck, throwing his features into relief. Kell stared at him, and he asked, "Is there something on my face?"

"You're too handsome," Kell murmured, half-annoyed by the realization. The suit he wore hung perfectly on his frame, emphasizing the contrast of power and grace. A man comfortable with his strength who felt no need to flaunt it. "You're unnerving."

"That's the nicest thing you've said to me since we met."

Kell reached for her seat belt, mumbling, "It wasn't a compliment."

"My mistake," retorted Luke, a shade of irritation in the response. "But I'll take what I can get from you."

"What does that mean?"

"What does that mean?" Luke repeated softly. Arousal, hard and insistent, returned as he placed a hand on her shoulder, angling her toward him. Soulful brown eyes watched him carefully, measuring. When he traced the flawless curve of her cheek, she didn't flinch, didn't pull back. She simply watched. Waited. Luke didn't intend to disappoint. "I find you gorgeous. Intriguing. Insufferable."

Wary, Kell lifted a hand to catch his wrist, intending to move his hand. Beneath the callused fingertip, her skin warmed, flamed. She tugged once. "The feeling is mutual. But I'd add arrogant and officious."

"Because I'm clear about what I want?"

"No. Because you try to take without asking. Touch without invitation."

"Perhaps. But then why are you holding my hand?"

She didn't know. Of their own volition, her fingers had curled around his wrist to hold rather than remove. Self-preservation warned that she should release him, make some pithy remark and suffer through dinner. She was here to ferret out information about the Griffin case, not to make out with the sheriff. "To keep it from straying again."

"Are you sure?" Luke slid his hand down, cradling the slender throat where her pulse beat wildly. "Tell me what you're thinking."

"That we need to go inside." Still, she couldn't stop looking at his poet's mouth. Which was moving toward hers. "What are you doing?" she asked, intending haughty, achieving breathless.

"I'm getting this out of the way."

Warm air skated over her lips, followed by a brush of silk. No, not silk, she realized dimly. His mouth skimmed over hers in a touch that barely seemed to make contact, yet seared through her like a bolt. Her breath escaped on a sigh, a shudder.

Luke concentrated, determined not to *take*, as he wanted to—almost desperately. A single point of contact rippled through his system on waves of sensation.

Her mouth with its permanent pout demanded that he explore slowly, fully. With the tip of his tongue, he traced the curves and dips, resisting the urge to crush. When her lips parted, he eased inside to test. Flavors exploded, the taste of her, another mystery to be solved. His hand lifted to stroke her hair, to match the silken skeins to the satin glide of tongue.

Unable to resist, unwilling to wait, Kell pressed closer. Too much, she thought raggedly, and wanted more. His kiss changed angles, the intensity increasing. Deeper now, with a hunger that echoed in her blood. She heard a moan escape, felt her hand tighten on his wrist. Holding on so closely, she didn't know if she wanted to ever let go.

And because she didn't, she forced her fingers to relax their possession. With a reluctance that ripped at her, she dropped his wrist and tore her mouth free. Blindly, he advanced, and she shifted out of reach, her spine straight against the door. She laid a palm against his chest, startling his eyes open. "Luke."

Instantly, he backed away, leaving a gulf between them. Shaking his head, he raised his hands in defense. "Okay."

"I can't do this."

Luke watched her, still, coiled. "Now or ever?"

"Ever."

"Wrong answer."

"I don't intend to be in Hallden longer than a weekend." She ignored the pang, and continued, "I find you attractive, yes, but I only agreed to dinner, nothing more."

"I haven't asked for more. Yet."

"And if you do, I'm warning you that you'll be disappointed."

"I won't, Kell, and neither will you." With that quiet vow, Luke climbed out of the truck and circled the hood to her door. He opened it and offered a hand to help her alight. "The chef here prepares a delicious trout amandine, if you like seafood. If not, the chicken Kiev is excellent."

Kell accepted the assistance and the advice warily, puzzled by the sudden affability. "How long has this been here?"

"According to Curly, Hervé is a tenderfoot. Only been in town for eleven years. Came from Montreal. He and Curly don't get along very well, particularly given his tendency to call the man Harvey." Luke tucked her hand into the crook of his elbow. He locked the car and guided her along the gravel path to the front door. "Curly is suspicious of food that requires precision cooking."

"As I recall, that suspicion extends to franks and beans," she offered dryly.

He nodded in amused agreement. "Peanut butter and jelly appears to suit him fine. When he's in an adventurous mood, he'll order from the pizza restaurant. Haven't been able to coax him to try Thai yet."

"Hallden has a Thai restaurant?" Kell asked in surprise. "Last time I was here, we were still celebrating the arrival of McDonald's to rival the Chevron gas station's chicken."

Luke ushered her inside the restaurant. "Town's gotten a bit larger since you left."

The maître d' greeted them warmly. "Sheriff Calder. Your table is ready. Gavin will seat you."

Gavin, a short, round man with ruddy cheeks and a bald pate appeared at their side. "Sheriff. Great to see you again. And who is this lovely woman?"

"Kell Jameson," Luke introduced, "meet Gavin Card, waiter extraordinaire." Luke decided not to mention that he'd arrested Gavin nine times for petty theft and attempted robbery before discovering a place for him at Hervé's.

"Kell Jameson, the lawyer?" Gavin's eyes widened in recognition. "I've seen you on television. You can get anybody off, can't you?" Losing the smooth accent he adopted for service, he unconsciously reverted to a New Jersey twang that belied his roots. "Mind if I get your card?"

Before Kell could reach into her bag, Luke covered her hand. "Gavin won't need your card," he corrected. "If he found himself in trouble, a lawyer would do him little good."

Gavin coughed lightly, hearing the warning clearly. "Right, Sheriff. Just a little stargazing." He scurried to pull out Kell's chair. With a practiced flick of the wrist, he spread a black linen napkin on her lap. He vanished for an instant, returning to fill their glasses with water and to offer Luke a bottle of wine he seemed to favor. Satisfied, he flowed through the menu options, highlighting recommendations. "I'll let you take a look and be with you in a few moments." Scurrying off, Gavin disappeared into the kitchen.

"Should I ask what that was about?" Kell inquired wryly. "I've never received such efficient water service before."

"Gavin and I have a long history in our short time together."

"You seem to have a knack for that." At his raised brow, she continued, "I have a difficult time remembering that we only met this afternoon."

"Time is irrelevant when facing the inevitable." Luke extended the basket of rolls that had appeared by his elbow along with the Chardonnay. "Don't you agree?"

She accepted the fragrant bread and the challenge. Breaking it open, Kell responded, "In general, yes. But the essential issue is what is inevitable."

"Given today's events, I'd be pleased to hazard a guess."

Taking a sip of water to quench a suddenly dry throat, Kell equivocated, "Too early to tell."

Luke studied Kell in the flicker of candlelight. Beneath the beauty he acknowledged, and the fatigue he could hear, he caught an occasional glimpse of an emotion he could swear was fear. Casually, he filled both their glasses with pale gold wine. "Why did you agree to dinner tonight?"

"I was hungry."

"Kell."

"I was," she insisted. She lifted her glass this time, as much for the taste as the shield. Luke Calder didn't strike her as a man to ask idle questions or to fish for compliments. Playing along, she looked at him, her head tilted in mock observation. "And I was curious."

"About me?"

"About you, yes. And about how Hallden has changed. I've been away a very long time."

"Sixteen years."

Of course, he knew, she thought. "Apparently, there are no secrets in Mayberry."

"Secrets are hard to keep anywhere."

She couldn't have agreed more. A lesson learned, impossible to forget. "If the secret is between more than one person, it's not going to stay secret for long."

"That's a rather dismal assessment of the rest of us."

"I'm a realist. One who knows that there are few people that you can trust at all, let alone with your secrets."

Gavin interrupted. "May I take your orders?" After committing the requests to memory, he collected the menus and headed off to another table.

"So who shares your secrets?" Luke's glance dropped to her hands. They were graceful, with long, tapered fingers bare of rings of any kind. He could feel them around his wrist even now, the firm grip belied by the supple, creamy soft skin. Now, those hands moved restlessly across the table. Not enough to distract, but sufficiently active for an observant man to note their near-constant motion. Desire stirred and he tore his gaze away. "Is someone pining away for you in Atlanta?"

"That's not your concern, Sheriff."

"I notice you call me 'Sheriff' in that dismissive tone whenever I ask a personal question."

"No, I don't."

"Actually, you do. In fact, you have yet to use my name. Are you afraid to say it?"

"Despite the gun and the terrifyingly huge ego, I'm not scared of you. Luke."

Rather than be insulted, Luke replied softly, "You should be."

Kell stiffened. "What's to be frightened of?"

"To start with, I think you're afraid that I'm right about the inevitable. And," he paused, speculating, "I think that whatever brought you back to Hallden isn't good news. In fact, it strikes me that you agreed to dinner tonight because you want to know something and don't want to ask."

Rather than deny the truth, she retorted, "That doesn't mean I'm frightened of you."

"No. But it does mean that you've got a secret. Otherwise, you'd have asked your questions at the Center and sent me on my way." He settled against the chair. "Well, go ahead and shoot."

Not expecting such a direct approach, Kell scrambled to adjust and marshaled her thoughts. Handsome and astute. A dangerous combination. "I don't have any questions, Luke," she said deliberately. "I received an invitation for a nice dinner, and I thought it might be fun."

"I appreciate that, but I don't believe you. Why drive the three hours from Atlanta to see Mrs. Faraday, only to check into a hotel? For that matter, why agree to dinner with me rather than catching up with her?"

"Because I had the mistaken impression that you wanted my company. I'm happy to return to the Center if you've changed your mind."

"No, no. I do want to have dinner with you. Like you, I'm curious." He bit into his roll and chewed thoughtfully. "An interesting coincidence that you'd pick today of all days to come back to Hallden. A town that you ran away from years ago. Why you'd register at a bed and breakfast rather than going home to the Center?"

Feeling a trill of apprehension, she punted, "Your hypothesis?"

"That Mrs. Faraday called you and told you about Clay Griffin's death."

The trill became a shriek. Instinct told her to abort the conversation, but she found herself replying, "She did. What she couldn't tell me was how or why he died."

"We're still waiting on the autopsy," Luke demurred.

"But you've seen the body. Was he shot?"

"Stabbed."

"In the heart?"

"Too romantic. No, in the leg." Luke lifted a hand when she would have continued. "My turn. Did you have a history with Clay?"

"We grew up together." Kell sipped at her wine, filing away his earlier answers. *A stab wound in the leg. Interesting.*

"Were you close?"

"No. But Eliza told me about the murder, and I wanted to check on her."

"After all these years?"

"A former resident was murdered. You think there's another reason?" she probed.

"Perhaps Clay knew something about you and your friends, and you're here to make sure no one else finds out what he knew."

Kell forced a dismissive laugh. "Clay knew nothing about me or my friends. He was a thug and a bully. According to Eliza, once he left the Center, he got worse. There's nothing Clay could have said about me before or after his death that would make me afraid of him either."

"Including the fact that he saw you at the Grove Warehouse the night it burned? You, Ms. Borders and Ms. Warner. It doesn't bother you that he knew that?"

"He didn't know anything," she lied, her face impassive. Yet, her heart thudded in her chest like a machine gun. Clay knew about the warehouse? How? They'd never considered that possibility. Or the ramifications. "I'm not sure what Clay thought he saw that night, but it wasn't us."

"His statement places you at the warehouse. In fact, he claimed that he saw the three of you running from the fire."

Kell smiled, eyes frosted over. "As an attorney, Sheriff, I'd have to commend you on your tactics but point out a couple of holes in your theory. One, I wasn't anywhere near the warehouse."

"And two?"

"Two would be that if his statement was true, the charge would be arson, and the statute of limitations on that ran out last year. I'd have no reason to be concerned if he or you believed his story. I couldn't be charged."

"For arson, you're right. But certainly, I could use it to guide my investigation."

"Investigation into what?"

"Murder." Watching her closely he explained, "Two men were found in the basement of the warehouse recently. They appeared to have died around the time of the fire." Leaning into the candlelight, he tested her composure. "A good investigator would check and see if the sole witness to the accident that may have killed them died because of what he knew. What do you think, Counselor?"

CHAPTER 7

"I think you have a vivid imagination, Sheriff," Kell replied quietly.

Luke studied her in the flicker of the candle. No stuttered attempts to rebuff his suggestion that she knew about the bodies before. No sudden rigidity of posture or shifting in her eye contact, moving down to indicate the coming of a lie. If Luke hadn't been watching for a tell, he might have believed her.

If. But Kell's graceful, lovely hands lay flat on the tablecloth, their impatient movement stilled. She maintained her unrevealing expression, her body angled subtly to reinforce her muted reaction. If he hadn't known better, he'd be convinced.

"You're quite good, Ms. Jameson." Luke offered the compliment sincerely. "If I didn't know better, I'd think that you had no idea what I was talking about."

"Sheriff, I don't know what you're talking about." Kell

stopped speaking, resisting the urge to add more. More than once, she'd counseled clients on police interrogation techniques. Answer only the question asked, and make your answer responsive but not revealing. Don't fidget and don't look up or down. Up indicated a search for a creative lie, and down showed guilt. Always keep eye contact and believe what you say. Even if you know it's a lie.

Topping off her glass, Luke added another question to his growing list. Did Kell Jameson and Clay Griffin have a history that stretched beyond a liar's statement to the police? Unlike some detectives, he found that questions were best answered by asking. "How well did you know Mr. Griffin, Kell?"

Kell gave a vague shrug. "As I said, we grew up together. Clay came to the Center when he was"—she paused, pretending to search for a number—"I think he was ten and I was seven."

"Did his parents die?"

"His mom. Clay never knew his father. His mother was a prostitute in Macon. Moved to Hallden a couple of months before she died. Mrs. F went to school with her, so she asked DFCS to let her take Clay."

"What happened?"

Kell sensed a trap and skirted the edges. "He didn't adjust well to living with fifteen other children. Every day, there was a new fight at the Center or at school. By the time he was a teenager, Mrs. F had no choice but to ask him to leave."

"Did he fight with her?"

"All the time." Seeing his raised brow, she added, "Not physically, no. Mostly yelling and storming out. Life with Mrs. F was tough, but better than most of us had ever had it."

"Including yourself?"

"Yes." She'd learned to explain her past with only a twinge of self-pity and shame showing. "One day my parents decided they preferred being a couple and they dropped me off at the Center. Haven't seen them since."

"How old were you?"

"Seven." She remembered the morning they brought her to Mrs. Faraday's house, the white mansion surrounded by hundreds of trees. Swing sets hung from magnolia tree branches, with kids gamboling across the manicured lawn. She'd never seen such a beautiful house up close. One where the shutters hung straight and no cars found graves in the front yard. "It was a week before my birthday."

"Kell."

Wondering why she'd offered that information, something she never mentioned, she flicked off his concern. "Didn't matter."

"That they left you before your birthday?" In his family, birthdays, like all holidays, were sacred family times. "It had to matter."

"It didn't," she said flatly. "Doesn't. Anyway, Mrs. F had a party for me. My very first one."

Because he could imagine Kell at seven, abandoned and overwhelmed, anger swelled. "Have you looked for them?"

"No, why would I?"

She appeared genuinely perplexed. Luke probed, "You have resources at your disposal that rival governments. Why not look for them? Find out why they left."

Kell lifted her wineglass. "I know why they left. They didn't want me."

The simple declaration kindled a rage in Luke that he struggled to smother. *How dare they?* How dare any parent leave a child because raising her became too hard? He'd grown up surrounded by affection and a rock-solid belief that his parents adored him. He could scarcely imagine waking up one morning to be told your parents had simply changed their minds. "I pity them."

"Why?"

"Because they missed a chance to know an amazing woman."

"You barely know me."

"You're right, but I think I can trust my instincts on this one."

As if on cue, Gavin arrived with their meals. Intentionally, Luke steered the conversation away from Clay Griffin and orphanages and murder. Understanding the declaration of a truce, Kell regaled him with tales of celebrity clients in exchange for detective stories straight from the source.

"The perp had the evidence in his mouth. But the idiot bit down on the tube, and it began to bubble. My partner thought he had rabies." Luke grinned. "Purple foam rabies."

Giggling uncontrollably, Kell asked, "What did he do?"

"Started to cry. He didn't realize the foaming was his fault. He offered to confess if we'd take him to the vet for shots."

The giggle became a full-blown laugh. "One time, Fin convinced Julia to drink Alka-Seltzer and Coke. The minute Julia had it down, Fin explained that according to urban legend, Julia would explode in five minutes."

"What did she do?"

"What only Julia would. She started telling me who would get each one of her dolls." Smiling at the memory, "However, she was very clear that Fin was to be robbed of any inheritance unless she apologized very nicely at the funeral."

"Very forgiving."

"That's Julia. Our collective conscience." She sighed, relaxed and nostalgic. "She could always convince Mrs. F to ease up on punishment."

"You miss them."

Kell pulled herself in. "Sometimes."

"Did you drift apart?"

"Our lives differed." She glanced at her watch. "It's almost eleven o'clock. And we're the last ones here."

Stymied by the return of her defenses, Luke admitted defeat. "I should probably get you home, then."

Together, they walked out to the truck. After helping her inside, Luke drove them through downtown and out to the Center. Unlike their drive to dinner, a comfortable silence filled the cabin. A bluesy guitar replaced the disconsolate saxophone. Kell relaxed against her seat, eyes drifting closed. When they fluttered open, Luke was standing outside her door in the Center's driveway.

"Your stop, I believe."

Kell smiled sleepily. "I'm so sorry about that. I've been in trial for nearly two months, and these last few days have been marathons."

"No apology necessary." He clasped her hand and held it as they strolled up the driveway to the wide, empty porch.

"Thank you for a lovely dinner, Luke," Kell said, turning to face him. Her right hand rested lightly in his left. "I enjoyed the meal and the company."

"Likewise." Stepping closer, he stroked his hand along her bare arm, coming to rest above her elbow. "I'd like to see you again."

"I'm only in town for the weekend."

"Then come back."

"I can't." But she wanted to. Very much. "I'm not from Hallden anymore," she murmured, as a reminder for herself as much as him.

"You're here now." Determinedly, Luke lifted her other hand and pressed it to his shirtfront. "I want to kiss you again. And again. And again."

"Luke."

"I want to know who you are."

"I'm a lawyer who came to visit an old friend."

"I want you to know me well enough to be able to tell me the truth."

At that, Kell realized she couldn't stay, couldn't

see him again. One day, if they continued to see one another, she would be tempted to tell him her story—but it was a story that belonged to two others, and they'd sworn to each other. "Good night, Luke."

He released her hands and took a step away. "Good night, Kell."

With a fond smile, she turned toward the door. Only to be spun around and into his arms. Before she could utter a protest, his mouth descended. In the instant before their lips touched, she braced herself, prepared for assault.

But this kiss tempted with softness, delighted with gentle forays that melted her against him. For seconds, hours, she stood in the circle of his arms, battered by a kiss that demanded nothing and offered solace and friendship. Her fingers caught at his broad shoulders.

Spanning her waist, Luke lifted her higher, eager to feel how well she would fit against him. Completely. Perfectly. Slowly, he lowered her to the porch and swept her mouth once more, barely sating the hunger that clawed inside.

Then he stepped away and bounded down the steps. He reached his truck and looked over his shoulder to see her standing there, hand half-raised to touch her lips. When he echoed the gesture, she turned slowly and walked inside.

Kell gently closed the door behind her. At this time of night, the children would be asleep. Conflicted, she dropped her keys on the side table and kicked off her heels. Scooping up the shoes, she marched past the stairs to the guest room.

"Nice dinner?"

Biting back a startled oath, Kell flipped on the overhead light and saw Eliza. "I thought you were asleep."

"Not until all of my kids are tucked away," Eliza reminded her, patting the bed beside her. She sat in a tufted chair reading a romance novel by lamplight. When Kell didn't move, she tapped the bed again. "Come and tell me about your night."

Flouncing to the bed, Kell dropped onto the handmade quilt Eliza had turned down in welcome. She sighed and drew her knees under her chin, wrapping her arms around her legs. "Which part? When he annoyed me beyond belief or the part where he kissed me senseless?"

Eliza let out a quick laugh. "The kiss first, of course."

"He's charming. Very charming. And entirely too smart," Kell accused. "First, he takes me to a lovely French restaurant."

"Hervé's."

Kell sighed. "The food was divine. And he made me laugh. Oh, Mrs. F, I haven't laughed like that since—"

"Since Findley and Julia."

"Yes."

"I missed hearing you all giggling in your bedrooms. Even though you were on your way to college, I always thought I'd have more time to get used to losing you."

"Mrs. F, I wanted to call you. So many times. But we—I—couldn't."

"I know." Eliza reached out and drew her into her arms. "I have to believe that if you needed my help, really needed it, you'd always know you can ask."

"I do know that. That's why I could stay away." Tears, held for decades, misted her vision. "I knew you'd let me come home."

"Will you tell me why you left?"

Kell nestled her head on the soft, warm shoulder. Smelled the hint of lilac, the scent familiar and wonderful. "One day, when it's safe."

Knowing she had to be satisfied with that promise, Eliza teased, "You enjoyed Luke. I never expected that it would take a policeman to get you to let that guard of yours down."

Sitting up, Kell brushed at the unshed tears. "Too far down, I'm afraid." The habit of pouring out her romantic troubles to Eliza returned easily. She gave the older woman a bewildered look. "I kissed him. Twice."

Eliza glowered mildly. "You were only out for dinner, Kell."

"Well," she defended, "the first time was an experiment. To see if I felt something."

"And the second time?"

"To prove that I did." Wistfully, Kell closed her eyes and recalled the glide of his mouth on hers, the impression of his hands at her waist. "It's been so long since I felt anything."

Of all her charges, Kell had been the most guarded, the

one slowest to warm to others. Eliza always understood her reticence and never pushed. The first time Kell had crept into Eliza's room after her first date, they'd talked about the boy for hours. After she'd convinced Kell to sleep, Eliza put the teenager to bed and wept. Tears burned in her eyes now, when she understood that in the years since, Kell had rebuilt the walls—higher and stronger. But that she still had a key.

"Luke Calder is a complicated man," she warned gently. "That easygoing demeanor hides some dark corners."

Kell shook her head swiftly. "Doesn't matter. I won't be here to find out."

"Do you think distance will make a difference?"

"I've only known him for a day, Mrs. F. This isn't love at first sight."

Wisely, Eliza said nothing about the note of uncertainty she heard in Kell's voice. Instead, she returned to Kell's comment about leaving. "If you're heading back to Atlanta, does that mean you learned something from him? Do they know who killed Clay?"

Chagrined, Kell moved to the edge of the four-poster. For now, she would keep Luke's mention of the Grove Warehouse fire to herself. "Actually, Mrs. F, I'm not sure what to think. The sheriff's office is waiting on an autopsy report. Those usually take three to four days, at best."

"Three or four days?" Eliza tried to hide her alarm and failed miserably. "If one of my children did this, Kell, I need to know now. This type of secret can eat away at you, break you."

The steady look Eliza directed at her had Kell fighting the urge to squirm. They'd never told her about the warehouse or the fire. Or the money. Fin's plan to create a diary meant they didn't have to. Julia swore not to tell, and to Kell's knowledge, didn't. Still, knowledge flashed in the hazel eyes that had seen through a thousand lies. This was one story, though, Kell couldn't reveal without permission. Instead, she tried for distraction. "I've got an attorney in my office working on getting the reports. I can probably find out what they know the same time the sheriff does."

"What will that do?"

"It will give us a lead. Help us figure out if someone here tried to avenge Nina or not." Kell explained, "The autopsy will tell us time of death and the height and weight of his attacker. We'll be able to eliminate a number of the kids based on that information alone."

"We?"

Hearing the note of hope, Kell relented. "I'll come back early next week, once I have the results. We can do our own investigation and put this to rest."

Eliza voiced the question that had plagued her since she found the knife. "What if one of my children did do this? I can't turn in one of my own, but my goodness, Kell, I can't allow any child in my care to become a murderer."

"We've got time, Mrs. F. On Tuesday or Wednesday, we'll know where we stand, and then we can determine how we react." Kell spoke calmly, reaching for the confidence that convinced others to place their lives in her hands.

With those same hands, she gripped Eliza's shoulders. "I'm not going to leave you alone again. I promise."

CHAPTER 8

In the hallway beyond Kell's room, a shadow length-
ened and turned. Silent footfalls traced a path across
the foyer and to the kitchen where the door stood
slightly ajar. The figure paused in the airy, open space.
Cabinets stretched along three walls, their surfaces
pristine. On the far wall, a butcher block squatted
on the granite. Slots held knives of various sizes and
shapes, each held in its place. Every one. Black mask
in place, he approached the block and found the knife
he'd been afraid to find. The one flaw in an otherwise
perfect plan. Because he'd relied on amateurs, an
obvious mistake had been made.

One that had to be corrected if disaster was to be
averted. One knife held the key. One knife worth killing for. Again.

He opened drawers slowly, searched methodically,
certain he would fail. The missing knife, the murder
weapon, had been taken from the victim's leg before

the police could find it and match it to the others. Logic assumed Eliza Faraday had the knife. That she had gone to Clay's apartment that night and recognized the weapon.

Leaving the kitchen, he crept into the study. The drawers were unlocked, a testament to Eliza's naïveté. After so many years, to still trust in the goodness of urchins born to hookers, thieves, and killers. To imagine that nature would be defied by a single woman's vain attempt at nurture.

He carefully removed each item in each drawer, making scant noise. The house had settled to sleep hours before, and he understood the Center's patterns. Which is how he'd slipped through the alarm before nightfall, had been privy to the touching scene between Eliza and Kell Jameson.

Another mistake left to reappear. His hand tightened in a burst of rage, snapping the item in his grasp. He opened his fingers and saw the plastic toy that had given beneath his fury. Kell Jameson and the other two had run that night, he recalled forbiddingly. When he would have acted, heads higher than his demanded no action. They wouldn't tell, the others had argued, wouldn't dare.

Then they'd vanished, the older two, and the younger one had been cautioned into quiet. For sixteen years, no one stirred the sleeping ghosts, no one dared. Until the need to act had become urgent. Time, for long their friend, had turned quickly. Decisions had fallen to him, and he'd made the choices others refused. Because he had the foresight to comprehend the full scope of their endeavors. To place the pieces into a whole.

Pieces that would fall apart if he didn't locate the knife. He straightened from the desk and moved to the bookcase. For hours, in silence, he removed each volume and searched the crevice of every shelf. As dawn approached, he considered the shelves near the door. In thirty years, she'd never mentioned a safe. Indeed, when he'd quizzed her about one, she'd laughed that she had nothing to protect, nothing to hide. Every resident was free to peruse the library's shelves, to borrow any book.

He examined the titles closely, noting their arcane topics. Bertrand Russell's *Introduction to Mathematical Philosophy* wedged between Diop and an anthropological text on race, gender, and religion. Surrounded by more books that no teenager would trouble himself to read.

Above him, noises began to creep through the house, signaling the waking of its residents. He moved faster, tossing volumes onto the carpet to land with muffled thuds. The dial resided behind a treatise on space-time. He steadied himself, and used the skills he'd learned over a lifetime. The tumblers of the old-fashioned safe revealed their combination with a disappointing ease. He opened the steel door and found the bundle wrapped in a kitchen towel. The worn fabric had not come from Eliza's kitchen, which meant he'd not be able to use it as planted evidence. A pity.

With haste, he replaced the thrown volumes, spurred by the pink light that drifted into the room. Room intact, he sped across the foyer into the kitchen. And collided with a small warm body. The boy stared up, mouth ringed by purloined milk. Before he could scream, he cuffed the boy hard across the temple. His free hand caught the tumbler of milk before it could crash against the linoleum, while the boy slid gracelessly to the floor. He set the tumbler on the counter and stepped over the fallen body.

In the growing light, he rushed behind the Center, weaving between its imposing oaks, emerging into the dense wood that concealed his vehicle. At the proper moment, the knife would make its bow, if his contingencies fell through. Kell's presence assured him that one or more would, but he cast aside doubt.

They'd worked for years, thriving and building and shedding those who betrayed their codes. Greed tempted ostentation, a trait he'd never displayed. His success, his power, required no outward validation of its existence. Empires grown from fallow ground and seized opportunities. Mistakes had been made, certainly, lives made forfeit because of them. One or three more would be meager prices for success.

After all, no one else had cared, why should they?

Kell burrowed deeper into her pillow, remnants of a pleasantly erotic dream clinging to the edge of memory. She recognized herself, and pretended not to know the identity of the man who'd done unspeakably wonderful things to her along a sparkling white beach. As wakefulness threatened, she tried to command herself back to sleep.

She'd spent the last ten weekends waking at the crack of dawn to focus on Brodie's defense, and for the first Saturday in recent memory, she was on her own timetable. No motions *in limine* or briefs to file to suppress evidence that would sink her client for sure.

For one glorious, hard-earned Saturday she would lounge about, slough off, and otherwise commit herself to intentional relaxation. The reason for her visit to Hallden had hit a brick wall. Without an autopsy or an arrest warrant, the Faraday case wasn't. She didn't have an alternate theory of the crime to follow up on, and any questions she might pose to the sheriff's department reflected badly on her client.

She had no choice but to stay in bed until hunger demanded she hunt through the Center's well-stocked pantry for sustenance. Visions of pancakes slathered in maple syrup set her stomach to rumbling. She flipped over, as much to quiet the sound as to avoid the sunlight that had the temerity to sneak through the lace curtains hanging at her window.

The shadowy figure of her fantasies had begun a fresh assault on her senses when a scream pierced the pleasant haze of sleep. From the sound, the screamer had been nearby. Kell vaulted from the bed, clad in the tank top and shorts she habitually slept in. She raced through the door and saw Nina standing in the doorway of the kitchen.

Kell crossed to her and saw Jorden lying prostrate on the cold floor. A bruise had already begun to darken the tender skin. "Nina, go call 911," she instructed tersely, moving past the immobile body to kneel beside Jorden. She located his pulse, and looked up to see that Nina had yet to move. "He's alive, Nina. Call 911. Now."

Eliza appeared in the entrance and clutched Nina's shoulders. She corrected Kell's instructions. "Nina, go into the study and call Sheriff Calder. His number is on the desk. Do not call the police, call Luke. Okay, honey?"

Nina nodded, her emerald eyes huge in the pallor of her face. She shifted past Eliza and ran to the study. Eliza joined Kell by Jorden's side. "What happened?"

"I don't know." Kell cradled his head in her lap, afraid to move him. "I heard Nina scream, came running in here and found him on the floor." She stroked the bruised cheek tenderly. "He's breathing fine and his pulse is good."

"That bruise isn't from the floor." Eliza covered her mouth for an instant. "Someone hit the boy."

"I think you're right." Kell angled her chin up at the counter. "He seemed to be getting a glass of milk. The milk is fine, but he's down here. My guess is that someone hit him."

"Not one of my children."

"No, of course not."

Kell knew the moment the true culprit occurred to Eliza.

"The knife!"

Kell nodded once. "Go, make sure it's wherever you put it. Luke will be here soon."

Eliza scrambled up, passing Nina on her way. She told the girl to report to Kell and then to wake the other children without alarming them. In her study, she shut the door and locked it tight. She moved to the second entrance, locking that door as well. But one look at the bookcase told her security had been breached. The volumes, carefully replaced, were out of the order she'd maintained for decades. Her hand trembled as she entered the combination and opened the safe. Papers and the stack of emergency cash she kept inside remained inviolate. But the knife and the towel it had been wrapped inside were both gone.

Putting aside the panic that bubbled into her throat, Eliza replaced the books and returned to the kitchen. Jorden had begun to wake, groaning softly. The brown eyes fluttered open and focused on Eliza. He jack-knifed up and threw himself into her arms, which closed around him fiercely.

"Ow."

"I'm sorry, sweetheart," she exclaimed, loosening her grip. "I didn't mean to hug you too tightly."

"No, ma'am, not that," he moaned into her chest. "My face hurts really bad."

Gently, Eliza stroked his back and kissed his forehead. "Do you know what happened, Jorden?"

"A man in a black mask punched me in the face," he announced, his voice muffled. "It hurt."

Kell crawled over to sit beside him. "Did you recognize anything about him?"

"No. He was taller than me, that's all."

Before Kell could ask another question, Luke pushed open the swinging door. He took in the scene in a glance and joined the trio on the floor. Without moving Eliza, he thumbed Jorden on the nose. "Hear you tried to catch a burglar with your face?"

Jorden giggled, his chest puffing out. He wriggled away from Eliza in sudden embarrassment and tried to stand.

Luke fastened a restraining hand on his shoulder. "Easy, Jorden. Take your time. Though, if it were me, I'd rather be getting a hug from two pretty women than standing up myself."

Relieved, because his face was on fire, Jorden returned to Eliza, though he decided it wasn't too manly to lay his head back down. "Do you really think it was a burglar?" he asked Luke excitedly.

"Won't know until I do an investigation." Luke sat on the floor and stretched his legs out, then removed his notepad. "Mr. Abrams, I'd like to take your statement."

"For real?"

"Absolutely." Luke took his time turning pages. "You're my eyewitness to the crime, aren't you?"

Kell watched the exchange and tried not to notice the way Luke reinforced the boy's pride and distracted him from his pain. Because if she gave him credit for kindness and sensitivity, she'd be in even more trouble than she'd already admitted.

Hoping to distract herself, she came to her knees.

"Kell, don't leave," Jorden demanded fretfully. "I might need a lawyer."

Smothering a smile, she explained, "You're not the perpetrator, Jorden."

"But the cop shows always make the guy talking to the police have a lawyer," he repeated stubbornly. "Can't you be mine?"

"Yes, Kell. Mr. Abrams desires counsel. Will you deny him his Fifth Amendment rights?" Luke teased in mock seriousness.

Deciding not to lecture either of them on the rudiments of the Constitution, and catching the approving look in Eliza's eyes, she sank down. "You may question my client."

Jorden explained in dramatic detail how the man had run into him, then punched him in the face. As he recounted the story, Nina and other children arrived in the kitchen. Eliza tried to shoo them out, but saw the expressions of worry and fear. They wanted to know what happened, and to know it wouldn't happen again. Slipping Jorden on to the floor between Luke and Kell, she quietly ushered the children into the kitchen. They took up posts along the cabinet, some sitting on the stools by the island. The older kids held the youngest ones as Jorden went through his story a third time, led by Luke.

"Did you hear anything when you came downstairs?" he asked a second time.

"No, sir. I didn't hear anything. I wanted to watch cartoons, but I can only watch them in the TV room 'cause I wake up early."

"Why did you come into the kitchen?"

"I was thirsty." He gestured to the glass. "Mrs. F gets

mad if you don't use a glass and we have to have milk or water in the morning."

"So you came down the stairs and into the kitchen. But you didn't hear anything?"

Jorden squinted in sudden thought. "Well, maybe."

"Maybe?"

"I heard a thumping noise maybe in the library." He ducked his head. "But I didn't listen too close."

Alert, Luke prompted, "Why not?"

Jorden slanted a look across the room at the other children, then leaned in to Luke and Kell. "They said that ghosts live in the library at night. I thought it was one of them."

Having told the same story herself, Kell patted his arm in commiseration. "I've heard the same thing. But I don't believe the man that hit you was a ghost."

The look of relief would have been comic under other circumstances. Luke asked a few more questions, admired the black eye, and sent Jorden off with Eliza to visit the emergency room. Main attraction gone, the other children scattered to begin morning chores, chattering excitedly about the dramatic events.

Luke lingered in the kitchen, and Kell decided to make coffee as a peace offering. And to keep her hands busy. "You were very good with him," she commented as she filled the glass pot.

"I left my rubber hose in my other pocket."

Kell smiled, then gave him a considering look. "He

was frightened and embarrassed. You made him feel like a grown-up."

A bit embarrassed himself, Luke scratched at the stubble he hadn't had time to shave in his rush to get to the Center. "I was a nine-year-old boy once. And I like Jorden. He's a good kid."

"Will you do an investigation?"

"Someone broke into the Center for a reason. Eliza told me she didn't see anything missing, and I expect who ever it was wore gloves. But I'll have Cheryl and one of my deputies come and dust for prints."

Nina pushed into the kitchen. Gone were the pajamas, replaced by a sundress, and, if Kell wasn't mistaken, a smidgen of blush.

"Kell, Mrs. F said that I should come and help you with breakfast." Nina smiled shyly at Luke. "Hi, Sheriff. I'm so glad you came to help."

"My pleasure, Nina." He returned the shy smile. "You look very pretty in yellow. I'll have to visit the Center more often. Surround myself with beautiful women."

Kell didn't have to hear Nina's sigh, since she could scarcely contain her own. A man who was kind to frightened boys and able to flirt gently with teenage girls nursing a crush. Her heart took another timid step toward a precipice. Then alarm skittered into Kell's eyes as the rest of Nina's sentence registered. "Help me do what with breakfast?"

Nina sauntered to the refrigerator and laughed,

practicing the husky sound she'd heard Kell make yesterday. On her, it sounded more like a cough. Abandoning the effort, she explained, "Mrs. F said you'd take care of breakfast while she took Jorden to the doctor. Faith went with her, and Brandon is upstairs supervising."

"Brandon?"

"Brandon McLean. Tall, skinny quiet guy. He's shy." Nina grabbed eggs and a carton of milk. "We usually have—"

"Pancakes on Saturday," Kell finished. "I don't know how to make pancakes."

Luke released a laugh too when alarm became abject terror. Realizing his task of saving the day had just begun, he beckoned to Nina. "If you can make sure everyone gets their chores done in thirty minutes, I'll make waffles."

"The ones with the blueberries?" she asked eagerly. "Mrs. F has some in the freezer."

"Yep."

Nina nodded and hurried out, remembering to slow down as she reached the door. "Thanks, Sheriff Luke. You're the best."

Left alone again, Kell finished preparing the coffee. "I can defend a cartel against drug possession charges while standing in the center of the drug boat, but I can't cook to save my life."

Luke grinned, already gathering his supplies. "Then I suppose that's one more reason you'll have to stay here. A constant supply of blueberry waffles." He located an apron to wear over his jeans and T-shirt.

Stopping behind her, he pressed a kiss to the nape of her neck. "Like your outfit, Kell," he murmured.

Kell shivered in reaction and hopped off the stool. "I've got to change."

As she pushed through the door, she heard him say, "Never on my account."

CHAPTER 9

As he expected, Cheryl and her team found no trace of the intruder except a jimmied lock on the kitchen door. After giving Eliza a stern lecture on safety, which included using the fancy security system she'd had installed a year ago, Luke went into his office to work on the Griffin case.

Curly greeted him, alerted to Luke's plans by Cheryl. "I swear you two are worse than mothering hens," he complained as he passed by the desk.

"Leave it to you and you'd spend most of your life here in this office," Curly responded. "Either that or hiding away in that rattrap you took a mind to rebuild."

"That rattrap is a diamond in the rough." Luke walked into his office, grateful for the coffee steaming on his desk. Mother hens or not, Curly and Cheryl took excellent care of him. Though they were as different from his squad in Chicago as night and day, both had been a close-knit team that looked out for each other. Almost always.

When the memory snuck in, Luke couldn't prepare for it. So he let the sorrow break against him, knowing that each time, the pain lessened. If four years had dulled grief and guilt to a razor's edge, perhaps by ten he'd be able to start the process of forgiveness.

"Thought you might want to take a look at this." Curly entered the office without knocking, a habit he'd never managed to pick up. He handed Luke a fax that Curly had already reviewed. "The lab in Macon says they've gotten backed up and won't be able to release the autopsy before Monday."

"Monday? It's a stab wound. All I need is a formal cause of death and some hint about the murder's particulars. I can't run a murder investigation without some shred of evidence."

"You know it was a knife," Curly offered laconically.

"Shut up." Luke read the fax, which included a short apology for the delay. "Tracy Hoover is still M.E., isn't she?"

"Yep."

"And she's usually fairly fast with turnaround."

"Yep."

Picking up on the responses, Luke rolled his eyes and let out a breath. "What else do you know?"

"Seems that Tracy's brother ran into some trouble in Atlanta last year. Didn't have money for a lawyer, so his sister called in a favor."

Luke's eyes became black slits. "Kell Jameson defended her brother?"

"Yep." Curly shrugged from his position on the

couch. "Can't confirm or deny anything, but I'm guessing we'll get the results around the same time Miss Kell does, give or take a day or so."

Luke cursed slowly and methodically, to Curly's amusement. As the tirade petered out, Curly offered, "Maybe you should focus on the other impossible case you've got in your basket."

"Don't have much of a choice, do I?"

"The knife is gone." Eliza repeated the sentence dumbly as Kell paced the study.

"Then someone else knows that you were at Clay's apartment." She stopped. "Are you sure no one saw you?"

"I was." Head bowed, Eliza felt the dread settle into her. First a murder, then a break-in that left one of her children injured. "Maybe I should tell Luke the truth."

"Then what happens? He will have the same thoughts that you did. If not you, then one of the children. They had access to the safe."

"My kids wouldn't do that," Eliza defended.

"Perhaps not, but it would be Luke's job to question them. To suspect them." Kell stopped walking and joined Eliza on the settee. "Our best defense is figuring out who did this first."

"How?"

"By eliminating the immediate suspects first. We know you didn't kill Clay. And, after last night, it's safe to rule out the children. The man Jorden described is bigger than anyone here."

"True." Trying again, she asked, "But wouldn't this convince Luke as well?"

Natural reticence about cops butted up against what she'd learned of Sheriff Luke. Grudgingly, she answered, "There may come a time when we have to turn to Luke, but we're not there yet. Until we have more answers, our best defense is to try and find out who else might have wanted Clay dead."

"But you're heading back to Atlanta tomorrow," Eliza pointed out, her voice neutral. "I'm not a sleuth, Kell."

Kell had already considered the problem. David would have a fit, but right now, she had priorities she'd forsaken for too long. "Don't worry, Mrs. F. I'll tie up some loose ends in Atlanta on Monday, and then I'll be back. I promise."

"What about the robbery?"

"Luke probably has a theory already. Let me see what I can find out." Kell bussed Eliza's cheek with a kiss. "Don't worry yet. But lock the door behind me."

Kell hurried out of the Center and climbed into her car, the dent from the errant ball gleaming in the sunlight. Rather than the surge of irritation she expected, she found herself wondering who won the game.

"I've been here too long already." Kell pulled onto the road, then she reached into her bag and removed her cell phone. For a dose of reality, she knew exactly who to call. The phone rang three times before Kell disconnected the line. She counted to thirty, dialed again and cut the line after five rings. Then she counted to fifteen, dialed and let the phone ring seven times. On the eighth ring, she heard the line connect.

"Hey, stranger."

"Hey, yourself," responded a voice that Kell had always thought belonged on a 900 number. Findley Borders lounged by a crystalline blue pool, three gold triangles covering inches of skin. An alabaster house rose behind her, reflecting the sunlight from the shimmering water. "You're early. We're not due for a chat until next month."

Kell smiled. "Sue me."

"Seeing how you got Brodie off, I'll pass," Fin demurred. "What's wrong?"

"Nothing."

Fin drew a knee up and draped her arm across. "Kell, you wouldn't be calling if there wasn't a problem. What gives?"

"I'm in Hallden." She waited a beat. "Clay Griffin is dead."

"Good riddance. Who's the hero?"

"Unknown. But Mrs. F might become a suspect."

Fin shot up on her lounger. "No way! She couldn't kill anyone."

"I know, I know. That's why I'm here," Kell explained quickly. "I'm trying to get a bead on who might have done it instead."

"Need me to look into anything?"

"Not right now, I just wanted you to know what's going on." Kell sped along the road, hesitating. "I think I like the sheriff," she confessed in a rush.

"As the killer? Old Patmos?"

"Not Sheriff Patmos. Luke Calder, the new sheriff. And not as the killer."

A low laugh came over the phone. "You've fallen for the fuzz."

Stiffly, Kell corrected, "I haven't fallen for anyone. I simply think he's very attractive."

Singing between giggles, Fin teased, "Kell and the Sheriff, sitting in a tree."

"Damn it, Fin, you're so juvenile!"

"And you're so tightly wound, it's about time someone had you acting like a girl."

Kell cursed again. "Why did I even call you?"

"Because Julia would gush and twitter. I'm your reality check."

Exactly, Kell acknowledged. "I've been here for two days. I barely know him."

"And he's already gotten to you? What's his mojo?"

"I don't understand it myself," Kell bemoaned. "I mean, he's built like an erotic dream, with a voice to match, but he's also smug and self-righteous and imperious."

"A perfect match for a woman who's cocky, too smart for her own good, and afraid to fail."

Grinding her teeth, Kell muttered, "Thanks for the compliment."

"I may not have seen you in nearly five years, but I know you, Kell. You're always in control, always three steps ahead. Maybe you like finding a guy who can keep up with you for once."

"After a weekend?"

"The weekend isn't what's bothering you, kid. It's the fact that you want it to be longer. Speaking of longer, we need to disconnect now. I'll get another phone and get the number to you."

"Fin, we can stop hiding soon."

"Not yet, though," Fin warned. "Plus, I've been a busy girl, K. Can't stop running now. Love ya."

The call ended abruptly, and Kell closed the phone. She needed to call Julia soon as well. First, though, she'd stop by the sheriff's department and prove Fin and herself wrong. But before she reached the turn-off for the office, a spectacle on the side of the road caught her eye.

A dingy red truck spattered with mud drunkenly straddled the road and the shoulder, one tire dipping into a ravine. Beside the truck, a small menagerie consisting of a goat, a pig, and three yapping dogs milled around aimlessly. A scarecrow of a man yelled orders to the animals, futilely waving what looked like a walking stick. Ahead of the pickup, she recognized Luke's truck. And the long-legged man yanking another goat along the highway.

Pulling to the side of the road, she emerged from the car and strolled up to the chaos. "Need some help?"

The elderly man answered first. "No, ma'am. Sheriff Calder's got me taken care of. Out for a drive and something scratched at my undercarriage, then Nadine got scared and jumped out of the truck. Before I could stop 'em, Rufus and Jezebel and Bobby Lee decided to follow. Old Hemp was too tired to make a real go of it. Lucky for me, I had Ernestine on the front seat, but she kept squealing something awful until I let her out."

In the distance, Luke swore at the goat, whom Kell assumed was the errant Nadine. He tugged at a rope he'd fastened around her neck, and the black-and-gray goat promptly sat on its haunches. "Hey, Luke!"

He glanced up and saw Kell, looking picture-perfect in white slacks and a matching top. For his part, mud tracks had fouled his khaki shirt, a fine partner to the jeans ripped by his tussle with the godforsaken spawn of hell Farmer Henry called Nadine. "What do you want, Kell?"

"Nothing really, just enjoying the show."

As if on cue, Nadine gained her feet and plowed into Luke, sending him sprawling into the ravine beside the shoulder. Farmer Henry let out a hoot of laughter. "Now, now, Nadine. Quit acting a fool and get back in the truck."

Kell jogged to the ravine and peered down at Luke. "Oops."

Levering himself up, he vowed, "Tonight, I'm making goat steaks. Join me for dinner?"

Laughing, Kell reached for his muddy hand and helped him climb up. "Eat Nadine? Why? She's just playing with you." For lack of a better option, Kell wiped her dirty palms on a clean part of Luke's shirt. For a second, her hands lingered on the firm mounds of muscle beneath her touch. When she realized she wasn't moving, she stepped away. "Sorry. I'm wearing white."

Luke swallowed past a sudden lump in his throat, ignoring the rush that hardened him instantly. He managed, "That evil goat escapes once a week. Next time, I'm going to let a car hit her."

Farmer Henry, who'd finally herded the other animals into the truck, ambled over to Luke. "Now, you don't mean that, Sheriff. Nadine's not a bad sort."

"She's rotten to the core, Henry. And she hates me." In answer, the goat sauntered over and began to nibble at Luke's pant leg. "Don't try flirting with me now."

Enjoying the show, Kell stood back as Luke tossed the goat into the pickup and closed the gate. "You a farmer in a former life? Look like a natural."

"Shut up, Kell," he cautioned. Rounding the side, he helped Farmer Henry into the cab and sternly warned, "I'm not coming out here again this week, Henry. Keep these animals at home."

"But they like going for a Saturday drive, Sheriff."

"This is your last warning," Luke repeated, but no one listening believed him. Henry waved as he drove off, and Luke turned to Kell. "What brings you into town?"

"You, actually."

"Do tell."

Kell shook her head. "I wanted to find out if you had any leads on the break-in."

"Nothing yet. I've got Cheryl and a couple of others on it. But who ever did this didn't leave much to go with. You have any theories you're willing to share?"

"None," Kell answered honestly. "I'm heading to Atlanta tomorrow."

"For how long?"

"Until I've got a reason to return."

Luke took her hand, and Kell didn't evade him. "Is seeing me a good reason?"

She hesitated, torn. "No, it can't be. Goodbye, Luke." She reached up and wiped at a smear of mud along his cheekbone. "Go get cleaned up."

Sunday morning, Luke carefully picked his way across the abandoned construction site, leaping over fallen cinderblocks and circling muddied pools. The Grove Warehouse project had come to a screeching halt last week when construction crews discovered two charred bodies during excavation. On his orders, the bulldozers had rolled out and the spooked owners were demanding they be allowed to relist the site for sale.

Walking to the exposed iron steps that led down into the basement, Luke recalled the original crime scene. Skeletal remains blackened by soot. One lay near the exit, where a chalk outline marked the position. The other had been deeper in the basement underneath a table. Dental records had identified one of the men, but his office hadn't received a hit yet that associated the other body with any missing persons records in Hallden or surrounding areas.

The death scene, then and now, bothered Luke. According to the arsonist reports, the fire had begun on the main level and swept through the warehouse. Unlike most warehouses, which were built on concrete slabs, this one possessed a basement level that protected the interior space from the heat of the flames and from earlier detection.

Blueprints pulled from the county planning office revealed no permit for a basement level. Indeed, if the bulldozers hadn't crushed the main levels, including a weakened subfloor, no one would have been the wiser. Instead, they discovered two burned bodies that somehow made their way downstairs to a section untouched by the conflagration.

Inside the space, Luke saw the scene he'd recorded in his earlier report. Laboratory tools preserved from destruction rested on workbenches around the room. Tests confirmed chemical traces of methamphetamines and cocaine. The drug lab had been shielded by concrete reinforcements, which did the two victims no good.

Moving deeper into the room, Luke paused when he heard a sound coming from above the stairs. A clicking noise sounded on the metal steps, reverberating in the cavernous space. Silently, he shifted to the nearest wall and plastered himself against the rough surface. And waited. Seconds later, the interloper came into view.

"What the hell are you doing here?"

Kell startled and spun toward Luke, her brain already reaching for a plausible story. To buy time, she exclaimed, "Luke, you scared me!"

He walked out of the shadows, face grim. "This is a crime scene, Kell. Not a tourist destination."

"I know." Kell waved a hand at the chalk outline. "But when you mentioned the fire Friday night, I wanted to see what happened." *Of all the damnable luck.* She'd contacted the sheriff's department before deciding to drive out to the Grove. The dispatcher told her that Luke was on patrol on the outskirts of town—the other side. If there'd been a chance of running into him, she wouldn't have come. She had no choice but to brazen out the encounter. "I represent criminals for a living. The mention of the warehouse raised my curiosity. Especially since you've considered my name in connection with it."

"Curiosity is a dangerous vice, Kell," Luke admonished as he closed the distance between them. "Wandering around dilapidated buildings is a surefire way to get hurt. Especially wearing shoes like that." He looked pointedly at the sleek brown shoes with their skyscraper heels.

The heels matched the trim chocolate suit she'd put on this morning. She'd chosen the outfit for the trousers and because these were her lowest pair of heels. Her travel wardrobe hadn't included casual outfits appropriate for the investigating a murder that implicated her.

"What are you doing here, Kell?"

"I'm on my way back to Atlanta," she explained. "This was on the way."

Luke frowned. "The freeway is north of the Center. This is south."

Oh, yeah. Recovering quickly, she corrected, "First, I planned to visit a friend that I haven't seen in years."

"A friend? Who?"

Plucking a name from her memory, Kell responded, "Mattie Cotton. She and I were on the cheerleading squad together." Hopefully, Mattie still lived on the farm her family had run for generations.

"You were a cheerleader?"

"I was co-captain." Kell made a furtive scan of the space. It was just as she remembered. Sterile, cold, and mean. Dangerous, even empty of what she'd seen then. Repressing a shudder, she asked, "Why are you here, Sheriff?"

"As I told you, this is an open investigation." One that became more convoluted by the day.

"Have you determined who the victims were?"

"We've got one name. Louis Pippin. A fairly renowned dealer in the meth trade back in its infancy, also dabbled in prostitution and extortion around the region. The theory is that he was trapped down here by the fire."

"But there's no damage to this room."

"Which is why I disagree with the theory. Chief Graves and I have a difference of opinion, but since the warehouse is outside the city limits, it falls into my jurisdiction."

"Chief Graves? Michael Graves?" She asked, not bothering to hide her revulsion.

"Yes. Mike made police chief the same year I became sheriff." Luke repressed a snort of derision. "Plans to run against me for the job in the fall."

"I remember him. He was a squirrelly man who always struck me as rather lazy and fairly dull. Barney Fife without the intestinal fortitude."

The accurate description startled a laugh from Luke. "No comment." He caught her elbow and steered them both toward the steps. "This is an active crime scene, Kell. I can't have civilians tramping around down here until we've completed our investigation."

"I understand." Grateful for the reprieve, Kell started up the steps. On the third step, she stumbled. Luckily, Luke was tight on her heels and caught her easily. Kell found herself wrapped against him, his arm braced on the banister to steady them both. "I'm okay."

"Okay."

Kell, for once, stood eye to eye with him. Mouth to mouth. Unable, unwilling to resist, she leaned in, closing the distance. "Just once more. For the road."

Softly, her mouth brushed his, and Luke accepted the caress, frozen. Her lips captured his lower one, her tongue slicking across the captive flesh. Murmuring to herself, she traced the contours of his mouth, a slow, tortuous exploration. When his arms closed around her, she slipped hers around his neck and dove. Tongue, lips, teeth met and mated, a frenzied kiss that shot sparks along heated skin. Luke reeled beneath the assault, desperate and eager. Her taste speared through him. Going under, he fisted his hands in her hair, needing an anchor.

Too soon, she pulled away. "Luke."

"Kell."

"I need to go. Now."

With effort, he forced his hands to open and she

turned away. They reached the first floor where rubble from the demolition made maneuvering tricky. He clasped her elbow and guided her out to her car.

"What was that?" he asked.

"An experiment."

"And?"

"And I need to go." She continued walking, head down. Kissing him had been an error in judgment, but one she couldn't regret. Not when her mouth still tingled with excitement. It was definitely time to go.

Beside her, Luke asked, "Did you know Louis Pippin?"

Kell barely avoided a stumble and, head still down, she pretended to consider the question. She shook her head in regret. "I don't recall the name."

Luke pulled her to a halt. "Really?" He watched as she answered, not her eyes but her hands. They lay still. A lie. Disappointed, he pressed, "Were you at the warehouse the night it burned down?"

Kell noted his attention to her hands and clasped them together. She tended to gesture when she got nervous, so she'd learned to control their movements in court. And for conversations like this. Interlacing her fingers, she replied calmly, "No. We were at the park, having a farewell picnic. Fin and I planned to leave that weekend. We took Julia out for a celebration." *Don't answer too much, keep it short.*

"Can anyone vouch for you?"

"That was sixteen years ago. I doubt anyone remembers what they did that long ago."

"Clay Griffin did."

"Or so he said."

"Why would he lie, Kell? Of all the people to blame, why did he pick you and your friends?"

Kell removed the keys from her pocket, signaling her intention to leave. "Because he was disturbed. Vindictive. Clay was angry with anyone who remained at the Center after Eliza made him leave. I'm not surprised he would concoct a story to the police about seeing us that night. But it simply isn't true."

Luke detested liars, especially the good ones. His job was to find the truth, theirs to hide it. Yet, he had no choice but to place Kell in that category. Which left one final question. "Where were you last Monday night?"

"On national television giving an interview for *CourtWatch TV*. During the rest of the week, I was gutting the prosecution. On Thursday, I was delivering a closing argument in front of a judge and twelve jurors and approximately seven million viewers. Where were you?"

"Calling a bingo game at the senior center." Hearing the belligerence, Luke understood he wouldn't get any more from her today. Instead, he plucked her keys from her clenched fist and opened the driver's door. "You should get that dent fixed soon. And next time you're in town, I'll have to convince you to let me drive this machine."

Kell sidled past him and turned in the space created by the open door. "I'm fairly particular about who gets behind her wheel. I tend to decline those who think I'm a murderer."

With a smile that belied his words, Luke cajoled, "It's my job to ask the tough questions. Surely you can understand that."

"I can. And you can understand if I don't believe you."

"Oh, you can trust me, Kell. With your car at least. I'm a very safe driver. I tend to take things nice and easy."

The conversation had shifted from alibis and cars to the attraction that arced between them. Determined to resist, Kell countered. "Nice and easy can be as dangerous as speed. Lulls you into complacency."

"You don't strike me as the type that has to worry. Anyone who drives a car like this recognizes the need to find a healthy balance. Otherwise, with this much power beneath your hands, you could forget yourself." Luke moved closer, caging her in. "But I always remember what I'm doing and with whom. It's one of my talents."

Kell lifted a brow. "One of? You have a high opinion of yourself."

"So do you. It seems we're well matched."

"But only one of us has the keys." Kell snagged them and ducked inside the car. She tugged the door shut, and a few seconds later, the window slid open. "Good luck with your investigations, Sheriff."

"Travel safe, Counselor." Luke stepped away from the car, remembering her kiss, knowing he'd see her again soon. Which is the only reason he let her go.

As soon as she reached the highway, she dialed.

"Julia Warner speaking."

"Jules, it's Kell." She heard the sudden intake of breath, realizing how she'd reacted to a similar phone call a couple of days ago. "Everyone is fine. Nothing's wrong," she rushed to add.

"If everything was fine, you wouldn't be calling," Julia corrected. In her living room, she sank onto the floor, clutching the receiver. "You're months ahead of schedule."

"There's been a development. Clay Griffin is dead."

"Clay? That's tragic, but I don't understand why this warrants breaking your sacred protocol."

"Mrs. F may be arrested for his murder."

"Preposterous."

Leave it to Julia to sum up the case in a single word. "I had to go to Hallden to check on her and find out what happened." Kell ran through her time in Hallden, skipping over her more personal encounters.

"So the sheriff knows about the warehouse?"

"He believes he does. But there's no way he can put it all together."

"What about Clay? We didn't see him that night."

"No, but apparently he saw us. I'm sure he gave an embellished report to Sheriff Patmos. Which means that we have to assume he also knew what happened."

"Oh, God."

"Right now, Luke has pieces but no real theory. We might have been at the warehouse. Clay might have seen us. The dead men might be connected to Clay somehow. It's all speculation."

"What should we do?"

"Nothing for now. The sheriff is waiting on the autopsy for Clay, and then we'll know if Mrs. F will be in danger."

"If she is, Kell, what do we do?"

"I don't know." Now came the question she dreaded asking. "Julia, did you ever tell her?"

"I swore I wouldn't."

"But you were young and alone. Frightened. I'd completely understand if you told Mrs. F. But I need to know."

"I didn't tell her. I swore I wouldn't and I didn't. Do you need anything else?"

"Don't be mad, Jules. I had to ask. I may be there for a while, and I have to know what I'm facing."

"Fine," she answered stiffly.

Ashamed, Kell wheedled, "I believe you. And I'm sorry I doubted you."

Julia sniffed loudly. "You should be. After all these years, how could you think I'd have told?"

"Because I'm a moron. So how long are you going to be mad at me?"

"At least for the next hour."

Kell grinned, knowing the crisis had passed. "Fin says hello."

"Got a postcard from her in February. Aruba."

"Which means she was probably in the South of France."

"Probably."

"We might have to meet, Jules. If Luke begins to figure it out, we won't have much time."

"And how well do you know this Sheriff Luke?"

Kell flushed. "I met him Friday."

"And you're already on a first-name basis."

"It's a small town, and I'm very friendly."

Julia scoffed at the description. "Since when?"

"Since Friday."

"Kell?"

"Fine. I like him. A lot. But not enough to put you two in jeopardy. No man is worth that."

"Is that the excuse you're going to use?"

"Excuse?"

"For why you won't let any man get closer than arm's length. Isn't that why you've kept David dangling since law school? Because you're afraid."

Feeling the description hit too close, Kell replied, "Leave it alone, Jules."

Undeterred, Julia continued, "You're one of my best friends, Kell. I want to see you happy. And you won't be, as long as you push every man away who might make you care. This has nothing to do with Fin or me. It's about you and your parents and being afraid to lose everything. Again."

The second shot was dead-on, and Kell grew cold. "Jules. I'm serious. Leave it alone."

Too soft-hearted to press, Julia relented. "I will, on one condition."

Grateful for the reprieve, Kell exhaled. "Name it."

"Let your guard down a little, Kell. Save Mrs. F, but let it go, just a bit."

"I'll try." Hearing her protest, Kell repeated, "I'll

try. But I can't promise, okay? Check the account in a couple of days. I'll let you know the status."

"Love you, Kell."

"Love you, Jules."

CHAPTER 10

"Autopsy's back, Sheriff." Cheryl halted in Luke's doorway, folder in hand. She hesitated to enter, given the sheriff's foul mood since Sunday. Self-preservation kept her on the threshold and close to the exit. She started her report. "Victim died of a severed femoral artery. Bled out in minutes."

"Don't just stand there, Cheryl. Come in." Impatiently, Luke waved her into the office.

"You sure it's safe?" she quipped as the door shut and she dropped into a chair. "I left my weapon in my desk."

"Very funny." Luke grimaced, well aware that he'd been in a bad mood. A few days that felt much longer. Ever since he watched Kell drive away. He felt like a randy teenager rather than the experienced man of thirty-eight he knew himself to be. Particularly given the brief acquaintance with a woman who had little compunction about bending the truth to suit her. Yet, he'd seen a core of loyalty in her that drew him in, found humor that held him. She was nothing like the woman he imagined himself falling for, yet he could no longer picture anyone else.

The contradiction infuriated him and hope kept him tied in knots. Every opened door had him looking for her, so he could either prove to himself he'd imagined their connection or convince her that he hadn't.

Either way, if he didn't curb his temper, he'd be working alone in the sheriff's department.

"I may have been a bit difficult this week," he offered in subdued apology, daring Cheryl to elaborate. Wisely, she remained silent, and Luke appreciated the intuition. In addition to pining for a woman he barely knew, he'd been waiting all week for a simple forensics report. Without a crime lab in Hallden, he often relied on the one in Macon, but the results didn't usually take this long. Another irritation he could hang on Kell Jameson. Restless, he lifted a pen from the desk and flipped it over his thumb. "Weapon?"

"Preliminary report describes it as a knife with an eight-inch blade."

"Sounds like a common kitchen knife." Which confirmed his initial impression. A stab wound to the thigh. Griffin barely had time to scream, let alone go for help. He'd been dead the moment the knife went into his leg. "Any DNA samples other than the vic's?"

"No, sir. No defensive wounds on the victim at all." Cheryl leaned forward, eyes troubled by the news. "But the coroner did make a note about the murder weapon. It wasn't made of steel."

"What do you mean?"

"The coroner reports that knife was made of," she referred to the report, "ceramic zirconia. The blow cracked the knife at the tip and left a fragment in the victim. Only ceramic does that. The stainless steel alloy typically used doesn't."

"Who uses ceramic knives? Hunters? Chefs?"

"She told me ceramic knives of this quality are hard to come by. Usually, chefs have them and maybe really advanced home cooks. Hunters would avoid them because of their tendency to chip against bone with heavy work. Plus, the blade has a unique signature too."

"Which is?"

"Coroner indicates that the blade has a slightly raised edge that angles at a sharper degree than other knives." She flipped the report cover shut. "We find someone with a specially made set of ceramic zirconia kitchen knives and we'll find our killer."

Luke processed this new twist, digesting the implications. Off hand, he could name three people who might possibly have a cutlery set like the one described in the report. Hervé Montague for one. Joel Welker, a local who prided himself on his barbequing skills and custom-designed kitchen. The third one had his neck itching in dismay.

Eliza Faraday. Her food and love of cooking was legendary. So much so that one of her former residents, an executive chef in L.A., gifted her with a set of exclusive cutlery. A bit of a gourmand himself, Luke had admired the knives last year when they arrived for Christmas.

Luke started to remind Cheryl, but held his tongue. The mention of Eliza Faraday as a suspect would create chaos in his office. Besides the fact that his chief deputy considered her family, nearly everyone in his office revered the woman—him included.

Still, her involvement would explain Kell's unexpected appearance. If Eliza was involved, she'd be wise to bring in the best defense attorney in the state. One who could poke around for information without raising suspicion.

One who could go out to dinner with the investigating officer and pump him for information. Then kiss him and leave his knees buckled for days.

Kell Jameson had occupied too much of his thinking, keeping his temper on a brink that required little to tip him over.

For now, he decided, he'd keep Eliza's potential involvement private. Gather as much information as he could before he brought Cheryl and the rest of the department into the investigation. His staff had been spread thin of late by a rash of break-ins. No sense in riling everyone up before he nailed his theory down. Eliza Faraday was the least likely candidate for murder, which, he knew, moved her up a notch on the suspect list.

He set his pen on the cluttered desk surface and lifted his copy of the report. "Get in touch with the coroner again and see if we can't determine the origin of the knife set. Who might have manufactured it and where. Shouldn't be too hard to trace. Let her know we'll consider her help repayment for the delay."

"I can take point on interviews," Cheryl suggested as she took notes. "We can begin with Chef Montague. He's the most obvious place to start, but I can't see why he'd have an issue with Griffin. Doesn't strike me as the vicious-murderer type."

"Agreed, but we need an alibi from anyone with means. But he could give us some help on where we'd find them." Making his plan, he instructed, "I'd like to keep this quiet for now, easy. Hervé knows me well, so I'll take the interview with him. You track down those knives. Also, pull his credit report and Joel Welker's."

Cheryl frowned. "You think Mr. Welker may be involved in this? He's eighty if he's a day."

"We can't ignore any possible suspect," Luke cautioned, as much for Cheryl as himself. "My gut says this wasn't a crime of passion, Cheryl. The killer knew what he intended to do when he entered Griffin's apartment. He brought the knife with him."

"I'm just having a tough time picturing a man built like the Pillsbury Dough Boy attacking a six-foot-tall man with the musculature of Clay Griffin."

"Fair point. What did the report say about the height and weight of the attacker?"

"Inconclusive. We're still waiting on toxicology to send us his blood work and the results on that gunk you found on his shoes."

"If he was under the influence, that would explain a lot. Right now, it appears that the victim knew his attacker and didn't try to defend himself. Drugs might mean he was incapacitated first."

"So our suspect list is Montague and Welker?" With a shrug, Cheryl capped her pen and rose. "I'll also get phone records for both of them. Griffin had a cell phone in his name, but the team also found several disposable ones in a drawer. We can drag the numbers and see who he'd been calling."

Luke rose and nodded in agreement. "Report to me when you've got something. Put the autopsy under lock and key. Engage the rest of the staff only as needed."

"Sheriff, is there something you're not telling me?"

He didn't like misleading her, but he didn't see a way around it. Sticking as close to the truth as possible, he hedged, "This is a sensitive case, Cheryl. Our suspect list is shaky and our motive is even shakier. I'd rather not start a witch-hunt or a panic until we've got a better handle on the facts. As much as I trust this team, information starts to travel fast. A secret between more than one person is not a secret anymore."

"Clever."

Luke didn't mention where he heard it. "Cynical, but true."

"I'll get right on it." Cheryl opened the door to the office, only to bump into a man standing at the door. "Chief Graves," she said politely.

Michael Graves had the wiry frame of a boxer and the instincts of a bulldog. Scruffy black hair refused to be sculpted by mousses and gels, preferring instead to lie limply at his nape. He reminded Luke of a used-car salesman or a tent-revival preacher, complete with D-list actor looks and caricatured charm. Only his eyes showed the shrewd calculation Luke had glimpsed on occasion. The pale blue scanned Luke's office, as though committing the dimensions to memory.

Recognizing the look, Luke stood. "Come on in, Chief. Thanks, Cheryl." From behind his back, Cheryl poked out her tongue, nearly startling a laugh from Luke. Covering his chuckle with a cough, he came around the desk to shake his colleague's hand. "Can I offer you something? I've got Coke and water."

"A Coke would be nice. It's hot as Hades outside." Each word entertained an added syllable, broadened vowels, and an undertone of false bonhomie that set Luke's teeth on edge.

"What brings you to my neck of the woods, Chief?" Luke asked as he retrieved a can from the refrigerator that squatted behind his desk. He filched a bottle of water for himself, wishing for something stronger. Visits from the police chief rarely left him in good spirits. He had no reason to hope today would prove different.

Ignoring the question, Graves picked a tissue from the box on Luke's desk and methodically wiped at the metal can. When satisfied, he levered the tab open and then broke off the metal ring. "Started collecting this as a child," he explained. "Have thousands of them now."

Luke silently mimicked the rest of the familiar gambit. *Coke oughta put me in a commercial instead of that there polar bear.*

"Coke oughta put me in their commercials instead of that there polar bear," Graves concluded with a hearty laugh.

On cue, Luke replied, "Should send them a letter. Maybe they're in the market for a new pitchman."

"Couldn't go into showbiz. Would take me away from the people I'm sworn to protect."

"Hollywood's loss, then." Luke reclined in his chair and took a swig of water. And waited. Like the story of collecting the metal rings from cans, he'd played this game with Graves before. Usually, his eagerness to remove the man from his office prompted him to speak first. But Graves's eyes glittered with an intentionality that warned Luke to wait.

Seconds ticked by as they slowly drank, Graves making a detailed study of the pile of paper on the desktop. Luke knew the instant the avaricious gaze honed in on the Griffin file. And he was prepared when Graves reached out casually to touch the folder. With an effortless swipe, he pushed the folder beneath another stack of papers and rested his forearm across the pile.

A flicker of annoyance marred the affable expression. "Don't want to share, Sheriff?"

"I'm happy to answer questions, Chief, but we've got some sensitive information in there that's not ready for public release."

"I'm not the public. I'm a fellow law enforcement officer who's afraid there's a killer running loose on the streets of Hallden. City streets." Aggravated, indignant, he stabbed a finger in the raft of papers strewn across the desk. "Clay Griffin was as much a resident of the city of Hallden as he was a county resident."

"Which fails to explain why you routinely ordered your cops to dump him in the county's section of the park when he got high."

"I did no such thing," Graves protested, almost convincing himself. "If some of my men made errors in judgment, all I can do is try to correct them. I'm here to offer you the resources of the Hallden Police Department, Sheriff. With three dead bodies on your sheets, I feel confident that we can help alleviate what must be overwhelming work for you."

Luke allowed himself a private smile at the unexpected generosity and wondered silently what Graves was after. The man had never had an unselfish impulse in his life.

Yet, despite his reservations about Graves, the police chief had a point. The murders had added exponentially to their plates, and his staff was pretty green when it came to murder investigations. The police department received the lion's share of resources, despite their smaller size. Perhaps it wouldn't hurt to bring Graves into his confidence.

"Griffin was stabbed in the leg. I'm working up a list of suspects. Mind giving me your thoughts?"

Graves smiled patronizingly. "I'd assume it was obvious, Sheriff. A crime of passion killed Griffin. A vicious stab wound sounds like an act of revenge."

Luke couldn't disagree. "Which raises the question of Clay's enemies. A rival doesn't make sense. The killer left nearly $3,000 in merchandise untouched. A drug dealer would have taken the electronics and anything else he could lay his hands on."

"True, true. Any girlfriends that we know about? An argument perhaps?"

"Neighbors didn't report any screams and there was no sign of a struggle," admitted Luke. The theory had several holes, that one included. "Crimes of passion usually exhibit more violence than a precise wound that kills the victim almost instantly."

"Passion can be cold, my boy." Graves shifted his attention to the file that peaked out from beneath Luke's elbow. "If I could take a look at the autopsy—"

Luke saw a hint of calculation in his cold blue eyes, heard impatience in the request. Graves had an interest in the autopsy that went beyond professional courtesy. Mild caution bloomed into full-scale resistance. Standing, he tucked the file deeper in the stack. "I appreciate the offer and the advice, Chief. We'll have a better handle on everything by next week." He came around the desk and ushered Graves to the door. With a twist, he released the latch. "I'll be in touch. Have—"

"Good morning, Sheriff." Kell sat perched on the low bench that held guests awaiting an audience.

Luke surveyed her greedily. Today's skirt was a deep crimson, halted at mid-thigh, revealing glorious legs that crossed at the knee. A slim white shirt buttoned after a substantial dip that had him hard and aching. Absorbing the reaction, he swallowed once. "Welcome back, Counselor."

Across the room, Curly took dedicated interest in some activity on his desk and refused to look up, despite a disguised snort of laughter.

"Kell Jameson?" Graves hesitated for a second, then stepped forward and lifted her hand. The move grazed her knee, as he intended, confirming by touch that the silken legs were indeed bare. "I don't know if you remember me. I'm Chief of Police Michael Graves."

"Yes, I remember," she returned smoothly as she gained her feet, moving them out of reach. "I believe you once referred to me and my friends as harlots in training. How do you do?"

Annoyed color swept beneath the pasty complexion. "I'm certain I wouldn't say that about such a lovely young woman. Perhaps you have me confused with someone else."

"Perhaps."

"And if you'd permit me to escort you to dinner, I could convince you."

Kell glanced at the gold band that gleamed dully on his finger. "Will your wife be joining us?"

Abruptly aware of their audience, Graves recovered swiftly. "Absolutely. Dinner would be at our house, of course. My Susanne is a fantastic cook. Best in the city, they say."

"They" being a community of one, if it was the same Susanne Graves Kell recalled. At community functions, Susanne had the unfortunate reputation of being the last to sell her packed lunches at a charity event. "I'm here for a short time, but I appreciate the offer."

Twice rebuffed, Graves mumbled a farewell and hurried from the department. Luke repressed a smirk until the door cleared. He turned and escorted Kell into his office. Before he closed the door, he called out, "Curly,

I'm going to need you to stay on duty for an extra hour tonight. Thanks."

Kell preceded him into the office, laughing. "Don't punish him on my account," she requested as she took the seat vacated by Graves. "I asked him not to warn you when I saw who was inside. You looked like you were having so much fun with the chief."

"Man's a barrel of laughs." Luke propped a hip on the edge of his desk. His jeans-clad legs lightly caged hers. "Back so soon?"

Better prepared this time, Kell launched into the cover story she'd concocted on her way into town. "Mrs. Faraday has decided to draft her will. That's why I came last week. We didn't have a chance to finish, so I made a second trip. Given her responsibilities, we're trying to be very careful."

Luke had to admire the lie. "So Eliza decided to change her will again?"

"Update it." Kell corrected smoothly. Even if he saw through the story, he couldn't disprove it. And the copy of the autopsy she'd received from her friend in the coroner's office meant she didn't have time to waste on a more elaborate story. "She's decided to add a codicil. Fairly routine, but I told her I'd help."

"That's kind of you," Luke said in clear disbelief.

He didn't have to believe her, Kell reminded herself. She simply had to keep him from zeroing in on Eliza until she'd figured out what really happened to Clay. Which wouldn't be easy, given her opposition. Her research on Luke revealed a twice-decorated cop with an uncanny ability to solve murders. During his tenure on homicide detail in Chicago, he had the second highest case-closure rate in the city. Good enough to be promoted to captain before he turned thirty-five. The file ended with a bust gone wrong, but the details were sketchy. The next year, he'd left Chicago behind for Hallden. A model cop with the skills of Sherlock Holmes right here in Hallden.

She'd known the instant she saw the analysis of the knives that, eventually, he'd circle around to Eliza. Kell simply had to get to her and the truth faster.

CHAPTER 11

"It's good to see you again, Kell."

"You too." She imagined herself prepared to see him again, to hear the rasp of sound that raced nerves into her belly. Two simple kisses twisted her in knots she had yet to untangle. Worse, she kept imagining what might be if she didn't have so many secrets to keep, Eliza's and her own. But the autopsy report lying in her briefcase held devastating possibilities that ruined any others. Kell pushed nerves aside and asked politely, "How have you been?"

"Good. You?"

Her mouth widened in a wistful smile. "I've been remembering Hervé's soupe de crouset." Unwillingly, though, her eyes flickered down to his mouth, recalling what had followed.

Luke gripped the edge of the desk when his hands yearned to touch. "I've been thinking about it too." He cleared his throat. "Excellent soup."

Kell's tongue darted out to moisten suddenly parched lips. "Best I've ever had. But too much of anything that good can be dangerous."

"You're not the type to shy away from danger, are you, Kell?" he challenged, his gaze fixed on her mouth.

"I only take calculated risks. Ones where I know I'll probably win."

He shifted his eyes to meet hers. "And you think you might lose?"

"I don't intend to find out," she warned.

"So you're here on business only. To update Eliza's will."

"That's the main reason, but I thought I might take a mini-vacation," she explained. "With the Brodie trial, it's been nearly impossible to avoid the cameras. Last weekend was the first time I've been able to relax in years." Which was true, Kell admitted. Despite the turmoil of return, she'd found a calm here that eluded her in Atlanta. It disturbed her that Luke played a prominent role in her respite. "I had some time coming, so I thought I'd head back and do a little bit of legal work between naps. Get reacquainted with old friends."

And new ones like Chef Montague, whom she hoped had a set of ceramic zirconia knives and an airtight alibi. She didn't want him to take the blame, but every person with access to the knives created reasonable doubt for Eliza. "I have quite a bit to catch up on."

With a smile that belied the speculative gleam he directed at Kell, Luke offered graciously, "Then, hopefully, I'll see you around."

Given the report they both possessed, Kell was sure it would be sooner than he expected.

Kell made a stop at the Center, then drove out to Hervé's. The half hour she'd taken had been spent reviewing her strategy and giving Luke time to make his next move. Like her, he'd know that a ceramic knife would belong to very few of Hallden's denizens. Chef Montague was the most likely person to own a set, and if he had one, it would muddy the investigation considerably. And nicely. Kell parked behind the restaurant, but she hadn't noticed Luke's truck in front. Disappointed, she crunched up the gravel path leading to the kitchen.

At a little past noon, she placed the odds of finding Chef Montague in the kitchen low, but she had to start somewhere. While she rapped at the door, she admired the restaurant in the sunny daylight. The single-level facility apparently belonged to a renovated home. Tucked away on the proper side of the Grove, the aged brick and high windows gave the space a comfortable air that suited its owner.

"Mademoiselle Jameson, you have returned," he greeted, bussing her hand with a Gallic kiss that seemed entirely appropriate. "I have a number of visitors for so early in my day."

He quickly ushered her inside. Luke sat at a sous chef's workstation where he tucked into a bowl of a creamy concoction with gusto. "Sheriff, we have another guest for lunch," Hervé announced delightedly.

Luke looked up and saw Kell standing beside the

shorter chef. "We have to stop meeting this way," he greeted coolly.

Kell watched his eyes glitter with annoyance, delighted by the response. Biting back a self-satisfied smirk, she joined him at the station. "I thought I'd ask Hervé if he'd be willing to share his recipe for the tartine we had as an appetizer at dinner." To toy with Luke, she filched his spoon and helped herself to a taste of soup. "Give me the recipe for this soup as well, and I'll be your lawyer for life," she promised.

Luke plucked his spoon from her fingers. "Get your own."

"Yes, yes. Please sit, eat." Hervé gallantly helped her onto a stool. "Unfortunately, I cannot part with my recipes," he explained regretfully. As he spoke, he crossed to the stove. He ladled soup into a bowl and removed a tray containing the tartines. He plated them with fluid, effortless motions while he spoke. "I do not share my recipes with anyone. Otherwise, I would have competition and I am too lazy and too old a man to fight."

Kell accepted the offered plate gratefully. Her stomach grumbled in welcome, reminding her that she'd failed to eat breakfast or lunch in her eagerness to get to Hallden. She bit into the pastry and savored the combination of walnut and goat cheese. "These are divine."

"My grandmother gave me the recipe as she lay upon her bed."

"I'm sorry," she consoled. "When did she pass away?"

Hervé blinked once, then grinned in comprehension. "No, not her deathbed. Her daybed where she lies in Montreal and watches her soap operas."

"Are you sure you will give the recipe to no one?" she coaxed, chuckling.

He shrugged, a flush of color sweeping his cheeks. "Perhaps one person. Madam Eliza, but only because she has the soul of a gourmand."

Alert, Kell sampled her soup. "Only Eliza? You don't think anyone else in Hallden loves food as much as she?"

Grudgingly, Hervé amended, "Of different culinary tastes, perhaps. Mr. Welker does demonstrate a flair for the grilling of food. And while her diner does not rival my restaurant, Azzie Preston is not a moron with food. She is possessed of a keen palate that has withstood the heresy of frying every morsel she serves."

Smiling consolingly, Kell urged, "Any of them have the technical skills to match your own?"

"Certainly, not. I am a master chef. They are," he huffed in disdain, "cooks. I have told my staff many times that one must marry artistry with aptitude."

"Hervé, will you show me that fancy knife set you are always bragging about to Gavin?" Luke asked.

The chef preened as he strode over to his workstation. An array of knives of varying lengths had been arranged for ease of access. Luke followed him, counting the number of knives and eyeballing their length. Several measured eight inches, few longer, most shorter. "I'm thinking about buying my father a set for his birthday. How many come in a traditional chef's collection?"

"Twelve." He removed a narrow, triangular knife with a long blade. "Ah, my Sabatier. These are the finest knives made, despite what the Germans would have you believe. Thiers-Issard has produced these gems for more than one hundred fifty years. Works of art, they are. Gavin tries to convince me to purchase from the Japanese with their new technology. Knives are made of good carbon steel, not fragile ceramic," he scoffed. "I tell Gavin to stay away from my knives, unless he wishes to test them from the inside."

Kell winced, as much at the image as the elimination of Hervé as a suspect. She shot a sidelong glance at Luke to gauge his reaction. For his part, Luke watched Hervé's demonstration of proper chopping technique, his eyes following the movements carefully. Rather than mild amusement at the older man's enthusiasm, Luke showed only genuine interest. When the chef brandished a six-inch blade and a sharpening rod, he moved to a safe distance, but maintained rapt attention.

"You try," Hervé demanded.

Luke accepted the blade and sharpener gingerly. He stroked the blade against the rod, sending sparks into the air.

"This is not a duel," Hervé corrected. "It is a dance. The blade requires the harshness of the rod, but should not be damaged. Bring them together quickly but gently. Merely a kiss. Do not force contact. Encourage it and they will do the work for you."

"Like this?" Luke drew the blade across the rod a few times, then lifted his eyes to Kell's. The annoyance hadn't disappeared. "Would you like to try?"

"No, thank you," she teased, "I prefer to watch."

"Apparently, watching isn't nearly as much fun." He held her gaze, eyes searing in their heat. "I haven't noticed that you have trouble participating when it suits you."

"It's a question of timing, Sheriff." She took another bite of tart. "I've been catching up on my Hallden news. Any more information on the murder of Clay Griffin?"

Appreciating her skill, Luke set the knife and rod down. Knowing she wouldn't let it go, he summarized, "Nothing yet. Chef, he ever come around here?"

"His kind is not welcome in my establishment, Sheriff," the chef intoned stiffly. "While I may have soft spot for the reformed rake, I do not countenance the debauchery of Mr. Griffin's ilk. The sale of illicit substances to children offends me."

"How do you know he sold drugs to kids?" Kell probed.

"One of my busboys," sniffed Hervé. "I was nearly forced to terminate his employment when I saw him making a purchase from Mr. Griffin. Not yet sixteen and already heading down a wrong path."

Kell latched on to a single word. "You didn't fire the busboy?"

"Oh, no. Not when Eliza requested that I give the boy a second chance."

"How kind of you. But you must have been furious with Griffin for bringing drugs to your door."

His eyes flared with anger. "*Absolutement!* I run a respectable place. Still, I am not so far removed from Mr. Griffin's station. I was outraged, yes, but I pitied him also. To prey on children for your daily bread is pathetic, no?"

"Of course."

"However, Griffin was prohibited from my restaurant. I am sentimental, not stupid. Plus, I showed him the very nice pistol I keep in my office. I am regarded as a fair shot, and Mr. Griffin believed me." He shook his head sorrowfully. "I wish ill on no one, but Clay Griffin cared nothing for others. A low, mean man, I believe."

A phone rang in the office, and Hervé excused himself. Luke set the knife and rod on the worktable. "Nicely done."

"Pardon?"

"The inquisition of the good chef. You slid answers out of him like a pro."

"I was merely making conversation." And hoping for other suspects. Alone, the mention of Eliza's well-known passion for cooking amounted to little in the way of evidence. Nevertheless, Luke's reaction had been informative. The cool brown eyes held steady, not showing a semblance of reaction. His lack of reaction tempted her to assume he had not clued into her as a potential suspect. But she doubted he would fail to follow up on such an obvious tip. "You seemed to be driving at some conclusion, though?"

"Police business. Nothing to concern yourself with."

"Then I can head out. I don't think I'll be making my tartines tonight."

"Where to next, Kell?"

"I plan to stop in to see Mrs. F." *And bring her up to speed on the knives.* Ms. Preston and Mr. Welker seemed unlikely culprits, but she would need as many alternate theories of the crime as possible. "What about you?"

"Cheryl dropped me off. My truck is at Jonice's for service. She was going to swing by and pick me up after her patrol. Maybe you can give me a lift instead."

"To the Center?"

"I have some things to discuss with Eliza. Cheryl can pick me up there."

Mind racing, Kell cast about for an excuse to keep him away from the Center until she had time to brief Eliza. "Alright. But I will be more amenable if I'm fed first."

Luke gave her a speculative and admiring look. "Food seems to be the center of our relationship. Where does it all go?"

"I've got nervous energy," Kell retorted lightly. "Would Hervé let you play in his kitchen too?"

"Not while I have breath," Hervé announced from the door. "I will feed you. Sit, sit. I will make you lunch."

Bustling around the workstation, he plied Luke with more soup and poured a generous bowl for Kell. Croque-madame followed, then Hervé excused himself to return a call.

"Why did you become a lawyer?" Luke asked as he nudged the plate of sandwiches across to her. He enjoyed watching her eat, taking obvious delight in every morsel. She ran the tip of her tongue across the slick mouth, catching a crumb. Heat surged through him, a brutal wave of arousal he was growing accustomed to fielding.

Unaware of the effect she was having on him, Kell lifted her shoulders once, her forehead knotted in thought. "I'd always wanted to be one, I suppose."

"The influence of *L.A. Law*, no doubt."

Kell hesitated, then shook her head. "It was Fin." The instant the words slipped out, she frowned. She didn't talk about Fin. "And the others. Being a kid without any power over your life is hard. Adults made all of the decisions, all the time."

"That's life, Kell. Children aren't equipped to make tough choices."

"Most aren't, but that doesn't stop the choices from being made." She chewed on her sandwich thoughtfully. "The law gives you power. You understand what the rules are, how they're broken. Why."

Luke drank from a glass of sparkling water. "The law doesn't tell you why the rules are broken. Lawyers either for that matter."

"Of course we do. In an opening argument or a closing statement, every sentence uttered on behalf of a client is a why. Poverty or neglect or greed, there's a reason. My job as a lawyer is to tell the jury why and help them see themselves making the same choice."

"Is that why most of your clients are guilty?"

"Ninety percent of my clients are not guilty in the eyes of the state of Georgia."

"What about your eyes?" Luke pressed. "Do you see them as innocent or guilty?"

"I don't care about innocence. That's not why I get hired. I produce results. Prove that the prosecution failed to meet its burden. Not guilty is the benchmark, not innocence."

"Are they ever innocent?"

Kell thought about Eliza. "Sometimes, yes. Not often, but yes."

"And how do you defend those clients?"

"With everything I can think of," she warned. "Innocence is rare in my world. I take it very seriously."

"Like I take the truth seriously." Luke stood, crossed to where she perched on her stool. He streaked a hand through her hair, coming to rest on her nape. Exerting a light pressure, he tilted her eyes up to meet his. The deep brown held suspicion and a fascination that fired his blood. Beneath the fall of hair, he stroked the tense line of her neck. "I dislike liars, Kell. Which is why you confound me."

She tried to swallow, but her throat tightened. "Lawyer, liar. People get the words confused quite often, but they aren't the same thing, Luke."

"I realize the difference, Kell, but you make it hard. For example, your hands aren't always honest." Giving away an advantage, he explained. "When you lie, your hands are still. It's the only time."

Shocked, she almost glanced down at them, but caught herself before reacting. In a scathing voice, she explained, "I'm a remarkably calm person, Sheriff. Some might even call me cold."

"They'd be foolish. Kell, you vibrate with an energy that you try badly to contain. Button it up in suits or not, I can see it. Feel it."

"Imagine it," she mocked, disturbed by the slow glide of his fingertips against her skin. Once, then again, her breath caught. "Let me go, Sheriff."

"I should. Like I should believe that you're capable of murder, but I don't." Instead, he plucked her hand from her lap, lacing the fingers with his own. "I think you're protecting someone. A few someones."

She jerked at her captive fingers, to no avail. Instead, he caught her elbow and slipped her from the stool. Kell refused to fight, and instead jutted her chin out defiantly. "You already have two mysteries to solve, Luke. I'm not one of them."

"Yes, you are. Any one who truly looks closely at you will see it. A Porsche? That car isn't a statement of wealth, it's an outlet. Power and raw energy that can pour out everywhere and leave you unscathed."

"I drive a Porsche because it's pretty. I wear nice suits because they make me look good. And I gesture because it helps me to think," she sneered.

"Liar."

"You don't know me." She whispered the denial, rearing away. Her hip bumped against the station and halted her retreat. "You know nothing about me."

He skimmed his thumb over the taut line of her jaw. The line tensed, and he resisted the urge to soothe. Edgy himself, he prodded, "I know what I see. A beautiful, brilliant woman who pretends to be aloof and hard-driving. Yet, she breaks a sixteen-year exile with a single phone call."

Her startled gaze flickered up to his. "Eliza didn't tell you that."

"No, you did. Just now." The tender glide of his fingers caressed her throat. Beneath his touch, her pulse jumped, scurried. "I can read you, Kell. Not completely, but better than you'd like, which scares the hell out of you. You're a mystery wrapped—"

"In an enigma," she finished mockingly, struggling not to lean into his touch.

"No, in a brittle shell that is perilously close to shattering." Frustration spilled into his voice. "Too many secrets to keep to yourself."

"And what about you, Sheriff? Why are you hiding in a tiny town on the edge of nowhere instead of in Chicago? What are you running from?"

Luke's hot eyes went instantly to frost. "We're not talking about me."

"Of course not," Kell challenged. "It's much easier to analyze someone else, isn't it? Let's see. You're a seasoned cop who threw away a promising career. Instead of catching real bad guys, you load goats into trucks and play country sheriff. All the women in town, and you find yourself attracted to me, the one woman who is dead wrong for you. Who lives too far away to make it real. Why? Because you're terrified that you can't handle the big stuff anymore. Hiding away here where the ugly parts of life can't find you."

"I'm not hiding."

"Yes, you are. Like the rest of us. The difference is, you won't admit it." She turned and walked to the back door. Halfway there, she tossed over her shoulder at Luke, "I may be a liar, but I'm not a coward, Sheriff."

CHAPTER 12

He caught her at the door, his hand snagging her arm in an unbreakable grip. Spinning her to face him, he warned, "You can't call me a coward and walk away."

Nerves wired, she yanked at the restraining hold, at the urge to stand still. "How are you going to stop me? I can go wherever I please, Sheriff. If I'm not under arrest, take your hand off me. Now."

Luke stared down at where his fingers manacled the slender forearm, and his eyes darkened with shame. He'd never manhandled a suspect, certainly not a woman. She twisted something inside him, a voracity that he'd never known. A desire that beckoned impulses he'd spent years taming. Releasing her, he moved away, hands lifted in apology. "I apologize. I didn't intend to frighten you." Or frighten himself with his reaction. The truth, it seemed, cut both ways.

"You don't frighten me," Kell conceded unwillingly,

intrigued by the play of emotions in the ebony eyes. No, his passion didn't scare her, but his analysis had. She detested how he saw inside her, how clearly. Insight like his was dangerous and, worse, compelling. "And I know you're not a coward. But stop trying to read me, Sheriff."

"You don't do such a bad job yourself, Counselor."

"Then we can call a truce. I won't look into you and you can stay the hell out of my head."

"I can't do that." Luke shrugged once. "You fascinate me. As does the real reason why you're here."

"I told you. To help an old friend."

Luke scowled at the lie masquerading as truth. He needed the truth from her if they were to protect Eliza. He wanted her to make the first move. Show the first hint of trust. But the short time he'd spent with Kell told him that would be next to impossible. So he'd break protocol first. In a low tone, he challenged, "You're protecting someone who might be a killer."

The bald statement hung between them. Kell darted a glance over his shoulder to the closed door of Hervé's office. "What are you talking about?"

Understanding her caution, Luke pointed in the direction of the front of the restaurant. Kell nodded and preceded him into the space. She chose a stool at the bar and slid onto the leather-covered seat. Calculation indicated that Luke's announcement warranted a change of tactics. Flat denial wouldn't hold him at bay. "Who might be a killer?"

"Stop playing games, Kell." Preferring to stand, Luke kept a safe distance between them. He tucked his hands into his pockets to keep them to himself. "Eliza, apparently."

"Do you really think she's capable of murder?"

Eyes steady on hers, he responded, "Yes. With sufficient provocation, anyone can take a human life. That's not the question. It's why."

"So? Why Eliza? Why kill Clay?"

He shook his head. "I don't know yet. But with the evidence I've got right now, she's batting one for three—means."

"The knives."

"Which you somehow knew about before you got here. Since you're part of the reason for my delayed autopsy." He saw the flicker of triumph and arched a brow. "Don't interfere in my investigation again."

"I will do whatever I think best for my client."

"What if that means bringing her into my office to make a statement? If she can clear this up, I can cross her off my list without raising her name as a suspect."

"Too soon, Sheriff. You can't prove that she alone has the means, and you haven't established that she had the opportunity. Or a motive."

"You're saying she has an alibi."

"I'm saying you've got no case."

"But I do have Georgia's best defense lawyer rushing to Eliza's aid, and that's a mighty powerful reason to believe she's guilty."

Kell hadn't considered that her presence would cast doubt on Eliza. Frightened, she said urgently, "I swear to you, Luke, she's not guilty. She didn't do this."

"Then help me prove it." Luke moved closer, his

voice low. "I have a duty to the law, and right now the evidence is pointing squarely at Eliza. But instinct tells me I don't have the full story." He closed the distance, still careful not to touch. "You and I both know that if I haul Eliza Faraday in for questioning, I damned well better have knife in hand and a string of witnesses. I won't, and that's gonna make this even messier."

"So what do you want from me?"

"A partnership. For a while. You and me trying to figure out what happened." That way, he could keep an eye on his prime suspect and prove his instincts correct.

"Together?"

"Quietly. If today is any indication, I'm going to find myself running into you anyway. Might as well work together."

"I won't compromise my defense of a client by breaking privilege."

"Won't ask you to. Because I'm not turning over all of my evidence to you. All I'm suggesting is that we coordinate. You start asking too many questions, and Eliza will become the public's top candidate. Hallden has changed over the years, Kell, and you don't know the landscape any longer."

"And you do?"

"Better than you." He extended a hand. "Trial run. We should talk to some of Clay's business partners."

"Drug dealers," she corrected.

"Sure. We know the means. Motive is the key," he said, echoing Kell's assessment. "We'll try it out today. The minute you think I've crossed the line—or vice versa," he challenged, "we call it and go our separate ways."

Kell studied his hand, still waiting for hers to slip inside. "And the other thing?"

"You mean the fact that I want you?"

"Yes, that."

He clasped his hands behind him. No, he wouldn't touch her again until she asked. He wouldn't risk it again. "That has nothing to do with this. I'm not going away." He held her eyes, his steady and direct. "Neither are you. You want me too, even if you're too stubborn to admit it."

"The fact that I enjoy your mouth is a poor reason to jeopardize my client."

Luke grinned at the exasperated compliment. "Usually not, but a good kiss shouldn't be underrated. But let's be clear. I want more than your mouth. I intend to have everything."

"I'm not a case to be solved." But the craving begun last week had followed her, taunted her. And now relief stood inches away. "I'm picky about who I sleep with, Sheriff."

"Me too. Counselor." He took another step. "I love your mouth."

Kell leaned forward, her lips parting on a sigh. "This is a mistake."

"Okay." He stood still, refusing to move any farther. This time, it would be at her invitation. No accusations, no remorse.

"One more time." With a muttered curse, she erased the distance between them, her lips pressed against the hewn, sensual mouth that haunted her. Terrified her. Parted in welcome.

Triumphant, Luke scooped her from the stool and into his arms. His hand cradled her throat, tipping her head to plunder. He sank inside, tasting and feeling and wanting in waves that crushed instinct. His hands skated over the rounded curve of her breast, found the indent of her waist.

She slicked her tongue over his and nearly buckled his knees. Somehow, wonderfully, he discovered only a gossamer weight beneath her jacket. The fragile silk proved no barrier to his explorations. With each gasp of delight he won, he promised himself another. If they had been alone, he would have dragged her to the floor to ravish and claim. His mind reeled with sensation, drowning out reason.

Kell felt herself going under and didn't care to surface. This madness, this delight, this man. She couldn't remember wanting anything else.

"Sheriff? Ms. Jameson?" Hervé called from the kitchen.

Luke stepped back, breaking their embrace. Kell swayed, then her spine stiffened.

"No more, Luke." She sidled around him. "I think you should call Cheryl for that ride. Please thank Hervé for lunch. I'll talk to you this afternoon. At the Center."

Before Luke could decide if he intended to stop her, she slipped out the door.

Kell forced herself to walk to her car slowly, unsure if Luke watched from the kitchen. Her hands fumbled with the door, but she stilled their trembling and climbed inside. By sheer force of will, she keyed the ignition and drove onto the road.

"Damn him, damn him, damn him." She repeated the mantra for a quarter of a mile, waiting for her pulse to steady. But she could still taste him on her lips, feel the imprint of his hands at her hips. Could still hear his insistence that she wasn't as controlled, as cold as she pretended.

He had no right to see inside her, to the woman that yearned for reckless rather than safe, for speed rather than sedate. He had no right to pry for her secrets and to make her yearn to share. Not so soon.

Not ever.

But she didn't believe the words any more than he did.

She sped along the highway, en route to the Center. Pushing aside her frustration, she concentrated on her first foray into detective work. She'd accepted a partnership with the man sworn to put her client in jail. Truth be told, though, she could see few flaws in his offer.

Hervé Montague possessed a brilliance for food, a delightful charm, and a knife set that bore no resemblance to the Griffin murder weapon. His loose connection with Clay wouldn't convince a jury of reasonable doubt.

Worse, still, he'd implicated her client by admiring her food artistry. She had been a fool to think Luke would not reach the same conclusions she had, that Eliza was on the short list of suspects. The other two people Hervé mentioned might provide some distraction from her, but not for long.

Working with Luke would be dicey, but she couldn't see a way around it for now. A strange alliance, to be sure, but one she'd leverage to save Eliza.

By her side, her cell phone rang. David's name popped on the screen and she engaged the headset. "Yes?"

"Have you been watching the news today?" He interrogated without preamble.

"Nope. I've just come from an interview with a possible suspect in the Faraday case. Unfortunately, he has no motive, and his preferred means of murder is a pistol." Kell had briefed him on the vague contours of Eliza's predicament, but had not gone into detail. "What's going on?"

"Police arrested Senator Francine Marley this morning for the murder of her husband and a second party."

"Who?"

"His boyfriend," David announced with spiteful glee. "Seems the Senator came home from Washington a day early to surprise the hubby, only to find him ensconced in their Buckhead manse in *flagrante delicto*. Unlike your suspect, her preferred weapon of choice is a SIG Pro, which is now empty of eight bullets."

"Eight bullets?"

"Shot them in the chests then took out their offending parts. Post mortem. Called the police and waited to be arrested." David waited a beat. "Her one phone call after being booked was to Jameson Trent. She specifically requested you as her attorney, Kell."

Kell clutched the steering wheel, breathless. "Senator Marley is a legend. This case could change everything."

"Exactly. We've had a good streak of luck with celebrities, but when you exonerate Francine Marley, that's the golden ticket."

"When's arraignment?"

"Today. Seems the judges all remember she used to sit on the state Supreme Court. She's gotten an expedited hearing."

The conflict occurred to her immediately. With their partnership fresh, Kell needed to be with Luke as he gathered evidence about Clay's background. Otherwise, she had little hope of gaining access. It made no sense to ask him to hold his investigation while she made the trek to Atlanta and back. David could handle the arraignment. "Then I'll need you to handle the hearing, David. I won't be back in Atlanta before Monday."

"Monday?" David protested. "You have to come right now. Senator Marley expects to see you at her arraignment this afternoon, and she will. The clerk agreed to get it on the docket at four, which will give you plenty of time if you leave now."

"I can't come until Monday," Kell heard herself counter. "Look, you'll get her out on bail and she'll get a preliminary hearing in the next thirty days."

"She'll demand faster."

"She'll learn to wait. Listen, David, I have a responsibility to Mrs. Faraday. The sheriff is homing in on her as a suspect. I can't leave until I know what he knows."

David issued an epithet. "Senator Marley has already wired us a one-million-dollar retainer. I don't have an engagement letter for the orphan lady. Find her a good attorney and get your ass to Atlanta. Today."

Impatience simmered, but Kell refused it release. She and David had been partners for years, and he wasn't being unreasonable. Except, for once, she needed to be selfish. An arraignment was a simple matter, and nothing would happen before Monday. She could follow up on more leads while he stood in front of a judge and entered a plea. "Which judge did we pull?"

"Lawrence-Hardy. She clerked for the court under Marley."

"Perfect. She'll grant a reasonable bail and give us the entire time on the pc hearing."

"Which you will be here to ask for. This isn't a negotiation, Kell."

"No, this is a partnership, David. I don't work for you."

"Absolutely right. You work for our firm, and our firm requires that its top attorney stop assuaging some misplaced guilt about escaping some drudge of a town and her Orphan Annie roots. Quit indulging delusions of Nancy Drew and get on the highway. You do the trials, and I make the business decisions. This is one of them."

"This isn't a function of guilt," Kell insisted. "I promised her I'd help."

"Then hire a P.I. and a lawyer for her, make your apologies and then come and do your job."

Understanding his frustration, she placated, "I'm sure you can use your guile to get the senator a reasonable bond and hold the case steady until I return next week. That's why there are two of us."

"There are two of us with very specific responsibilities. I handle the quiet, ugly matters like tax evasion and corporate espionage and associate pay. You do the big, flashy murder trials and accidental rapists. We aren't public defenders, Kell. We keep rich, guilty defendants out of jail for an exorbitant fee, and we've just hit the mother lode."

"David." His assessment struck her like a blow. Slick, oily shame churned in her belly, and she could hear Luke's question ringing in her ears. Why did she become a lawyer? To save the lives of spoiled, amoral clients intent on self-destruction? Or to protect and defend the innocent when she found them? In her heart, she knew the answer was both, but the chance to defend the actually innocent came along infrequently.

Ahead of her, the sign to the Faraday Center for Children greeted her, its familiar ivory and blue logo extending a welcome. Beneath her hands, the Porsche's engine roared quietly as she drove up the inclined driveway to the car-port.

"You still there?" David asked impatiently.

"Yes."

Assuming he'd won, David briskly moved on. "I think Malikah should sit second chair. She'll appeal to the jury as a young Senator Marley. Nice contrast to you too."

"No."

Slashing through her name on the pad, he conceded, "Fine. I'll put Doug on it."

"I meant no, I'm not coming to the arraignment."

"What?"

"I made a commitment to Eliza, and I'm not leaving her unprotected. You can handle the arraignment, and the prelims. I'll have a better handle on things here by the weekend, and we can map out our strategy when I get back to Atlanta."

"If you don't come back today, Kell, and we lose the Marley account, I will consider it a breach of our partnership agreement. You know what that means."

The loss of her partnership draw and a fairly public dispute that could leave her reputation in tatters. "Senator Marley should be reasonable, David."

"She might be, but I'm not. Be in Atlanta by four or I'll have you served with termination papers."

On the lawn, children raced around in the damp summer air, impervious to its sapping heat. She spotted Jorden on a swing, next to a pretty young girl she suspected was the one who'd gotten him punished last week. Without Eliza, they would be scattered to the mercies of foster care systems and other homes. She couldn't, wouldn't be responsible for that fate.

"Send them to me in Hallden," Kell replied firmly. "I'll email you the address." She pressed the button that disconnected the call. Immediately, the phone shrilled for attention.

"Hey, Ms. Jameson!" Nina stood at the car window, waving. "Mrs. F told me to keep an eye out for you," she explained through the glass.

Kell cut the engine and stepped onto the gravel walk. "Good to see you, Nina."

"You okay?"

"Yes, why?"

"You look, uh, despondent."

Kell gave a chuckle. "Excellent word. And an apt description. I've just ruined my life." Tucking her hand inside Nina's arm, she led the girl up to the house. "How was your day?"

CHAPTER 13

In the library, Kell flopped across the settee, bare feet tucked into the space between cushions. Eliza would kill her if she caught her with shoes scuffing the furniture. She'd been lying prone for most of the day, closeted away from the bustle of chores and supper. Her guest room had been tagged for cleaning, hence her banishment to the nearest room with a flat surface.

Across the room and beyond its bay windows, dusk settled around the Center. Cicadas began their nightly serenade to the tree frogs that inhabited the woods behind the house. Night birds chirped in delighted chorus.

She didn't notice. In fact, she hadn't paid attention to much in the twenty-four hours since she'd tossed her career away in a fit of what she could only explain as madness. Rolling onto her side, Kell emitted a wretched moan of agony. After all, she'd carefully exorcised what remained of her scruples over the course of her career, selecting clients and defending cases that shredded any sense of honor. She'd selected a law partner with the soul of a piranha and the ethics to match. Jameson Trent, LLP thrived on cases with the most venal clients and the highest profiles. That's how David made his money and Kell achieved her fame.

The perfect partnership.

In an instant, though, she'd cast avarice and fame aside for what? Her head throbbed in sympathetic counterpoint to a queasy stomach. To do good. Damn her. Eliza Faraday managed to locate that one last spark of redemption she'd imagined quenched. Now, she had an innocent client.

She hated innocent clients.

Innocence meant caring about the outcome more than the performance. For every other case, the verdict simply capped off what she was hired to do. Create reasonable doubt for the guilty. This time, she'd be obliged to prove her client not guilty.

"Are you going to lounge around all day?"

The gravelly voice with its distinctive timbre pitched her stomach into somersaults. She remembered the way his hands nipped into her waist, stroked her skin. Another in a litany of mistakes. Biting off a curse, Kell rolled over to face the back of the couch, presenting her stiffened spine to the intruder. "Go away, Sheriff."

Luke shut the library door with a firm click and strolled farther into his favorite room in the Center, ignoring her command. High shelves stood packed tight with leather-bound volumes and flimsy paperbacks.

Ever since he arrived in Hallden, Eliza had served as an unofficial lending library. She welcomed those who appreciated her collections.

He had a difficult time picturing the friendly, gentle lady who'd welcomed him with tea and cookies plunging a knife into a defenseless man. But Luke had seen more than his share of inexplicable crimes. Eliza Faraday didn't strike him as a killer, but he'd been wrong before.

Banishing suspicion, he moved to the section of bookcases where Eliza maintained her stock of espionage novels. The shelves stood next to the end of the settee where Kell appeared to be sulking, if he read her body language properly. He focused on the titles and tried to not stare at the length of leg exposed by the criminally abbreviated skirt hiked up trim, coffee-toned thighs.

Instead, he forced himself to skim the titles, looking for one he hadn't read before. Swallowing past the familiar tightness in his throat, he said neutrally, "Nina tells me you've been hiding in here all day."

"Nina talks too much," Kell muttered into the cushions. She was in no mood for banter with him. All she wanted was peace and quiet and a place to sulk in private. As though reading his mind, she drew her legs in close and wrapped her arms around her knees. "I have a headache, that's all."

"You were fine yesterday."

"Now it's today," came the snippy reply. "Did you come to quiz me on my medical status or are you here for something specific?"

"Headaches make you testier than usual," Luke commented, drawing out a title by Cussler. "I didn't know that was possible."

"Keep pushing."

The snarled warning brought a grin to his face. He greatly preferred a feisty Kell to the limp, despondent woman curled into a tight ball of misery on the sofa. Whatever had knocked her back, he knew his presence had the prolific effect of igniting some passion from her. As much as he wanted to cross to her and soothe, annoying her would no doubt be more successful. Glancing over his shoulder at her, he mocked, "What's got you pouting? Break a heel on those expensive shoes?"

"Pouting?" Very slowly, Kell levered herself over to face him. Her legs stretched out, finding purchase on the armrest. Resentment surged through, a molten sweep that bared her teeth. A huge part of her problem stood in front of her. Mocking her. "I don't pout."

"Could have fooled me." Luke moved to lounge against the sofa, and he trailed a finger along the slender ankle resting on the arm. Desire streaked through him, a visceral race of blood and need. Deliberately, he kept his touch light, amused and aroused when he felt her arch against the light stroke. "Other than a smirk, I didn't realize your mouth had another expression."

Kell sat up, eyes spitting fire at the insult. Worse, her flesh tingled where he caressed absently, her pulse jumped erratically. Wrestling for control, she jerked her leg free and shot, "Perhaps if you paid less attention to my mouth and more attention to your case, you wouldn't need my help."

If he had paid less attention to her mouth, Luke admitted, he'd probably have recognized why she'd come to Hallden in the first place. Instead of responding, he batted her legs off the cushion and took a seat. "What happened to you after you left the restaurant, Kell?"

"Nothing." His sitting forced Kell to scoot over, and she abruptly became aware of the expanse of skin her position had exposed. Discreetly, she tugged the raised hem to a more appropriate length. "I got some bad news. Nothing I can't handle."

"I doubt there's much you can't handle, Kell." He lifted her hand, his voice gentle. She wouldn't appreciate sympathy, but he couldn't resist. The odd mixture of stoicism and vulnerability caught at him. Folding his hand over hers, he nudged, "Something upset you. What was it?"

She ran her free hand through her hair, wearily smoothing errant strands into place. "There's nothing you can do."

"I can listen."

The simple offer pulled at her. He didn't demand answers, didn't wheedle for information. Where his hand clasped hers, warmth trailed along her skin, a companionable feeling that she'd missed without ever knowing she wanted it. Him. She shook her head in bemusement. "You do that well."

"What? Listen?"

"No." She smiled, a brief turn of lips that evaporated as quickly as it appeared. "You make me forget that I don't know you, and I don't like you."

Not offended, Luke turned her captive hand over, his fingers linking with hers. "We do know each other, Kell. That's what scares you." When she frowned, he corrected, "Disturbs you."

"Maybe."

"Well, it disturbs the hell out of me." Stroking his thumb along the creamy smooth skin, he urged quietly, "Talk to me."

The impulse to share confounded Kell. She'd kept her own counsel for so long. Yet, the thought of confiding in Luke brought a comfort that unsettled. She opened her mouth to refuse his offer, only to hear herself confess, "I lost my job yesterday."

Luke merely rubbed his thumb along the ridge of her knuckles. She wouldn't look at him, he noted. But her admission was progress. He probed, "Why would David Trent dissolve your partnership? You're the heart of that firm. Twice the lawyer he is."

Warmed by the defense, Kell asked, "You know him?"

With a sound of derision, he explained, "I know of him. Practiced criminal work in Chicago for a while. I never met him in court, but my colleagues did." His mouth tightened. "He wasn't renowned for his ethics."

"David plays to win," she defended automatically. In warning, she added, "So do I."

"You protect your clients. That's not the same as Trent's antics." It wasn't a question.

Shame had her flushing lightly. "I win my cases, Luke. By fair means or not so much."

"Do you lie in court?"

"By legal standards, no."

"And by yours?" The answer mattered, more than he'd have expected. "Have you broken your oath?"

"No. But give me a few more years with David," she laughed mirthlessly. "I defend clients who can afford to pay our fees, and they pay for a bit of flexibility in our moral codes."

"So what happened?"

"My moral code did battle with my partnership agreement. I'm not sure which one won."

"He doesn't want you defending Eliza?"

"David didn't mind my client detour at first, but—"

"But what?"

"He wasn't happy, but he understood. Until I told him I wasn't returning to Atlanta to take over the case that can make our firm a household name."

He understood instantly. "Your firm picked up the Marley case?" he asked, impressed despite himself. "Every defense firm in the country is going to chase that one."

"And she picked us." Restive, Kell withdrew her hand from his and rose. She walked to the window seat and flicked at the drapes that had been drawn against the afternoon sun. "I refused to come back for the arraignment."

Luke watched the jerky movements, concerned. "Because of Eliza."

She clenched the fabric, outrage warring with disappointment. "David considers my refusal to come to Atlanta a breach of our partnership agreement. He threatened to serve me with termination papers."

"It's your firm," Luke protested. "He can't simply kick you out."

Grudgingly, she admitted, "I'd do the same to him if our positions were reversed. This case is my personal crusade. It won't help the firm. I'm putting my whims first."

"Protecting someone you love?"

"Yes."

A fact that disturbed her more than she expected, Luke judged. He gained his feet and followed her to the window. Resisting the urge to touch, he reached past her to open the shades. Twilight dappled the magnolia tree that dominated the view. A scent rose from her skin, lighter than he'd expected, though he knew the scent by heart. Not the floral of a garden, but a crisp fragrance that teased his senses with its directness and undertone of sensuality. How appropriate, he acknowledged wryly. "Are you going to fight him?"

"How?" She'd grappled with that all evening. "I drafted the agreement. He's on perfectly solid ground. We have to agree on major cases, and a retainer like Marley's would certainly take precedence. I know because I wrote the agreement."

"Oh."

"Yes, 'oh.' I'm making the choice to stay here rather than earn a million-dollar retainer."

"Why?"

She turned to him now, her eyes direct and level. "Because I believe Eliza is innocent. I don't think she had anything to do with Clay's death."

"I want to believe you. Believe her." He placed his

hands on her shoulders, noting the play of muscle beneath his touch. She was strong, tense. "Let me talk to her."

"I can't do that, Luke. She's my client, not yours." Kell shifted into attorney mode, grateful to leave behind the sentimental woman who welcomed a shoulder to cry on. "Until I'm satisfied that you've exhausted all other leads, I'm going to advise her to not speak with you."

"You're perilously close to a line neither one of us wants crossed," Luke retorted, holding up a hand before she could respond. "I suggested that we work together, and I intend to stick to my word. But the minute I have reason to suspect Eliza Faraday of murder, friendship and this partnership can't matter. Neither can whatever is between us."

Pulling her shields back into place, Kell took a step away. His hold on her shoulder didn't falter, but she refused to fight him. "Will you tell me the whole truth too, Sheriff? Why you fled Chicago?"

"There's nothing to tell."

Kell laid a hand on his cheek, drawing his eyes to her. "The difference between us, Luke, is that I'm at least honest with myself. And I can leave well enough alone."

Taking her at her word, Luke dropped his hands and moved away from her touch. He fished in his pocket for his keys. "Go change into something more comfortable."

"Why?" she asked suspiciously.

"Because we have work to do, and you can't be wandering around town in that skirt."

Kell glanced down at her dress, baffled. "It's perfectly respectable."

"If you didn't have legs like that, maybe. But I can't take you anywhere if those are on display. And put your hair in a ponytail or something."

"Should I smear dirt on my face?" she sniped.

"I'd say yes, if I thought it would help. You're too gorgeous for this kind of work," he complained aloud.

"What work?"

"For visiting Clay's old haunts. The drug hells of Hallden." He propelled her to the door, stopping to twist the knob before guiding her into the foyer. "You've got five minutes, and then I leave without you."

CHAPTER 14

White blossomed magnolias and cheery songbirds avoided the Red District of Hallden, as had prosperity and hope. Narrow alleys masqueraded as streets, winding between mobile homes and shotgun houses, screen doors framed by burglar bars. Kids scampered along the broken pavement, passing clusters of men wreathed by clouds of smoke. The occasional streetlamp flickered pale yellow streams of light onto the inhabitants of the district, illumining the forgotten.

Luke parked his truck in the driveway of a whitewashed brick dwelling, its dirt yard already home to a dark sedan of indeterminate age and origin. He killed the engine and flicked the headlights to bright. He turned to Kell.

"I would take you inside, but I can't."

"Because your informant won't talk if he sees me, right?"

"You've done this before." He should have expected so. In fact, he'd debated bringing her along tonight. But with Graves nipping at his heels, he had to move fast if he wanted to keep Eliza's name out of the case. Experience warned him that Kell would find her way here eventually, without him. "Then you know the drill."

"Don't talk to strangers should cover it," she answered dryly.

"Stay in the truck until I come to get you, okay?" Ebony eyes studied her face for a hint of fear or argument. But he saw neither. Another surprise. The lady was full of them. "I'll only be a couple of minutes."

Kell merely nodded. "Leave the keys, though." She reached down to her purse and removed a novel. "I'd like to listen to the radio."

The keys dropped into her waiting palm, and she watched silently as he stepped from the truck and strode up the sidewalk to the front door. A sharp rap brought a hand to the curtains hanging in the windows. Ruffles drifted into place, and seconds later, the door opened a crack. Luke quickly slipped inside, disappearing from Kell's view.

She flipped open the pages of the romance novel she'd tucked into her bag. After the third pass at the same sentence, she admitted defeat and shut the book. Thoughts raced through her mind at a clip that allowed for little else.

Like how she came to be back on the side of town she'd vowed to escape as a child. Garret Street hadn't

changed much in the years since her parents had
bundled her off its sidewalks and over to the Center.
Indeed, if she remembered correctly, the white house
they were parked in front of belonged to Mrs. Harris,
a crotchety old woman who'd threatened the neighborhood children with grave bodily harm for trespassing
on her property.

She and Anamaria Akins used to pick flowers from
the azalea bush that squatted beneath the old lady's
window, she recalled wistfully. Pink flowers with the
loveliest fragrance. Anamaria's favorite color.

After Kell was sent to Faraday Center, Anamaria
had teased her mercilessly. Called her "garbage girl,"
thrown away by her own parents. The wound, long-
since healed over, ached sharply as she furtively
watched a group of teen boys approach in the rearview mirror.

Returning to Hallden reopened too much. The life
she'd built in Atlanta required locking away sentiment
in favor of the goals she'd set for herself. No longer
a victim of poverty or neglect or a charity case, she'd
made Kell Jameson a brilliant, feared attorney, polished hard and solid as diamond.

With a flaw that could ruin any value she'd gained.

"Hey, lady, wanna come play?" A young man leered
outside the passenger window, laughing with his
friends. Whipcord lean, scars marked a face gone sour
with malice. Hooded brows shielded dark eyes, and a
permanent sneer lay below a nose broken by at least
one fist. His guttural tones demanded, "Come on out,
let me show you a good time."

Kell opened her book again and calmly read the next few pages. Beyond the window, the teenager and his friends grew louder and lewder. She resisted honking the horn, unperturbed. A lifetime among their kind had dulled the instinctive fear she might have felt.

As she continued to ignore the taunts, the six or seven teenagers surrounded the truck. The vehicle began to rock, shoved from both sides. Kell jostled inside the cab and considered her options. Ignoring them wasn't working. The teenagers' randy hostility required an outlet.

Before she could act, from the rear of the truck, a new boy approached and hissed an alert. "Man, wrong chick. This is the sheriff's truck," the young man warned anxiously. "Better not let him catch you hitting on his woman."

"I'm not afraid of a pig," the ringleader boasted, making a snout with his finger. He echoed his claim by snorting loudly. The raucous sound drew chortles from the cluster of young men that circled the truck. A couple, though, moved away and faded into the shadows.

"See ya, man."

"Run, punks. I don't care." Goaded, he pounded on the window. "Unlock the door, lady, and let me show you what a real man can do. Don't make me come and get you."

Kell calmly inserted the key in the ignition and, when the engine engaged, slid the window down a few inches. A hand could reach inside, but not touch anything. "What's your name?" she inquired softly.

"My friends call me Doc, but you can call me Daddy,"

he suggested, resting his fingers on the open rim. To test the give, he jerked at the pane of glass, which held still. "Why don't you get out of that truck and come ride something much harder?"

"Because I have taste," she replied casually. "And a forty-five tucked in my purse that will make your equipment an amusement park ride if you don't walk away from this truck in the next thirty seconds."

"You expect us to believe a lady like you's got a gun in there?"

Kell tilted her head back to make eye contact through the window. "Actually, no. I expect you to continue to harass me and make me fear for my safety. At which point, I can shoot you and claim self-defense."

Hoots of appreciative laughter met her comment, and Doc wriggled in embarrassment. "I ain't afraid of you."

The wiry teenager who'd issued the warning about Luke's truck rushed over to Doc. "Dude, I recognize her. She's that lawyer from *CourtWatch TV*. Nina says she used to live at the Center."

"Your girlfriend knows her?"

"Nina's not my girlfriend," he dismissed brusquely. "But this is her. I saw her at the Center last week." Catching himself, he added, "When I went by to drop some stuff off for my grandmother."

"For real?" Doc leaned closer to the truck, peering inside. "The hot one? She doesn't look like her too much."

"They all wear more makeup on TV," one of the boys offered. "Plus, she's usually in them short skirts."

"What's your name, lady?" The question came from a shorter boy, who Kell guessed to be around sixteen. "You really that lawyer that got Brodie off?"

"Kell Jameson. And, yes, I am an attorney." Doc had faded away a few paces, leaving room for his friends to crowd closer to the window. Kell realized she'd rarely have a better chance to ask questions. "Who are you?" she asked the sixteen-year-old.

"Martin, ma'am." He had a soft voice that lilted over the address.

"Nice to meet you, Martin." She pointed at the one who'd recognized her. "And you?"

"Tony. Tony Delgado." The baseball cap he wore tipped low over his brow. He gazed out from its brim quietly. "One day, I might want to go to law school."

"You ain't goin' to law school," scoffed Doc. "Only kinda lawyer you'll be is a jailhouse one."

The remaining boys laughed, and Tony dipped his head lower. "It's just a thought."

Sympathy thrummed through her. "I grew up down the street, Tony." She inched closer to the window, lifting her voice to carry into the knot of young men. "Before I moved to the Center."

"For real?"

"For real. Mrs. F made me go to school, and I studied. Got decent grades. Then I went to college and law school." She gestured to the far end of the street. "I think I lived in that house down there. It used to be blue."

"That's where I live," Martin volunteered shyly. "I never met a real lawyer before."

"She ain't nothin'," Doc protested, his sway over the posse slipping. "A TV lawyer, man. Blowin' you up for nothing. None of us is goin' to college. Which is why I know how to make mine right here at home."

Kell filed away the reference, although Luke already likely knew Doc well. "You might not go to college. That's up to you." Screwing up her courage, Kell killed the engine. The key gripped tight in her hand, she alit from the truck to stand near the boys. Immediately, she was grateful to Luke for insisting on the jeans and T-shirt, coupled with the flat brown sandals. "I'm here working on a case," she opened.

"What kind?" Martin sidled next to Tony. Doc continued to mutter in the background, but the other teenagers fell silent.

"I'm a defense attorney. I don't work for the cops." Kell could tell when the connection occurred for Tony.

"Then why are you in Sheriff Calder's truck?"

"I'm visiting town, and Luke is a friend of mine. But while he's inside, I think you guys can help me."

Sensing a trade, Doc reasserted himself, shoving Martin to the side. "You looking for information?"

"Depends on whether you know anything or not." Kell stopped, watched Doc carefully for a beat. "If I hear something worth knowing, that man gets my card. Which entitles him to a free legal session at any time."

"What if I don't need a lawyer? What if I need a lady?"

"Then I assume you'll have to go to the Grove to find her." Kell winced internally at the crass suggestion, but the chuckles from the others bolstered her courage. "I'll trade advice for answers. Any takers?"

Tony took a step forward, only to be blocked by Doc's arm. "Whatcha want to know?"

"Clay Griffin." She scanned the faces in the broken light. "What can you tell me?"

Doc's face blanched and he gave a quick shake of the head. "Sorry, lady. We've got curfews. See you around." In seconds, she could hear tennis shoes slapping the pavement as the boys ran off. Tony gave her a fleeting look, then he sped into the darkness.

"What the hell are you doing out of the truck?" Luke raced to her side, eyes combing the street for danger. Catching her arm in rough hold, he growled, "I told you to stay inside. This area isn't safe."

"No, it's not," she agreed quietly. She pulled free of Luke's grip and pressed her fingers to her mouth. "I used to live on this street. A blue house with four rooms. Bedroom, kitchen, living room, bathroom. My dad was the janitor at the Crystal Pony, a strip club in the District." A baby wailed in the distance. "Mom danced there, I think. I remember her clothes, all sparkles and shiny."

Fascinated, Luke said nothing.

"One morning, when I was in second grade, she woke me up and told me to pick out my favorite toys. Didn't take long," she murmured. "I had a stuffed whale that I'd gotten for Christmas or something. Mom shoved the rest of my stuff into a garbage bag. Told me to get in the car."

Knowing what happened next, he couldn't stop hands from catching her face, turning her to him. "Kell."

"I remember asking why I wasn't taking the bus to school. I always took the bus with Mattie and Anamaria."

He stroked her cheek, felt a drop of moisture beneath his thumb. "What did they say?"

"Mom said that Dad got her a better gig. A traveling road show." She smiled wanly. "No children allowed."

"They abandoned you."

She released a breath, deep and shaky. "They saved me. My God, Luke, if they'd kept me."

"You'd still be the woman you are today. Smart and tough and savvy."

She disagreed. "I'd probably be an exotic dancer like my mom. Or a petty crook like my father. But they saved me from that. They gave me away to a woman who cared that I learned, that I saw myself as more than—"

Kell broke off, and Luke tipped her eyes up to meet his. "More than what, Kell?"

"Just more, I guess. Mrs. F always told me I could be more." Her fingers curled around his wrists. "She made me a better person than my parents could have, Luke."

"Eliza raised you, yes, but you made yourself. We all do. Every day. You chose the kind of woman you want to be, Kell. Not Eliza. Not Trent. Not your clients."

"But—"

"But nothing." Frustrated, he shifted his hold to her shoulders and gave them a brief shake. "You outgrew that blue house a long time ago, darling. And the people inside."

"Perhaps. But I can't disappoint her, Luke. No matter what."

Luke leaned close and pressed a soft kiss to her startled mouth. "You may not have to. Come inside and meet some of my friends."

CHAPTER 15

Luke and Kell sat on a sagging flowered couch whose springs had seen better days. Kell had correctly identified Mrs. Kathy Harris as the domestic who maintained a painfully clean lawn with two azalea bushes that crouched outside beneath her windows. She also remembered the elderly woman to be a busybody and a gossip. Two useful traits, she imagined.

The plastic slipcover squeaked meekly as their host joined them. She extended two glasses of a syrupy yellow liquid identified by smell as lemonade. "Luke here tells me you're one of Eliza's children."

Mrs. Harris eased her bulk deeper into the well-worn hollows in the flattened cushions. Her words echoed in the cramped space, in part, Kell assumed, because of the hearing aid that lay unworn on the scarred coffee table. "Said you're a big city lawyer now. Got that actor fellow off."

"Yes, ma'am. I practice law in Atlanta." Kell sipped

at the nearly solid liquid, grains of sugar floating amidst errant bits of pulp. Repressing a cough, she asked, "You've lived here for a while, haven't you, Mrs. Harris?"

The creased face squinted in the dimly lit room. A naked bulb shone from a tabletop lamp, a poor partner to the overhead fixture clouded with dust. Behind thick bifocals, Mrs. Harris peered into Kell's face, bending forward until they were nearly nose to nose.

"I'll be a monkey's uncle," she muttered in stereo. "You're Doreen and Nate's child, aren't you?"

"They were my parents," she replied neutrally.

"Sorrier waste of flesh I don't know I've ever seen. Best thing they ever did in life was send you to Eliza," she announced in her booming voice. "Never came back for you, did they?"

"No, ma'am."

"Good riddance, I say. Peddling Doreen's skin for money like a pimp. Nate had a mind as sharp as a tack. Figured out early how to get that girl to make his money for him."

"I'd rather not talk about my parents, Mrs. Harris," Kell interjected. With a cursory look at Luke, she prompted, "I'm here to ask you about Clay Griffin."

"Told Luke here the same thing I'll tell you. Don't wish death on any one of God's creatures. But that boy had a streak of pure evil in him, sure as I'm sitting here. Whoever took his life didn't do much a sin, Lord forgive me." She punctuated her plea by pressing a beringed hand to her heart. "Sold dope right out on the street every night. Tried to recruit my grandson to help him. Ran him off with my shotgun."

"Mrs. Harris is quite the marksman," Luke complimented. He touched Kell's shoulder lightly in warning as he took over questioning. "You were telling me earlier about Clay in the last few weeks."

Mrs. Harris took a deep draught from her lemonade. "My grandson told me about him. How Clay had been flashing more money around here. Tony thought he had expanded his territory."

"Tony Delgado?" Kell asked.

Narrowing her eyes, Mrs. Harris cocked her head. "How do you know my grandson?"

"I met him outside," Kell explained quickly. "He was with some other boys."

"Hoodlums, more likely. Probably with that Doc Reed. One of Clay's salesmen." She sneered the description.

That conformed with her brief exposure to Doc. She said to Mrs. Harris, "Tony mentioned he wants to become a lawyer."

The broad face broke into a crooked smile. "His father is a hard worker, married my Viola twenty years ago. Raised that boy right. Mostly. Goes to class, gets good grades. Smart as a whip."

Kell smiled appreciatively. "You must be proud."

"I am."

Knowing how Mrs. Harris loved to brag about her grandson, Luke steered them back on topic. "Did Tony tell you where Clay's new territory was?"

Mrs. Harris shifted her focus to him. "He didn't

know. All Clay would tell him was that he had found a better score. Not drugs. Offered Tony a job working with him on it."

"Tony said no?" Luke set his untouched lemonade on the coffee table. He figured consuming a second glass would lead to diabetic shock. The news about Clay's change in career didn't jibe with the intel he'd received from Graves. "When was this?"

"About a month or so ago. Tony went with him to a plant to meet Clay's employers, but he said they didn't seem quite right."

"Were they selling drugs, Mrs. Harris?" Kell rested a hand on the older woman's where it lay on the plastic cover. "Did Clay ask him to help?"

"Tony said they weren't into drugs. But he couldn't figure out what they wanted him to do. All Clay told him was that he'd have to run a few errands for them before he could be trusted with more responsibility."

"Can he identify the men he met with?" An eyewitness to potential suspects other than Eliza would legitimate a shift in his focus.

Kell had the same thought. Urgently, she asked, "Did he describe the men to you? Where he went?"

"Now, hold on," Mrs. Harris demanded. "I agreed to talk to you, but I'm not putting my only grandchild in trouble. Sheriff, if you plan to arrest my Tony for going on a job interview—"

Luke stood and stepped over Kell to crouch beside Mrs. Harris. He placed a calming hand on her shoulder. "Tony didn't do anything wrong. Kell and I think he may have seen something that can help us figure out who wanted to harm Clay."

Astute eyes studied Kell's. "This one won't spare my grandson if she's got someone else to look after."

Kell stiffened at the accusation. "I wouldn't let another man go to prison to protect my client, Mrs. Harris. Unlike my parents, I do have scruples."

"Not that I've seen on television. Anybody who watched that trial knew Brodie was guilty as homemade sin." Mrs. Harris took another drink from her nearly empty glass. Worry crept into her voice. "You made that jury believe what they wanted to believe. How do I know you won't trick my Tony into saying something that will get him in trouble? What do you care if he winds up hurt? What do you know about protecting somebody's child?"

"I won't allow her to do anything to harm Tony, Mrs. Harris." Luke patted her hand. "You've got my word on that."

Hackles raised, Kell stood. "While I appreciate the sheriff's pledge to you, Mrs. Harris, I don't need to manipulate a defenseless boy to defend my client. I wouldn't put your grandson in harm's way. I'm not my parents—I do have some integrity." She spun away and hurried to the door.

"Wait a second!" Mrs. Harris called out.

Kell ignored the summons and grabbed the doorknob. Unfortunately, the elderly woman had secured the door against any possible intruder with three deadbolts and a chain. By the time Kell finished undoing the final lock, Luke had levered Mrs. Harris from the sofa.

Surprisingly firm hands settled on her shoulders. Mrs. Harris didn't attempt to turn her, but simply held her still. "I apologize, Miss. That was wrong of me. We each make ourselves up. We borrow from people that we meet, from what we see in the world around us. You took something from those two ne'er-do-wells who brought you into this world. And another piece of you came from Eliza. Heck, standing here right now, something of me is adding to who you are."

Kell turned. "I won't hurt your grandson, Mrs. Harris."

"Okay. I'll believe you." She leaned heavily on Kell as they slowly returned to the couch. "Luke, go fetch my phone."

Luke completed his errand and handed the receiver to her. She punched in a phone number. "Viola? Send Tony down to see me."

"Is everything alright?" her daughter asked.

"Right as rain. Tell him I need to see him now."

"Does this have something to do with why the sheriff is at your house?"

"You live two blocks away. How'd you know about that?"

"Tony told me. Is he in trouble?"

Mrs. Harris watched Kell as she responded, "No. The sheriff has questions for him. I'll be right here to listen to his answers."

Luke led the women into small talk while they waited for Tony to arrive. A timid knock sounded at the door, and he got up to let the teenager inside.

He began to greet him, but before he could, Tony

babbled, "Sheriff, I tried to warn Doc not to mess with her, I swear. I didn't come and get you 'cause I didn't want to leave her alone."

Behind Luke, Kell frantically tried to catch Tony's darting, distressed glance. "Tony, please come here."

The young man rushed over to her, his expression wreathed in apology. "I'm sorry, Ms. Jameson. Really."

"Sorry for what?" Luke demanded. "What the hell happened out there?"

"Nothing important," soothed Kell. She crossed to Luke and touched his shoulder. In an undertone, she hissed, "We'll discuss it in the truck. Sit down."

Luke glared down at her, then took a breath. "Later," he warned.

"Later," she agreed quickly. "Tony, thank you for your help this evening. Now, the sheriff and I have a few questions for you about Clay."

As he had earlier, Tony paled at the mention of Clay's name. He cut a look at his grandmother. "I don't know anything about him."

"Stop lying, boy. I've already told them about the job offer." Mrs. Harris swatted at his leg. "What have I told you about lying?"

"To not say too much when I do," he answered smartly.

Mrs. Harris chuckled. "And not to tell strangers that your grandma taught you how to lie." She pointed to the chair that sat next to her post on the sofa. "Sit down and tell the sheriff what you told me."

Warily, Tony took his assigned seat. "Um, Clay tried

to recruit me to work for him a while ago, but I said I couldn't. My folks would have killed me."

"Of course." Kell smiled warmly. "I understand from your grandmother that you're doing well in school."

"Yes, ma'am. I'm planning to go to college next year. If we can find the money."

Luke picked up the thread. "So when Clay told you he'd gotten a better job, one that wasn't about dealing, you were interested."

Kell frowned, bothered by the story. "Why did he offer the job to you, Tony? You'd already turned him down once. I would think Doc would be a better candidate to work with Clay."

"Clay didn't trust Doc." Tony explained, "Last year, they got into a fight because Doc was skimming profits. Not enough so Clay could prove it, but we all heard about it."

"Is that why he came to you?" Luke asked.

"That and I've got a car. My dad and I rebuilt the engine last summer."

"He needed someone with their own transportation," he surmised.

Tony's head bobbed nervously. "He came to pick me up for the interview with his employers."

"Where did you go?" Kell eased forward until she could watch Tony's eyes in the light.

"A place off of County Road is all I know. When we got close, I had to put on a hood."

Luke probed, "Why did Clay say that was necessary?"

"He said the project they were working on was confidential. Until I got hired, I couldn't know the location."

"But you remember it was off County Road," confirmed Kell.

"Yeah. Seemed stupid to make me wear the hood though. Clay called the place an office, but where we stopped was more like a metal shed. He took me inside to meet with these two men in suits."

"Can you describe them?" For the first time, Luke pulled out a small notebook. "Tell me what you remember."

"The first guy was skinny and really, really white. Had these blue eyes that almost had no color. Brown hair, but stringy like. Second guy was black. Built kind of like you, Sheriff, like a running back, only shorter."

"Anything else you remember?"

"It was kind of weird. There was a third man, but he stayed in the back, behind this wall. Like the guy in the *Wizard of Oz*. He didn't ask any questions most of the time, but he did speak once."

"Did you recognize the voice?"

"Not exactly. It sounded familiar, but I couldn't tell why."

"Would you know it if you heard it again?"

"Don't think so. I'm not great with that stuff." Concerned, he focused on Kell. "Do lawyers have to be able to do that? Recognize voices?"

"No." Kell offered another encouraging smile. "But the best ones can recall details. Close your eyes, Tony."

He did so immediately. "What now?"

"Picture the first man. Tell me about his clothes."

"Suit. Blue with the white pinstripes. Had on a tie that matched his eyes, that blue. Like ice. He wore a ring on his pinky finger, gold with a ruby. Had some writing on it." Tony's eyes popped open. "I remember thinking that I might get one too."

"Why?"

"Because the black guy had one too. Same ring, only his stone was green. An emerald."

"How do you know they were the same ring?"

"The writing on them. Both had a symbol, like a"—he closed his eyes again, squinting to recall the memory—"a triangle with a circle cutting through the bottom of it."

The description set off alarm bells in Luke's head. He'd seen that symbol himself recently. Where eluded him for now, so he concentrated on the boy's story. "Tony, why didn't you take the job?"

Chagrined, Tony squirmed beneath the sheriff's inquiring look. He'd sound like a punk if he told the truth. But one look from his grandmother had him squaring his shoulders, prepared to be embarrassed. "I liked the suits and the rings, man. I mean, Sheriff. Both of them looked sharp, and even Clay didn't look like a druggie much anymore. But they gave me the creeps."

"Why?"

"I don't know." He frowned. "All the James Bond stuff was weird. They told me I'd be in security at their plant. When I asked where the plant was, that's when the voice in the back spoke. He told me that I'd find out everything I needed to know later."

"What did they say they produced?" Kell asked quietly.

"Wouldn't tell me. And when I asked where the plant was, they wouldn't tell me that either." He shook his head. "Didn't seem right. I finished talking to them and Clay drove me back to the District. He came by the next day, and I told him I'd rather not. He told me I was being stupid."

"Why?"

"He said that drugs were the old way to get rich, that he'd found a better way. Legit, you know?"

"Did he say anything else?"

"Said that the deal was he had to provide his own staff. He liked me because I didn't sell with Doc or the others. Kept myself clean."

"Was that the last time you spoke to him about it?"

"No. Last week, Clay comes by driving a Hummer. Black, tinted windows, rims, the works." Tony remembered feeling like an idiot when the SUV slowed to follow him and his friends. "He rolled down the window and called my name. Said 'Hey, Tony, I hope you like delivering pizzas for a living. Look what you've missed.' Then he showed me his ring. It had a blue stone."

Tony stared down at his shoes. "Next thing I hear, Clay is dead."

CHAPTER 16

Kell knocked on the office door the next morning. Luke waved her inside. "What are you doing here?"

"My job." She scanned his desk, brightening when she saw the tabbed folder. "Can I take a look at the evidence file?"

Luke didn't bother to cover the folder. "Absolutely not."

The answer wasn't unexpected, so Kell didn't protest. Their partnership played close to the line as it was. The county's chief prosecutor would have Luke's badge for sharing their files before discovery required the release. His accession would have amazed her, and forced her to question his competency.

To show there were no hard feelings, she added, "Just thought I'd try. But we're both clear that I'll find out some how, right?"

Luke spared her a piercing look. "Don't end-run me, Kell."

"Define *end-run*. Come on, Luke, I've got resources at my disposal that I intend to use."

He replied firmly, "Involve Cheryl or anyone on my staff in this, and I pick Eliza up."

"You wouldn't." Her response wasn't a challenge, but a statement of fact. Luke deplored the possibility of arresting Eliza as much as she did. He was unlike any lawman she'd ever encountered, a distinction that weakened her resolve to keep distance between them. Rather than jump to obvious conclusions, he struck her as methodical and intentional, willing to explore possibilities. Justice as a goal rather than a lucky coincidence.

Cops, in her experience, went after the low-hanging fruit, the easy answer. Their willingness to take a crime at face value didn't mean they were lazy or didn't care, but that they accepted the truth of human behavior—most crimes weren't premeditated. People killed for passion or gain or revenge. Prove those motives, and prove your case. Her career had been built on convincing jurors of alternate theories. Dulling passion, denying greed, saintly clients who decried revenge.

"Does your team know that you suspect her?"

"Not yet. But I will have to tell them soon. We've got a couple of days at best, Kell, then I have to move on the evidence we've got."

The weekend, she summarized. By Monday, he'd be at the Center, warrant in hand.

"Why the rush?"

"Politics." He sneered the word. "This is an election

year, and the county commission isn't keen on having unsolved murders playing in the papers while they run for office."

"Aren't you up for reelection?"

Luke lifted his shoulders dismissively. "I don't solve crimes to win elections. But I'm risking my career on this one. The Palace is on the county line, which means Chief Graves could raise a claim to jurisdiction. He'd love to have this one under his belt by November."

"He wants your seat," she guessed.

"This would be his first murder." Luke didn't mention that the other two corpses lying in the county morgue weighed down his argument that he could handle the cases without help. He'd prioritized Clay Griffin, and he'd decided to align himself with Kell to disprove Eliza Faraday as the killer. All choices that he'd have to answer for eventually. "Tell me what you thought of Tony."

"Smart. Ambitious. Perceptive enough to refuse Clay's offer." A frown creased her brow. "I'm still at a loss as to why Clay would recruit him, though. If his employers had money, they could have hired outside help to act as security. It strikes me as very odd that they'd hire a kid from the District."

Luke had the same reaction. "Tony and Clay have a connection that he didn't tell us about. I'll talk to Cheryl, see what she can find out."

"He's dating Nina." Kell made the admission, regretting the words the minute they escaped. But Cheryl would discover the truth easily, and perhaps telling Luke would engender a trade of information. "When

I was waiting for you last night, Doc teased him about dating Nina."

"Which connects him to the Center." Luke began to flip a pen in tight, controlled circles. "This keeps coming back to Eliza."

"Conveniently," protested Kell.

"But not too conveniently," Luke considered aloud. "A set of knives that she might own. A teenage love affair with one of her wards. A former resident who held a grudge." He slanted a look at Kell. "Then there's you. A potential witness to another set of murders, implicated by the deceased. Another connection to Eliza."

"You can't prove that one has anything to do with the other."

"Not yet, Kell." The threat hung in the air between them, then Luke continued. "I believe what the evidence tells me." His eyes held hers steadily. "For Eliza's sake, and yours, you'd better hope it starts telling me something new," he warned flatly.

Kell heard the threat, and her stomach tossed anxiously. *Calm down*, she admonished herself. *Think about the case, the evidence. What do you know?*

Then it hit her. The autopsy report she'd received listed samples sent out for lab analysis. She'd have to tip Luke off to her source, but the more she worked with him, the less she worried about his motives. "The chem labs. Has Cheryl gotten the reports back on what you had sent out for analysis?"

Luke cursed silently. The material he'd found on Clay's hands and shoes were hold-backs, information he didn't intend to release to Kell or anyone asking. At his direction, Cheryl had placed the materials under seal and sent them to the Atlanta lab separately. Yet, somehow, the defense already knew. "Exactly who have you got on the inside?" he asked, incredulous.

"I've got friends, Sheriff."

Kell's sources slipped her a copy of a classified autopsy, why shouldn't she also know about the samples he'd sent out for analysis? Tony's mention of a plant had triggered the same train of thought for him. "I want to know if I have a leak in my office. If they're telling you, they might be sharing information with Graves."

"No one in your unit," she assured him. "What can you tell me?"

"Apparently, you know exactly what I do. Nothing yet. The chemical analysis hasn't been completed yet."

"What type of material was it? Metallic? Blood?"

"No comment." He kept his eyes blank, giving nothing away.

She continued to press. "According to Tony, there are at least three men who might be involved in Clay's murder. Did you find prints at the scene that you can't identify?"

"Of course I found prints. We're talking about a dealer's house."

"Whose?"

"People. Kell, I'm not going to give you the file and I'm not going to tell you the contents either."

"Then how exactly are we working together?"

He set the pen down. "By letting you tag along on an

interview. And by not bringing your client in for questioning. Seems like you've got a good deal."

"Give me something more to work with, Luke. We're supposed to be sharing information."

"No," he corrected. "We're sharing interviews. I draw my conclusions and you draw yours."

Kell rummaged in her bag for a pen and paper, frustration bubbling. "This would go much faster if you'd cooperate," she mumbled crossly. "I won't tell the D.A."

"I'm sure you won't as that would implicate your client."

"Fine," she conceded peevishly. "But you can't mind if I speculate aloud, can you?"

"Be my guest."

In her mind, she replayed Tony's description of his time with Clay. Three men, two he could identify met him at a makeshift office. No distinguishing characteristics, but identical rings for the front men. She looked up from her notes. "Did you find Clay's ring among his personal effects?"

The question was met with silence. Kell ticked off a *no* on her legal pad. "Any signs of a struggle in the apartment? The autopsy indicated he didn't put up a fight with the killer, but was anything in the apartment disturbed?"

More silence.

"So Clay Griffin, lowlife drug dealer abruptly cleans up his act. He cuts off his sales and begins to recruit security for a new venture. A company that had no name, no location, and no product."

"But plenty of seed capital," Luke added meditatively. "Enough money to finance an expensive car and a change of wardrobe."

"Did you find new clothes?"

"Can't say that we looked." Luke calculated how many laws he'd have to break to do what occurred to him. "I'll deny it," he cautioned.

"Deny what?"

"Be ready to meet me tonight at the Center."

"I assume my attire will be the same."

Luke permitted himself a grin. "See you at eight."

"Where are we going?" Kell asked once they'd pulled onto the highway. She'd spent most of her Friday reading the materials she'd requested on Clay. In defiance of an embargo by David, Malikah overnighted a packet that confirmed what Kell had already known. Clay's later years had been a series of arrests and paroles that abruptly ended a year ago. She mentioned as much to Luke, who didn't seem surprised.

"That's where we're going. To Clay's apartment." He made a quick U-turn and headed down the county road toward the Palace. He'd noticed a car in his rearview, and figured if it was a tail, he'd find out for sure. "I thought it might help you to see where he was killed. Based on what Tony told us, the crime scene team may have overlooked something. But when we get to the motel, I need you to stay in the car until I come and get you."

"Sure."

Not a ringing agreement, but he'd take it. "Ten minutes. That's it." Soon, the truck parked in an alley behind the motel. "Lay down on the seat," he instructed. "No one can see you, okay? Graves can't find out I brought you to a crime scene."

"Got it." Kell didn't say thank you, but she understood how tough a choice he'd made to break procedure. Whether he admitted it or not, he trusted her more than he thought. "I'll be right here."

"I'll get the key from Purdy, the super, then I'll come through the service door over there." He gestured to a black metal door beside a grimy Dumpster. "When I motion to you, come on. Keep your head down."

Kell agreed, and Luke left the truck. He emerged from the alley, checking the area for stragglers out looking for trouble on a Friday night. Palace residents paid for four walls rather than the illusion of safety or privacy. From a window above his head, he heard a vicious argument about a man's prowess and his ability to demonstrate the same on a regular basis. Heavy, vicious metal poured into the damp air, evoking a scream demanding silence. Right about now, Curly would be accepting a call from that floor to report the noise pollution.

Anticipating the dispatch, Luke reached into his pocket for his cell phone. While the call connected, Luke scanned the area once more. A sleek black car parked on the opposite street, windows tinted for maximum impenetrability. Down the block, the usual motley collection of vehicles grazed the curbs. Purdy refused to pay for parking or to invest in a plot of land for more than the handful of cars that crowded into the meager spaces he provided.

"Hallden Sheriff's Department."

"Ruth?"

"Hey, Sheriff." Ruth Lee doubled as dispatcher, but rarely on weekends. "Curly told me you'd be calling in."

"Where is he?"

"Got a message from him an hour ago. All he said was that he had an emergency, would I sit for him?"

"Doesn't Donald have his poker night tonight?"

"Sure does. He won't miss me until after midnight." She yawned widely, the sound clear across the lines. "What can I do for you, Sheriff?"

"Get a report about excessive noise at the Palace?"

"Just got it in before you rang us up," she acknowledged. "Was about to send out Sergeant Little."

"Don't bother. I'm in the vicinity. I'll take it from here."

"Okay. Also, Sheriff, there's a message for you from Chief Graves."

"When did he call?"

"Not ten minutes ago. He didn't say it was urgent, so I hadn't planned to bother you on your night off."

"Thanks, Ruth." He disconnected the call and dialed Graves at home.

"It's the Chief."

"Chief, it's Sheriff Calder. I got your message."

In his study, Michael Graves straightened in his La-Z-Boy, sucking in the damnable gut that overflowed his belt despite the twenty-five sit-ups he performed daily. He'd been practicing his speech ever since he got word of Calder's activities tonight. Boy had no right to be poking his nose in areas where he didn't belong.

"Hear you've been patrolling on my side of the fence, Luke, my boy. Interviewing folks in town tonight."

"I've been pursuing leads, yes. We have to go where the evidence takes us, Chief," Luke returned mildly. "The police department and the sheriff's department have long respected that, haven't they?"

Graves coughed once into the receiver, a tone of obvious disdain. "I suppose. But down South, we observe the usual courtesies, Sheriff. I wouldn't have minded a ride along."

"Appreciate the offer, but I had it under control."

He pounced on the opening. "Yes, I understand that you've added a new member to your force. Ms. Jameson changing careers?"

Damn it. Luke kept his tone even. "Ms. Jameson wanted to visit old friends in the neighborhood, and I offered her a lift."

Liar. Smugly, Graves dug in. "You and Ms. Jameson are seeing quite a bit of each other. Her second trip here in as many weeks, and both times, she spends her evenings with you."

The emphasis on *evenings* didn't escape Luke's notice. Antagonism welled, but he tamed it ruthlessly. Graves's insinuations provided him with an excellent out. Sooner or later, he'd have to explain Kell's presence, and sooner had just arrived. He simply had to hope Kell wouldn't rip out his throat for lie. "Ms. Jameson and I have discovered that we share a number of mutual interests. We find it difficult to be apart."

Envy coated Graves's reply as he thought of the pinched faced, spindly harridan waiting for him upstairs. "Why, Luke, you old dog. Didn't know you had it in you. We might have to go out for drinks one night and compare notes."

Like his rage, Luke kept his disgust hidden as he approached the front door to the Palace. "Was that all, Chief?"

"I'd appreciate a courtesy call the next time you go hunting in my neck of the woods, Sheriff. Wouldn't want to get you caught in some crosshairs."

"And I wouldn't want to fire back," Luke issued his own caution. "I'll keep you filled in as necessary, Chief. Have a good night."

CHAPTER 17

Luke hung up the phone and hissed out a breath. Graves obviously intended to keep tabs on him and the investigation. Instinct told him that the police chief's interest stemmed from more than professional rivalry. A comment Graves made at the sheriff's office nagged at him. *Passion can be cold, my boy.*

So far, not one shred of evidence indicated a crime of any passion or feeling. But maybe he'd overlooked something in the apartment. Something that would catch his eye this time, or that Kell might see.

He buzzed Purdy's intercom from the street, noting that new security had been installed. When no response came, he leaned on the button until a voice barked out for him to enter.

"This ain't no Ritz Carlton," Purdy blustered as he forced open the door with one hand. The other clutched a soup can, ringed with dark brown stains.

"We ain't got bellmen waiting on sorry—" He cut his eyes up at his visitor for the first time. "Oh, Sheriff. It's you." Standing taller, he reached down to zip the pants he'd been lounging in. "Didn't know you was coming by tonight. Would have waited, waited up if I'd known."

Luke dismissed the apology with a wave, sight fixed on the rotund man's sweating forehead and no lower. "You can go back to your activities, Purdy, after you get me the key to Griffin's place."

Purdy waddled around the front desk. "When's that unit gonna be free to rent, Sheriff? It's been a while. Folks has been inquiring about rentals. Decent folks, the kind that pays on time."

Both of them knew Palace apartments came open every day, and that no decent person would seek out the Palace for a haven, safe or otherwise, if they had a choice. "Another week at most, I imagine," Luke explained. "Until we've got a handle on this, I can't risk losing access."

"Well, at least give me a schedule of your visitors. Chief Graves had me running up and down them stairs all afternoon yesterday."

"Graves stopped by?"

"Uh, huh. Told me you two had joint jurisdiction on this one, seeing as how the northwest corner of the motel is in the city proper." Purdy spat into the soup can. "Police won't come when I call for help, no siree. Always telling me to report it to the sheriff. But suddenly, he's here with state folks, poking around after a drug dealer."

Luke flattened his hands on the grimy front desk. "How many people came with him, Emmit?"

"It was him and two men. A black guy and a white one." He leaned forward, whispering conspiratorially, "Didn't look like police to me, I'll tell you that. One of 'em wore an earring. Diamond stud. And both had these prissy rings on their fingers."

The men that Tony described. "You asked Chief Graves about them?"

"Sure did. He told me they were from the DEA for Georgia. I'm guessing that's why they dressed so flashy. Them undercover types, like on television."

Luke worked hard not to grind his teeth or release the string of curses hurling in his brain. That son-of-a-bitch, he thought, had been keeping tabs on his investigation and tampering with his evidence. Probably had someone follow him to Mrs. Harris's place, which prompted the check-in call.

Someone who might right now be in the alley with Kell.

"Emmit, the key, please," he commanded tersely.

Aware that he'd revealed more than he should, the old man dropped the length of metal into his open palm. He circled the counter warily, waiting for the eruption. "Leave it in the drop box when you're done, okay, Sheriff?"

"If you don't mind, Emmit, I'd like to keep it for the time being. There's only this one, right?"

"Well, I've got my master, you know."

Calculating, Luke reached into his wallet and removed three twenties. He extended the bills and instructed, "No, you don't. Got lost in your apartment somewhere, didn't it?"

Emmit gave him a knowing glance, snipped the money from Luke's fingers, and shoved them into his pocket. "Can't find the darned thing nowhere." He looked around, as though checking for eavesdroppers, then added in a whisper, "Want I should call you if the police chief or his buddies come again?"

"Please." Luke clapped Purdy on the shoulder. "I won't forget your assistance to the Hallden Sheriff's Department."

Puffing out his chest, Purdy nodded sagely. "Damned police won't do for me, I ain't got no call to do for them." Then he turned and toddled down the hallway to his apartment.

As soon as he disappeared, Luke jogged across the entryway and down the first floor hall to the service door. He shoved through the metal doors, sparing a second to flip the bottom latch, and headed for the truck. In the gloomy alleyway, no light permeated the shadows.

He couldn't see her figure in the truck, and adrenaline coursed into fear. Skidding to a stop at the passenger window, he hauled at the door, his fingers unsteady on the handle. "Kell? Kell?" He whispered harshly. "Are you in here?"

She popped up at the sound of his voice, eyes wide with concern. "Luke? What's going on? What's wrong?"

Without wasting a second, he lifted her out of the truck and slammed the door. He clicked the locks with his remote, then dragged her with him to the service door. Once inside, he kicked the stand up and pulled her into the hallway. "This way," he directed, taking the stairs two at a time.

Kell followed silently, aware that his sudden urgency had a purpose. Grateful for her weekly bouts of torture on the elliptical machine, she kept pace with him as they climbed up to the fifth floor. The questions that crowded on her tongue remained in check until he sliced through the police tape. She noticed that the seal on the door had been broken.

Furious at the breach, Luke keyed open Clay's door and ushered her inside. When the door shut tightly behind them, he flicked on the light. Weak light crested over the chair that had fallen earlier. He noted that the open drawer had been pushed in, that the couch had been shifted several inches. Crimson stains stared up from the beige carpet, and he heard Kell's swift intake of breath.

"You okay?" He extended a hand to her to draw her closer. "I assumed you've been to your share of crime scenes."

"I have," she acknowledged wearily, "but not for anyone I knew." She dropped his hand and approached the blood that had ruined the carpet. Bending, she murmured, "Clay and I were friends once. I guess I'd forgotten that."

"The man who died in this apartment wasn't the boy you knew."

"Maybe. Maybe not." She looked up at him, the wide brown eyes drenched with sympathy and skepticism.

"It all stays inside us. Every part of the past. You can't escape it, can't deny it."

"So you work hard to fight it." Luke moved forward and heaved her to her feet. His hands framed her face, forcing her eyes to his. He kissed her once, softly, reassuringly. A brush of mouth to mouth that soothed them both.

Kell absorbed the touch and the comfort. "Sometimes it's hard to remember that."

Understanding, Luke released her and gestured to the outline taped to the floor. He'd made a decision downstairs, when Purdy told him about the police chief. "Clay wasn't killed because of who he'd been as a child. He died because of choices he made as an adult. And I have reason to believe those choices involved Chief Graves."

"Graves killed him?" she asked, stunned.

"I don't know," Luke admitted. "I'm not sure what the hell is going on here. Clay turns over a new leaf, comes into some money and tries to recruit Tony to help him. Then he's murdered in his apartment, only no one hears or sees a thing. Now I find out that Chief Graves has been in this apartment, with two friends that sound familiar."

Kell's eyes widened even further. "The men that Tony met? Are they cops?"

"Not likely. I know everyone on Graves's force. None of them match the boy's description." He carefully circled the outline and the chair. "When I left last week, this drawer was half open. The couch was flush against the wall. Both have been moved, as though Graves was looking for something."

"Clay's ring," she surmised. "How did you know they'd been here?"

"The super told me, thought I already knew." Striding to the kitchenette, he found a hand towel. "There's been a lot of interest in this drawer," he explained as he returned to stand by the dresser. "I wonder what else was supposed to be inside."

Slowly, Luke took the drawer out and held it out for examination. The flimsy plywood construction showed no evidence of a false bottom. Inside, the tan interior bore trace stains and some dust, but nothing that signaled at its meaning.

Behind him, Kell peered into the open space left by the empty slot. Using her shirttail, she tested the remaining handles. The other two drawers proved similarly unremarkable. The top one could be removed like the second drawer, but the bottom one only extended part of the way before stopping because of a mechanism that halted it halfway.

"They've been picked clean," she noted. "Was there something inside when you came the first time?"

"No. This one was standing ajar, and the other two were closed. After we photographed the scene, I had the team check them for contents. All empty."

Kell studied the bottom drawer from her position and noticed a broken edge in the corner where it would move no further. Below the empty space, a flash caught her eye. "Luke, come here."

He crossed to her side. "Did you find something?"

"Maybe." She gained her feet and shifted to the right side of the dresser. Giving an experimental tug, she said, "It's bolted to the wall."

"Purdy is cheap." Luke cocked his head at her. "What are you thinking?"

She grabbed his hand and gestured inside the open space. "See the bottom panel?"

"Yes?"

"Look closely."

Luke bent his head, nearly stuffing it inside the hole in the dresser. He inclined his gaze to the left and then to the right. And saw it. "There's something stuck behind the dresser."

"You can't get to it by removing the drawers. That's why they didn't find it."

"We have to get it out."

Kell rose and hurried into the kitchen. "Once, Fin and I decided to snoop in Mrs. F's attic. We'd been reading Trixie Belden or something, and Fin was certain that one of the cabinets in the attic had a false bottom." She found a butter knife lying in the sink, unwashed. Flipping on the water, she sprayed the knife clear of what she assumed to be congealed jelly. She gave it a quick swipe with the discarded dishtowel and knelt beside the drawer.

"Turns out, cheap plywood doesn't really care for being prodded and poked." Kell wedged the knife into the shadowed slot where the wood joined the sideboard. She prised the wood from its mooring, hearing it splinter with satisfaction. "This type of wood is its own false bottom," she pronounced, removing the fractured board. The bottom removed, she levered the back free of the sides and the entire drawer collapsed.

Luke squatted down and helped her remove the broken pieces. "Did you find anything in the attic?"

"A game of Twister and a month of extra chores." She smiled at the memory, and reached into the now open space. "Fin would definitely have preferred jewelry." Using her shirttail, her fingers closed around the shiny object and lifted it into the light. "Clay's ring."

"Which Graves knows about."

Kell sat back on her heels. "Graves doesn't strike me as a criminal mastermind, Luke. Seems more likely to be a pawn of the other two."

Because Luke agreed with her assessment, he nodded, studying the loop of gold with its blue stone. "But we can't underestimate him. He's been tailing me and he knows that I'm working with you." He filled her in on his conversation with Graves. "In fact, I'm fairly certain his man has reported to him that we've been in the apartment for more than twenty minutes. If they didn't find anything, they're going to be wondering if we did."

"What do we do now? Take the ring to your office?"

"Can't. I'm not sure one of my officers isn't feeding him information."

"Then what do we do?"

Luke stared at the ring, then slanted a grin at Kell that had her stomach wobbling. "We go to the safest place I know."

"Where's that?"

"My house."

CHAPTER 18

Ivy climbed white railings and tangled with vines of honeysuckle. A slate roof sloped low over shutters that framed the picture windows on either side of the broad front porch. Potted plants hung from the porch ceiling, and an old rocking chair rested in the corner.

Luke led Kell up the cobblestone walkway, her elbow firmly in his grip. Crabgrass peeked through the stones and he made a mental note to spray in the morning before heading into the office. He noted in approval that the lawn had received its scheduled mowing from Cheryl's son.

Pride swelled as Luke watched Kell take in the 1820s farmhouse he'd spent the better part of three years rehabbing. From the hunter green shutters too dark to distinguish in the moonlight, to the refinished floors inside, every detail had been his vision. Hours of labor on weekends and his infrequent days off had been poured into his house, along with the remorse that had weighed him down for nearly four years. He'd rebuilt himself, and this house. But when Kell remained silent, pride faltered unexpectedly.

As though she could read his mind, she finally murmured, "It's perfect. Though not exactly what I expected."

"Which part?" he teased as he unlocked the front door with its original hardware, rescued from the basement.

"It's so, well, homey."

"Fixed it up with my own two hands," he explained. Beneath the porch light, his eyes caught hers and held. "I'm very good with my hands."

Before she could respond, a black bullet shot past them. Luke whirled her aside as a second mound of fur, this time a golden yellow, bounded out after the first. "Meet my roommates, Jekyll and Hyde."

Kell watched as the black dog rolled across the midnight lawn in ecstasy, while the golden retriever observed from a safe distance on the rocker. "I take it the lab is Hyde?"

"Excellent observation. Jekyll tends to be the instigator. She prefers to incite Hyde into action and enjoy his comeuppance." He guided her into the living room and gestured her to a leather sofa. Instead, Kell wandered around the room, taking in the space.

A shade richer than jade adorned the walls and accented the hardwood floors polished to a high shine. The marble mantle displayed a trio of photos that included a tall man in dress whites next to a beautiful woman garbed in the same. The woman held a small bundle, which she assumed to be an infant Luke.

In the second photo, Luke towered over the couple, this time the one in uniform. She spotted the CPD insignia on a flag behind him and figured out that it was his graduation. A third photo showed Luke in a CPD T-shirt, his long arms slung around the shoulders of two men who laughed up at the camera. Behind them, four others made faces and rude gestures at the picture taker.

"Who are these guys?" she asked, turning to Luke with a smile.

"My squad," he answered shortly, leaving the room to check on the dogs. He propped the front door open, inhaling the scent of honeysuckle and the other wildflowers that grew out behind the house. He looked at that photo everyday, and it never got easier to see them smiling at him. Unaware how badly he'd soon fail them all. Pushing away his melancholy, he returned to the living room. "Have a seat."

Kell sat, still thinking about the photograph. In her research, there'd been mention of a tragic accident that killed several members of the same squad. His squad. Kell started to ask, but Jekyll shuffled in, bored with Hyde's antics. She sniffed once at Kell, then sauntered past her into the den. Deciding not to press, Kell asked instead, "How long have you had them?"

"They came with the house." With a practiced motion, he unclipped his holster and set it on a sideboard laden with unread catalogs and magazines. "The owners were moving into an assisted-living facility, no pets allowed. They dropped the price five percent when I agreed to adopt."

"Smart."

"Yep. The dogs were already named, which should have warned me." He returned to the foyer and whistled for Hyde, who gave a disgruntled bark but padded inside.

Hyde, unlike Jekyll, decided to investigate the newcomer. A wet nose pressed against Kell's hand and she stroked his grassy coat. "Aren't you beautiful?" she crooned, and the dog panted with delight.

"Keep rubbing his fur like that and you'll have to take him home with you."

"No pets allowed in my condo. The chair of the homeowners association is allergic." Kell had never owned a pet, never really wanted to. But the soft rumbles beneath her hand as she pet Hyde brought a moment of regret. "Nice dog," she crooned softly. Wanting to continue petting him, she lifted her hand and tucked it in her lap. No sense in getting attached.

Luke noticed the wistfulness and filed the reaction away. He snapped for Hyde's attention and shooed him into the den. "Want something to drink?" he asked, walking toward the kitchen, which opened off of the living room. Bumping open a swinging door, he called out, "Water, wine, or beer?"

"Any chance you have a Coke in there?"

"One Coke coming up." He returned with two bottles dangling from his hand.

Kell accepted the chilled soft drink in its signature container. Tipping the soda down her throat, she released the sigh she'd held back. At his raised brow, she explained, "I haven't had a real Coke in years. Used to be a Friday treat at the Center. Cold Coca-Cola in the glass bottle."

"We had them on base. One of the perks." He lifted a bottle of pale amber ale to his lips. "However, tonight seems to require something a little harder."

Grateful for the opening, Kell rushed to ask, "What's going on, Luke?"

"I'm not exactly sure. But the upshot is that I have sufficient evidence to believe Eliza is innocent."

"Good," she replied, but the tension clustered at her shoulders remained. Ever since she discovered the ring beneath the dresser, he'd been in an easy, even lighthearted mood. The austerely handsome face had relaxed, become more mobile. More attractive, if that were possible.

Nerves born of uncertainty and apprehension jittered when that chiseled smile flashed at her. To distract, she commented, "Your colleague may be implicated in a murder, and he's trying to sabotage your case. Yet you are remarkably sanguine."

"Michael Graves and I don't see eye to eye on much," Luke said evenly. "Apparently, he thinks that by scooping me on the Griffin murder, he'll have a better shot at my job."

"Or?"

"Or the Chief of Police is a conspirator in a murder."

The ebony eyes shifted from light to dangerous in an instant. "And if he did have something to do with Griffin's death, then he's going to be looking for a scapegoat."

Disquiet settled over Kell as the implication sunk in. "Why would he target Eliza? Why even think of her?"

"I don't know that he has," Luke cautioned. "But while Graves isn't a bright man, he's not an idiot. Your sudden reappearance will tip him off eventually."

"Then I can leave. You think Eliza is innocent, which means you won't arrest her." She set the bottle on an oak coffee table that appeared handmade. More of Luke's handiwork, she imagined. "Unless you have another reason for me to stay."

A hundred reasons, most of which included the bed upstairs, Luke thought hungrily. But now wasn't the time to mention the desire that had become a permanent ache whenever he thought of her. "The longer you stay in town, the more he'll speculate. You leave and he might not look her way."

Contradicting herself, she countered, "You did."

"Because I knew about the knives. Graves and Eliza don't get along well. She thinks he harasses her children."

"He always has." Kell recalled a particularly nasty winter afternoon the year Julia arrived. "Once, he trapped Fin and Julia and me in a closet at the general store. Accused us of stealing."

"Had you?"

Kell took no offense. "That time, no. Julia had on

a pair of leather gloves that she'd received from some relative. The store owner swore they belonged to him. Graves demanded that Julia produce a receipt." Bitterness flared again. "What thirteen-year-old carries around receipts, especially for gifts? Anyway, when we refused to give the gloves to the owner, he shoved us into a utility closet. Propped something under the door to keep us inside."

"My God."

"It was worse than you think. Fin is claustrophobic." Kell winced at the memory. "She just sat on the floor, moaning and rocking. Julia and I begged him to let us out, even offered to give him the gloves."

"How long did he keep you inside?"

"Two hours. Until Mrs. F came to get us. One of the others found her and told her what had happened."

"No wonder you hate him."

"He's a loathsome little toad who preys on the weak." Kell swigged from the bottle of Coke, abruptly thirsty. "So how do we catch him?"

"We can discuss that over dinner." Luke stood and snagged his bottle. "Come into the kitchen, and I'll wow you with more of my culinary skills."

Kell followed him through the swinging doors and stopped short, impressed. The kitchen was a wide, airy room complete with a butcher block island and long, deep counters. Where the living room had been painted in shades of green, the kitchen boasted lemon yellow walls and touches of auburn and sage. "All I seem to do around you is eat."

"The way to a woman's heart, I hope."

Luke installed her on a stool at the island and set out an impressive array of pots and pans. He dumped handfuls of pasta into boiling water, sprinkling in a handful of spice. On a separate burner, onions sizzled with garlic, to which he added a splash of wine. She'd been given the mundane task of salad making, which stretched the limits of her skills.

She enjoyed watching him cook, the easy grace of movement, the intensity that flared as he puzzled over a vegetable. Not a simple man, she knew, but one who came with layers and corners that one could easily over-look. Like his reaction to her question about the photo.

"Who were the men in the photo, Luke?"

He hesitated briefly, holding a spoon above the pasta. "I told you. Guys from my precinct in Chicago."

Kell sliced a cucumber carefully, but looked at Luke. "Do you stay in touch with them?"

"No."

"Why not?" she probed, needing him to tell her the truth. For once, she understood his constant pressing for more from her, knowing she had to demand the same. "Talk to me, Luke.

His eyes, already so deep and dark, went black and cold. "There's nothing to talk about."

Rather than retreat, she pressed. "Are they the reason you left Chicago?"

"Yes."

Although she'd figured out part of the answer, she asked, "Did you have a fight? Get kicked off the force?"

"No." He flicked off the heat below his sauce and turned to face her, his lean face dangerous. "I killed them all. Okay?"

Stunned, she dropped the knife and it clattered to the floor. "What happened?"

"Exactly what I said. I killed six of my best friends."

Kell slid off the stool and came around to where he stood at the stove. She covered his hands with her own, oblivious to the heat that rolled from the burners or him. "Tell me what happened."

He supposed he owed her. After all, he'd been pulling at her for honesty. It was his turn to reveal a truth. "A stakeout went bad. I was their commanding officer. Had a suspect under surveillance for child pornography." He jerked his hands free and moved past her into the breakfast area. "We got a tip that he was expecting a large shipment of tapes from overseas. I ordered the team to follow him to the docks. We didn't have time to arrange for more back up."

Kell said nothing, but she came around the island and stood, waiting.

"We reached the docks and the slip where the ship was unloading. But he wasn't expecting tapes and DVDs."

Comprehension dawned in a wave of horror. "No."

"We could hear the children crying in their boxes. Stacks of crates filled with stolen children. I didn't want to call in or wait for orders. I told them to take the docks. Without waiting for more backup." He could hear the gunfire erupting around them. Hear the first of his men fall. "We scattered, trying to get to the children and pick off the transporters. It took five minutes maybe. Five minutes to wipe out six of my men."

"Did the children—"

"The kids were safe. I managed to secure them after the firefight stopped."

"How many?"

"Twenty-three. Crammed into these boxes like animals."

"And the suspect and his crew? Did they die?"

Luke smiled then, a gruesome twist of lips that chilled her blood. "Most of them were shot by my men. The bastard in charge is serving ten consecutive life sentences in general population."

"Good."

Her reaction shocked Luke into focusing on her. "What did you say?"

"I said good. He deserves whatever he gets." She reached behind her for her soda, and passed Luke his beer. "I won't bother to tell you that their deaths weren't your fault."

"Thanks. A dozen shrinks have already tried. Put me on medical leave until we all realized I couldn't stay in Chicago."

"You did what you were trained to do. And I will tell you that you're stupid if you keep that photo on the mantel out of guilt."

"Excuse me?"

"Those men sacrificed their lives following a man they trusted, doing something they believed in. And you demean their memories by regretting that."

"You have no idea what you're talking about."

"I am very familiar with making choices that leave you feeling sick to your stomach, shaky with regret. But someone has to make the choice to act, and that's what you did. To the best of your ability."

"And my men be damned?"

"No, and your men died with honor. Which is more than I can say for most."

"For yourself?"

Kell shut her eyes and shook her head. "One confession per meal," she quipped, her voice forcibly light. "I think your pasta is overheating."

CHAPTER 19

"Soon," Luke threatened lightly, deciding not to push. For now. Wounds that had never quite healed over pulsed too raw for him to do battle. But, he promised, her turn would come. Instead, he turned his attention to the pasta, barely saving it from ruin. "I've got a Chardonnay chilling in the refrigerator."

"Got it." She gratefully accepted the reprieve and fetched the wine. A quick hunt through his cabinets revealed glasses. Before she could ask, a corkscrew appeared by her elbow. "Anything else?"

"Salad dressing should do it." He reignited the burner beneath the saucepan, then coated the pasta with the contents. Cooking settled him, the creation of a meal to satisfy at least one keen appetite. As she moved around his kitchen, Kell made it nearly impossible to ignore the brilliantly painful twist in his gut or heavy beat of desire. He wanted her more each time he came near her, and walking away became more of a trial.

One that would end soon.

Aware of her temporary escape, Kell skirted around Luke in the kitchen, finding tasks to keep her out of reach. After placing the dressing on the table, she gathered plates and utensils. There was an order to his kitchen, not rigid or controlled but seamless and competent.

She understood that about him, but the rest, the anguish and loss, that had shocked her. He didn't wear his grief like a martyr, the way some might have. Neither had he buried it, pretending his past had vanished by leaving Chicago. No, she realized, he'd found another outlet, a way to honor their memories through serving another community. Protecting those whose lives he shared.

A man like Luke didn't become a cop. He'd always been one. Would always be. Standing for others, making their worlds safe, whether he knew their names or not. A man like Luke couldn't have made the choices she had. She doubted he'd ever find himself so deep that they'd be necessary.

Which doomed whatever grew between them, she admitted. Attraction, respect, even, if she were to be honest, affection, couldn't compensate for their differences. A sheriff and a defense attorney.

"Stop it."

Looking up, she caught his gaze over the island, felt the tension rise around her. "Stop what?"

"Figuring out why this won't work."

"I didn't say a word."

"But that mind of yours was processing all the angles."

Caught, she plowed ahead. "You and I don't share the same codes, Luke. We're on opposite sides."

"That's not true." He flattened his palms on the butcher block. "I have a goal, and so do you. To get the answers. We just ask different questions."

"It's not that simple."

"Because you want to make it harder. Then you can ignore how I make you feel."

"I don't feel anything that I can't forget once this is over."

"It won't be over, Kell." A promise, a threat, blazed from ebony.

Before she could react, he'd banked the emotion, leaving only a cool watchfulness that had her taking a half-step away. "Dinner's ready."

"What?"

"Dinner. Pomodoro and fettucine." Balancing the bowl and garlic bread he retrieved from the oven, Luke led the way to the table. Kell had laid out dishes and utensils, and he efficiently ladled pasta onto their plates. He offered her a slice of bread, butter melting onto the platter. "Come and sit down."

She heard the unspoken truce and accepted. Taking a seat, she quipped, "I think my arteries just clogged." *Worth it,* she decided, *if the flavors match the smells.* "Between Hervé and you, I'll have justification for a whole new wardrobe to capture my expanding waist-line."

"Italian food demands sacrifice." Filling her glass, he smiled at her over the rim. "And confidence, which you've got in abundance."

"You find me arrogant?"

Luke pondered the question as he swirled pasta onto his fork. "Arrogant isn't the right word. You've got the brains to prove your point. Insolent, maybe. On the edge of pretentious, absolutely."

Kell bristled. "I am not pretentious."

"Says the woman driving a sixty-thousand-dollar car."

"Perhaps the issue is your fixation on my Porsche. First you tell me I have it to let out my energy and now it's proof that I'm ostentatious."

Luke lifted his wine, sipping thoughtfully. "Kell, I would never describe you as ostentatious."

Taking the bait, she insisted, "Then how would you describe me? Besides insolent and pretentious?"

"Complicated." He swirled pasta around his fork, considering. "Part of what fascinates me about you is your ability to say almost nothing and somehow manage to fill the entire room. No wasted motions, no flashy ways. There's confidence and control, all crowding against that block of fear that keeps you hiding away."

"I appreciate the psychoanalysis," she scoffed. "How much do I owe you?"

"An honest answer. For once."

"Try me."

"Have you thought of me?"

"Of course," Kell equivocated. "Your job is to put my client in prison."

"That's not what I mean and you know it."

Luke reached across the table and plucked her glass

from suddenly nerveless fingers. Dark eyes focused on her, dragging her into their ebony pools. She resisted the undertow, but felt herself being swept under. "Tell me."

"I've thought of you. Too much."

"And what did you think?"

"Turnabout?"

"Fine."

Kell cocked her head to study him. "A man shouldn't have a face like yours in real life."

"Sorry," he mocked.

"You've learned to balance your strength with a softness I didn't expect."

"I'm not soft."

"No. But you are kind. To impressionable boys and starry-eyed teenage girls. To ex-cons and murder suspects." She held his eyes, wanting him to know this much at least. "I like you, Luke. You're a good man."

"Kell."

Abandoning caution, she finished, "And I thought about your mouth. The way you kiss me. Like there's nothing else in the world."

"There isn't." Heat thundered in his veins, hardened him in a swift rush that left dinner forgotten. He stood, drawing her to her feet. "Let me show you."

Kell swayed once, dreamily. Warily. "I don't know."

"Learn," he ordered as his mouth captured hers.

She braced for invasion, ready to be swept away. But he baffled her with a glide of his lips against hers, a teasing foray that opened her mouth in protest. Even then, he held back, wrapping her tight until she could feel only him. Everywhere.

Softly, inexorably, he tested the contours of her lips, the damp heat urging him inside. Reaching for patience, Luke sank down onto the chair she'd abandoned and settled her across his lap. Her eyes fluttered open, her fingers clutched at his shoulders. When she tugged him closer, patience fled.

Heat, a conflagration, searing at his senses. Cool, the feel of her hair tumbling beneath his seeking fingers. The cotton shirt he'd insisted upon frustrated his hands as they streaked down over generous curves. A button flew free as he forgot to wait. Touch, taste, take. The litany poured through him, shook him.

More, she thought dizzily. More of the slick of tongue against tongue. More of his hands skating along her skin, building desire with a stroke, a touch. Unwilling to wait, she twisted against him, slanting her mouth to claim. His scent punched through her, a spice that drove want higher and higher. In concert, she fumbled at the slippery buttons that defied her urgency.

When his thumb crested the rise of her breast, she moaned and retaliated, nipping at his mouth. A dark laugh rose between them, hers, his.

Luke thought to sate himself, but found only a deeper hunger. Energy jolted through him and he dragged her impossibly closer. Mindless now, only wanting to be inside, he lifted her to his mouth, licking at silken flesh that pouted for his attention. Then he drew her inside, reveling in her cries.

The shrill of a cell phone broke through the haze.

Ignoring the sound, Kell fastened her mouth to his throat, laving the strong column, enjoying the gallop of his pulse. She'd wanted, but never craved. Needed, but never yearned.

A second melody joined the first, the cacophony of sound too much to ignore. Cursing, Kell and Luke broke their embrace, chest heaving with labored breath.

He caught her cheek with an unsteady hand. "We have to check, right?"

"Yes," Kell agreed, rising reluctantly. Her phone in her purse, discarded in the living room. Luke grabbed his phone and flipped it open while she rushed to answer the imperious demand.

"Calder here."

"Luke, it's Ruth. You need to get over to the Center right away."

At the sound of the unflappable Ruth Lee's near hysteria, Luke's blood cooled immediately. "What's going on, Ruth?"

"I just got a call from my friend Annie at the police department. Sheriff, Chief Graves is on his way to arrest Eliza Faraday for the murder of Clay Griffin."

"Call Cheryl and tell her to meet me there." Luke snapped the phone shut and snatched up his holster. Fury warred with disgust. He should have seen this coming, should have known that Graves would figure it out. He reopened his phone and dialed.

Adjusting his shirt with his free hand, he strode into

the living room. Kell stood at the door, eyes fierce and angry. "Nina said they've searched the Center and plan to arrest Eliza. Chief Graves is in the kitchen with three officers. She needs me to come now."

"We're going." Luke caught her hand and twined their fingers. "We'll figure this out."

He bundled her into the truck, climbed inside, and gunned the engine. In a rare show, he put the lights on top and whirred the siren. The fifteen-minute trip was over in seven. Kell jumped from the truck before he placed it in park. Two marked vehicles blocked the driveway, their lights flashing blue and white in the silence.

Catching up with her, he warned, "Don't say anything. Let me handle this."

Kell jogged up the path, her response nearly a snarl. "She's my client. My responsibility." One that she'd neglected to make out like some oversexed teenager. "I should have been here."

"But you weren't." Luke caught her arm and whirled her around to face him. "Whatever Graves is doing, this is not a game to him. If you don't do as I say, I won't be able to help her. Or you." He clamped his hand over her protest. "Or the children inside this house. Graves has a plan and we don't, so let me figure one out."

Shoving his hand away from her mouth, Kell argued, "I'm not a damsel in distress, Sheriff. I know how to take care of my own."

"Yes, you do. And for now, that means trusting me."

Kell could feel the adrenaline rage through, the vicious kick of guilt that she hadn't been here. She shunted both aside with effort and focused on the smart move. "Okay. I will trust you. For now." Her fingers gripped his arm in a bruising hold. "But I won't risk her. Do you understand?"

"I understand. Come on."

CHAPTER 20

The tableau as they entered the kitchen told Luke the story. Chief Graves prowled near a black granite countertop, brandishing a chef's knife with its lethal eight-inch blade. Two officers had been posted inside, a burly redhead composed of equal parts muscle and flesh. His partner was only slightly smaller, in height if not dimension. Luke recognized both men. The taller was a good cop, if a touch lazy, and the shorter one hadn't left much of an impression.

For her part, Eliza stood stoically at the entryway from the kitchen to the dining room, her tiny frame stiff and unyielding. The shorter officer waited at her side, steel glinting in the light. Luke held Kell's arm until he saw the cuffs. "Go on."

Kell dashed to Eliza, hands outstretched. "Mrs. F?" She nudged the officer aside, noting his look of chagrin. "Have they read you your rights?" she demanded.

"Yes, dear." Eliza nodded once, her hazel eyes steady and unshaken. "Chief Graves also gave me this." She handed Kell a sheet of paper. Kell accepted the document and skimmed the contents quickly.

Luke didn't have to read the paper to know what she held. He stepped into Graves's path and the older man faltered in his confident stride. "A warrant to search the Center, Chief? Which judge did you wake up to get that?"

"Judge Majors. She found my evidence compelling," Graves announced slyly. "I also have a present for you." He shoved an envelope at Luke.

"This is my case, Graves." He fingered the envelope. "Griffin died in my territory."

"Then you should have been doing your job." He eyed Kell, ran his tongue across his fleshy pink lips. "One of our citizens is being denied justice due to a personal bias on your part. Would have expected better of you, Luke. Didn't think you were the type to screw the lead suspect's attorney." Graves laughed spitefully. "Hope she was good."

The punch knocked Graves on his ass and had the two officers charging Luke. He easily evaded them, then held up his hands in surrender. "Don't try it, Lancy."

"Arrest him," Graves cried from his sprawled position on the floor.

The redhead, Lancy, watched Luke carefully. He'd worked for him for a month before being lured away by Graves to the police department, a decision he still regretted. Better pay couldn't paper over the differences between Graves and Calder. He folded his arms and shook his head at his boss. "I don't think he's gonna take another swing, Chief."

"I said arrest him. Assaulting an officer. Dereliction of duty," he shrilled. Blood poured from his face and dripped onto the crisp white shirt he'd chosen for the evening's drama. He'd even called ahead to the news station, and they were supposed to have a camera waiting on his return. A tape he intended to play as the central commercial for his election to sheriff in November. Ruined. "I think he broke my freakin' nose."

"Elevate it," Lancy advised. He left Luke's side to grab a towel and held it out the chief. "Here you go."

Graves snatched the cloth and pressed it to his nose, yelping with pain. "Don't make me give the order again. Place him under arrest. Now."

Potter, the second officer, helped Graves to his feet. Like Lancy, he'd once worked under Luke and was reluctant to arrest him. The entire business had him unhappy. Being more cunning, he tried a different tack. "Chief, with all due respect, you really think we should arrest the sheriff? Won't you have a hard time explaining why he hit you?"

Graves jerked his hand free and adjusted his badge. While it may be good press to portray Calder as a bully, the image of him as the weaker of the two wouldn't translate well on film. Not when he alone had been harmed. He blustered, "Fine. But I want Eliza Faraday in cuffs and in the squad car. Now."

Shoving his hands in his pockets to keep them away

from Graves's throat, Luke prodded, "What are the charges? Owning a set of kitchen knives?"

Graves corrected smugly, "Not just any knives, Calder. A knife described as the murder weapon in your autopsy report." He snatched up a folder, blood staining the cover. With relish, he waved the blue folder at Luke. "According to your own lab reports, Griffin was killed with a ceramic knife. My investigation revealed that she received an identical set last December, Sheriff." He sneered the title. "Eliza Faraday not only has the knife, she had a reason to want Griffin dead."

Luke's expression betrayed nothing. "What's your theory?"

"I don't need theory. I've got witnesses. Ones who heard Eliza Faraday threaten to kill Clay Griffin on the day he died." He jabbed a finger in Eliza's direction. "That's why she called Ms. Jameson in to help her. Because everyone knows that her specialty is guilty clients. Until now, though, I didn't realize how far she'd go to get them off."

"Luke, no," Kell warned as he took a menacing step toward Graves.

Graves skittered back until he slammed up against the counters. His foot landed in a spot of blood, and he tumbled to the linoleum floor again. Officer Potter scrambled to assist, only to be batted away.

Gaining his feet again, he snatched the cuffs from Potter and approached Eliza. "Eliza Faraday, you are under arrest for the murder of Clay Griffin." With one hand, he clipped the handcuffs onto her wrist and turned her to secure the other. "Bag that set of knives," he instructed.

From the doorway, Nina burst into the kitchen, protesting. "This isn't right! She didn't do anything." Several of the older children followed on her heels, demanding her release.

Eliza shook her head sternly. "Nina, take everyone into the family room." When the girl opened her mouth to protest, she gave her a stern look, the "Hard day" look every child recognized. "No argument. Kell will join you in a moment and explain what's happening."

"We know what's happening," Nina countered, pointing a trembling finger at Graves. "That idiot thinks you killed Clay because of what he tried to do to me."

"Young lady, show some respect to your elders," admonished Graves in a falsely avuncular tone. "Being a foundling isn't an excuse for bad manners."

"And being in power isn't an excuse for stupidity," Nina retorted, unabashed. "Everyone knows that they booted you out to give Sheriff Calder the job because you were too lazy to do anything."

Kell appreciated the outrage, but judged that in Graves's current mood, Nina would soon find herself in an adjoining cell. She whispered to Eliza, "Don't say anything until I get to the station. I'll be there as soon as I can."

With that admonition, she took Nina's arm and dragged her toward the door. "Come on, everyone. Right now. Don't give them any more reason to be mad at Mrs. F."

The thought that they could be hurting Eliza widened several eyes, and slowly, they filed out of the kitchen while Kell held the door open. When the last one had slunk out, Kell made eye contact with Luke. "Will you go to the station with her? I need to talk to the kids."

Luke nodded, and he crossed the room to stand with Eliza. Judge Majors had issued a legal search warrant, and he had no grounds to stop her arrest. It was sheer force of will that had kept his face blank when Graves revealed his evidence. Evidence Kell hadn't told him about, evidence he'd failed to gather himself. Fury rose, aimed squarely at his own behavior. Graves's assessment of his conduct wasn't far off the mark. Sentiment and attraction kept him from doing his job. It wouldn't stand in his way any longer.

"Chief Graves, I plan to accompany Mrs. Faraday to the station. If you have no objections?"

Thrown by the change in demeanor, Graves gave a short nod. He released her arm, and motioned to Potter to escort the prisoner out. In awkward procession, he led Eliza through the foyer and out to a waiting vehicle. Lancy guided Graves, whose nose continued to bleed into the towel. Luke secured the kitchen door and decided to check on the kids before following.

In the foyer, Jorden waited for Luke. "She didn't do anything, Sheriff," he said mutinously. "Mrs. F wouldn't kill anybody."

Luke bent down, bringing their eyes level. "The police have to follow orders, Jorden. Just because Mrs. F has been arrested doesn't mean that she's guilty. They simply need to ask her more questions about what happened."

But Jorden was having none of it. "I know what happens when y'all arrest people. They go to jail and don't come back."

Before Luke could answer, Kell appeared behind Jorden and placed a comforting hand on his shoulder. Jorden glanced up, eyes welling with angry tears. "She can't go to jail. You've got to help her."

"I'll get her out, I swear."

Luke shot Kell a look that warned of lying to the boy. After all, Graves wasn't half in love with her. Willing to overlook procedure because of eyes the color of mink and a mind that could distract him from his duty. Rising, Luke gave Jorden a serious look. "I need you to trust me, Jorden. I won't let any harm come to Mrs. F and I'll do my best to bring her home." He extended his hand. "Will you trust me?"

Jorden glanced over his shoulder at Kell, then back at the sheriff. Reluctantly, he placed his hand in Luke's. "Yes, sir. Thank you, Sheriff."

"Run into the family room and tell Nina I'll be right back," Kell instructed with a squeeze to the thin shoulder beneath her hand. Jorden dashed away, leaving Kell and Luke in the foyer. Alone.

"You lied to me." The accusation was flat, cool.

Kell shook her head, a sensation suspiciously like loss crowding into her gut. She shunted it aside in favor of professional pride. "I didn't lie to you. I simply didn't break privilege and tell you what my client revealed to me."

"It's true, then? Graves does have a witness that heard her threaten Griffin."

She affirmed, "There was a fight, but Eliza didn't do this, Luke. We both know that regardless of what Graves has, his hands aren't clean either. He broke into the motel for a reason."

"To show me up and take my job," Luke ground out. "A job I don't appear capable of performing, given the current situation."

"Eliza is innocent," she protested, reaching out to him. When he evaded her touch, she dropped her hands to her sides. "She's innocent. You know that."

Luke stormed, "Maybe she is, but proving that is no longer in my control, is it? I know you couldn't break attorney-client privilege to tell me everything, but dammit, Kell, you owed me something. I put my neck out for Eliza, and the least you could have done was trusted me with a sliver of the truth."

"At what point in the time that I've known you should I have revealed that my client might have a motive for murder? When you learned that she probably had the only knife set capable of matching your evidence? Or maybe when we figured out the police chief might be involved?"

He was in no mood for logic. On some level, he'd thought they'd become real partners. Self-disgust spewed out. "I know that rather than do my job, I allowed myself to be sidetracked. Now, if Eliza isn't guilty, I've made proving that a hell of a lot harder by falling for you."

Panic skirted beneath the pride. "You haven't fallen for me. Three kisses don't make a relationship."

"No, they don't." Luke gave her a long, considering look. "Honesty and trust do, though. We've never given either a try, have we?"

Frozen, Kell watched him as he strode out the door and down the stairs to his truck. The engine roared as he circled the cul-de-sac and headed into town.

CHAPTER 21

In the family room, the inhabitants of the Faraday Center watched Kell with varying degrees of hope and futility. She did a quick headcount. Four on the couch, two on the loveseat, one sitting on Nina's lap in an over-sized armchair. All but one seat taken, Kell headed for an empty ottoman near the fireplace, searching for the right words to allay the alarm that enveloped the room. "Mrs. F is going to be okay," she began. "I need the younger children to go to your rooms so I can talk to the teenagers."

"They've arrested Mrs. F for murder," Nina inter-rupted harshly. "We all know what happened, Ms. Jameson. Don't treat us like regular children." A chorus of voices echoed her demand.

"Kell," she corrected mildly. She looked around, noting that while the youngest children were absent, several of the kids present hadn't yet reached puberty. "How old are you?" she asked the delicate girl seated on Nina's lap. Wispy blond bangs settled above corn-flower blue eyes, enhancing the air of fragility.

"Eight and a half," she replied timidly. "I'm Casey."

"And you?" Kell pointed at a lanky teenaged boy who leaned negligently against the wall. "Brandon, isn't it?

He shuffled uncomfortably. "Yeah. I'm fourteen."

Jorden piped up. "Kell, the police are wrong. Sheriff Luke said so. And we want to help Mrs. F. Wouldn't you?"

Despite their ages, Nina and Jorden were correct. These weren't normal children to be spared reality. They'd seen enough of human behavior to understand how the systems worked. Kell released a defeated breath. "Alright. Everyone can stay. But nobody talks about this to anyone outside the Center. Okay?"

Several heads nodded, echoing those who announced their agreement. Nina spoke up first. "Is the sheriff with Mrs. F?"

"Yes, he went with her to the station. As soon as I get you all settled in for the night, I'll call someone to come and stay with you, then I'll go down there myself."

"Do the police know about Clay hurting Nina?" asked Brandon.

"Yes." Kell rose and stood in front of the mantel. "Someone told Chief Graves that he came to the Center and tried to hurt her." She looked around the room ex-pectantly. "I have to know who told him. You won't be in trouble, but I must know."

"You're an adult. You might be trying to trick us."

The speaker was a girl, maybe thirteen, with caramel-toned skin and deep brown eyes rife with suspicion. The resemblance to Jorden was unmistakable. Kell recalled that her name was Faith. "I'm not."

"Why should we trust you?'

Trust had become a commodity in short supply lately, Kell thought derisively. But with good reason. She withheld information to protect those she loved, and she had no reason to expect these kids to do any less. "Because, Faith, I'm here to help Mrs. F."

"So?"

"So if I don't know the truth, I might get her in worse trouble." As she had tonight. Kell cast about for a way to earn their confidence. With a solemn look, she focused on Nina. "You understand attorney-client privilege, don't you?"

Nina nodded, turning to the group. "That's when a lawyer can't tell the cops or anyone else what you tell her. Like a pinky swear. If she breaks her promise, she gets in trouble and can't be a lawyer anymore."

Faith considered the deal. "I don't think anybody here told."

"No one?" Kell glanced at Brandon, who stared down at his shoes.

"I don't think so." Following her gaze, she shook her head forcefully. "Brandon wouldn't tell either." She marched up to Kell. "No one talks to the cops, ma'am. We just don't."

"Then how did the chief find out?"

Faith shot Nina a look and received a nearly imperceptible nod. "That day, Clay wasn't here alone. Tony and Doc were here too."

Nina bowed her head and muttered. "I wasn't supposed to let anyone come over while Mrs. F was running errands, but Tony just showed up."

"Is Tony your boyfriend?" She already knew the answer, but trust had to be earned on both sides.

"Kind of." Nina raised her eyes to Kell. "He's not like Doc or those guys he hangs around with. He's really smart. Likes school a lot, and he wants to be a lawyer like me."

"Tony's seventeen, right?"

"Yes, ma'am." Embarrassment flushed her cheeks. "We haven't done anything, if that's what you're thinking."

Kell offered a reassuring smile, aware of the rapt attention being paid to Nina's story. "That afternoon, Tony stopped by to say hello, correct?"

"Uh, huh. He was giving Doc a ride home. I went out to the car to say hello. Faith came with me."

Faith picked up the story. "Doc was acting weird, telling Tony that he had a meeting. Tony told him that if he was in such a rush, he could walk to the District."

"Doc took Tony's cell phone. I didn't know who he'd called at first," Nina continued. "Ten minutes later, Clay drives up."

"He had a Hummer," added Jorden.

"Black with chrome rims," another boy piped up, eager to contribute.

"When I realized Doc had called Clay, I sent every-one into the house." The green eyes flashed with re-membered anger. "Mrs. F told Clay not to come to the Center."

"How did you know?"

"I'm in charge when she's not here. Brandon and me."

"Why was Mrs. F angry with Clay?"

Brandon spoke up. "Because he tried to get Jorden and some of the other guys to deal for him," he ex-plained in a soft voice. "I stopped him, and I told Mrs. F."

Kell returned her attention to Nina, but Faith inter-jected. "I took everyone inside and Nina tried to make them leave."

"I told Clay and Tony to leave, and they said yes." Nina dropped her eyes. "I was stupid. Tony and Doc drove off first, then Clay. I stayed outside to pick up toys, and I heard another car. I thought it was Mrs. F."

"Clay had come back." Kell could guess the rest. "Then Mrs. F found you and Clay by the gazebo."

"Not just her. Tony and Doc too. When Clay didn't follow them, Tony came back. He helped Mrs. F stop—" Her voice broke and Casey wrapped her slender arms around Nina in comfort.

Briskly, Kell summarized, "Either Tony or Doc told the chief about Clay. Would Tony do that?"

"Absolutely not," Nina protested. "He swore we wouldn't talk about it to anyone. I believe him."

Having met the young man in question, Kell tended to agree. "Is there anything else that I need to know?"

"Mrs. F used to give Clay money," volunteered Jorden. "Envelopes full, once a month. Until he tried to hurt Nina."

Stunned, Kell tried to mask her amazement. "For how long?"

Faith shot Jorden a fulminating glance. "She stopped giving him money last month."

"When did she start?"

Nina hesitated, then answered, "At least as long as I've been here. Eight or nine years. Like clockwork."

Reluctantly, Faith confirmed, "We thought he worked here when we were little. The last Friday of every month, Clay would wait out by the kitchen. Mrs. F would pass him a white envelope and he'd count the money on the steps."

"Did he ever give her anything?" Kell probed quietly, afraid of the answer.

"Mrs. F wasn't buying drugs, Kell. She wouldn't do that." Nina frowned. "I assumed she was trying to help him out, since he used to be one of her kids. That makes sense, right?"

It did. But what worried Kell was that Eliza felt comfortable admitting to threatening him and to going to his apartment, but conveniently forgot to explain ten years of blackmail payments. She interlaced her fingers and lifted them beneath her chin. "Until I tell you to, no one is to mention this. Not to Sheriff Luke or the police or anyone else. If they ask you what you know, tell them you need to talk to me first, okay?"

Eight heads dipped in agreement. Nina tapped Casey's leg and the younger girl slid off her lap. Standing, she instructed, "Kell has to go to the station to see Mrs. F. Everyone go upstairs and get ready for bed. Faith and I will come and check on you in a few minutes. Brandon, go take a look at the little ones and make sure they're asleep."

Troops dispatched, Faith and Nina flanked Kell. "We can stay here by ourselves. Mrs. F doesn't like it, but between the two of us and Brandon, we're nearly forty- -five."

Kell chuckled appreciatively. "While I agree that you can handle yourselves, we should avoid giving the police any cause to question Mrs. F or the Center."

A knock sounded at the door, and Jorden yelled, "I'll get it."

Kell and the girls hurried from the room to stop him, but Jorden was jerking the door open when they arrived.

Curly stood on the doorstep, cap in hand. "Sheriff told me the young'n's needed a babysitter." He grinned at Jorden. "Shouldn't you be in bed already? Or has there been some excitement around here?"

Waving him in, Kell sent warning looks to the trio. "The kids are upstairs getting into bed and these three are on their way. I'll be gone a few hours, most likely."

"Take your time, Miss Kell. I'll just find me an old movie on the television and wait until you can bring Eliza home."

"Are you sure this is okay?"

"Curly watches us whenever Mrs. F has to be out of town," Faith explained. "I'll get your foot tub."

"One glass of lemonade coming up." Jorden raced out of the foyer and into the kitchen.

Nina smiled reassuringly at Kell as she headed up the stairs. "It's okay, Kell. He does this a lot."

Kell regarded the situation dubiously. The Curly Watson she remembered was a curmudgeon who despised children. "When did you have the change of heart, Curly? You never used to like kids."

"Back then, I wasn't courtin' Miss Eliza." He gave Kell a wink. "That's our little secret, okay?"

"Not the first one I've learned tonight." Kell retrieved her purse from the kitchen and briefly updated Curly. "I plan to wait at the station until I find out if she'll be arraigned tomorrow."

"Tomorrow's Saturday. Judge Majors doesn't hold court then."

"Eliza's not spending the weekend in jail."

"If anyone can spring her, you and Luke can." He sobered suddenly. "If Graves gets away with this, he'll try to run Luke out of town next. You can't let that happen."

"I won't. Luke's not going to lose his job because he did the right thing." Not again.

"Good, good." Curly smiled and gave her a none-too-gentle shove out the door. "Go earn your money, girl."

Across town, Luke pounded on an ornate door inset with glass and etched with swirls. He ignored the brass knocker and discreet doorbell in favor of brute force. White hair appeared in the glass inset, above a wrinkled face that had been burned by the sun more than once. "Luke Calder? What in the devil's unholy name are you doing at my house at one in the morning?"

"I came to see the judge, Dr. Majors. It's urgent."

"It had better be a matter of life or death, or I'm liable to make it one," he retorted gruffly. "Mary? Come on down. It's not a robber, just a lunatic sheriff."

Judge Majors appeared on the landing, hair covered in a pink satin cap. "Sheriff Calder, what are you doing here?"

"Trying to find out why you issued a warrant for the search of Eliza Faraday's home without consulting me."

She descended the steps, silent until she stood beside her husband. With a withering voice, she replied, "I wasn't aware that I required your permission to execute my duties, Sheriff."

"When you give another office a search warrant for one of my cases, I'd like to think I'm entitled to the courtesy of notice."

A scowl formed between her brows. "Your case? Chief Graves assured me that he held jurisdiction over the Griffin murder. He showed me an autopsy report. Plus an eyewitness statement."

"My report. My case." He decided not to respond to the issue of the statement, since he'd yet to read it, though he figured his copy was in the envelope Graves gave him. Assuming it did support the chief's position, he was curious about the source.

The judge noted the omission, but did not comment.

Instead, she asked, "Were you not preparing to search the Center?"

"No, ma'am. I had another angle I wanted to pursue first."

"And where is Eliza now?"

"Based on Graves's theory of the case, he arrested her for murder. She's being booked as we speak."

Judge Majors tapped her mouth. "I can't do anything tonight, Luke." She held up a hand when he began to argue. "But I will convene a special session of court tomorrow at ten A.M. for her bail hearing."

"Thank you, Judge."

"Don't thank me yet. Based on what I read this afternoon, I don't think the warrant was an overreach by the chief."

"If she's guilty, Judge, I won't stand in the way of prosecution. But I'm not sure she is," he said flatly. "However, what about jurisdiction? Can Graves just step in?"

"The murder occurred at the Palace, correct?"

"Yes, ma'am."

"That motel, if I recall correctly, straddles the city line."

"But the room itself is in the county," he argued.

"Perhaps," she cautioned, "but you don't come to this argument with clean hands, Sheriff. The chief tried to tell me his observations about your relationship with Kell Jameson."

Luke stiffened. "I've done nothing to compromise my investigation."

"Perhaps," she repeated firmly, "however, I'd ask

you to consider whether you can be more helpful to the delivery of justice by fighting over jurisdiction or by completing your investigation." She inclined her head, and walked him toward the door. "I'll see you in court tomorrow morning, Sheriff Calder. Good luck."

CHAPTER 22

Officer Potter showed Kell into the waiting room with efficient courtesy. "Mrs. Faraday is completing processing. She'll be allowed to speak with you shortly."

"Thank you, officer." Kell sat in the folding chair he indicated and laid her briefcase on the metal table. Her client would sit on the opposite side, facing the two-way mirror that ran the length of the wall. She noted a speaker in the upper left-hand corner of the room. Apparently, a lawyer meets her clients in the same room that interrogations take place. Convenient for the police, a nightmare for the defense. Something she'd keep in mind.

For now, she smiled wanly at the officer. "Officer Potter, may I trouble you for some water, please?"

"Right away, ma'am." He zipped from the room, leaving the door to swing shut behind him.

Kell understood the routine of awaiting clients

in the sterile confines of a police precinct. The act of taking fingerprints and filling out index cards of vital, yet ultimately useless, information filled hours of a cop's time. Forms typed in triplicate to travel with personal effects, to record the breaking of a case on pages to be sent along to the prosecutor. Case files built from such small matters, like the weight of a suspect or his tendency to limp as he walked. In Kell's world, those pages contained nuggets of gold, that when displayed properly before a judge or jury resulted in acquittal—usually in the form of reasonable doubt.

She relied on the sloppiness of overwork, the drudgery of habit for a blank to be missed or a sheet to be overlooked.

She doubted that would work this time.

Her client had no alibi, perfect motive, and kept the means sitting on her kitchen counter. Rubbing at her eyes, Kell plotted her next move. She'd find out where Judge Majors lived and beg the judge to hold an early bond hearing and set a fast trial calendar. By then, hopefully Luke's pique would have passed, and he'd be willing to resume their sleuthing. Eliza's main hope of freedom rested on determining who else wanted Clay Griffin dead.

Officer Potter reentered the room, a bottle of water in hand, as well as a napkin. He set both on the table. "Need anything else?"

"Is Sheriff Calder around?"

"He's at the front desk. Should I tell him you're here?"

"Yes, please." She twisted the cap on the water and took a long drink. Talking to Luke was necessary, and she didn't expect him to make the next few minutes easy.

As she wiped her mouth, the door swung open. Luke walked in, holding an identical bottle. He gave her a dispassionate look that betrayed nothing. "They've got Eliza in processing."

"Officer Potter told me. How long until I can see her?"

He flipped the second chair around to straddle the seat. "Fifteen minutes, probably. Graves keeps three men on shift at a time. He demanded Lancy take him to the county hospital for X rays."

"You have a solid right hook."

"He's got a weak face."

Kell smiled, but sobered when Luke did not return her tentative smile. All business, she acknowledged, an ache forming in her chest. He was livid, she understood, but he had to know she was doing her job. Protecting her client.

"Does the chief respect the privacy of the counsel interview?" she questioned, eyes edging to the mirror.

"Yes. He's not that stupid." Luke opened his water, swigging half the contents at once. He swiped at his mouth and offered in a low voice that signaled he didn't completely agree with his own analysis, "I've talked to Judge Majors. She's agreed to hold a bond hearing for Eliza in the morning."

Pleased, Kell asked, "Did you discuss jurisdiction?"

"Yes. And jurisdiction is a question at issue that she

doesn't intend to take sides on. The location of the motel gives Graves plenty of cause to follow any leads he sees fit."

Including a possible conflict of interest between the sheriff and the chief suspect's attorney. Kell skimmed her eyes over his tight mouth and icy gaze. The witness statement would have to come up eventually. "Do you want to know about the witnesses, Sheriff?"

He inclined his head. "For a change of pace."

Smarting, Kell explained softly, "The afternoon that Clay died, he attacked Nina Moore at the Center." Luke straightened, and Kell placed a hand over his, drawing him back. When he slipped his hand free, she put hers in her lap. "She's fine. Eliza arrived home in time to stop him from doing more than scaring her. But there were two eyewitnesses to the scuffle. Tony Delgado and his friend Doc Reed."

"Tony was visiting Nina."

Kell filled him in on the story of the attack, writing notes on a legal pad. She decided to keep the payoffs to Clay to herself for the moment, a choice that gave her conscience a twinge. She hated to lie to him again, but until she heard from Eliza, it wasn't her information to share.

"My guess is that Doc is Chief Graves's informant. If Doc helped Clay sell drugs, he'd also probably have been brought in on whatever Clay'd gotten into next. He has a reason to try and pin the murder on someone else."

"Doc's a petty criminal," Luke mused. "He doesn't have the brains to orchestrate a cover-up. If he'd been at Clay's apartment that night, I promise you, he'd have stolen the television and video game."

"Then either Graves is heading this up, or he's working with the people who are. Luke, can I assume you still believe Eliza?"

"For now," he yielded. "Graves is working too hard to make her look guilty." Luke sent her a baleful look. "You've helped."

"Yes. I did. Still, we can't keep having this fight, Luke. I maintained client confidentiality," she sighed, pinning him with a look of exasperation. "I'll admit I didn't tell you everything. Neither did you. For good reason. Until tonight, we had very separate agendas. And we may have them again."

Knowing she was right didn't soothe the raw feeling of betrayal. He imagined they'd gotten closer, that she wouldn't have let him be blindsided by Graves and the powerful ammunition he carried. But he'd entered this arrangement with his eyes wide open. "What do you suggest we do?"

"Exactly what we have. Share relevant information and work together to find out who wants Eliza in prison for murder."

"We have to assume Eliza knows something or has something they want. Either that or she's simply a convenient scapegoat."

"Convenient? They used a specialty knife that could be traced back to her and almost no one else."

"Then there's another reason for targeting her that you're not telling me."

Kell bristled. "I've told you everything I can, Luke."

Which, she thought desperately, wasn't exactly a lie. The money and missing murder weapon weren't her secrets to reveal. Not when Luke still harbored a shadow of doubt.

"I guess that will have to do for now." He swung his leg around and stood. Rounding the table, he bent close to her ear. "Graves may have pissed me off, but he was right. I have compromised my judgment. I adore Eliza, and I'm falling in love with you."

Her mouth opened, and he nipped at her ear, a brief jet of sensation that would have buckled her knees, had she been standing. "Fair warning, Kell. I won't forget dinner or our interrupted dessert. Neither should you."

Before she could respond, he stood up and strode out.

She was still sitting in the same position when Potter brought Eliza into the room. "Thirty minutes," he explained, "then lights out for all prisoners."

Eliza winced at the description, taking the seat Luke had abandoned. "Who's minding the children?"

"Curly Watson came over. He told me he's watched them before."

A pretty blush crept into the pale cheeks. "He's a very good friend."

"Another secret you've been keeping, Mrs. F."

"I beg your pardon?"

"A relationship with Mr. Watson. Paying Clay Griffin blackmail." Kell shifted forward, incensed. "What you do with your love life is your business, Mrs. F, but you should have told me about the money."

The older woman met her furious gaze with look of equanimity. Calmly, she asked, as though seeking the time, "How did you find out?"

Her ire rose at the banal inquiry, and Kell explained angrily, "You have very observant children. According to Nina, these payments have been going on for nearly a decade."

"More like sixteen years." Eliza held Kell's accusing glare without flinching. "I made the first payment in September 1991."

Kell fell back against her chair, terror racing through her, displacing outrage. "No."

"Clay came to see me a few weeks after you and Findley disappeared. Told me he'd seen you three in the area near the fire and that he had proof you were somehow involved." She kept her voice low, intent. "Julia was still under my care. I couldn't allow him to ruin her life. So I gave him the money."

Her stomach hitched, another layer of guilt churning acid. A silly act, a desperate choice cascading across the years. In a dull voice, she asked, "How much to protect us?"

"The first time? Five hundred dollars. A paltry sum for my children," she explained fiercely. Eliza gripped her chin and forced her to look at her. "Wherever you were—are—you're mine, Kell. Always."

The words eased but didn't erase the shame. "When did he come back?"

"October. Said that he'd be visiting every month for as long as I wanted him to stay silent. The payments got bigger every year, and he got greedier." Eliza focused on the wall behind Kell's head, debating. Sighing, she went on. "After you won your first big case, he brought me a copy of a news article about you. He demanded a thousand dollars."

"Four years ago?" Kell quickly did the math. "That's almost fifty thousand dollars since then." She blanched at the sum, thinking about the funds moldering in a bank vault. Her car, her wardrobe cost more. All owed to Mrs. F. Everything. "How in the world did you pay him? Why didn't you call me? You don't have that kind of money."

"Actually, I do." Eliza managed a short laugh at the look of amazement. "Didn't you ever wonder how I managed to operate the Center? I don't fundraise or solicit donations, and one of my conditions for accepting children is that I will not take aid from the state."

"I guess I never really thought about it," she admitted dazedly. "Where's the money coming from?"

"My family. I have a substantial trust fund that's administered by a foundation established by my great-grandparents. The Metanoia Foundation. It holds the land and produces a respectable income."

"Land besides the Center?"

"I own the six hundred acres the town knows as the Grove and another five thousand acres between Hallden and Taylor County."

"My God." Kell took a shaky drink of water. "You're rich."

"I have adequate income for my needs," Eliza conceded. "Though the land is not in use. My parents were early environmentalists. They refused to allow the land to be harvested, and I have respected their wishes."

"Where is the money from, then?"

"Wise investments in the stock market after the Great Depression, plus a few companies my mother seeded with her capital." She folded her hands primly on the cold metal surface. "Paying Clay would not be motive for murder, dear. I had the money to spend."

"And then some," mumbled Kell.

"However, after Clay's attack on Nina, I did go to his apartment to tell him that if I ever saw him near the Center again, the payments would cease. But I never got the chance."

"Does anyone else know about these payments besides the children and you?"

"I don't know if Clay told anyone, but I doubt it. The foundation is administered by a bank. The account manager would be aware of my regular withdrawals, but not their purpose. I draw monthly amounts of substantial size, so the payments wouldn't be noticeable. I do not have to account for my actions, but there would be a record of them."

"Who are the trustees for the foundation?"

"I am the sole trustee, under the trust's terms. The Georgia Bank manages the trust, according to my wishes."

Kell noted the bank name on her pad. "What happens to the foundation once you're—"

"I will die eventually, Kell. You can say it."

"What happens?"

"I've willed that the money remain in the trust for the operation of the Center. The Center inherits my fortune, since I am the last of my line."

"And if you go to prison?"

"I don't know." Eliza frowned, her eyes shadowed with fresh worry. "I've never asked."

CHAPTER 23

For a Saturday morning, the Hallden County Courthouse was packed. No fewer than two reporters from
the local paper had been dispatched to record the
proceedings. Cameras typically filming county fair
competitions or weekend fender-benders set up in
the hastily created press section of the courtroom.
Curious neighbors who'd awoken to the latest gossip
crowded in pews that rarely held more than a dozen
or so watchers.

Kell muscled her way through the knots of onlook-
ers who clogged the aisles. Three hours of sleep had
her bleary-eyed and her temper on a short leash. She'd
been awoken at six by Nina, who reminded her that she
was responsible for placing a healthy meal on the table
by seven. Curly had taken his leave around three A.M.,
which left Kell on her own.

Luckily, the kitchen came well stocked with a variety of cereals and assorted fruit. Even better, Cheryl

Richardson appeared at eight with her sons in tow and a reprieve. After dispatching the children for morning chores and bringing Cheryl up to speed, she'd sprinted through a shower, a hasty bowl of cereal, and shimmied into her battle armor. The charcoal St. John, with its conservative hem, was matched with black pearls at her ears and throat. Power heels from Ferragamo completed the look and earned her a whistle of envy from Cheryl as she rushed out the door.

A scan of the room revealed a preening Chief Graves talking with a reporter, arm gesticulating impassionedly. He stood at the prosecution's table, next to a lean man with a clean-shaven scalp that towered over his squat frame. She admired the perfectly shaped bronze dome, as few men handled the look well. Kell couldn't see his face, but she assumed he represented the D.A.'s office.

She didn't need to look around to know Luke wasn't there.

Pushing aside the bitter ache of disappointment, she cut across a row of seats and came out on the far aisle. She was in sight of the defense table when a reporter caught her eye and waved a microphone in her direction. Light flashed as bulbs popped in her direction. "Is it true that Eliza Faraday killed Clay Griffin in a lover's quarrel?"

Hearing the shouted question, another one barked out, "Are you having an affair with Sheriff Calder? Is that why Chief Graves had to take over the case?"

"Is Sheriff Calder going to resign his post pending an investigation?"

Kell dropped her briefcase on the table and turned to the gathering bank of cameras. Most lawyers attempted to belay the inquisition with "no comments" or simply brushed off the press. But she knew better that a reporter with answers tended to list toward your side. Give them short, pithy answers or quotable phrases. Never affirm what you could reasonably deny. And always take the tough questions. Potential jurors appreciated what appeared to be honesty and journalists got higher ratings. A win-win.

She faced the camera fronted by a slender woman of indeterminate years, which Kell guessed placed her at about forty-five. The sleek bob of black hair framed a clever honey-toned face that seemed to expect resistance and hungered for it. Kell assumed the question about Luke had come from her. "Yes?"

"Ayanay Ferguson of Channel 13. Is it true that Chief Graves removed jurisdiction of this case from Sheriff Calder because of a cover-up involving you and the sheriff?"

Kell's eyes hardened, but she avoided the instinctive defense of Luke or herself. The first moment she kissed him, she'd put her reputation in jeopardy. So be it. But her client was Eliza. "Eliza Faraday has dedicated her life to the service of Hallden's most vulnerable children. I find it abhorrent that one man's quest for power should be built on flimsy evidence and nasty rumor." Unable to resist, she added, "Jurisdiction has not been transferred. While I understand the Attorney General is looking into the propriety of the police department's actions, my concern isn't with who arrested my client. It's why. The evidence we've seen so far calls into the question the competence of the police department or what they consider reasonable suspicion. Apparently, Chief Graves found a crumb and decided to call it a loaf."

Amused but unconvinced, Ayanay shoved her microphone forward. "Do you deny having an affair with Sheriff Calder?"

"Unequivocally," Kell replied shortly. What hadn't happened before would certainly never happen now. "Next question?"

A man she recognized as the anchor for Channel 7 pressed through the pack. "Was the defendant having an affair with Clay Griffin?"

"No. And I'd strongly recommend that you check your source." She glared in Graves's direction, and heads swiveled to follow. "I'd also remind everyone that this is an election year for an ambitious man who saw the job of his dreams taken away four years ago. Due diligence requires examining every possible motive, for this heinous murder and for the vicious prosecution of a pillar of the community."

Out of the corner of her eye, Kell saw Eliza being led into the courtroom and lifted her hands. "Judge Majors agreed to a Saturday arraignment due to the highly unusual witch-hunt instigated by Chief Graves. I would only ask that my client be given the benefit of due process and a chance to clear her name."

Officer Potter guided Eliza to the table and dispersed

the reporters to their pen. Eliza settled into her chair, spine stiff, face drawn.

"Did you get any sleep at all?" Kell asked in a hushed tone.

"A wink or two." She turned to Kell. "Did the children do their chores?"

"Yes, ma'am. Cheryl Richardson brought her boys over to play with them, and she'll stay until we can take you home." Kell patted the hand balled into a fist on her lap, worried at the whitened knuckles. For all her calm, Eliza was terrified. "We'll get you out of here today."

"Do your best," came the subdued response.

The tone of defeat worried Kell more than the bags hanging beneath fatigued hazel eyes or the clenched fists. She searched for words to bolster Eliza's spirits, but the bailiff entered the gallery.

"All rise." The bailiff, a veteran of thirty years, had only seen one other case draw so much attention. On that day too, Eliza Faraday was in the courthouse. But not as the defendant. He gave his assistant the signal, and the judge appeared on the dais behind her chair.

"You may be seated." Judge Mary Majors instructed from her wide leather chair, hand-picked when she first took the bench. Luxury and comfort mattered, especially when meting out justice. A judge distracted by discomfort or personal issues became insular and overlooked the minutiae that made judges necessary. Just as importantly, she appreciated the supple give of the upholstery, its silent glide as she closed the distance between herself and the court.

Eliza started to sit, but Kell tapped her elbow in warning. On the other side of the courtroom, the prosecutor remained at attention.

Judge Majors gave a signal to the bailiff. "Mr. Mundy."

"Docket number 780-R–491, the *State v. Eliza Faraday*."

"Caleb Matthews for the State," announced the prosecutor.

"Kell Jameson for the defense."

Judge Majors bent forward, eyes steady and impassive. "The defendant is present and in custody. I'll hear from the People on bail."

The prosecutor folded his hands behind him. "Clay Griffin was brutally stabbed to death in his apartment, Your Honor. The defendant was heard threatening the deceased earlier that afternoon. She also owns the only locally known set of the weapon used in the murder." He stopped speaking, and Chief Graves reached over the railing separating them, hissing instructions. Graves jabbed a finger in Kell's direction. Caleb jerked his elbow free and returned his attention to the court. "Sorry, Your Honor."

"Does the State have something to add?" Irritation at the misbehavior coated the question.

"No. We ask that the defendant be held without bail until trial."

"Chief Graves appears to disagree with you," she prompted. "Is there additional information the State would like to offer the Court?"

"No, Your Honor."

"Defense?"

"Eliza Faraday has a spotless record, Your Honor. Her career is serving children, and without her presence at the Center, their lives will be put at risk."

Judge Majors reclined slightly. "Overstating the matter a tad, aren't you, Counselor?"

"If I stray into hyperbole, Your Honor, it is simply zealous defense of my client's good name. The purported witness statements come from former drug dealers associated with Mr. Griffin, and I would argue are not reliable."

"We're not at trial, Ms. Jameson. Please stick with arguments relevant to the matter of bail."

The reproach stung, but Kell adjusted. "What is known, however, is that Eliza has lived in Hallden for nearly her entire life and does not pose a flight risk."

Caleb interjected, "This is a second-degree murder case, Your Honor. Holding the defendant in custody is customary."

"Customary but not mandatory," Kell reminded the court. "This case and this defendant deserve the benefit of Your Honor's doubt. However, we would not be opposed to a high bail, to satisfy the People's concern."

Judge Majors studied Eliza, mouth pursed in consideration. "Bail is set at $1 million, cash or bond."

"Your Honor," Kell spoke quickly before the gavel could fall. "The defense requests a preliminary hearing be set to dispose of this matter before more damage can be done."

"The State agrees," Caleb said, surprising Kell with his concurrence. "If it pleases the Court."

"The defendant is not being held in custody, Counselor. A preliminary hearing will be set within thirty days, as the law requires."

"Excuse me, Your Honor, but given the precipitous nature of the State's case, we'd request a speedier hearing. My client would like to have this specter removed as quickly as possible." More importantly, Kell needed to know what else the prosecution had in its quiver.

"Be careful what you wish for, Ms. Jameson. I have a room on my calendar for this Tuesday, or your client will have to wait until October. Your choice."

Tuesday? Three days to prepare for a probable-cause hearing without her team or the mountains of resources she typically had at her command. Eliza tensed beside her, and she knew the decision was out of her hands. "We'll take Tuesday, Your Honor."

"Preliminary hearing is set for Tuesday, September twenty-third. Court dismissed." The gavel sounded and the judge disappeared into chambers.

Eliza released a pent-up breath, her body sagging for an instant. "I can go home?"

"Yes, as soon as we can post bail." Kell gathered her materials, including the bond paperwork she'd arranged earlier using one of Eliza's accounts. She'd fret over her rash decision to move ahead with the hearing later. Since it seemed the day to take chances, she faced Eliza. "I need your permission to do something."

"You're not a child, Kell. You haven't needed my permission in quite a while."

"For this, I do." She met Eliza's questioning look squarely. "I want to tell Luke what you told me last night. All of it."

"If you think it's best. Alright."

Kell frowned. "That quickly. You don't want to know why? You're not worried?"

"Kell, my dear, you don't place faith in others easily. If Luke has earned your confidence, then he has mine. I've known him for quite a while now, and I know he's someone I can rely on. I'm simply pleased you agree."

Pressing her hand to Eliza's cheek, she advised, "Thanks, Mrs. F. I have a bondsman on standby. I'll have you at the Center and back to the children by lunch."

Chief Graves stormed around Assistant D.A. Matthews's office, voice raised in outrage. "Why the hell didn't you tell the judge about Jameson and Calder?"

"Because it wasn't relevant."

"Not relevant?" Graves squealed. "It proves that I had to take over the case. And that Calder can't be trusted."

"Jurisdiction isn't my concern, Chief. I'm responsible for prosecution—no matter who brings me the case."

The even temper stoked his rage higher. Impotently, Graves growled, "It's your fault she's out on bail. Cross me again, and I'll have you prosecuting jaywalkers and litterbugs."

For his part, Caleb Matthews reclined in his seat, unperturbed. Michael Graves reminded him of a law professor he'd once had. A Napoleon of a man convinced of his native superiority, a belief belied by all available evidence. On his desk, the Faraday file lay open to the eyewitness statement, supplied by Graves. "When you've finished your tantrum, perhaps we can review the case file."

"Tantrum? Why you pissant! When the D.A. hears about this—"

"By the time the D.A. hears about this, he won't interfere," Caleb reminded Graves solemnly. "He's on vacation in Aruba for three weeks, which means you'll have to deal with me. And let me explain how I work." He lifted a sheet from the file. "Statements should be notarized. I don't introduce evidence that has your signature as the witness."

Graves protested, "I always sign witness statements."

"Not in my cases. This statement will need to be retaken. I'd be happier if it were corroborated by someone who didn't refer to himself as 'Doc.'"

"He's my witness."

"Then I'll expect you to have the notarized versions in my office on Monday. Jameson is taking a gamble on a Tuesday prelim, which leads me to think she knows something we don't."

"She's bluffing," Graves asserted confidently. "She didn't know about the eyewitness last night. Her entire strategy has been about boffing the sheriff."

Caleb ignored the remark, masking his distaste. Instead, he riffled through the file until he reached the autopsy report. "This is a copy of the autopsy. Where's the tox screen or the lab report?"

"I haven't received that from Calder yet," Graves answered stiffly. "I told you, he's engaged in a cover-up."

"Because he didn't share his evidence with you?"

"Because he's boning the defense attorney and doesn't want her client to go to jail."

Fed up with the snide remarks, Caleb demanded, "Do you have proof of a relationship between Sheriff Calder and Ms. Jameson?"

"I will have it. It's just a matter of time."

"Until I receive incontrovertible proof, no more mention of an affair will be made to the press or to the court."

"You can't tell me what to do."

"You're right. I can't. But I can ask the court for a gag order to prevent you from talking. Break it and the judge will hold you in contempt of court."

"Whose side are you on?"

"I work for the people, Chief Graves. Same as you." He thumped the evidence file once. "You made a premature arrest on circumstantial evidence. You don't have the murder weapon, you don't have a provable motive, and you've made the defendant seem sympathetic."

"I have not."

"Attacking a woman who takes care of orphans and accusing her of killing a drug dealer. If the public doesn't see her as the victim instead of Griffin already, it's simply a matter of time. I've seen Kell Jameson work. By jumping the gun on this, you've given her first blood in the media war."

"We're in Hallden. Not Atlanta."

"Doesn't matter. People will be riveted, and now they have to choose sides. The grandmother who rescues abandoned children or the drug dealer who"—he picked up the witness statement—"apparently tried to rape one of her kids." He tossed the page down onto the desk. "The best hope we have of conviction is that you do manage to find a murder weapon and another witness who doesn't have a rap sheet as long as this one does."

Graves caviled, "If you think we'll lose, why did you agree to an early p.c. date?"

"Strategy. A Tuesday hearing on probable cause gives Jameson less time to win over the jury. As a matter of fact, my first motion will definitely be for a gag order." Graves sputtered, and Caleb held up his hand. "It makes sense. She's superb on television."

"Then I'll tell our side of the story."

Caleb cleared his throat. "With all due respect, you're way outside her league." He reached for a second folder, with Luke Calder's name on the tab. "Sheriff Calder's service record was on my desk. I assume you provided it?"

"He's been involved in a cover-up before. No reason he wouldn't do it again."

"The shooting in Chicago. Yes, I read it. According to the report, he was cleared of wrongdoing."

"Then why did he quit his job and move across the country?" Smirking, Graves smacked at the report. "A wrong cop is always wrong. He let his men get killed and now he's letting that girl cloud his judgment."

"Maybe." Caleb examined the folder thoughtfully. "Find me proof of an affair, and I'll bring it to the judge."

"Good. Very good."

CHAPTER 24

Luke scanned the crime lab report a third time, absorbing even less than his first two passes. Coffee, gone lukewarm, slid down his throat with the jolt of caffeine he required after a sleepless night. Recriminations chased frustration, snarled with an impotent rage. Graves had stepped over a line Luke never should have drawn. Still, in an endless loop, he played the last two weeks in his mind, trying to decide what he'd have done differently.

He rejected every scenario that ended with avoiding Kell.

In his gut, he didn't buy the evidence against Eliza, strong as it was. As a cop, his job was dispassionate observation, but that was a crock. Cases required strong feelings, instinct as much as evidence. And instinct screamed that Graves's zeal to pin the murder on Eliza had nothing to do with law enforcement.

"So what else is there?" he muttered. Hopefully,

he'd find the answer in the chemistry report, assuming he could focus long enough to decipher its conclusions. This morning, he'd burned through his store of favors to get a fax of the preliminary findings. Downing the rest of his coffee, he forced himself to concentrate on the lab tech's analysis. Then he saw it. "Bingo."

He grabbed the phone and punched in the number to the Center. Jorden answered on the first ring. "Faraday Center."

"Jorden, is Kell there?"

"Yes, sir. She brought Mrs. F home like she promised. You wanna talk to her?"

"Please." Focused now, he reviewed the tech's description of the evidence bag he'd sent along. More tests would be forthcoming, but his initial theory had Luke springing up from his chair and shoving his gun into the holster.

"Luke?"

"Put on some jeans and sneakers. I'll be out to pick you up in fifteen minutes." Without giving her a chance to respond, he hung up the phone. Swinging through his door, he called out, "If Chief Graves stops by, lock the doors."

En route, he dialed Curly. The obscene greeting brought a grin. "Long night?"

"Had me playing nanny until the crack of dawn. What do you want now?"

"Property records. I'm heading out to County Road, Route one-forty-eight. Find out who owns all that land between Hallden County and Taylor."

"Any particular name I'm looking for?"

"Not yet. But if a name pops out at you, do a background check for me."

"Will do." Curly frowned into the phone. "Watch your back, Luke. Graves is serious about this one."

"I know. Hopefully in a few hours I'll know why."

"Thanks for coming, Kell." Luke drove away from the Center. "I appreciate it."

"Where are we going, exactly?" Kell asked, still a bit groggy. She'd lain down for a power nap, only to have Jorden banging on her door with a message from Luke. Despite the summons, she'd been waiting when he arrived and taken up her now-regular post in his truck. "Did you learn something new?"

"Curly found some information that might help Eliza." Before she could interrogate him, he continued, "I hear Caleb Matthews agreed to a hearing in on Tuesday?"

"Yes," she answered. "He seems to be confident."

"Matthews is good. So good, I'm surprised you were able to get bail posted so fast." He nodded approvingly. "Eliza must have been relieved."

"She'll be relieved when all of this disappears." When her reputation no longer lay in tatters to be picked over by a press that typically covered nothing more exciting than a failed bank robbery. "The kids are anxious. The younger ones keep crying, and the others are afraid to speak. They don't trust that I'll save her."

"They don't trust the system," Luke corrected. "She's been their bedrock, and now she's shaken."

"I know. I know." Kell rested her head on the seat, eyes closed against the afternoon sun. "I've never seen her like this. So—diminished. Mrs. F is a bulldog. But watching her in court today, she seemed frail. Almost broken.

"Graves has threatened everything she holds dear. The Center. You."

"Me." Me and Fin and Julia, still causing her grief, she thought despondently. "I can't let him do this to her, Luke. It's not right."

"If this were another case, another client, what would you do?"

"I'd break their story. Find witnesses to undo theirs, hire experts to contradict the ones they put up."

"So we'll do that." Luke caught her hand, and her eyes fluttered open. He kept his attention on the road, his words calm and certain. "I'm in, Kell. Completely."

Moved, she asked, "What about Graves? The election? This isn't just about Eliza. He's trying to destroy you too."

"That means you'll have to do a hell of a job."

"What can you tell me about Caleb Matthews?"

"Assistant D.A. Straight arrow, doesn't play games."

"All lawyers play games," Kell scoffed.

"Well, fewer games than most. He's up from Brunswick. Been in Hallden for a year or so."

"He doesn't seem to care for Graves. Had a dust-up in court."

"About what?"

"You and me, I think. Graves appeared irritated

when the D.A. only mentioned the witnesses and not that other stuff."

"Our delayed affair?"

"We're not having an affair."

"Not for lack of my trying," Luke quipped without amusement.

Kell muffled a laugh at the note of irritation. "Where are we going, Luke?"

He gestured out the window. Stands of pine rolled past as the truck bumped along the county road. "According to the lab report, the material I found on Clay's hand and in his boots came from a wood-processing facility. Pine and other wood refuse. The stuff on his hands has tested as an alcohol, only thicker. I thought it smelled like pine."

"Pine-scented alcohol?" Kell tried to recall her chemistry classes from high school. "Could it have been a cleanser?"

"A janitor's job that paid enough for a Hummer?"

"What's your theory?" she countered.

"I'm not sure. Which is why we're going to see where Tony did his interview."

"We're looking for a mysterious office in the middle of the woods."

"Hopefully, Curly will call in a few minutes with some help to narrow it down."

"Help?"

"I asked Curly and Cheryl to pull property reports on this land out here."

Kell flinched, nearly invisibly. But Luke, who'd

become attuned to her every expression, caught the re-action. "What is it?"

"I think I have to tell you something else."

Resigned, Luke rolled his eyes. Without another word, he slowed the truck and pulled to the side of the road. The asphalt was empty of cars, had been for the last twenty miles. He gritted his teeth, preparing. "Tell me what?"

Kell wondered about her decision, and the conse-quences for holding back. He claimed to care about Eliza, to be falling in love with her. Worry about making the wrong turn for Eliza bumped squarely into an emotion she refused to name. She, who made a career of bold decisions, feared that her choice in the next few minutes would alter all of their lives. But if he was in—truly in—then she owed him as much of the truth as she could spare. Shifting to face him, she confessed, "Two things. Neither will sound good, but you have to know that Eliza didn't do this."

"I've placed my career on the line, Kell. If I didn't think that she was innocent, Graves wouldn't have been in court today. I would have."

He might still, she thought, casting her mind about for another tack. Nothing occurred. In for a penny, she decided bleakly. "First of all, the land is owned by a foundation. The Metanoia Foundation."

"Metanoia Foundation?" He tried to recall ever hear-ing the name, but drew a blank. "How do you know they own the land?"

"Because Eliza Faraday is the sole beneficiary."

"And when did you learn this gem?" he asked, his voice bland, eyes dangerous.

"Last night. This morning, I mean." She took a breath and plunged. In self-defense, she fixated on a spot outside her window. "When she told me that Clay has been blackmailing her for years. Sixteen years."

"Blackmail." He repeated the word, softly, ominously. Knuckles tightened until bone stretched skin. "Is there anything else?"

His calm acceptance raced a chill along her spine. Before she could regret it, she spit out, "The murder weapon. I know where it is. Or, where it was."

"Where was it?"

"In the Center. Mrs. F had it, but it was stolen the night of the break-in."

The explosion she braced for didn't come. After several seconds passed, she twisted to face him, confused. "Did you hear me?"

"Yes."

"And?" She tried to read his expression, but the taut face was blank. Tight mahogany skin stretched over the high cheekbones and along the squared jaw, revealing nothing. "Luke?"

"And what, Kell? What do you want to hear me say?"

Concerned, she touched the back of his hand, startled when he slipped it out of reach. "I'd like to know what you think."

He faced her then, eyes flickering with disdain, and she thought she glimpsed a flash of hurt.

Incredulity dripped from his words. "What I think?

I'm absolutely certain that you don't actually believe I can think. Because if you gave me credit for a single brain cell, we'd be having a different conversation."

She scrubbed a weary hand over her eyes and reminded him, "I only found out about the foundation this morning at the jail. This is the first opportunity I've had to tell you."

"And the murder weapon? When did you learn Eliza had stashed it in the Center?"

"Earlier."

"So, Eliza was at the crime scene the night Clay died. But she didn't kill him."

"No. She panicked, Luke. That night, she did go to see Clay to tell him she wouldn't be paying the blackmail any longer. After he attacked Nina, she refused to give him anymore. She drove to the motel, went to his apartment. She said the door wasn't closed completely, and she heard sounds." She broke off, trying to read his reaction.

He betrayed nothing, simply motioned for her to continue.

"She entered the apartment and saw him lying on the floor. She tried to help him, but before she could do anything, he was dead."

"Why didn't she call the police?"

"He was dead, Luke," she reminded him. "And when she tried to help him, she recognized the knife. She couldn't call it in."

Luke comprehended instantly. "Because she thought one of the kids had done it."

"Exactly." Kell moved restlessly. "She took the

knife and hid it. When she got back to the Center, she didn't check her stand. She'd freaked out and didn't think about the obvious proof that it wasn't one of the kids. The knife she found at Clay's was still in her set."

"Someone had a duplicate knife."

"Exactly." Wanting him to understand, she stressed, "If she hadn't taken the murder weapon with her, you'd have made an immediate match and arrested her."

"Instead, now the murder weapon is in the hands of the killer, again," he rejoined. "That knife is evidence that now has her fingerprints on it."

"She didn't kill him."

"I know that," he dismissed impatiently. "But the person with the murder weapon can turn it in and we'll have her finger prints on it. With Clay's blood. Did she try to wipe it down?"

"I doubt it. Eliza isn't a criminal mastermind."

"No. That's why she's got you."

"Yes," she gave him a level look. "That's why she has me."

Luke refused to feel remorse for the potshot. He reminded himself that she'd withheld information and put them in this morass. But he'd have all of it. Now. "What's the reason for the blackmail? Are you going to tell me what Clay held over her that was so terrible, she paid him for so long?"

"I can't," she murmured, regretting her silence. "I'm sorry, I can't."

Without a word, he left the truck, engine idling, the

sound loud in the sudden silence. He strode toward the tree line, long, angry strides that ate up the ground.

Grimly, Kell removed the key from the ignition and trooped after him. "Luke. Luke!"

He gave no sign of hearing her, except to lengthen his stride.

Kell sped up, jogging to close the distance. She grabbed his arm and skipped around to block his path. "What's wrong now? I thought you wanted me to be honest with you. To tell you the truth."

"The truth about everything, Kell." He shook his head in disgust. "But you can't do that, can you? Every time I think you finally have some faith in me, you prove me wrong."

"Of course I have faith in you." Angry now, Kell stood her ground. "Eliza gave me permission to tell you about the blackmail and the rest of it. Once I knew it was safe to tell you, I did. Luke, I'm doing what I'm supposed to do. Defending my client. But when will you decide you can have faith in me?"

"What?"

"You keep asking for my trust, for my faith, but what about you? I'm a defense attorney, Luke. My job is to protect my client, no matter what."

"And protect yourself." Luke hated that she had to, that she might still need to. Her secrets kept him helpless, forced to stagger around her world blindly. Vicious disappointment rode him and he lashed out, "Clay blackmailed her for almost twenty years, and you don't think I know why?"

"You don't."

"Of course I do." Pulling himself in, his tone was clipped, icy. "Their bodies are lying in the morgue."

Kell swallowed. "Those men have nothing to do with Eliza's innocence."

"No, that's all about you. And don't say I don't have faith in you. Hell, I've broken a dozen regulations because I do believe in you. As much as you'll let me."

"Then stop acting like I've lied to you about what's going on," she spat out. "I've only ever asked you to help me save Eliza. Never anything else."

"That's true." He gave a short, bitter laugh. "You won't tell me about what happened sixteen years ago. Why two men are dead and you and Findley Borders ran away from Hallden."

"You're the detective." Kell slapped at his chest, anger spilling over. The hit pushed him back a pace. "You want to know what happened, figure it out."

Chest and ego smarting, he ticked off, "Eliza paid blackmail to Clay Griffin beginning right after you skipped town. To keep him from telling the police that you had something to do with the warehouse fire. Am I wrong?"

Kell looked away, refusing to answer with another lie. "It's complicated."

Luke closed rough hands around her arms, fingers digging into flesh. "Everything with you is complicated, isn't it?"

She welcomed the bitterness, matched it with her own. "Sometimes."

"No, all the time. And each one puts me in jeopardy of losing my job." He relaxed his grip slightly, spoke in harsh tones that shook her. "A job I love, but am willing to put at risk for you." Giving a derisive snort, he added, "For a woman who doles out information like I'm the one on trial."

She didn't shrug off his grasp. "Luke. You can't really believe that. I care about you. Respect you."

"Respect me?" He stared down at her, bemused at the earnestness. At every turn, she deceived him and yet, like a fool, he came back for more punishment. "I think you're a damned good liar who is going to have to tell me the truth. All of it."

"I can't."

"And I can't act on blind faith any longer," he warned bleakly. "Over and over, you've asked me to accept your version of the world, and I have, like some infatuated rookie cop."

"You don't believe Eliza killed Clay."

"No, but I'm not so sure about you and that fire, Kell. I don't think you killed those men, but you do know more than you've told me. More than these trickles of information. I deserve the whole, ugly, unvarnished story." He slipped his hands up to her throat, tilting her eyes up to his. "I'm in, Kell. All in. But you'll only come half the way. What am I supposed to think?"

"That I'm doing the best I can."

"Do better." Incensed ebony eyes bored into dismayed brown. "Give me something to hold on to. Something that proves that I'm not making a fool of myself here."

"These aren't my secrets to tell, Luke. By God, if they were, you'd be the one I share them with. Believe me."

He released her then, unwilling to touch. With one hand, he flicked aside her plea. "Why should I?"

"Because."

"Give me a real answer." His request was low, almost anguished. "Why, Kell?"

"Because I may be falling in love with you too."

CHAPTER 25

"I'm doing my best." The admission emerged on a ragged sigh. Defeated, she turned and headed toward the truck.

Luke touched her shoulder. When she stopped, he challenged, "You can't say that and walk away."

"I didn't expect you to believe that either," she snapped wearily. She refused to struggle against him, to make more apologies for choices made long before they met. Turning, she bowed her head. Her hands clenched and unclenched. Not wanting to see his reaction, she confessed, "I care about you. I care about your career. But you're not the only one who's lost something in this."

"Your partnership." He slid his hands down to capture hers and their restless movement. "I'd forgotten."

"Yes. My partnership." She gave a short chuckle, failure rich in the sound. "Probably dozens of clients who will be told a variety of stories as inducement to stay with David. Stories that are true. I did toss aside a major case. I did abandon my practice for a personal crusade." *I let myself become involved with the last person I should want.*

Because he knew she needed it, even if she didn't, he shifted to fold his arms around her. Emotions knotted inside him, a tangle of two codes of justice that could not coexist. His demanded truth, hers mandated loyalty. Dropping his chin onto her head, he muttered, "We make a terrific pair."

Her forehead pressed against the ridge of his bicep, giving into comfort. "Someone wants Eliza in prison, Luke. They know too much, about her, about me. About you. And they've got Graves to pull the levers to accomplish whatever they're trying to do."

"So you'll prove she didn't do it."

Leaning against the firm band of his arms, she looked up at him. "I can't do that without you."

"Well, you've got me."

He bent his head and covered her mouth with his. Desire, impatient and fierce, clawed at him, mingled with frustration. With effort, he battled off the urge to crush her lips beneath him until he'd sated the anger that roiled in him still. Instead, the kiss was as much a balm as a warning. Her taste spun inside him, crowded his senses until all he knew was that soon, one of them had to break.

Ending the kiss, he laid a hand on her cheek. "I know you're doing your best."

"Thank you."

"Try harder."

Deliberately misunderstanding, she slipped free. "Help me figure out who's behind this, and I will. We have until Tuesday. Then I have to convince the judge that Grave's evidence is worthless."

Luke thought about what they knew already. "We can try to discredit Doc, but the kids heard the threat, as did Tony. Plus, we shouldn't underestimate Caleb Matthews. He's a good man, but he likes to win."

"Great."

"So our best bet is finding this building Tony was taken to and pointing the finger at someone else." Luke fell into step beside her as they returned to the truck. After helping her inside, he pulled onto the lonely route. "I talked to him again this morning. According to what he remembered, Clay drove for nearly an hour on County Road before they reached it."

"Was it on the route?"

"No. He remembers feeling a gravel path that jutted off the main road. The building was about a quarter of a mile inside."

Kell filed away the information, watching the road carefully. "What did the lab say about the sample you sent in?"

"The substance I found appears to be a pine resin."

"Appears to be?"

"Tests were inconclusive. The lab tech who wrote the report says the sample I sent doesn't match any resin he's ever worked with. In fact, he's sent the sample to the university for analysis."

"When will they have the results?"

"A week." Understanding her concern, he reassured Kell, "We'll just have to find something else."

"What do we do about the knife, Luke?"

He shared her concern. "I don't know. But one worry at a time, okay?"

Green rolled outside the windows in unbroken waves. Luke kept his speed at a sedate 55, which earned snide comments from Kell. Curly had called to confirm Kell's assertion that the land was owned by the Metanoia Foundation. With instructions from Luke to keep this information to himself, Luke returned his attention to their slow hunt for the building.

"Can we speed it up, Sheriff?"

He slanted her a knowing look. "Remember what happened the last time you were caught speeding?"

Duly chastened, Kell subsided into silence. The road stretched longer, winding across low hills and precious little else.

"There!" she exclaimed, as a trail veered off into the woods. "Make a U-turn. There's a road to the left."

Maneuvering the truck, Luke guided the vehicle off the highway and onto a gravel path rutted by storms and disuse. At a quarter of a mile, he slowed to a crawl. "I don't see a building out here."

Disappointed, Kell suggested, "Let's go farther."

He drove deeper into the woods, the gravel track giving way to hard packed soil. Brush littered the road, branches snapping beneath the tires. At half a mile, he recommended, "There's nothing out here, Kell. We should get back on the main road and continue looking."

"Okay."

Luke reversed the truck in a neat three-point turn and aimed toward the spot where they'd entered. A squirrel darted in front of them, and he slammed on the brakes, swerving to miss the tree rodent. As he pulled the truck under control, he glimpsed a flash of metal behind a screen of trees.

"It's here." He shoved the truck into park and leapt out. Kell followed on his heels. Quickly, he stripped away the false cover of limbs to reveal a driveway. A metal building, identical to the one Tony described, lay in a clearing.

Limbs broke beneath their feet as they scrambled over fallen trees to approach the clearing. Nearly half an acre had been stripped of trees and foliage, a brown wasteland in the midst of high stands of pines. Stumps rose from the stripped ground, and wide gouges in the earth indicated the recent presence of heavy machinery. Machinery that was nowhere in sight.

Motioning Kell behind him, Luke removed his gun, senses on high alert. They crept toward the building in silence, aware of every rustling leaf. As they neared the building, he waved Kell into a spot behind a jagged tree stump. Alone, he advanced slowly to the front door, bent low beneath the visibility of the window. A padlock secured the metal shut. He peered inside the dim interior through the lightly frosted glass. Luke crept around the side, eyes cutting the area for movement. The circuit of the building revealed a tank and a small generator, but little else. The building itself was little more than a glorified shed. Four walls and two windows that overlooked the path they'd taken to reach the building, and an exit he found as he came around the rear.

Once he'd assured himself the building was unoccupied, he returned for Kell. "Both doors have been padlocked. Windows are made of fiberglass." Lawful entry required a pair of bolt cutters and a search warrant. He explained as much to Kell.

"Do we have to go back?" She worked hard to temper her impatience. Judge Majors was unlikely to grant another warrant or take any further special measures during her weekend, and Kell understood why Luke would be loathe to ask. "I guess we can wait until Monday."

"I didn't say that. Wait here." He disappeared down the path and returned with an oversized pair of pliers. He situated the cutters and the lock gave way. He removed the ruined lock and made short work of the doorknob with a violent kick. "Let's take a look."

Stray particles drifted inside the building, but the interior was unexpectedly pristine, if stuffy with a strange odor. A floor had been laid with cement that echoed dully beneath their feet. Silver tables lined the walls, loaded with vials and machinery. The wall Tony mentioned cut into the rear of the space, creating a cubicle. Luke pressed a pair of latex gloves that he'd stored in his pocket into her hand.

Kell snapped the gloves into place while she counted nearly a half dozen workstations similarly outfitted, each posted with a metal stool. "This looks like a lab."

"Yep. There's a waterline that connects to a tank behind the building." He pointed a gloved finger up to the low roof. "Forced ventilation. Explains the smell."

Luke crossed the room to a table near the exit. On the surface, a sticky glob clung to the surface. He leaned down to sniff. The pungent scent hadn't dissipated in the stuffy space. "This is what I smelled on Clay's hand."

Kell hurried to join him. "Smells like pine trees and alcohol." She gestured to the station she'd been examining. "That one has a different odor. Less sharp than pine, but with the same goo on the table and in the vials."

"A laboratory set up in the middle of a forest." Luke removed his phone, aiming the camera at each table. He snapped several photos from each angle. "The county hasn't authorized a logging operation out here, and this doesn't resemble any drug lab I've ever busted."

"I'm not sure this is a logging operation." She pointed out the back window to the heavily grooved landscape. "That looks more like clear-cutting than a harvest operation."

Luke raised a speculative brow, and she explained, "One of my clients was a timber farmer."

"Timber farmer?"

Prowling the room, she corrected, "Actually, he strip-mined thousands of acres in Washington State. Timber farming was a sideline." She squatted beneath one of the tables, checking the underside for any hint of ownership.

Luke took the other side of the room and began crawling along the floor. The building's construction was solid, if shabby. No air escaped between the floor and lower wall. Metal sheeting on the outside had been reinforced with more concrete inside. "Why did a timber baron hire you?"

"Allegedly, he killed his partner for trying to embezzle a share of the profits." She frowned thoughtfully as she checked for marks on the vials. "Police had him cold, since he had possession of two of the victim's fingers."

"And you got an acquittal?"

"Mistrial. The judge neglected to mention a substantial investment in one of his ventures. Lost his house and his wife in the bankruptcy."

Luke shrugged, deciding to keep his opinion to himself. He lithely gained his feet, brushed at his dusty knees. "So we have an abandoned building with a miniature chem lab set up in the middle of the woods. What the hell is going on here?"

"If I had to guess, I'd say that someone is experimenting with tree resin."

"Thanks, Sherlock."

Kell didn't take offense. "Middle Georgia has a fairly diverse array of tree species," she offered in explanation. She wandered into the cubicle, but found nothing more incriminating than a pencil lodged beneath a worktable in the area. Lifting the pencil, she carried it out by the eraser to Luke. "When we were in high school, the science teacher was cute. I paid attention."

He slipped the pencil into an evidence bag he'd

brought inside. Perhaps the user had chewed on the pencil and left behind DNA. "What did you learn?"

"That resin is the tree's natural defense. Functions as the immune system." She tipped up a black unit outfitted with knobs and dials. Other than a production label, there was no hint of its utility. "But it has limited use for humans, other than for eco-friendly products."

"Whoever slashed through those trees out there isn't a friend of the environment."

"Agreed." Kell made a final circuit, finding nothing. "I need to do some research on this area and the trees in this forest. Any one who would go to the trouble of hiding this thinks it's worth the cost."

"And perhaps worth killing for."

CHAPTER 26

Outside, slate gray clouds dimmed the endless sun-light. As they picked their way across the clearing, a fat drop landed on Kell's nose, followed quickly by a steady torrent that chased them to the shelter of the truck.

Luke boosted her into the dry interior, water sleeting in a summer shower. He ran around the bonnet to climb inside, his T-shirt plastered to his chest. With quick motions, he started the truck and fired the heater.

"You okay over there?" he asked, scrubbing at the rain on his face using the bottom of his shirt.

"Hmm, hmm." Kell murmured, captivated. Hardened muscle rippled across his exposed skin, flattening into an abdomen that stuttered her pulse. Rain glistened on firmly molded arms, beaded on closely cropped hair and luxurious eyelashes that enhanced masculinity rather than weakened it. Abruptly, she became aware of the ebony eyes watching her appraisal.

A slow grin curved the chiseled mouth, throwing the planes of his face into beautiful relief. "Come here."

"Why?"

He held out his hand, palm upward. The low, gravelly voice with its sensual drawl repeated the summons. "Come here, Kell."

Mind blank, heartbeat racing, she made one last effort at fending off the inevitable. "This will only drag you in deeper."

"I've already gone under."

Knowing her choice was made, she slid across the leather bench, laced her fingers with his. "I want you. Terribly."

Luke slipped his hand beneath the wet fall of hair, raked his fingers through the strands. Carefully, he drew his thumb across her brow, along the high line of her cheek. At her mouth, he brushed at droplets that clung to the ripe curves. "You entrance me."

"Oh."

"Oh," he repeated. "This face stuns me every time. I think I'm prepared for it, then you look at me and I forget my name for an instant. Every time."

"Luke."

He skimmed his free hand along the soaked T-shirt, lingering at the dip of her waist, the taut globes that shuddered beneath the thin material. "Then there's this body. Long, endless legs in those heels designed to break a man's will. And none of it prepares you for the smarts behind those doe eyes or the heart." He covered her breast lightly. "Or the heart that tries to hold too much."

"Luke," she said his name again, urgently.

"Yes, Kell?"

"Drive."

In the hushed light of his bedroom, Luke let his hands trace the contours of her body, memorizing every line. The rounded invitation of hip, the indentation of waist. A contrast formed, of softness and resilience and he thought he understood both. His lips grazed the silken sweep of her mouth, nipped at the slightly crooked corner. "Lovely," he whispered.

Kell laid her hands on the broad span of his chest, tugged impatiently at the damp shirt. Shivers danced across her skin where he touched, where her fingers met unyielding muscle. Here was the strength she admired, the stubbornness of will that annoyed. Want stirred restlessly and she dragged at the cloth, muttered, "Help me."

"Indeed." Lifting his arms, he waited until she tossed the shirt onto the floor to reach for the hem of her top. "Your turn."

Slowly, torturously, he bent and drew the cloth upward, stopped inch by inch to sample the satin expanse at her navel. Her bra fell unheeded beneath his nimble touch, and he dipped his head to draw the perfect globe into his waiting mouth. When her knees trembled, and her hands sank into his hair, he laughed in delight. "We've got time, darling."

"I like speed." Tormented, she twisted against him and he let go reluctantly. His hands busied at her waist, fumbling to release the wet denim from her hips. Distracted, she caught a flat, firm nipple between ungentle teeth. And revelled in the moan that broke from his chest. She tested him with heated flicks of tongue that sampled the warm saltiness of flesh. A hot, wet line tracked the arrowing of hair that disappeared at his waist.

He caught her high, and her arms twined around his neck to hold. "Now, Luke," she demanded.

Unable to resist, his mouth crushed down on hers, plunging inside to take what had been too long denied. Heat, vicious and wonderful, pushed him to dive deeper. Flavors he'd sampled before became a banquet to savor. Piquant and sweet, spiced and delicate, her taste flooded his senses, weakened him.

He swept her into his arms, carried her to the waiting bed, a stretch of deep green that he slept in, too often alone. Impatient now, he ripped at the spread, shoving the tangled cloth out to the carpeted floor. She arched across the crisp white sheets below, her skin rich against the cotton. Control vanished as she bowed up, offering him every pleasure he'd imagined.

Clothes vanished, removed by eager, careless hands. The smooth perfect breasts fit his hands, his mouth. She writhed against him, a challenge to draw more from her. With his fingertips, he skimmed the dampened flesh for moments, for hours. Once he'd learned the lush, strong body by touch, he employed his other senses. The scent of her, that intriguing blend of clean and sultry, dazed him. The sight of her, taut with desire, humbled him. He slicked his mouth across her waist, dipped lower to sate and destroy. When she broke beneath his mouth, he streaked up to begin again.

Thrilled, overwhelmed, Kell moved beneath him, ranged over him and launched a deliberate assault of her own. At the ridge of his shoulders, she strung kisses that trailed along the strong column of his throat, the square lines of his jaw. Mating their mouths, she sank into his kiss, afraid she'd never want to leave. The body she explored trembled for her, and she could only give. In a whispering silence, she nipped here, licked there. Where hard grazed soft, she lingered, testing his discipline, her skill.

He bucked under her command, a shock to a system he thought had felt everything. But in every movement, every fevered touch, he learned a new ecstasy, a terrific agony. Breath shuddered out of him, her name a litany. He dragged her to him, rose above her. "I need you. All of you."

"You have me. Anything."

"Love me," he demanded, taking her up once more.

Afraid she did, Kell kissed him, a merger that spoke words she wasn't ready to say aloud.

Arousal, ravenous and craven, bent to a stronger, more fragile need that consumed her. She opened for him, and he plunged inside, dragging her to him.

The rhythm caught them both, drove them to demand then offer. Endlessly, wonderfully, they fell into the greedy darkness and fought to give more than either could have imagined. An explosion, his, hers, theirs, brought twin cries and release.

Kell lay still in the darkness, unable to lift her head. The firm pillow beneath her cheek beat an unsteady tattoo that curled her mouth into a sleepy, satisfied smile. Already, they'd made love twice, and exhaustion demanded her surrender. "Well."

Shifting to draw a tangled sheet over their cooling bodies, Luke couldn't repress a smirk of his own. "Yes, well."

"Tired."

"Rest." He drew her across his body, her head tucked into his shoulder. Her leg slid between his and he felt himself stir, impossibly. Moonlight snuck through the window, cresting the long, naked limbs in a glow. She slept with intensity, body a ready spring even in sleep. Tenderly, he stroked his hand along the narrow column of her spine, pushing the sheet to her waist. She wasn't voluptuous or slender, but somehow gave the impression of both.

A woman of duality, he acknowledged in the darkness. Somehow, he'd fallen in love with both women. The vibrant, arrogant attorney who flouted every rule he held dear and the fiercely loyal orphan who risked all to protect what she loved.

For her, he knew, he'd be willing to bend, maybe to break. And he wondered what that would cost him, if she refused to have him in the end. An ache, brutal and greedy, spread through him and he drifted into sleep, a frown between his brows. Her name on his lips.

The scent of coffee pulled him into wakefulness. Kell stood at the end of the bed, wearing one of his blue shirts and nothing else.

"I thought you might have to go into the department today," she said, almost shyly, as he accepted the steaming mug. "Figured I wouldn't poison you by trying my hand at breakfast."

"Today is Sunday." He sipped at the cup, grateful for the hit of caffeine. "Cheryl's got the morning off, so yep, I've got to go in." Watching her, remembering waking her at dawn, he turned and set the cup on the bedside table. "In a few hours or so."

Kell took a step back, eyes wary.

Luke noted the movement with irritation. The defenses that had disappeared last night were firmly in place once more. Not yet, he decided. "Kell."

"Yes?"

He drew the cover back in bold challenge. "I believe I owe you one."

She hesitated for a second. Studied the rigid length of him, considered the drawled invitation. She shrugged philosophically and dived onto the bed with a laugh. "Fair's fair."

Kell shimmied into hopelessly creased jeans and settled for a borrowed T-shirt from Luke's closet. Pleasurable aches sang along her skin, and she caught herself smiling smugly into the mirror as she tried to bring some order to her tousled hair. A hot shower had washed away the remnants of fatigue, despite Luke's decadent interruption.

Today, though, required focus. Tuesday's hearing gave her a chance to probe the prosecution's case for weaknesses. Doc's eyewitness account of the fight had been delivered to the Center, as had the forensic evidence linking Eliza's cutlery set to the source of the murder weapon.

What Caleb Matthews didn't have, wouldn't have, was the murder weapon. The possibility of it appearing hung like a weight around her. But she felt curiously light, knew that she owed some part of her good spirits to Luke.

No one before Luke had burrowed so deep, reaching the part of her she held inviolate. Before him, she could count on one hand the opinions that mattered to her, the women who held her steady on the questions of right and wrong. Now, there he was, stripping away secrets and layers of protection, revealing her to his eyes. What stunned her, confounded her, was that he refused to look away.

Even when all the evidence pointed not only to Eliza's guilt, but her own.

Two bodies in a morgue and two women half a continent away. And a lie told so long, it had become her only truth.

"Kell, you need to see this."

Luke called to her from the living room, and she brushed aside the brief descent into maudlin musings. "I'll be right there."

She glazed her mouth with lipstick and swiftly bound her hair into a modified French braid. Scooping up her shoes from the bedroom, she found Luke looming over the coffee table, paper in hand.

Reading his mutinous expression, she asked, "What's in there?"

"An interview with Doc Reed where he claims now not only to have heard Eliza threaten to kill Clay." He lifted his head to meet her concerned expression. "He says he saw her at the Palace Motel on the night of the murder."

Kell allowed herself a brief moment of worry. Doc's newest statement placing Eliza at the scene connected the threat at the Center and the confiscated knives, and she had no idea how to break that link.

Taking the paper from him, Kell scanned the story, looking for a hole. "Can you bring him in for questioning?"

Luke affirmed, "I still have this as an open case. If he's a material witness, I can bring him in."

"Do it."

CHAPTER 27

"I want Doc Reed and Tony Delgado here in twenty minutes. Separate rooms." Luke issued the order as he stormed into his office. The glass door slammed, rattling the pane and the sparse crew of deputies who knew what set him off. He spread the crumpled pages of the *Hallden Telegraph* onto his desk. The cover story featured Doc Reed in an ill-fitting suit on the stoop of his family home.

"She came at him with a butcher knife," the article quoted. "Mean old lady said that if he ever came by the Center again, she'd kill him. That night, Clay and I were playing video games. I got bored and decided to go. I was leaving the motel and I saw her in the lobby. She had something shiny in her hands, but I didn't get a real good look."

Just enough information to paint a picture and place the weapon in Eliza's hand, Luke noticed. He dropped behind his desk and plucked the receiver from its base. "Caleb Matthews, please," he told the operator.

A tinny voice recited the number and Luke punched it into the phone. On the second ring, Caleb answered. "Caleb Matthews."

Luke heard a hint of irritation, wondered who else had been bothering the D.A. this morning. "Matthews, this is Sheriff Calder."

The irritation shifted into wariness. "Sheriff. Didn't expect to hear from you on a Sunday morning." He waited a beat. "I assume you've seen the paper this morning." As had he. Apparently, his threat of a gag order hadn't scared Graves into better behavior, an oversight he'd fix on Tuesday. "Our star witness has been busy."

"Very talkative," Luke acknowledged sardonically. "I suppose Graves and I have put you in a tough spot with this one."

Caleb gave a low chuckle. "I must admit, Hallden isn't a dull town. Haven't been in this kind of turf war before, though. Usually, this kind of wrestling match is between locals and the feds."

"Run into much of that on the coast?"

"With drug trafficking, I've had my share of arguments with the Justice Department." He cleared his throat. "But my checkered past with the feds isn't the reason you've called."

Luke fingered the paper with Doc's soulful mien in four-color spread. Fancy for the *Telegraph*. "I've ordered my deputies to pick up Doc Reed and Tony Delgado for questioning as material witnesses."

"Graves has made an arrest in the case, Sheriff. You could give the defense grounds for appeal."

"I don't agree with Graves that Eliza Faraday is guilty."

"Cop instinct or something else?" The question was bald, but direct. "Graves has made some pejorative allegations about you and Ms. Jameson." Anticipating Luke's explosion, he inserted mildly, "I won't allow gossip to dictate my prosecutorial decisions, Calder. But two eyewitnesses and a link to the weapon are pretty strong evidence."

"Not enough to convict."

Caleb had the same concern, but the choice had been taken out of his hands. His attempt to put the case on hold had been thwarted by the D.A. after a plaintive whine from the police chief at 8 A.M. "Graves's arrest may have been premature, but he's got the big three."

Means, motive, and opportunity. Luke had brought successful cases to D.A.s with less. "As long as I still have an open case file, I intend to pursue my own theory of the case."

"Want to let me in on it?" Caleb challenged, displeasure clear.

Luke smiled, understanding the other man's annoyance. "Not yet. But you play it fair, Matthews, so I wanted to let you know what I'm doing."

"In the spirit of sharing, you should know I intend to call you as a witness for the preliminary hearing. As the chief investigator on the scene, you've got to describe what you found."

"I found a dead man and a lot of reasons to doubt that Eliza Faraday is the killer," he warned.

"All I'm asking for is that you tell the truth."

His tone left no doubt he questioned Graves's ability to do the same. Luke sympathized, and found himself offering advice. "Watch out for him, Matthews. Do what you have to on this case, but keep your eyes open."

"Thanks for the warning, Sheriff. Have a nice day."

"Did you see anyone outside the motel?" Kell stood in the study, pacing the thick carpet. "Anyone at all?"

"No. I was scared, certainly, but not witless," snapped Eliza. "I looked out the door and there was no one outside. I walked quickly to my car and drove directly home."

"Any cars pass you on the street?"

"I don't think so," she admitted. "Once I started driving, I concentrated on making it to the Center as fast as possible. I needed to check on the children."

"They were all in bed?"

"Yes, every one of them. But the knife was mine, I thought, so I assumed one of them had beaten me home." She leaned forward, voice edging toward hostile. "I don't believe the boy saw me. I'm certain he didn't."

Careful of the fraying temper, Kell stopped near the desk, changing her tone. "Did you ever have any runins with Doc? Maybe he tried to recruit some of the boys for Clay?"

Eliza sniffed disdainfully. "Doc Reed knew better than to ply his trade here. He rarely stopped by, unless Tony brought him."

"Does he have any reason to lie about what he saw?"

"Money. A favor from the chief of police," Eliza volunteered wearily. "Perhaps I should simply tell the police exactly what happened. I didn't kill anyone."

"You know as well as I do that's not the answer. Graves and others have put a tremendous amount of effort into making you look guilty." She pointed to the open copy of the *Telegraph* splayed across the immaculate desk. "If they held back this statement until now, Graves must be feeling some pressure."

"I still don't understand why they've targeted me." Eliza lurched from her chair, hazel eyes bewildered. "I've operated this Center without blemish for decades. Until now, I didn't realize I had an enemy that hated me so badly, he'd try to ruin my life."

Kell had pondered the same thought since leaving the building she and Luke discovered. "Mrs. F, do you have a copy of the trust documents for the foundation?"

"Of course." Eliza opened a drawer to a filing cabinet and removed a thick binder. "I meet with the bank annually to review our investments and operations. Here are the annual reports from the past three years. The rest are in storage, but I can retrieve them."

Kell accepted the binder and sank onto the settee. She opened the cover and replied absently, "Yes, if you could get them."

"Certainly," Eliza replied, but she halted at the door. A wave of affection rushed over her, calming nerves jangled by tension. Of all her children, Kell had been the one who pretended best. To be independent and aloof, but she'd always been the ringleader and the one Eliza counted on to watch after the others. Losing her had broken Eliza's heart. Kell wouldn't know that the scholarships for college and law school fellowships bound her to Eliza during those missing years.

She regretted the distance, the birthdays celebrated alone. Yet, she couldn't bring herself to regret the woman she'd become. Confident and accomplished, with a compassion she tried vainly to disguise.

"Mrs. F?" Kell glanced up and saw her paused in the doorway. "Something wrong?"

"No. Nothing at all." With a slight smile, she turned away. "I'll just be a moment."

Doc Reed slouched low in the ladder-back chair, legs stretched out beneath the wooden table. The unblemished surface tempted him to scratch his initials into the top, but the stern officer standing in the corner gave him pause. Doc spent his fair share of time in rooms like this, usually waiting for his mom to come and get him. At eighteen, he'd aged out of misdemeanors solved by parental tears and into more serious matters that required lawyers and hearings. But he'd bought himself a get-out-of jail free card and got his picture in the paper to boot.

His new best friend happened to control the comings and goings at the police department, a good friend for a man like him to have. Doc thumbed his nose and sniffed loudly. "Any time y'all want to start things up, I'm ready. I'm on a schedule."

Outside the door, Luke examined his prey. Faded jeans sagged low on hips covered with plaid boxers, a deliberate display. The tanned arms bore the musculature of a regular basketball player, the face bespoke several fights won and lost. A consummate bully and liar, they'd met more than once. Youthful indiscretions escalated steadily into petty crime and low-level drug sales.

Luke swung into the room and dismissed the deputy he'd placed on task to guard Doc. "Harold Reed?" he read the name from the file he carried. Cajoling didn't work with Doc. Antagonism did.

Sneering, he corrected, "Name's Doc."

"License says *Harold*." Luke dropped the thick file onto the table, but didn't sit. "Harold Francis Reed. Prefer me to call you Francis?"

"Prefer your teeth in your throat?"

Luke leaned in until their foreheads nearly touched, eyes level, voice a hum of menace. "You threatening me, Francis? Please say yes."

Doc glared at the sheriff, calculating the odds if he rushed him. He was tall, but the sheriff had him by at least five inches. Bigger than him too. Insult yielded to reality. "Name's Doc," he repeated sulkily.

Easing back, Luke flipped open the file to the article he'd clipped from the paper. "Francis, I want you to tell me a story."

"What kind of story?"

"Make-believe. Like the one you told the reporter."

Bristling, Doc folded his arms. "I told the reporter exactly what I saw. That bitch Mrs. Faraday running out of the motel. Carrying a knife."

"Describe the knife for me."

Ready for the question, Doc retorted, "I didn't see

the whole thing. Just the shiny part, the blade. She was trying to hide it, but I could still see it."

"In the middle of the night?"

"Streetlights," he responded smugly. "Plenty of light."

"What time did you see her?"

"Around one. I was already outside, waiting on my ride, when she came flying out with the knife."

"One A.M.," Luke repeated. "Who was coming to pick you up?"

"A friend."

"You have friends?" Luke filled his tone with disbelief. "Why didn't you drive yourself?"

"'Cause I don't have a car." A situation that Graves promised to remedy soon. "So I called one of my boys to get me."

"Which one?" He held a pen poised over his notes. "Give me a name and a number."

Doc reached for a name, someone with a car. "Tony Delgado," he blurted out. "Yep, Tony came to get me."

"Tony and Clay were tight?"

"Naw. Tony was a lightweight. Couldn't hang with Clay and me." The smirk flashed a single gold tooth at Luke. "But he does what I tell him to."

"Like pick you up in the middle of the night?" Luke smiled then, a thin spreading of the lips that held only threat. "You sure about that?"

"I already said so." Doc squirmed in his chair, feeling the first trickle of unease. "Tony came to pick me up, and while I was standing on the curb, I saw Mrs. Faraday."

"Now, that's fascinating, Francis."

"What is?"

"That Tony gave you a ride."

Knowing he was caught, he improvised. "Um, he didn't."

Luke straightened. "Didn't give you a ride? You said he did."

Doc shook his head, grinning in triumph. "No, I said I was waiting for him to come pick me up."

"But he didn't?"

"No. He never showed."

"I thought he did what you told him to? Which is it, Francis? Does Tony do what you tell him or did he leave you standing on the street corner like a hooker?"

Flustered, Doc cast about for a suitable lie. "His mom wouldn't let him come. He couldn't do anything about that."

"Then how did you get home, Francis? After you see Mrs. Faraday running out of the motel with a knife, after your friend leaves you stranded on the street, exactly how did you get home?" Luke rose and circled behind him. "Did you go upstairs to Clay's apartment and ask him for a ride? He had that nice car, that Hummer. Did you bang on his door and when he didn't answer, did you go inside?"

Seeing the trap, Doc sprang from his chair, bumping into the table. "No way, man! No way you're gonna make me seem like I killed Clay! I want a lawyer!"

Luke advanced on him, forcing his back to the wall. He crowded, but did not touch the younger man. "You're certainly entitled to an attorney."

Doc feinted right, but Luke countered him easily. Unable to get around him, Doc complained, "Then I want to go. You can't keep me here if I'm not under arrest."

"I can if you're a material witness to a murder. But, you do have the right to an attorney now," Luke explained softly, forcing Doc to strain to hear. "See, Francis, you are the last person to see Clay alive except for the killer. That makes you a suspect, not a witness. Whoever is telling you what to say already knows this. But I'll go and get you a lawyer."

Doc heard *suspect* and his stomach knotted. He grabbed Luke's sleeve, stopping him. "I didn't do no murder, man," he whined. "It wasn't me."

Before Doc could finish, Graves burst into the room. Florid color turned his skin a motley hue, and the broken capillaries on his nose deepened to purple. "Don't say another word," he screeched to Doc.

Grateful for the distraction, Doc ducked under Luke's arm and skittered behind Chief Graves. "I didn't say anything," he groveled, knowing in a few more seconds, he would have.

Rounding on Luke, Graves huffed out, "Intimidating a witness. I'll be on the phone to Judge Majors about this, you mark my words."

Calmly, Luke propped a hip on the edge of the table. The livid interrogator disappeared, and he offered meditatively, "You've been telling anyone who'll listen, Chief, that I haven't been sufficiently zealous in my pursuit of Griffin's killer. I can't imagine the judge objecting to my interview of a material witness, can you?"

Trapped, Graves blustered, "I'm taking him with me. He needs to review his statement."

"By all means," Luke invited, rising and standing at the open doorway. "He definitely needs to practice."

Doc flushed red as Graves dragged him from the room. His sagging jeans fell lower, tripping him as he stumbled out.

Luke followed slowly. "Is Tony in the other room?"

"Yes, sir," the deputy responded, eyes dancing with merriment. "Graves left with Doc. Boy barely kept his pants up."

Luke grinned, "He waived his rights. If Graves hadn't shown, he'd have spilled his guts."

"Graves has good timing, then."

"Yes, he does," Luke agreed, a thought occurring. "Evan, you're friends with Lancy at the police station, aren't you?"

"Went through the academy together."

"Give him a call and see if you can't get us a copy of the intake log for the night of the Griffin murder."

"Sure thing, Sheriff. Should I tell him why?"

"Nope. And if he can keep the request to himself, I'd appreciate it."

Luke knocked on the Center's front door a few minutes past dusk. When it opened, four curious pairs of eyes greeted him, none of them belonging to Kell. "Hey, kids. Is Kell around?"

"What's behind your back?" Jorden asked baldly. "Is it a gun?"

"No."

"Is it a grenade? I saw this cool thing about grenades on television. Once you pull the pin, it blows up. If you don't let it go in time, your hand blows up too."

"No, Jorden, it's not a grenade either."

"Then why are you hiding it?" Fear struck and Jorden stepped forward belligerently. "Is it handcuffs? Are you gonna arrest Kell?"

Embarrassed, Luke brought the clutch of tulips around for inspection. "No, I'm not here to arrest her. They're flowers. For Kell."

"Oh, they're beautiful," Nina sighed.

Faith smirked, "Really pretty, Sheriff. Flowers for your girlfriend. You going on a date?"

"A real one, for a change. If one of you nosy urchins will get her for me."

"I'll do it," Casey piped up and ran for the guest room. She banged on the door. "Kell! Kell! Sheriff Luke has flowers!"

Kell opened the door and saw Luke standing in the foyer, surrounded by more of the children. Tulips wrapped in paper bloomed in a profusion of color. Smoothing at her hair, she crossed the floor to greet him. She stopped beside the children, aware of their rapt attention. "Hello, Luke."

"Oh, to hell with this." He pushed the flowers into Nina's hand and reached for Kell. Seconds later, his mouth closed over hers in a searing kiss, that had the girls giggling and the boys making a variety of noises, from disgust to encouragement.

Summoned by the noise, Eliza joined the throng at the door. "Luke."

He broke the kiss and smiled at Eliza. "I'd like to steal Kell away for a picnic, if you don't mind."

"Not at all." Eliza plucked the tulips from Nina's reluctant grasp, and shooed the kids into the family room. "Kell, Luke, you go and have fun."

Before Kell could speak, Luke bundled her into the truck, a picnic basket at her feet. "What's all this?" she asked sweetly.

"A real date. Our first one." He twined their fingers. "No interrogation or sleuthing. Just you, me, fried chicken, and a good bottle of Chianti. If you'll have me."

Pleased, touched, she leaned forward for another kiss, a soft one that sank him deeper still into love. "Thank you," she whispered, resting her head on his shoulder.

"For what?"

"A perfect evening."

CHAPTER 28

On Monday morning, Jorden answered the door at the Center. "Hey, Sheriff Luke." He bit his lip, then launched like a missile. Luke caught him mid-flight, and unexpectedly strong arms wrapped themselves around his neck, tightening fiercely.

"You said you'd get her home, and you did," the boy mumbled gratitude into Luke's shoulder. "I'da said so last night, but there were girls around."

"I made you a promise, didn't I?" Luke patted the thin back, felt the relief sigh out. "But we're not done yet, Jorden."

Jorden loosened his hold and Luke set him down, a hand resting on the bony shoulder. "Kell has to go to court with her," he announced solemnly. "Nina says she's real good, though."

"One of the best." Luke scrubbed his hand over Jorden's head. "Where is she now?"

Jorden pointed to the library. "No one's allowed in

to bother her," he whispered conspiratorially. He'd already made that mistake twice. The first time, she'd been nice. Second time, she nearly threw a book. "Gets real mad if you interrupt her while she's thinking."

"I might have a way around that."

Jorden weighed the odds, but gave the sheriff the thumbs up anyway. Man to man. "Just remember to duck," he warned as he ran out the front door.

Luke took the advice and stealthily entered the library from the study. He found Kell sprawled across the library floor, papers strewn around her. From his vantage point, the pages were spread haphazardly, but she appeared to have a system of order. Books not taken from Eliza's shelves were stacked three deep. Tabs and highlighters of every color imaginable speckled the rug beneath her.

Brief white shorts framed legs he'd dreamed about last night. She held one bent at the knee, sandal dangling from her toes. Wires trailed from earphones, and he heard violins playing a raucous symphony. Obviously intended as a deterrent for chatter, he surmised.

In silence, he turned the lock at the study and made his way to the other entrance, footfalls making no sound. Locking the second door, he approached in a crouch. Judging his angle, he dove, grabbed her and flipped them both in a smooth roll.

"Are you crazy?" Kell demanded as she fell against his chest, shock, amusement, and arousal rippling through her.

"No, I'm hungry." Rolling her free of the scattered

pages, he fastened his mouth to hers. Need pummeled him, weakened him. He explored her mouth slowly, wringing a ragged moan from the lithe, curved form beneath him. She pressed against him, and he wanted to ravage. So he forced himself to savor.

Her lips fused to his, and she sank under his kiss. When it changed, when the heat mellowed and touch softened, she sighed. Here was pleasure and belonging and friendship. She floated with him, content to crest gently as he sat up, draping her across his lap.

"I missed you." Luke stroked at the length of hair that had escaped and snaked along her cheek.

"Me too." She allowed herself to brush her mouth across his, once, then a second, longer foray. Finally drawing back, she explained, "I wish I could have stayed last night, but Eliza is nervous, very anxious. I didn't want to leave her here alone."

"I understand.'" He twined the dark silk strands around his finger. "But we'll have to do something about it. Maybe a work-release program. Making love under the trees was glorious, but I may have to arrest myself if we do it again."

"What do you suggest?" Kell captured his earlobe, traced the whorls with the tip of her tongue. When his breathing stuttered, she turned her attention to his throat. "I don't think Mrs. F intended the library for such uses."

In retaliation, he cupped her breast through the tank top, drew his thumb slowly across the hardened tip. "I can be very discreet." He felt her tremble in reaction and captured her mouth, eager for one last taste. Reluctantly, he released her, setting her on the rug beside him. "I actually came with news. I got distracted last night."

Kell surfaced and brought her knees in to rest her chin. "Your interview with Doc? How did it go?"

"Pretty good until Graves showed up." Luke scooted away, requiring the distance. "He wasn't there that night."

"You're sure?"

"Almost." He described the interview. "I had Tony in the other room. He denies ever receiving a call from Doc. In his version of the story, after Clay attacked Nina, he and Doc had a fight about Doc's association. Doc told Tony to mind his own business, and they parted company a little after seven."

"Was Doc involved in the murder?"

"He's a bully, but he doesn't have the stones for murder. Yet." Luke recalled his tough-cop routine with satisfaction. "If Graves hadn't burst into the room, I'd have had the entire story."

Kell frowned. "How did Graves know you'd brought him in?"

The same thought had occurred to Luke. "I've got a leak in my office. The same person who tipped off Graves about the autopsy must have called."

"Do you know who it is?"

"I have my suspicions, but I'll worry about one problem at a time." He stood, and reached down to help her to her feet. "Are you ready for tomorrow?"

Kell started to fob him off with a cocky remark, as she would anyone else who asked. Yet, once more, he was different. "I haven't been this concerned about a probable cause hearing since my very first one."

"What happened then?"

"It was a purse-snatching case. A teenage girl with three priors. She liked designer bags." Kell smiled at the memory. "Last one she grabbed was a Coach." At his blank look, she explained, "Retail price of twelve-hundred dollars."

"For a purse."

"For a Coach handbag. Anyway, the sticker made the theft a felony. She was seventeen, but with her other convictions, she was looking a prison time." Kell wandered over to her research, stared at the high-lighted pages with their streaks of yellow and green. "She got caught running into a lingerie store and the bag flew into the display. I got the cop to admit that he didn't actually see her with the purse in her hand, and the victim never got a good look. D.A. decided not to prosecute."

"Nice job. But I'd have gotten the arrest to stick."

"Not against me. I'm very good."

Luke slipped his arms around her waist. "I know. So does Eliza."

"She trusts me. After everything I did to her, she still trusts me."

"You have that effect on people, Kell." He tipped her eyes up to his. "I love you."

Kell froze, unnerved by the declaration. She tried to cover. "Are you sure? The fall alone should have killed you," she quipped shakily.

"I do love you, Kell." He raised a hand to caress her

cheek. "I love how smart you are. How loyal and tenacious."

Heart pounding in her ears, she responded blandly, "I sound like a cocker spaniel."

"Don't joke. Not about this." Luke brought his other hand up to frame her face. Love, powerful and tender, moved through him. It had to be here. Now. "I admire you. The woman you've made of the girl who grew up here, thrown away by those who should have protected you. I understand why you defend your clients. To you, it's not about right or wrong. It really is about defense—standing for those who might be harmed by a system that doesn't always get it right."

She drew a shallow breath, willing her heart to quiet. "What do you want from me?"

"I want you to love me too. To trust me."

"To tell you about the warehouse," she guessed.

"Yes." He felt her stiffen. "No, not because I have to hear the story to help Eliza. Or to help me close a case. I want, no, I need you to want to tell me. To trust that I can keep your confidences. For you and your friends."

"And if I can't? If I can't take that risk, even for you."

"Why not?"

"Because it's not my story to tell." Owing him honesty, she added softly, "And if you knew all of me, you wouldn't feel the same."

"Kell."

She broke away, stepped back. "You won't. You couldn't."

"I know you're not a murderer, Kell. As sure as I know myself, I know that about you." Taking a step toward her, he let himself plead. "Trust me. Please."

Sorrow cascaded through her, shaking and rending. "I can't do that, Luke. I'm sorry." Then, for the second time in her life, she fled.

In the guest room, she hastily dialed the number, before she faltered. David answered curtly, "Jameson Trent. David Trent speaking."

"It's Kell."

David bolted up, and rushed to close his door. He didn't need the associates to overhear this conversation. "The prodigal daughter returns."

"Not quite. I'm still down in Hallden."

"I know. You've got prelims tomorrow." Anticipating her question, he replied, "The Atlanta stations have been picking up the feed. CTN did a piece this morning. Your little *pro bono* case is the talk of the nation. Matron accused of vicious murder, defended by orphan done good."

Kell hadn't watched the broadcasts. "I hadn't noticed."

"Perhaps you should stop canoodling with the handsome sheriff, if the gossip columns are to be believed."

"Luke is in the Atlanta papers?"

"Full column on his heroic acts in Chicago. You two make great coverage. They've got a picture of you from the Brodie trial and a grainy one of Calder. Rugged jawline, looks excellent in black and white."

Bemused, Kell sank onto the bed. Luke would go ballistic when he found out. Eager to talk about anything but him, she asked quickly, "How goes the Marley case?"

David paused before responding. "The good senator called this morning. Despite her earlier decision to take her case elsewhere, your good deeds have convinced her that you'll do wonders for her image. She's offered to add fifty percent to the retainer, if you'll take the lead."

"One point five million?"

"Retainer. And she's agreed to bill out at our top rate, which, coincidentally, is now seven hundred and fifty dollars an hour."

"David, that's extortion."

"That's business." Abandoning pride, he cajoled, "So, will you come back?"

"I thought you'd dissolved our partnership."

"Hyperbole. I learned it from watching you." He braced for rejection, ready to offer more. "Kell, come on. We've been together forever. Forgive and forget, and I'll add no more lewd comments to the pot."

She stared at the closed door, where Luke had likely already stormed off. He wouldn't be back. The pain of loss was a steady throb, the sharp bite a reminder of what she did well and what she didn't.

"Let me take care of this tomorrow, and I'll be in the office on Wednesday."

CHAPTER 29

Caleb Matthews approached the witness with a single sheet of paper. The navy suit, cut along the same dramatic, lean lines as its wearer, hung perfectly. Kell could only be grateful that Judge Mary Majors was an audience of one and purportedly happily married. Behind her, in the filled gallery, murmurs about the handsome D.A. drifted up to Kell. Had she faced a jury of Eliza's peers, the piercing golden eyes that met hers briefly would have guaranteed him at least one juror on swoon alone.

Tracy Hoover, the medical examiner from Macon, relaxed in the witness chair, a veteran of preliminary hearings. She greeted him warmly, not immune to the effect of those eyes.

"Dr. Hoover, is this the pathology report submitted by your office to the Hallden Sheriff's Department?"

"Yes, it is."

"Please read what is indicated as cause of death."

Dr. Hoover placed half-glasses on her nose. "Exsanguination. Mr. Griffin bled to death."

"Did you determine the cause of the exsanguination?"

"His femoral artery had been severed." She looked at the judge. "Someone sliced his left leg open and left him to bleed out."

"In your diagnosis, did you draw any conclusions about source of the wound?"

"From the marks on the skin and damage to the femur, I determined that the source was a knife. Blade about eight inches long. Ceramic construction."

"Ceramic?" He leaned closer, curiosity wreathing question. Even though this was only a hearing, the uniqueness of the blade was essential to connecting the defendant to the wound. "How do you know?"

"Carbon steel knives, the kind most of us have, are virtually unbreakable. They dull and tarnish, but they don't break. Ceramic, on the other hand, keeps its edge longer and doesn't absorb the human oils that corrode steel. The downside, however, is that a ceramic tip will snap off if it strikes a hard object with sufficient force."

"Did you find evidence of that in the deceased?"

"Yes. During an internal examination of the body, we located a ceramic fragment that we traced to a specific brand of knife sold primarily to chefs. The manufacturer is a Japanese company that specializes in this particular knife construction."

"Thank you, doctor. Only a couple of additional questions. Did you conduct a tox screen on the victim?"

"He registered a blood alcohol level of point-O-2,

below the legal limit. We also found traces of cocaine in his system, but he hadn't ingested the substance in a number of weeks."

"And did you establish a time of death?"

"Based on lividity and taking into account the state of decomposition, I estimated the time of death to be between midnight and four A.M. on the night in question."

Caleb nodded. "No more questions, Your Honor."

"Ms. Jameson."

Kell approached the M.E. empty-handed. She had several questions, many of which she already knew the answers to. "Dr. Hoover, did your autopsy reveal the height or weight of Mr. Griffin's attacker?"

"No. Due to the angle of the wound, the perpetrator could have been as tall as six five or as short as five two."

"What about Mr. Griffin?"

"He was," she referred to the report still in her hands, "five ten, one hundred and ninety pounds."

"And did the victim show any signs of a struggle? Any defensive wounds on his hands or body?"

"None."

"Is this common? That a man would sit quietly and allow himself to be brutally attacked without taking any steps to defend himself? Especially if he outweighed his attacker by nearly fifty pounds?"

"Objection." Caleb rose, ready for the question. "Calls for speculation."

"Objection sustained," the judge ruled, but her gaze

lingered on Eliza's diminutive frame, as Kell intended.

Satisfied she'd made her point, she released the witness.

"Mr. Matthews."

"I call Sheriff Luke Calder."

From the second row, Luke rose and approached the stand. As he passed Kell, he didn't turn. Kell, unaware she'd expected any reaction, felt the deliberate snub pierce a heart she imagined numbed.

Greeting the bailiff, Luke took the oath and then his seat.

Caleb approached. "Sheriff Calder, you were the chief examiner at the scene, were you not?"

"Yes."

"Did you examine the body on site?"

"Yes."

Caleb winced internally at the monosyllabic responses. He spared a quick look at the judge, who also noted Luke's recalcitrance. He asked, "What did you observe?"

"The victim had already come out of rigor by the time we received the summons from his neighbor. When I arrived, my chief deputy had secured the scene and was taking photos. I examined the body and noted that the likely cause of death was the hole in his thigh."

"Did you secure a murder weapon?"

"No. A review of the apartment revealed a single knife, which did not appear sharp enough to inflict the wound."

"Did you send it for testing?"

"I did not. Given the condition of the butter knife, I saw no reason for analysis. Both my chief deputy and I determined on-site that it was not the weapon."

"At a later time, after receiving the autopsy, did you revise your opinion about the knife in the victim's apartment?"

"No. The autopsy indicated that the knife in the victim's apartment did not match the wound."

"Did your investigation reveal anything more about the knife?" Caleb looked at Eliza and Kell, leading Luke's gaze. "Any unique characteristics?"

But Luke had been a witness a hundred times and he knew the trick. His flat eyes remained focused on Caleb. "I interviewed persons of interest who had reason to own the knives described. However, I did not locate the murder weapon."

"Did you interview the defendant?"

"No. Before I could do so, Chief of Police Michael Graves obtained a search warrant for her home. He confiscated a cutlery set from her kitchen, but I have not been privy to any determination about the knives taken."

"Did you also have occasion to interview a Mr. Harold Francis Reed, also known as Doc?"

"I did."

"What did you learn?"

Luke located Doc slunk low against a bench in the rear of the courtroom and sneered lightly. "From Harold? Not much that I found useful or compelling."

Caleb refused to smile. Sternly, he asked, "Was a statement taken?"

"Not by me."

"By whom, then?"

"By Chief Graves." Luke indicated the chief with a jut of his chin. "Graves has taken all witness statements associated with this case that I am aware of."

"Thank you."

Kell rose slowly, her stomach listing, heart lodged in her throat. "Sheriff Calder."

"Counselor." The look he gave her bore no trace of the affectionate lover, the irritated partner. Wintry and remote, he stared through her.

She rushed through her questions, as much to avoid any question that could incriminate Eliza as to move out of his line of sight. Finishing up, she asked, "Have you reached an opinion about my client's role in this matter?"

"Objection!" Caleb sprang from his seat. "Calls for a conclusion."

"Indeed it does," Kell argued. "Sheriff Calder has been essential to this case from its start. By the prosecutor's own testimony, he has been made privy to the autopsy and the witness statements. Certainly, he can render an opinion based on his observations and seventeen-year history as an officer."

Judge Majors frowned thoughtfully. "Objection overruled, unless the prosecution has other grounds for objecting."

Kell blanched, her eyes drawn helplessly to Luke. The

cold remained, and he watched her with the passion of a stranger. No one intercepting his glance would have imagined that two nights ago, they'd been wrapped in each other's arms.

Graves heaved over the rail and whispered frantically to the prosecutor. Wisps of conversation rose in the courtroom. *Harlot. Bias. Blackmail.* In the crowd, the whispers were echoed as the story of the sheriff and the defense attorney repeated through the throng.

Caleb brushed Graves aside and turned to the judge. "No, Your Honor. No additional grounds."

"Then, Sheriff, you may answer the question."

"Based on my review of the evidence and my personal observations, I do not believe Eliza Faraday killed Clay Griffin. I find the eyewitness statements to be inconclusive at best, more likely fraudulent. And based on my personal bias, I think Chief Graves has strung together theory and conjecture and looped it around the most convenient target."

"No more questions, Your Honor."

"Sheriff, you're dismissed."

Luke stepped down from the witness stand, hand in the pocket of his jacket. As he passed the defense table, he slid a folded sheet under a folder on the desk. Kell lifted her startled gaze, but he took no notice. Neither did Caleb, who'd been accosted by Graves, the older man purple with outrage.

"Mr. Matthews." Impatience shimmered in the judge's words. "Any more witnesses?"

Caleb jerked his elbow free of Graves's anxious clasp. "I call Harold Francis Reed to the stand."

While Doc strolled up the aisle to the witness stand, Kell unfolded the sheet of paper. The faxed heading read Hallden Police Department. In the center of the page, the words *Arrest Log* leapt out at her, with the date of Clay's murder typed below. Further down, four columns lined the page, headed by the words *Name, Charge, Time of Arrest, Arresting Officer.* Puzzled, she skimmed the names. At *12:47 A.M.* her eyes widened in astonishment.

After being sworn in, Caleb led Doc through the events at the Center. He bragged about Clay's prowess with women, how Nina had been sniffing after him for weeks. Kell laid a restraining hand on Eliza when he suggested that rather than an attack, she'd interrupted a planned tryst.

Clearly offended by his star witness, Caleb hurried through the testimony. Doc repeated his claims about visiting Clay and seeing Eliza rush out at one A.M., knife in hand. He introduced the notarized statements given to Chief Graves and released Doc to Kell's interrogation.

Standing behind the defense table, she began, "Mr. Reed, it is your assertion that you personally witnessed my client leaving Mr. Griffin's motel, is it not?"

"Listen, bitch, I've already said this three times."

Judge Majors whipped her head around and bit out, "You will watch your mouth in my courtroom, or you will find yourself spending several nights in a cell."

A smart-assed comment rose in his throat, but he caught Graves's malevolent look and subsided. "Fine. But she shouldn't be asking the same stupid questions."

"Indulge me." Kell crossed the floor, fax in hand. "I simply want to be certain about your *story*."

"It ain't a story," he corrected loudly. "I'm telling you what I saw."

"At one A.M."

"Are you deaf? Yeah, at one A.M."

"Mr. Reed, are you capable of astral projection?"

"Ass-what?" Doc's eyes bulged and he twisted to face the judge. "You gonna let her talk to me like that?"

Judge Majors smothered a laugh and shot Kell a stern look. "Please rephrase."

"I apologize, Your Honor." Kell tapped her nails on the witness stand. "Are you capable of being in two places at once?"

"Like a clone? Naw."

"Then can you explain to the court how you managed to be on the street outside the Palace Motel at one A.M. while you were being booked into the Hallden City Jail at 12:47 A.M. on the charge of public drunkenness?"

Murmurs rolled through the crowd. Kell ignored them, continuing, "I have in my possession a copy of the intake log for the Hallden City Jail on the night Clay Griffin was murdered."

"Objection." Caleb rose to face the judge. "The log hasn't been authenticated and is therefore hearsay."

"What about it, Ms. Jameson?" Judge Majors inquired.

"Your Honor, I am not offering this log as evidence for the truth of the matter asserted. The log is presented simply to impeach the witness."

Judge Majors nodded. "Objection overruled. You may proceed."

Kell turned to Doc, who squirmed deeper into his seat. "According to the log, you were in the process of being strip searched, I believe, at the time you swear you saw my client leaving the building."

"I didn't—I don't . . ." Doc stumbled over his excuse, trying to catch Graves's attention. The liar told him that the record of his arrest had been destroyed, and that if he cooperated, Graves would make sure he didn't have to worry about being arrested. Now Graves just sat there, pretending not to know him. He'd put a stop to that. "Chief Graves told me what to say. He made me write it down over and over again, made me practice."

Kell shifted to block Doc's view of the chief. "When did he ask you to lie to the court?"

"On Saturday, after Mrs. Faraday got out of jail. He came by my house and promised me he'd make the charges disappear if I just swore out the statement he gave me."

A chorus of boos began in the rear of the courtroom, rolling over Kell like a benediction.

"That's a goddamned lie," Graves thundered from his seat. "The punk is lying."

"Sit down, Chief Graves!" barked the judge, her equanimity ruffled by the outbursts in her typically serene courtroom. "If I don't hear absolute silence in the next five seconds, I will clear this courtroom."

Silence rushed in, and Kell waited for the judge's next words. "Young man, do you realize that you have committed perjury in my court?"

Doc hunkered down, eyes downcast. "Yes, ma'am."

"Which time? When you swore you saw Eliza Faraday or when you accused Chief Graves of falsifying statements and suborning perjury?"

Perplexed, Doc answered awkwardly, "The first one. The one about Mrs. Faraday."

Judge Majors turned to Kell. "Any further questions for this witness before he is taken into custody?"

"One, Your Honor." She watched Doc for pregnant seconds, then asked, "Did Clay Griffin attack Nina Moore?"

"Yeah. He had me distract Tony by getting him to take me home, then he caught Nina out by the gazebo. Told me he wanted to get a taste of whatever she was giving Tony. Tony figured something was up and drove us back. If Mrs. Faraday hadn't come, he probably would have raped her for sure."

"I'm done with this witness, Your Honor."

"Bailiff, please take the witness into custody." She shot a fulminating glare at a wheezing Graves. "I advise you to remain seated for the duration of this hearing, Chief Graves."

Kell returned to the defense table, and stood, waiting for recognition by the court. The judge nodded. "Based on the evidence presented by the prosecution, I move that this court find no probable cause to hold my client on the charge of second-degree murder. They have failed to establish that she is the sole owner of the type of knife in question or that she had ever been seen in the vicinity of the victim's apartment. Her threat against Mr. Griffin occurred when he posed imminent harm to her ward, and she did not take any physical action against him."

"Mr. Matthews?"

Caleb gained his feet, his posture ramrod straight. "Based on the testimony currently before this court and the evidence in the possession of the State, we do not have adequate evidence to proceed with the charges at this time."

"I appreciate the candor of the State, Mr. Matthews. The court hereby dismisses the charges against Eliza Faraday. Mrs. Faraday, you are free to go."

Eliza embraced Kell, tears streaming. Friends and well-wishers swarmed them, including several former residents of the Center. Kell struggled to see above their heads, to find Luke. In the rear of the courtroom, Luke stood stiffly and pushed through the doors, never looking back. She gathered her papers quickly and helped guide Eliza out of the courtroom and into an empty conference room.

Finally alone, Eliza grabbed her hands, bringing them to her cheek. "Kell, I don't how to thank you. You saved my life."

"No, I didn't," Kell demurred. "But if I did, I'm glad I could return the favor." Her throat closed and tears pressed against her eyes. "I never thanked you, Mrs. F, for saving me. For helping me become a woman you could be proud of. I hope I've made you proud."

The hands holding Kell's tightened. "Every day, honey. My goodness, don't you know that I'm proud of you every day?"

"Even after what, after what happened?" Kell sniffed. "After Clay hurt you because of me?" Freeing one hand, she knuckled away tears that streamed down her cheeks. "You weren't supposed to get hurt, I swear. I didn't mean for any of this to happen."

Eliza dropped Kell's hand to catch her chin in a firm grip. "I know that, Kell. Don't you think I know that? Children make mistakes, baby. Even one of my daughters."

"Daughter?"

"Of course you're my daughter. I grew you as much as she did, and then I got to watch you grow yourself. I couldn't be prouder, Kell. Not ever. Come here." Eliza wrapped her eldest daughter in her arms and held her while she wept.

At the prosecution's table, Chief Graves raged at Caleb, who methodically packed his briefcase, ignoring the invective showered over him. "How the hell did you lose this case?" Graves shrieked, his already flushed face growing ruddier by the second.

"The only reason I'm not having the bailiff place you under arrest," Caleb snarled, "is that I want to give Sheriff Calder the pleasure. I strongly advise you to go home and put your affairs in order."

Fury morphed into horror. "I can't go home," he shrilled. "Arrest me. Right now." He clutched at Caleb's arm, his eyes wide with a terror that dilated the pupils to saucers. "For the love of God, Matthews, place me under arrest."

Caleb scowled at him, confused by the alarm. "What

are you afraid of, Chief? Doc is already in custody. No one is going to attack you on his behalf."

"You don't understand. They'll be angry about this. I failed, and I got caught. They don't forgive mistakes."

"Chief, if you are truly frightened, I can have you placed in protective custody. The sheriff's deputies can escort you to your residence."

Graves sagged against the table, horror giving way to resignation. "Won't help. They've gotten inside already."

"Who has?"

"Stark." Graves stood up, ran unsteady fingers through gray hair damp with perspiration. "This isn't over." Before Caleb could react, he pushed through the crowd and out into the corridor.

Kell and Eliza stood surrounded by media and townsfolk, but she saw Graves emerge. He beckoned to her with frenzied motions. Elation demanded good sportsmanship, and she wove through the knots of people to join him.

"Yes?"

Graves huffed mightily, his breath a wheeze of stuttered air. "Don't stay here. They know you're back."

The polite smile faded. "What are you talking about?"

"Stark. This." He snatched at her wrist, prying her fingers open. Kell wrestled to free herself, but the thick fingers clamped tight. Smacking her palm, he forced her to make a fist and shoved her aside. "They know about you and the others. Be careful."

It happened so quickly, she barely registered the act.

One second, he charged to the exit, forcing his way outside. In the next, a shot rang through the courthouse. Screams filled the corridor, and Kell watched as Graves raced across the macadam. Another shot shattered the window of a car nearby, but Graves managed to peel away. No shots followed.

Caleb, who'd been steps behind in the courtroom, ran out, but Luke reached her first. Hands gripped Kell's shoulders, turning her into Luke's embrace. "Kell, come with me. It's not safe here."

"They shot at him."

"The police are already looking for the gunmen," Caleb said. "Get her in a room."

"Kell, come on." Without waiting, Luke pushed her toward the room she and Eliza had vacated earlier. He kicked the door shut and settled onto a chair, cradling her shuddering form.

In the safety of the room, he ran his hands across her body, searching for wounds. "Were you hurt, love? Kell, talk to me."

"I'm fine. Fine." Then she opened her palm. "Luke, look."

"What is it?" Luke spoke to her, his voice an eerie echo. He gently lifted her hand. A gold band lay in the center, with an onyx stone.

And a triangle intersecting a circle.

CHAPTER 30

"He was afraid for me, Luke. He gave me this and warned me that they knew I was back."

"They? Who was he talking about?" Luke knelt beside her, chafed hands gone cold as ice. "What did he say to you?"

She shook her head, as every nightmare chased away for sixteen years returned with a vengeance. "That they knew about me and Findley and Julia," she replied, her head bowing in defeat. Against her palm, the ring bit deep into skin. "He called them Stark. Said they weren't finished."

"Finished with what?" Luke captured her chin and forced her eyes to meet to his. Discarding comfort, he chose the harsh reality she favored. "Talk to me, Kell. Don't be a coward."

"They know who I am. What I did." She opened her hand, the ring in the center. Surging from the chair, she muttered, "I have to go."

"No more running, damn you." Luke pressed her back down, determinedly. He plucked the ring from her fist and dropped the circlet into his pocket. She followed the movement of his hands, fixated on the threat it represented. "Look at me," he instructed softly.

After a moment, she managed to do as he asked and focused. "It's too much, Luke."

"You don't have to tell me what's going on." He pressed his forehead to hers wearily, his hands unsteady on her shoulders. "But please, Kell, for once, let me help you."

A shudder vibrated through her. Too many years of holding in the truth. But now, more than ever, she had to remember Fin and Julia. Her next steps would determine their futures. Again. "Listen to me," she begged in a voice thin with fatigue and grief. "I will tell you everything, but not yet. Not now."

Knowing that trust had to stretch both ways, he kissed her forehead tenderly. "What can I do?"

"My friends, my sisters, Findley Borders, and Julia Warner. They're in danger. I need you to bring them here, where you can protect them." She gripped his lapels suddenly, demandingly. "Only you, Luke. You can't tell anyone else. It's not safe."

"Okay, I'll get them. I'll protect them."

"And Eliza. She's still in danger. I'm not sure how it all fits together, but it does."

Questions gathered like a storm, but Luke held off. He'd promised her time, and he'd deliver. "Anything else?"

Kell shook her head once. The door behind them opened and Caleb entered, with a visibly shaken Eliza in tow. He shut the door firmly on the reporter that tried to squeeze her way inside. Without preamble, he confirmed, "They didn't find the gunman. Graves also got away."

Luke stood, Kell's hand still in his. Eliza joined them, brushing at her damp brow. She asked briskly, "Are you hurt?"

"I'm fine," Kell responded, voice steadier. She could see the panic beneath the stalwart expression, felt warmed by the gruff care. Like Luke, Eliza knew better than to coddle. Kell welcomed the lack of sentiment and assured her, "I wasn't hurt."

Luke took the opportunity to grill Caleb. "Did anyone see the shooter?"

"No. Shot came from outside. It looks like they were waiting for him." Caleb gestured to Kell. "Other than Ms. Jameson, no one seems to have noticed anything out of the ordinary before it happened."

Before Caleb could pursue his line of questions with Kell, Luke challenged, "You know what this means, don't you? About the Griffin case."

Caleb didn't mince words. "Mrs. Faraday didn't kill Clay Griffin. Yeah, I know." He thought of his last moments with the police chief, the bizarre request. Hopefully, someone in this room would have some answers. "Graves was frenetic in the courtroom, too eager to have her convicted. When the judge dismissed the case, he all but confessed that some plan had fallen apart. He begged me to arrest him."

Luke smiled, a feral turn of his mouth. "It would have been my pleasure."

"Did he tell you why he was afraid?" Kell asked quietly. If Graves had been frightened enough, he may have allowed a clue to slip. Some indication of what or who Stark was. She insisted, "Did he say anything at all about who might be after him?"

Caleb grimaced. "I brushed him off, damn it. He told me that Stark would get him. I didn't ask who or what Stark was. Hell, I dismissed it and him. But I am listening now." He focused on Kell. "Do you know Stark?"

Kell didn't blink. "No. I don't know him." *Them.*

Luke had learned her tones by now, knew the cadence of her voice. Taking his cue, he dropped her hand to approach Caleb. "I'd be grateful if you'd contact Chief Deputy Richardson in my office. We'll need to have a team look for the sniper, but I have to assume he's already fled. I'm putting out an APB on Graves."

"Lancy said he was on point. They've already started setting up roadblocks."

"Good, but Graves's men aren't equipped for this and they may be in on whatever is happening. Richardson isn't. We can trust her."

"They won't like it."

"They'll get over it. She's got more experience, and she's not looking for her boss. Tell them they don't have a choice. Never mind, I'll do it." Luke glanced at Eliza, who met his worried eyes over Kell's bowed head. "You should take Kell home. I'll be over as soon as I can."

"Fine. For now. But I'm not Graves, Sheriff. I don't play dirty, but I'm not going anywhere." Caleb turned to the door. "I'm sorry, Ms. Jameson." He reached for the knob, prepared to face the barrage of cameras, wondering if the verdict and the shooting were connected.

"Caleb, wait." Kell opened her eyes and studied him carefully. She owed him what she could give. "You're in danger now. Graves marked you as being on the wrong side."

"Of what?"

"Of whatever killed Clay Griffin. You're not safe anymore." She clasped Eliza's hand tightly. "None of us are until Graves is found."

Caleb didn't argue. "Then what can we do? How do we find out who's after us?"

She looked at Luke. "We trust him. I'll do my best to help find Stark, but you can't let anyone else know what Graves said to you. Not until they arrive."

Caleb's even temper flared. Cutting his eyes between Kell and Luke, he demanded, "Who the hell is Stark? Until who arrives? Someone needs to explain what's going on here."

"You know everything you can right now, Matthews. As soon as I can tell you more, I will." Luke doubted that would be enough, but he had more on his mind right now than satisfying the D.A. "One step at a time. I'll fill you in."

Realizing he wasn't going to wring any more from either of them, Caleb left the room, allowing himself the satisfaction of a slam that shook the door. Eliza took Kell's hand, leaned down to her ear. "Trust him, honey. And trust yourself." She straightened and bussed

Luke's cheek as well. "I'll make my own way home."

"No, have Deputy Little take you. You don't travel alone right now." Luke started to open the door, but Eliza forestalled him.

"Stay here. I'll find him." With that, she exited the room, leaving them alone.

Kell stood abruptly and her chair tipped over, knocking against the table. Luke shifted to right it, but she placed a hand over his.

His eyes met hers and he waited. "What is it, Kell?"

"I've had three people in my life that I could count on. And sixteen years ago, I lost it all. I made a stupid, careless decision and I couldn't take it back. Couldn't fix it." Tears, so long denied, threatened once more, but she refused them release. "I figured out a long time ago that I could take care of myself. I didn't need them— Mrs. F or Julia or Fin. I would be successful on my own. I dated, but never because I wanted a partner or a true lover. I didn't need anyone."

"No, you didn't." Luke wondered if she'd practiced breaking his heart. "I get it, Kell. You don't rely on anyone. You're smart and self-sufficient and a damned good attorney. Eliza was lucky to have you in there today."

Kell's eyes widened. "I forgot to thank you for the fax."

"No, don't thank me." He tugged his hand from beneath her, certain if he stayed in the room any longer, he'd beg. "I'll bring your friends here and set up protection for you and Eliza and Caleb." He took a step back, desperate to escape. "Need anything else?"

"I need you to listen to me."

"Listen to what, Kell? To more reasons why I can come only so close and no closer? I get it. You lose people. Your parents, then your friends. So no more trusting and no more losing. I finally get it." He walked slowly to the door, wondering how he could move when his life had shattered around him. "I'll have someone take you home."

"Luke, wait." Fear stabbed through her, but she ignored its warning. Love equaled pain and loss and devastation. And, if she were brave, happiness and joy and a partner she could trust. Even if she lost this time, she had to try. "Wait, please."

He spun around, rage replacing grief. "No, you wait. You once accused me of being a coward, and you were right. I did leave Chicago so I wouldn't have to face that damned precinct every morning. I ran away, hoping that if I didn't look back, my past wouldn't follow me. My failure to protect my squad."

"That wasn't your fault."

"No, it wasn't. I get that. Just like I get why you want to protect your friends. But what I learned that you haven't yet is you can't outrace your past, Kell. You can't finesse it or outtalk it. You can't escape what happened before. Because it made you who you are."

"What did it make you?"

"Ready. To find the only small southern town to rival Chicago in body count. To find the only lawyer who can not only convince me her client is innocent, but cajole me into helping her prove it." He leaned against the door, defeated, but determined to have it said. "To find the only woman I could love, especially when she lies to me to protect those who count on her."

Kell came to him, stopped in front of him. Ebony eyes watched her warily, greedily. The threat of tears vanished, replaced with relief. Her heart, already full, expanded as she realized the truth she'd refused to admit. Had to tell him. "I wasn't finished, Luke. I was afraid. Then I met you. I met a man who saw through me, inside me. A man who didn't flinch. You understand me, even the parts I don't. You love me."

"Yes."

"And I love you too. I love how brave you are. How sweet you can be. I admire the choices you've made, especially the ones that cost you the most." She caressed his cheek, the hard stubborn line of his jaw. "In all my life, I've never told another man what I need to tell you. I love you. Always. Completely." She inhaled sharply, drawing his mouth to hers. "I love you."

She kissed him, and he caught her up, binding them together. Trust, she'd found, didn't require a loss of control, a ceding of herself. With Luke, the leap of faith would never be reckless.

Suddenly, Kell reared back, remembering. "Oh, God. I forgot."

Luke set her feet on the floor and asked slowly, "What didn't you tell me this time?"

Kell squirmed under the severe gaze. "Um, I told David I'd rejoin the firm."

"When did you tell him you'd come back and when is he expecting you?"

"I talked to David last night, and we patched up our differences." Quickly, she added, "And I agreed to return tomorrow. The Marley trial. The press will be there. They'll want to cover it."

Luke maintained a slippery grip on his temper and disapproval. Neither would stop her. "Tell Marley to go to hell. This Stark, whatever they are, aren't going to disappear. You can't ignore this, Kell."

"No, they won't disappear." Arms still wrapped around Luke's waist, Kell gathered herself. Fear had seeped away, replaced by a steely determination. The enemy had revealed itself, if for just a moment. Now, she was prepared. "But I'm still going to Atlanta. For a client conference. But I'm coming home to Hallden."

"Thank God."

"That's the arrangement. I agreed to rejoin the firm, on the condition that I spend most of my week here." She glanced away, then met the opaque eyes, hers dancing with mischief. "I thought I'd set up an office in town. Commute. A compromise."

"Are you sure?"

"Yes." She came to him again, taking his hands, locking their fingers. "I love you. If you can be patient a little while longer, I'll tell you everything." She kissed the knuckles with their fading bruises. "I'm all in, Luke. If you want me."

He kissed her, a merger of promises, of souls.

"I love you, Kell Jameson. All in."

AUTHOR'S NOTE

Kell's story began years ago, in a very different form. Eventually, she grew too large in my imagination to be one person and was too alone to defeat her enemies. And so lived Findley Borders and Julia Warner—sisters and friends torn apart by a deadly secret.

For Kell, who must learn that trust is not a weapon, Luke is a partner and a friend, a combination she never thought to find. As Stark continues its reign of menace, join me as we learn of Fin's courage and Julia's resilience, and watch them find each other and their soulmates in the chapters to come.

I eagerly welcome your comments and questions at www.selenamontgomery.com, by email at selena_montgomery@hotmail.com or by mail at:

P.O. Box 170352
Atlanta, Georgia 30317–0352

Happy Reading,
Selena